HOOD WR

BLOODLINE

OF A KANE

A NOVEL BY BOBBY DENNIS JR.

PUBLISHED BY HOOD WRITTENS PUB.
PROMOTIONS BY CUM UP PROMO.
Cumuppromo@aol.com
www.hoodwrittenspub.com

For information on how individual consumers
Can place orders, please write to, e-mail, fax or visit
us on the web.
HOOD WRITTENS PUB. or
CUM UP PROMO
3522 Gladys St.
Jacksonville, Fl. 32209
Fax: 904-598-2418
E-mail: cumupromo@aol.com
www.hoodwrittenspub.com

For orders other than individual consumers,
HOOD WRITTENS PUB. allows a discount on the
purchase of (10) ten or more copies of a single title
order for special markets or premium use.

For orders purchased thru the above named
affiliates.
We offer a 25% discount off the sale price for
orders being shipped to prisons including, but not
limited to federal, state,and county. We truly feel
y'all pain.

PUBLISHED BY HOOD WRITTENS PUB.
PROMOTIONS BY CUM UP PROMO.
Cumuppromo@aol.com
www.hoodwrittenspub.com

BLOODLINE
OF A KANE

A NOVEL BY BOBBY DENNIS JR.

PUBLISHED BY HOOD WRITTENS PUB.
PROMOTIONS BY CUM UP PROMO.
Cumuppromo@aol.com
www.hoodwrittenspub.com

Note:

This novel is a work of fiction. Any resemblance to real people, living or dead, actual events, establishments, organizations, and/or locales are intended to give the fiction a sense of reality and authenticity. Other names, characters, places and incidents are either products of the author's imagination or are used fictitiously, as are those fictionalized events & incidents that involve real persons and did not occur or are set in the future.

Published by:
HOOD WRITTENS PUB.
3522 Gladys st.
Jacksonville, Fl. 32209
www.hoodwrittenspub.com
Cumuppromo@aol.com

Library of Congress Catalog Card No: To be supplied
ISBN: 0-615-12928-5

BLOODLINE CREDITS:
Story By Bobby Dennis Jr.
Edited by Kim Grier and Ausha Rogers
Text formation by Ausha Rogers
Cover work by Adolfo Latorre al@adolfolatorre.com or
www.adolfolatorre.com
Printed and pressed by Instant Publisher

"DEDICATION"

This book is dedicated first and foremost to Father Yahweh who blessed me with the ability to tell a story. To my mother and father Betty Ann and Bobby Dennis who provided me my life and for the way I was raised, because I had to go thru there to make it here! To Ausha Rogers who believed in me from the start, I love you bro and that goes without saying. To Azaryah "Lalisa" Rogers thanks a million lil sis for holding the team down, dreaming the dream, being a conduit as well as a rock! Love you lil sis, see you in Cancun! To the brothers and sisters who lived and died for the game, you provided the stories I just narrated them. Lastly I'd like to thank the Florida D.O.C and their policy of not letting prisoners in disciplinary confinement have library books and the unnamed correctional officer that took the one I smuggled in; couldn't have done it without you! A word to those who hated and didn't believe. I told you!

Bobby Dennis

BLOODLINE
OF A KANE

BY BOBBY DENNIS JR.

BOOK ONE OF
KANE FAMILY SAGA SERIES

BLOODLINE
OF A KANE !

The year was 1860, slavery still abounded . The economic situation in the northern states was drastically falling apart, while the south flourished . The north was all for abolishing slavery, as that one move would break the south's stranglehold on the United States fragile economy . The south was in an uproar, and there was talk of breaking away from the union. Southern states and their elected officials were preparing to break away. Slavery provided the south with what appeared to be an unlimited as well as cost effective supply of labor. The north was basically industrial, the south agricultural, they supplied the nation with foods, textiles and other goods.

In the spring of that year a young slave girl, 15 years old, named Amanda ran away from a big plantation near Charlotte North Carolina. The plantation was the Kane plantation. They didn't grow cotton, corn, or wheat. What they grew were slaves ...

Since importing slaves had been outlawed, the country sought to grow its own. On the Kane plantation, they grew only enough food stuffs to feed the slaves and the Kanes. A work force was necessary , so they had to have an overseer, his name was Elmer Spivey. He was a tall, thin, potbellied redneck with dirty blonde hair, stained and cracked big yellow teeth, a wispy mustache and beard. A weak looking chin, and washed out pale blue eyes. He was a mean and cruel man, as well as a terrible task master. Only 30 years old he looked nearly twice his age, and had worked for the Kane's for 10 years. He lived on their property with his wife Lucy, a brown haired mouse of a woman. She was small of stature, and scared of her own shadow. Elmer had instilled the fear with numerous beatings.

She was his first cousin, and they had wed when she was 13. At 22, she looked 50. They had five sons ranging from 2 to 7, tow headed boys each one of them.

Elmer had also fathered at least 15 more children from slave women, and made sure they were quickly sold. There was one slave woman who wouldn't have him. A big, jet black slave, named Bessie. She was 30 years old, and finely built. Big firm breast, trim waist, big thighs, a big perfectly shaped butt, and a lovely spread of hips. She was a pure blood Zulu from the coast of Africa. She traveled across the middle passage in the safety of her mother's womb. Her mother Cissy, had been sold off years ago when she was a small girl. She tried to remember the strange language her mother spoke to her as a child. The rhythmic cadence that gave her such joy. Bessie was the favorite of the plantation owner, one Thaddeus Matthew Kane.

Thad Kane as he was known far and wide, was a big strapping man with brown hair and eyes. He was a kind man, and treated his slaves well. One thing he wouldn't do was take a slave's word over the word of a white man, and the slaves knew this. He was 40 years old. His family were among the first to settle in North Carolina, so he was well respected throughout the state.

His wife was Elisabeth Kane, a robust woman of 35. She had bore him two children, John Ellis Kane and Rebecca Louise Kane. John Ellis as he was called, was the mirror image of his father at twenty, a tall finely built young man. He had sired 8 or 9 children with slave women, but his father promptly sold them.

Rebecca at eighteen was a beautiful woman with alabaster skin, her one fault was that she loved black men. She had a mean streak and where she got it was a mystery. She had been forcing the slave boys and men to have sex with her, since she discovered what sex was by peeping in the slave cabin.

Thad Kane was Amanda's father. Bessie was her mother, the only slave woman Thad had ever had. Amanda was a fine girl at 15, full breast, thick thighs, a beautiful butt, the only thing that marred her figure was that she was pregnant.

Elmer had been at Amanda, but Bessie warned him and he ceased, because Thad Kane had a fondness for Amanda. Facially her and Rebecca resembled, but at 15 her body was more lush and full. She was a big girl, inherited from her parents. Thad Kane had warned all of the men to stay away from Amanda.

A pure blood Mandingo who came to America at two and was twenty two then, by the name of Josh, fell in love with her and she with him. Her pregnancy was the result of their affections.

Rebecca had come across them making love in the barn. Amanda was Rebecca's companion, and body servant. She slept on a pallet in Rebecca's room. Rebecca had taught her to play with her vagina, and they pleasured each other.

When Rebecca caught them, she was on her way to have sex with the stable hand. She watched Josh make love to Amanda and fingered herself to orgasm. A few days later she confronted Josh, and explained the penalty for violating her father's order to stay away from Amanda. She told him there was one thing he could do to ensure she won't tell.

From that day on Josh had sex with her. The fly in the ointment, was that Elmer stumbled up on them. She tried to lie and say it was rape, but Elmer had watched for a while and knew that wasn't the case. He black mailed her into having sex with him.

Elmer took to punishing Josh for every little infraction, Josh rebelled and was chained to the whipping post. As Elmer whipped him, Amanda attacked him, and was chained to a post next to him and whipped. When Elmer released them, Josh knocked him down and kicked and stomped him with his bare feet. Elmer pulled his pistol and shot Josh dead.

That night as Elmer slinked between the slave cabins to have sex with a slave name Bertha, Amanda waited in the shadows with an axe. As he passed her she stepped out and swung the axe, and cleaved his head in two. The axe stuck in his trunk as Amanda had swung it with such force.

She took off running. She was six months pregnant. She had no idea where to go, she just ran towards the mountains.

The next day there was an uproar, and they looked to see who was missing. Thad Kane had knew who had killed Elmer and why. He didn't call in the sheriff. They buried Elmer and John Ellis took his place as overseer.

Elmer's wife was allowed to stay on the land, she was given a deed for ten acres. Thad Kane sent hands to help her plant and harvest her crops, and soon she took up with a big light skinned slave named Bo. She bore him five sons, and at the tender age of 28 she died. Her six years with Bo, were the happiest days of her short lived life.

Bo took up with a bright yellow slave woman named Della, and they raised the ten boys. The civil war started in 61', and ended in 66', and the ten acres became Bo's.

At the time of Elmer's murder Thad never sent any one after Amanda, he just let her go. Rebecca couldn't be consoled, so Thad sent her up north to a finishing school. Bessie bore him a son, then the war came. Both Thad and John Ellis joined the Confederacy, he as a Colonel and John Ellis as a Lieutenant. Thad was wounded and lost his left arm. John Ellis was killed. Elisabeth killed herself when she got the news.

Rebecca came back to run the plantation. She had been gone for three years, but her hunger for black men had not abated. She took up with a half white slave named Tandy, who had taken over as overseer while her father and John Ellis went to war.

When Thad returned in 65', the place was almost as he had remembered, most of the slaves remained though many had run away. Bessie was there with his five year old son, a boy who could pass for white. He looked just like his father, but he would be bigger. Thad moved Bessie into the big house, and named his son after him.

Rebecca and Tandy lived in the big house and she gave birth to twins, both boys which she named John Thaddeus Kane and Ellis Matthew Kane.

At first Thad was enraged that his daughter would fuck a black man, and have children. They had some terrible rows, but Bessie opened his eyes and he radically changed his views. He became extremely progressive for his time. They kept their domestic arrangements to themselves, and the plantation prospered. He had buried gold, and it got them through the lean times. After the war, the Kane plantation was one of the few places that made money and grew. The community learned that they were co-habiting with blacks and held it against them. The blacks in the area did business with them, and soon Thad was buying up land dirt cheap.

He gave all of his ex slaves two acres and a mule, and they sharecropped with him. He never cheated them, and spent most of his time with blacks. He and Bessie had four more kids, three girls and a boy. Tandy and Rebecca had four more children.

Thad junior, John, and Ellis Kane, took over after their parents died. They all married poor white women and the line went on.

The Kane plantation still stands today, still owned by the Family who now own and operate Kane International, a big consortium. You would never know they had the blood of a Zulu from a royal line. So in a sense they are Blue Bloods, and all are lily white or so they think.

* CHAPTER # 2 *

Amanda ran towards the mountains. For three months she hid during the day, and walked in the dark of the night. She wore out her shoes and walked barefoot until the blisters were gone. Her feet were hard and callused. Her clothes hung in tatters. She was nine months pregnant when she stumbled sick and exhausted into the Cherokee Indian camp. There were other runaway slaves who had become part of the tribe, not many, maybe 10 or 12 men, women, and children. The women of the tribe ran to her as she fell in the camp. They took her to a Teepee and did their best to minister to her. They went and got the camp Shaman, who turned out to be an ex-Buddhist Priest turned trapper and mountain man.

He was Chinese and his name was, Tan Lao Tzu. The Cherokee called him Yellow Bird and believed him to be a medicine man. He was 25 years old and had been in America for 10 years. He came with a bunch of Monks to minister to the Chinese railroad workers. The Monks were slaughtered along with a group of railroad workers by the Irish railroad workers, who resented them because they worked for cheaper wages and the Irish felt they were taking their jobs. Tan Lao Tzu escaped and walked from California to North Carolina and had done many things in those 10 years.

He was a small man, 5' 4" tall and weighed 145 pounds, but there was not a man there that could best him in combat. Hand to Hand or with weapons, Lao Tzu had mastered the art of Kung Fu by the time he was 14. He was an expert with any bladed weapon and the bow. He could ride a horse better than most and taught himself how to use firearms. He was good with both pistols and rifles, he was a dead shot. He knew how to use an array of different herbs that were used as medicine. He had been with this band of Cherokee for five years and he spoke their language, Chinese and English fluently with no accent. He had a Cherokee wife who was the daughter of the Chief, who was named Standing Bear. His wife's name was Sparrow and his son was Little Bird who was just a year old. He dressed in buckskins just like the Indians and his skin was turned a yellow brown by the sun. He looked in every way like one of them, the difference was in the eyes and he wore his head bald.

Sparrow came to their Teepee and said. "There is a woman who needs your help. She is not of the people, she is a dark one."

"Show me," he said.

She lead him to the Teepee where Amanda lay and as soon as he saw her he fell in love.

Amanda showed no hint of her white blood, skin wise and her hair wasn't exactly straight, but it wasn't kinky either. Her skin tone was a deep nut brown, her eyes were round and dark, and her lips were full and sensuous. Her face even in pain was beautiful.

He kneeled beside her and checked her as best he could in the feeble light. He could see she was pregnant, her stomach swollen and smooth. It seemed like if you pricked it, it would burst. He spoke in a combination of English and Cherokee and told the women to get hot water and cloths.

Amanda's water broke and gushed from between her legs and she was running a high fever. Quickly he mixed some herbs with hot water and held it to her lips, she sipped, coughed, then drank the rest. She looked into his eyes, she had never seen eyes like his, they were beautiful. Weakly she mustered a smile. He held her head and looked at her. When she smiled, he looked at her and knew he had to have her as his wife.

Most of the men had two or more wives, his wife Sparrow was only 15. He didn't know her age, but he was sure she wasn't much older. He feed her more of the potion, then said. "Your child is arriving, do you understand,"

"Yes," she replied.

The women returned with the things he requested. He spread her legs then kneeled between them.

"Just do as I say and every thing will be alright." he said.

"I trust you pretty eyes." she said.

He smiled, felt her stomach, then said. "In a minute I want you to push the baby out."

Two women held her hands. "Push, push hard," he said.

She pushed and pushed until it felt like something

was ripping her apart.

"Push, push hard," he said. "I see it."

She screamed and pushed, the head popped out.

"Push, push," he said.

She pushed and screamed with tears rolling down her face. The baby was squeezed out and Lao Tzu pulled the baby from her, cut the cord then tied it. He told her to push again, she did and the afterbirth came out.

"You have a son, and he is as black as a Raven. A beautiful and healthy boy. How will he be called?"

"His name is Raven Kane." she said with conviction.

"So it is." said Lao Tzu, and handed the baby to her. He was black as midnight with a head full of dark curly hair. She held him to her breast where he sucked her big nipple into his mouth. She looked at Lao Tzu again, and blessed him with a big smile.

"I'll leave you now." he said. "I'm Lao Tzu, they call me Yellow Bird."

"I'm Amanda Kane, they call me Mandy."

"I'm pleased to meet you Mandy." he said then left the Teepee and went to see Standing Bear.

Standing Bear was a very big man, barrel chest, big arms, and legs. His hair was past his shoulders, raven black, tied in two thick braids, with buckskin ties and clumps of bear pelts on the ends.

"Welcome Yellow Bird." he said. "I see from look in your eyes it is very important matter. What is it?"

"A woman came into camp tonight, a dark one. She is mine." Lao Tzu said.

Standing Bear smiled then asked. "Does she know this?"

"She just gave birth to a son, I delivered him. I will have this woman." said Lao.

"Good for you, but you know if someone else lays claim, you will have to fight for her." said Standing Bear.

"I would die for this one." said Lao.

"I must see this one for myself if she has so much inflamed you." Standing Bear said.

"She is beautiful," said Lao.

Standing Bear looked at him, then said. "I'll see." Lao left the Teepee and walked silently into the dark night.

    *   *   *   *   *

The next morning Lao Tzu went to the Teepee where Amanda was the night before. He brought her a buckskin dress and moccasins for her feet, and a bowl of food. He ducked thru the entrance as she lay there asleep with the baby in her arms.

The baby was wide awake and quiet, his eyes followed Lao as he came across the room. Lao had never seen such awareness in one so young, or the eye control. He knew this would be a great one with the proper training and he planned to be the one to train him. He took the baby and held him in his arms, and moved one of his hands from side to side in the baby's face; then up and down. He watched the baby's eyes as he moved his hand, the eyes moved in sync with his hand. The baby never once turned his head, or made a sound. So Lao grabbed him in both hands and tossed him into the air time and time again and the baby just smiled. Lao tickled him and he laughed, so he held him to his chest and said aloud. "You will be my son."

"It looks that way to me." Amanda said.

Lao turned to her and looked into her eyes and they smiled at him.

She had awaken when she felt him take the baby from her arms. At first, she didn't know that it was him. She cracked her eyes, saw that it was him, the man with the funny name and pretty eyes. She watched every thing he did and saw that her son never uttered a sound. She had been around many babies and most of them cried through the night, but her Raven was a quiet one. The only sounds she heard from him was when he sucked her swollen breast, the next time was when pretty eyes tickled him.

She didn't know where she would go from here, or what she would do. She was ill prepared to travel, now that the baby was born. She could leave him with pretty eyes who she knew would take care of him, but what would she do after that? She would take a few days to regain her strength, then plan her next move.

Lao had looked in her eyes the entire time she was lost in thought and she was unaware of his intense stare until he spoke.

"You will stay with me, you and the boy. He will be my son and you my wife."

"What if I don't want to be your wife?" she asked.

15

"In time you will, you have no place to go nowhere to turn. It's obvious you're running from something, I'm simply offering you something to run to. Take your time, regain your strength, today you will move in my Teepee. Sparrow will be your sister, Little Bird your son."

"I don't know pretty eyes, let me think about it."

"There is no time to think about it. When the Braves see you, one of them will make the choice for you as I have." he said.

"I have never seen a man like you before, you look kind of like an Indian, but your eyes and skin are different. What kind of man are you?"

"I'm from the land of chin, or china as these in this country say. I come from a land far away, as do your ancestors here." He said. "Put these on." He gave her the dress and shoes he had brought.

"Eat this." he passed her the bowl of food he had brought.

She stood and held the dress against her. He saw the lush swell of her breast, the roundness of her stomach, the plumpness of her sparsely covered pubic mound and the generous curves of her hips.

She pulled the dress over head and again he drank in the loveliness of her naked body. The soft buckskin dress fit tight on her. He knew that over the coming months as she matured all of the excess weight would melt away from her. She would really be a sight to see. Then she sat and hungrily devoured the food.

When she was done he passed her the baby, then said. "Come on, I'm taking you to your new home." She took the baby and followed him.

Standing Bear's tribe numbered about 400 people, mostly women, children and the elderly. About 150 were warriors. The tribe had nearly 500 horses and that's how a man measured his wealth. Lao had twenty horses and by their standards he was wealthy.

As they walked across the camp, the people watched. The Brave's watched the sway of Amanda's buttocks and the full round swells of her breast and made obscene gestures. Lao Tzu walked with his head held high, Amanda a few paces behind. As they came to the Teepee, Sparrow floated out with Little Bird riding her hip. Lao had told her of his plans and she was glad to be getting a sister and mother for her son.

16

The women did all of the camp work and skinned the kills the men made, so she was glad for the extra help. She was like a princess in the tribe, but did the same work as the other women.

Sparrow was a beautiful woman, shapely but small. She stood about 5' 1" and weighed about 100 pounds. She had a boyishly slim body with curves at the breast, hips and buttocks. Amanda on the other hand was at least 5' 9" or 10" and weighed 150 pounds. She was tall as most of the men in the tribe. Very few women were her size, though many were heavier and wider.

Sparrow hugged her, then said. "Welcome sister, we will do well together."

Amanda hugged her as the crowd stood and watched.

A big Brave with bow in hand, and a quiver of arrows slung over his back. A knife and Tomahawk at his waist, dressed in breechcloth and leggings stepped from the crowd and grabbed Amanda's arm and pulled her away from Sparrow's embrace.

"Night Bird you come with me." he said.

Amanda snatched her arm free and he reared his arm back, and shot a wicked slap towards her face. Before the blow landed Lao blocked it and turned it away.

"Brother you would discipline my woman?" asked Lao.

The man who's name was Coyote looked at him, then said. "The woman is not yours, I stake claim to her!"

"You have no right to stake claim to her, I delivered her son who is now my son. She is my woman and that is not a claim that's a fact." Lao said.

Coyote pulled an arrow out of his quiver, held it in front of Lao's face and snapped it. "At noon, to the death,"

"As you wish," said Lao.

"That's what you meant when you said a Brave would make the choice for me?" asked Amanda.

"Yes that's it," Lao replied.

"What will happen now?"

"One of us will die during the fight." he replied. "Whoever wins, you're the prize."

If you were the daughter of a Brave I would have paid the bride price of two or three horses, but since you're not then there will be a contest. He made the challenge so he sets the rules. Rarely is it ever to the death. One fall or first blood, but this runs deeper than you I'm afraid. I'm an outsider here Mandy and some of the Braves resent my status. I'm considered a Shaman, or Medicine Man by them. If I had been Cherokee he never would have made the challenge because they usually hold the Shaman up to high esteem. It borders on worship. The Shaman they had before I arrived, left after I did some things he couldn't. He thought his medicine had failed him and that the spirits favored me.

It had nothing to do with spirits, but my knowledge of medicine and medical techniques was greater than his. I tried to explain it to them, but I was not as skilled in their language as I am now. That was almost five years ago."

"What will you do, he's so much bigger than you?" asked Amanda.

"I will kill him and take my prize." he said.

He looked at her, touched her face and smiled. She looked so uncertain.

"You will get to know me and I will tell you of my past, but from this day forth I want you to know that the truth will be our bond. Trust me, never doubt me, or you may plant the seed of doubt in my heart and a moments indecision could cost me my life. I'm confident in my abilities and after today you will be too."

"Alright pretty eyes,"

They all went into the Teepee where they sat and talked. Sparrow explained to her their duties and acted as if she knew Lao would win. Her confidence lifted Mandy's spirits. What Sparrow knew and had seen, was that no man had ever bested Yellow Bird in a physical contest no matter which.

They sat and Sparrow taught Mandy how to build a carrier for her son, so she could strap him on her back and work. She also showed her how to rig a sling so she could carry him in the front and let him suckle while she worked.

Lao Tzu went and checked the sun, came back, and said. "It is time." He grabbed his weapons and the women followed.

*   *   *   *

They came to an area that was marked off around a Buffalo wallow, almost the entire tribe was there. Standing Bear stood at the edge of the wallow and waited as Lao Tzu and Mandy approached. She would stand there at the edge and watch.

Coyote stepped from the crowd with a 10 foot leather strap that had loops at both ends. He and Lao Tzu stood before the Chief.

"Coyote you made the challenge. What is it to be?" asked Standing Bear.

"A death match!" said Coyote as he snapped the leather strap. "Let him choose the weapon!"

"You should choose the weapon that will make your death more merciful and swift, great warrior." said Lao. He turned to the assembled tribe then said. "Who will father this Brave's future children? Let those men now take his wives. His words have brought death upon his head as you will see. He has had time to think clearly about the type of contest, he chooses death. Any two men who stand in front of me will be cut down like standing grain at harvest. Coyote I give you this time to do your death dance, for the spirits on the wind whisper your name."

Coyote looked at Lao Tzu then spat in the dust to show his contempt, and said. "Big talk for a little yellow bird."

Standing Bear grabbed the leather strap, tested it, then made a loop over each man's left wrist and drew it tight.

Coyote pulled a foot long knife, then jumped in the shallow depression in the earth. It was about 10 feet around.

Lao Tzu jumped in and pulled his big knife. No sooner had he done so than Coyote attacked. Blade held in an underhand stabbing motion, sharp end up.

Lao Tzu had expected such a move and used his strapped arm to block the strike. He spun and was behind him, and said. "You should be dying now."

Coyote spun and whipped the leather low in an attempt to tangle up Lao's legs, and throw him to the ground.

Lao leaped over the strap and raised his left hand in the air in a rapid motion, then quickly snapped it down. The leather strap moved swiftly like an ocean wave and with a snap like a pistol shot, slapped Coyote in the face. The strap lashed across his lips, nose and his right eye, raising a welt and bursting his lips. It tossed sand in his eye and momentarily blinded him, he screamed. "AHHHHH!"

Lao moved in close and shouted. "I will show you mercy once again, throw down your weapon and concede!"

The tribe roared. They knew that if he threw down his weapon he would be exiled from the tribe. Coyote wiped at his eyes, then charged Lao who calmly stood there. As their bodies met Lao let Coyotes momentum drive him backwards. He rolled, placed both feet in Coyote's stomach and flipped him thru the air. Coyote landed on his neck and shoulders with a jarring thud, the wind knocked out of him.

Lao Tzu continued his roll. He used his hands to propel himself skyward, then he landed astraddle Coyote and plunged his knife down into his heart. He stood, pulled his knife from Coyote's chest and plunged it into the ground. Then he removed the strap from his wrist and began to do the death dance.

He danced around Coyote's body and sang to the spirits, soon after the tribe joined in. He stopped the dance, walked to Amanda, and said. "Let's go." They walked thru the crowd, and Sparrow fell in beside them as they walked to their Teepee.

*   *   *   *

Inside the Teepee, Lao sat on his bed of Beaver pelts. There were three beds and Amanda sat and watched Lao, cause she had never seen a man move as graceful as he. It seemed as if he was doing a elaborate dance as he fought, and now she understood his words and trusted his ability to defend them.

He watched as she held Raven to her breast to feed and the boy wrapped his lips around the big nipple. His hands clasped to the side of the swollen breast. He saw him suck, as the milk squirted into his mouth.

"He will be a great man. He is going to be big, I can tell by his bone structure." said Lao.

"Pretty eyes you're a strange man , you seem to see things far away as if they were close." said Mandy.

"In my short life I've been many things and I've tried to absorb as much as I could about nature and people. In the watching I've learned I come from a superstitious people, who believe in many spirits and gods. Much like the people I live with now. That is basically my reason for staying with them , because they seem so much like my people except they are more primitive. My people are more advanced in areas, but their customs and traditions are similar. Even some of the words are the same. I've found myself wondering if they are perhaps a branch of my people that migrated here centuries ago. We are similar in appearance, except where the skin and the eye's are concerned. These are a great people, nomadic and very warlike, but honest and true to each member. You will see as time passes."

"You're assuming I'll stay and are making plans for my future. I was a slave pretty eyes and I ran away. Not just from slavery, but from people controlling me, my thoughts and actions." she said.

"We are all slaves to something. The difference being, some things we chose to be slave to, some things we are obligated to be slave to and some things we are forced to be slave to by nature or circumstances. Take for instance Raven, you are a slave to his needs. You will serve him, defend him and nurture him, because as his mother you're obligated to do so. As for staying here, you will be slave to me because you choose to and also because circumstances will prevent you from doing any thing else. You are black and if you left here and were to get captured, you know what your fate would be. Being wise you would choose the lesser of the two evils and in the end you will be a willing slave to me. Your love for me will dictate that."

"But I don't love you." she replied.

"Not to worry, because in time you will." he said with a smile.

"You seem mighty confident in that."

"Never forget the words I told you. I have confidence in my ability no matter what it is I face. I attack it with the thought, I can be successful. You and Sparrow will help to reinforce my confidence and I will grow stronger for it. I'm highly respected in the tribe and as my woman you will be too. You will be expected to lead by example and you will never fail to be first to fulfill your duty. In everything, you will be representing us as a clan and I expect you to do us proud. In the days to come Sparrow will teach you your duties. We will be in this camp until the next full moon, then we will leave because hunting season has begun and there will be much work to do. Build your strength and prepare yourself, for you will play a large role in the future of the tribe, as will Sparrow. I don't want any division in our clan, we will work together as one. Sparrow will help to raise your son and you will help to raise hers. In two years time their training will begin."

"Their," she asked questioningly.

"Raven and Little Bird. In time they will be the greatest warriors this tribe has ever had. Each family group is attached to a clan. By virtue of Sparrow being my wife, we're a branch of the Bear clan. So we represent the head of the clan, the others will follow our lead. Do you understand?"

"I think so." she replied.

"Let's eat." he said, and Sparrow and Mandy left the Teepee and went to the cooking fire.

          *   *   *   *

Throughout the day Sparrow took Mandy thru the camp, introducing her to the females who were the head of their clan. It was then that she found out the name they had given her. She had heard the Brave Coyote call her Night Bird, but paid little attention to it. The women called her Night Bird, Sparrow alone called her Mandy.

"Why do they call me Night Bird?" she asked Sparrow.

"Because you came in the night, and you are affiliated with Yellow Bird. You even named your son after a bird, so Night Bird you are to the people." said Sparrow smiling.

"Yours' are a strange people, I don't know if I will be able to fit in." said Mandy.

"Be yourself, there is no need to try and fit in. Do your duty as the woman of Yellow Bird and the people will mold themselves to you. You have come into the tribe as a wife of the elders of our people, so you will be expected to lead. The people will look to you for inspiration. Never must you seem undecided or unsure, but be confident. It is human to err. If you make a mistake, it will not be held against you. The people will assume the spirits didn't favor you in the action and go on. I have been Yellow Bird's wife for three winters, and he has taught me much. The use of herbs, weapons and the usual style of fighting; not to mention his way with a woman. He will teach you these things too. Most is done in secret. I follow the traditions of the people, but my heart is far from them. We must lead by example and his teachings will help us to do this. I will teach you what I know, trust me there is much to learn. We have a lifetime together, we will be sisters so there is much time."

As night fell they went to the Teepee. After they had bathed in a cool stream that flowed behind the camp, they came in with bowls of food. A fire burned in the middle of the floor. Lao Tzu sat, eyes closed in a lotus position, hands upturned resting on his knees, deep in meditation.

Sparrow raised a finger to her lips telling her to remain silent. Mandy listened to the strange words that Lao Tzu chanted as he sat, immobile as stone. He stopped, opened his eyes, looked at them then smiled. They smiled back.

"How was the rest of your day?" he asked Mandy.

"It was filled with wonder and surprise. I've seen so much it has been difficult to absorb it all." she answered.

"I understand, but absorb it you must. I'm sure Sparrow has told you of your standing in the tribe, so you must learn quickly. Tomorrow before dawn I will begin to teach you about plants, herbs and their uses, plus the rudiments of Kung Fu. I will teach you to speak the languages of Chin and the Cherokee. At first they will seem difficult, but in time they will be second nature. The language of Chin is so we can communicate in the presence of others in secret. It is a language that only we and our offspring will speak, no one else."

"Let us eat." They sat and ate the food they had prepared. Sparrow had made two small beds for their sons and she placed them among the pelts. In minutes they were asleep.

Sparrow, Mandy and Lao Tzu removed their clothes. The pelts the boys laid on were behind Mandy. Her bed lay at an angle towards the foot of Sparrows, whose lay at the foot of Lao's. Sparrow lay on top of the pelts naked, the flickering light from the fire danced across her body.

Mandy could see Sparrow's hand moving over her slim body, pinching at her stiff nipples. Rubbing across her stomach to her pubic mound, then staying there and jerking back and fourth. She couldn't see Sparrow's fingers dipping in and out of her cunt, but she knew what she was doing.

Mandy got hot and slipped her hand between her legs, and rubbed her finger over her clit as she squinted her eyes to see Sparrow better.

Lao Tzu moved from his bed and kneeled above Sparrow's head. Mandy saw him and looked at his penis. It was hard and throbbing, as she watched him watch Sparrow.

23

She noticed that his penis was much smaller than Josh's, but it was fat and thick. She watched as Sparrow grabbed it and brought it to her mouth, and sucked it in. Mandy had never saw anything like it before. Sparrow sucked him like a baby sucking a tit, and she found it strangely erotic. She watched as he straddled Sparrow's head, then he leaned forward and buried his face between Sparrow's legs. She saw his head moving, but didn't know what he was doing. So she crawled over between Sparrow's legs, then she lay down so she could see what Lao was doing. She saw that he was using his tongue to stab and lick her cunt. She saw his tongue slide in and out of her, saw her hips rise and fall as the tongue plunged in and out of her. He raised his head, opened her lips and flicked his tongue against her clit. Then he pushed two fingers inside of her and pumped them in and out. It was a strange sight but she found it exciting and she stroked herself as Rebecca had taught her. Sparrow's ass rose faster and faster as Lao licked at her, then she rose completely from the pelts and Mandy heard a high wailing scream.

"I eee"…"Ohhhh"…, as Sparrow's orgasm shook thru her.

Mandy stroked her clit faster and felt the sensations as her orgasm approached. Lao Tzu raised his head and looked into her eyes. Mandy's body spasm and she froze as her orgasm washed over her. Lao looked as she shook thru it. He rose and turned, and Mandy saw his short, thick shaft. It was glistening with saliva, as he moved between Sparrow's legs. She crawled to where she could see.

He held his rod to Sparrow's cunt and slowly slid it in. Sparrow moaned as he pushed it deep ummm"…"ummm,"

He thrust in deep slow strokes and looked at Mandy, as his rod slid in and out of Sparrow.

Mandy watched as Sparrow's slot seemed to swallow his shaft. He thrust faster and faster, as Sparrow's hips rose to meet him. Mandy's hands again went between her legs. Soon Lao was drilling into Sparrow, his penis a blur.

"Yes"…"yes"…Sparrow moaned as he piston in her faster and faster. She moaned then screamed, "Ieeee"…as she came again, then he exploded in her. He thrust in her until her orgasm subsided, then turned to Mandy who was stroking her clit furiously.

He pushed her back and spread her legs. "You are not ready yet. It will be at least a moon, but I will take care of

24

you." he said.

He put his head between her legs, and licked at her clit with solid strokes. He lifted it, pushed it and rolled it. His tongue battered it until her hands reached down to hold his head, then she shook and moaned.

"Oh my"…"oh"…"oh"…"yes" as she came.

He rose, pulled her into his arms and held her tight, then said. "Rest Mandy".

Before dawn the next day Lao Tzu and the women feed the boys, then headed off into the woods before the camp was awake. Only the sentries posted around the perimeter of the camp were awake. Mandy's first lesson was to learn to walk in the woods silently. Lao and Sparrow taught her. They came to a clearing in the woods and Sparrow taught her how to rig a sling so the boys could hang from a low lying branch.

Lao Tzu started her off with breathing and balance exercises, and some elementary kicks and punches. For two hours he patiently taught her.

Mandy was much bigger than Lao and Sparrow, but Lao was much stronger despite his small frame. Each day he taught them Kung Fu and how to use herbs and medicine.

Moon after moon the lessons continued as the seasons passed. Winter was approaching and the big hunt was near. The tribe would kill many deer and buffalo to dry for the coming winter.

Lao Tzu taught Mandy how to use the bow, knives, pistols and rifles until she was a dead shot. He taught her to ride horses and in time she rode as well as any Brave, even with Raven strapped to her. She was one of the fastest runners in the camp, and her strength and skills became legend.

By September she was taking small bands of women out on hunts, this had previously been unheard of. She taught them to use the bow, though not the Kung Fu. She and Sparrow led the young women and their confidence grew.

Lao Tzu was proud of his women and the role they had come to play in the tribe. When the big hunt came they would not play the traditional role the women played, as skinners and packers. They would ride to the hunt with the men.

Lao Tzu had taught them well.

*CHAPTER # 3 *

The tribe had moved farther south to the border of Florida, because the winters were less harsh and there was little or no snow fall. They had hunted their way south and as faith would have it they didn't encounter any hostile tribes.

As they settled at the Florida, Georgia border, they built their camp. They didn't hunt close to the camp, they went 15 miles or so away. They didn't want to spook the game close to camp, because they would need it to take them thru the winter.

Their hunting party consisted of 30 Braves, Lao Tzu and his women. They had brought along 20 horses to pack their kills back to camp. As they rose from a depression, they spotted a group of fat antelope grazing about a quarter mile away. They dismounted and hobbled their horses, they would travel the rest of the way on foot. They were all armed with bows, knives and tomahawks. They didn't carry any firearms.

Mandy and Sparrow were dressed like Braves in loincloths of buckskin, buckskin leggings and shirts. They both wore long braids with buckskin head bands adorned with feathers. Lao Tzu wore the same except for the headband, in its place he wore a buck skin cap he had fashioned from which hung yellow feathers. He was the only one in the tribe to wear the odd headgear.

As they crept towards the unsuspecting antelope, Lao Tzu thought he detected movement on the other side of the clearing. He signaled with his hand and his whole party fell to the ground. He scanned the area using his peripheral vision to try and spot any movement. They lay still for several minutes and he didn't see any thing, so he motioned them to move closer. Once they were in bow range he signaled them again, this time they all notched arrows and chose a target. They watched Lao Tzu and he nodded.

As the 33 arrows streaked toward the herd of antelope there was a sudden barrage of gunfire, 20 antelopes fell to the ground as the arrows struck their targets, an even larger number fell to the shower of lead.

Lao Tzu and his band notched more arrows, and lay in the deep grass waiting. A minute later, about 60 Cree Indians rose from the bush and rushed to the fallen antelope.

Lao knew that once the Cree saw their arrows, they would know the enemy was close. As soon as the Cree were in range Lao Tzu and his band unleashed a deadly hail of arrows, notched their bows and launched another wave before the first struck, then another.

Twenty of the Cree fell to the first group of arrows, ten to the next and four to the last wave. Lao pulled his tomahawk, leaped to his feet and attacked the stunned Cree. His band followed on his heels screaming their war cry.

"AYEEEE"...

The Cree, taken by surprise were stunned by the whistling death that claimed 34 of their brothers and were overwhelmed by the ferocity of the attack. Lao, his women and the Braves waded into them with raised tomahawks. Lao, a buck knife in one hand and a tomahawk in the other fell upon the Cree like a whirling Dervish. His tomahawk chopped into the neck of a Cree and almost decapitated him. When he wrenched it free he watched blood geyser in the air from the severed artery. He spun and in a underhand stroke buried his blade deep into the stomach of another Brave, disemboweling him. When he pulled his blade free, the man's intestines spilled from the gapping wound. He continued to hack and slash his way into the band of Cree.

Mandy behind Lao and to his right, attacked a Brave who was aiming his rifle at Lao. She spun and tossed her tomahawk in a pin wheeling arch. The blade cleaved into the center of his forehead and lodged deep in his scull. As she ran to retrieve her weapon, a Brave loomed in front of her. She leaped from the ground in a side thrust kick that caught the Brave in his throat, and sent him reeling back choking. She pulled her knife and slit his throat. The blade severed his windpipe and artery. A gush of air escaped and his blood spurted out and sprayed over her in a mist.

She dropped and quickly pried her tomahawk from the dead man's head and brain matter oozed from his split skull. She turned looking for another Cree.

Sparrow rushed behind Lao on his left and had notched an arrow. She aimed at a Cree Brave and released the arrow, it struck the Brave in his eye and punched out of the back of his head. She dropped the bow and pulled her tomahawk, attacking a Brave who was closing in on Lao's blind side. As the Brave was raising a tomahawk of his own, and rearing back to throw it, Sparrow moved in just as his arm was swinging forward. She swung her tomahawk and caught him at the wrist. The tempered steel of her blade had been honed to razor sharpness and it cleaved thru skin, muscle and bone. The hand holding the tomahawk was severed from the arm and it flew thru the air with the tomahawk still clutched tight in it. The Brave screamed as blood squirted from the stump. Sparrow spun in the same motion and buried the blade in the center of his face.

In less than ten minutes the battle was over. They had killed the Cree, but they lost ten Braves in the fight and another six were wounded. Lao and his wives went to find the Cree's horses and they found them in a rope corral in the woods. Ninety horses in all were found. They lead them back to where their band waited. They helped load the antelope and their dead, then they left the area quickly and rode back to camp. They had scalped all of the Cree and counted coup. The bloody scalps hung from their bows and the bridles of their horses.

Mandy and Sparrow had taken five scalps apiece and were the talk of the camp. The warriors told the tale of their bravery in battle and their share of the horses made them wealthy in their own right.

The Cherokee moved their camp, because they knew the Cree would soon be looking for their brothers.

* CHAPTER # 4 *

Winter came and went. It was not as harsh as the previous winters as they were near Florida, but it was cold nonetheless. The game was plentiful and they began to move north as spring approached.

In 1861 the Civil War began and there were battles fought all over the south. The Cherokee moved farther north skirting the battles that waged all around them.

The next two winters were harsh ones, the old and the young died by the dozens. They continued to move north as the war escalated.

The tribe became smaller and smaller as death, disease and war with hostile tribes took its toll. The births of fatherless children and merging with runaway slaves would swell their numbers from time to time, but the onslaught of the cruel, merciless winters and even crueler battles would thin out their numbers.

In 1866 the Civil War ended, but the hostilities between the tribes continued as they had for centuries. The Civil War had been the white mans' war and had no effect on them, except it turned the white man's attention from the Indian problem for a minute.

The Native Americans had been at war with each other forever it seemed and there was no peace treaty for them. They were a nomadic people who moved from season to season, but it seemed game was getting scarce as the white man flooded the land. The Native Americans killed for food and never more than they could eat. They gave the herds time to replenish themselves.

The whites were much different, in that they killed for hides and tallow, leaving the carcasses of the dead animals to litter the land. The buzzards and carnivores feasted on the many corpses the white's left behind rotting. They killed off great numbers of the buffalo, that once covered the land as far as the eye could see. They decimated them until there were thin scattered herds left.

The whites were like a force of nature as they

ravaged the land, destroyed the wildlife and chopped down the great forest. They brought in their domesticated cattle and began fencing off the range. They raided the native American burial grounds, settled on their tribal hunting grounds and attempted to deny them rights of passage.

It was only natural that the natives would rise up and fight for their way of life. It was at this point that the whites did to them the same thing they did to the buffalo. They decimated them, called them savages, when by right they were the savages. The whites were merciless as they slaughtered the natives in the thousands. They littered the land with their corpses again providing the buzzards and carnivores with a grisly feast.

In 1857, the so called Indian Wars were raging full fledge. The Native Americans were being killed for both real and imagined threats. They were being driven off their home lands and herded onto reservations, miles away from their home land where they had lived for centuries. There was no regard for tribes, so they were mixed with other tribes who had been their mortal enemies.

They were beaten, bruised, killed and maimed, yet still there were pockets of resistance. In some the fighting spirit lived on, and they would choose their day to die.

Standing Bear and his band of Cherokee were among the ones who chose to fight. They had moved deep south into the swamps of Florida, that would become known as the Everglades.

By the time Raven was 15 years old. He was the biggest man in the camp and he would grow bigger. He stood 6' 3" and weighed 220 chiseled pounds. He wore his hair in two thick braids that hung down his back. The only warriors in the camp who could stand with him were his father and brothers.

Little Bird's name was now Eagle. He was 5' 8' and weighed 170 pounds. He wore his head completely bald like his father and at 16 was a great warrior.

Lao Tzu had fathered four more children, three from Mandy and one from Sparrow.

Mandy bore him two sons, Falcon 14 and Hawk 13, both were mighty warriors. Falcon was 5' 11" with slanted eyes that were a hazel color. He wore 180 pounds and could only be beat in a physical contest by his father and Raven. Eagle could fight him to a draw and only his strength prevented him from loosing. He was light complexioned with long jet black hair that he wore in a single braid, which he wrapped around his neck.

Hawk at 13 was 5' 11' and weighed 170 pounds. He was cocoa brown complexioned with long jet black hair that he wore in two braids. He had the slanted eyes of his father and was the fastest runner in the camp.

Sparrow had bore him a daughter. She was 14 and her name was Dove, she was Raven's wife. They had a son who was a year old and Crow was his name. He was as dark as his father, but bore the slanted eyes and silky jet black hair of his Chinese and Native American grand parents.

Mandy bore him a daughter also. Her name was Swallow and at 12 she was as big as Sparrow. She had breast, ass and hips that promised her size would equal her mothers. She was a shade darker than her father, her skin a golden hue. Her eyes slanted, her lips full and inviting. The Braves were in constant competition for her.

She was betrothed to a Brave name Wolf, who was half black half Cherokee. His mother was a runaway slave who lived with the people for nearly 20 years. He was 18 and stood almost 6 foot tall, weighed 190 pounds and was a warrior. He would wed Swallow as soon as he brought Lao the bride price of seven horses.

*   *   *   *

Lao Tzu and his family were legendary in battle. Lao, his wives and four sons had counted coup on many of thier enemies. The women were just as fierce in battle as the men.

Mandy and Sparrow by that time were experts at martial arts. They started the children off in training and Lao finished them off.

Dove was a great fighter, but she fought only her mother and brothers. She was 5' 2" and wore 100 pounds. She and Swallow had yet to engage in battle with their band, but if called they could.

Lao Tzu and both of his wives were still young, he forty and they thirty. He had formed his own clan. The Bird Clan and they were the fiercest among the Cherokee. Close to them camped the Seminoles, who they were friendly with.

The Seminoles were comprised of Indians, runaway

slaves and other Native Americans who were exiled from their own tribes. They often went on hunting parties together.

Raven and his brothers spoke four languages by this time and from constant contact with the Seminoles they were all fluent in Spanish. Rarely did they come in contact with white men, they knew the trouble it would bring. They ventured from the camp days at a time.

On one such trip they had been deep in the swamp trapping beaver and fox. They had four pack horses loaded with salted yet green pelts and they headed to the trading post which was a weeks ride from the camp.

Their small band consisted of Raven, Eagle, Falcon, Hawk, Wolf and another half-breed named Cougar. Cougar was the son of a runaway slave and a Cherokee woman. His sister Willow was the wife of Eagle and they had a son who was now Little Bird.

Willow had two sisters who would be the wives of Falcon, and Hawk. Fern and Violet were theirs as soon as the bride price was paid. Three horses apiece.

The men had the horses as they were the wealthiest clan in the tribe. Lao and his sons often went out on raids of settlements and other tribes.

As the six Braves rode up to the trading post they noticed a group of horses with blue and yellow saddle blankets, with crossed sabers and the legend U.S on the corner.

Raven and his brothers could read, Mandy had taught them as Rebecca taught her. Lao had furthered their education and they read and wrote both Chinese and English. They knew the horses were army because they had fought them many times before.

The six Braves were all dressed traditional, except Raven and his brothers wore holstered pistols that hung gunfighter style on their hips. Raven wore two holsters crisscrossed that hung on either side. Eagle wore his pistol in a cross draw rig.

They carried Colt Peacemaker 45's, Winchester lever action 30-30 rifles and the four brothers carried several knives. Each had one strapped at their calves and one at their waist. They all carried tomahawks and their bows and quiver of arrows were strapped to their horses. The six men bristled with weapons.

They each wore loincloths, leggings and calf high

moccasins. None of them wore shirts, but they all wore vests held together with beads and decorative colored quills from porcupines. Each wore wide leather bands around their heads except for Eagle, who wore a buckskin cap of his father's design.

From Raven's headband hung big, blue-black feathers from the bird of which he was named.

Falcon, Hawk and Eagle all wore feathers from their name sakes. And Cougar and Wolf's headbands were decorated with pelts.

They dismounted and each grabbed a bundle of pelts and entered the trading post.

The trading post was a big squat building made of rough hewn logs. It was one big room with make shift tables and drunken white men, both soldiers and civilians. There were squaws and black women sprinkled throughout the place, whores each one. They were sitting in the laps of the men smoking, drinking and laughing as the men groped them beneath their ragged dresses.

The man who owned the trading post was named Sam Purdy. He was a big man and he ran the place with his brother Seymour.

Seymour was just as big as Sam and they both were rattle snake mean, pig eyed men. They ran the whores and fucked them too. They had built cribs behind the trading post where the men could take the women. For 50 cent per thirty minutes they did good business, as they were the only trading post, slash whore house in fifty miles or more. The only other women in the area were Squaws and the wives of settlers. And it was dangerous to molest either, so the eight women were kept busy. None were older than twenty two, but you couldn't tell by looking at them. They were all hard eyed and seasoned. The liquor had taken it's toll on them.

As Raven and his crew came to the counter and laid down their pelts, Sam Purdy offered them a drink.

Raven and his band never drank the white man's fire water. They had seen its results so they turned it down.

Sam Purdy turned up his lips, sneered then asked. "You too good to drink with us nigger?"

Raven looked in his eyes and said. "I didn't come to drink, I came to trade. Every time we come here we never drink, yet each time you offer us that filth. It seems to me that you should've learned by now we don't indulge in your filthy habits, so you can stop trying to encourage us!"

A big man in the uniform of the U.S Calvary with captain bars on his shoulder spoke up.

"You talk mighty uppity for a nigger. I've never heard an ex-slave use such perfect language, besides you're dressed like a savage."

Raven turned to the man and said. "I've never been a slave, and it is you who dress the part of a savage."

The captain looked at him in shock, then said. "Nigger I'm of a mind to teach you a lesson for that smart ass mouth!"

Raven looked to Sam Purdy and said. "We came to do business not make trouble." He laid his rifle on the counter and looked Sam in the eyes.

Eagle and Cougar had moved to the back of the big room and each took a corner as they saw trouble rising.

Wolf and Hawk spread out, so they could cover the front.

Falcon stood beside Raven with his rifle pointed towards the floor. The drunken soldiers and civilians never noticed the positions the men took, they were concentrating on the conversation at the counter.

The captain who's name was Seamus O'Rourke grabbed Raven's shoulder and turned Raven to him, and shouted. "Nigger don't you never turn your back when I'm speaking to you!"

Raven's hand shot up in an open handed blow that struck the Captain on the side of the face and ear. The blow cracked like a pistol shot and knocked the Captain from his seat. He crashed to the floor in a stunned heap by the force of the blow.

Sam Purdy screamed, "nigger you're a dead man!" and reached under the counter for a shotgun he had there. Before his hands closed over it, Falcon's rifle had swung in a rapid arch. And with devastating force slammed into Sam's head behind his ear. Sam collapsed to the ground unconscious.

There were ten other soldiers in the place besides the Captain and six civilians including the Purdy's. Seymour Purdy sat at a table playing cards with two of the civilians and three soldiers. They had all passed in the play when the confrontation began. When Seymour saw Raven slap the Captain to the ground, he started to rise. He pushed his chair back and reached to his waist for his pistol that hung there. It was a big Colt Dragon.

He pulled it from his waist and was bringing it up, when Hawk fired his rifle. The big 30-30 slug hit Seymour in the middle of his chest, crushed his breast bone, ripped thru his heart and exited in a spray of blood and gore. The force flung him back into his chair, which toppled over backwards. When the big slug hit him, reflexively he pulled the trigger.

The big pistol discharged in a plume of smoke and fire. The bullet struck a man sitting across from him in the face. The slug destroyed the man's nose, plowed thru his head and blew the man's brains out of the huge exit wound it made in the back of his head.

The room burst into total chaos, as the soldiers and civilians stood clawing for their weapons. Three men sat at one table, two had whores in their laps. They stood quickly dumping the whores to the floor. All three were fumbling for their guns.

Raven's hands streaked down, pulled his two Peace Makers and fired off four quick shots as soon as they cleared leather. All three men were punched back, as the rounds hit them. Each man took one to the heart and one took one in the neck. The bullets shredded their hearts and blew out of their backs in a shower of blood, lungs, and pulverized heart muscle.

Falcon had his rifle at his waist working the leaver and firing in one steady motion. He opened fire on a table of four soldiers. One of the 30-30 slugs ripped thru a man chest and crashed into another man's forehead. The force had been decreased to a degree, but there was still enough to penetrate and puncture the man's brain.

Eagle pulled his pistol and fanned the hammer, killing two soldiers before they could undo the flaps over their pistols. Both were head shots, that scattered bone and brain in the air.

Cougar fired his rifle methodically, killing two soldiers with heavy slugs to the chest, that pinned them to the chairs.

Wolf fired round after round into the men. He shot one soldier in the face, blood and brains showered from his head. He shot a civilian in the side, shattered his ribs, punctured both lungs and pulped his heart. The slug blasted from his other side in a spray of blood, bone shards and various mingled tissues. In less than two minutes they had killed 15 men.

Sam Purdy and Seamus O'Rourke were the last white men alive. The whores crawled in the blood and gore screaming.

Captain Seamus O'Rourke looked at the carnage and whispered, "oh my god". Then he looked up into the dead eyes of Raven and begged. "By the blessed mother of god please don't kill me. Please Jesus"...

Raven shot him in his pleading mouth and the bullet ripped out of the back of his head in a spray of blood.

Falcon stuck his rifle over the counter and shot Sam Purdy in the head and blew his brains out.

"Be quiet!" Raven shouted in a loud voice. The women stopped their screaming and watched the six Braves.

"You will help us to clean up this mess." Raven said to the women. The women all nodded yes.

Hawk and Cougar hitched up the wagon they found in the barn. Then the six Braves loaded the bodies in the wagon and dumped them in the woods. It took them two trips. They had stripped the bodies first, the wild animals would do the rest. They buried the saddle blankets and clothes, then changed all the brands on the Calvary horses.

Raven, sent Hawk and Cougar back to the camp to get Lao Tzu and the entire Bird Clan, plus Fern, Violet and the woman he chose to be his wife. They took the horses they got from the trading post as bride prices.

Raven told them to bring back Wilber O'Gilvey, the only white man who lived in their camp. He was a trapper who had two Indian wives. It would take them three days to reach camp riding in relays and another seven or eight days for the clan to reach the post. Ten or twelve days at the most.

In the mean time Raven set the women to cleaning the trading post. Raven, Eagle, Falcon and Wolf changed into white man clothes that they got off the shelf. Wolf got one of the holsters and a pistol from those they took off the dead men. Raven chose to dress in all black. Black jeans, black shirt, black vest, black boots and a black low crowned Stetson that previously belonged to one of the dead men. The others chose an array of colors and set up shop in the trading post.

The first customers that floated thru were Indians. Raven dealt with them fairly. They were surprised at the prices they got for their goods and word spread quickly.

Raven had read the books and knew who was supplying the Purdy's. Most of the suppliers brought their goods to the post, but Raven knew they would have a problem dealing with a black man. That's why he had sent for Wilber O'Gilvey, he would front the operation for the clan. Lao Tzu, Mandy, Sparrow, Dove, Swallow and the other wives would really run the place.

* CHAPTER # 5 *

Fourteen days had passed by the time Hawk and Cougar returned to the post. Hawk came to Raven and they embraced, then he said. "Father wanted to come with us, but after a lengthy discussion he came to the conclusion that it would be better if he stayed with the clan."

Raven nodded his head. Raven was dressed like the white man and Hawk stared hard at his elder brother as they walked into the trading post. Raven refused to sell strong drink to the other tribes, but he gave them all a fair price. They sat in the post catching up on what news there was of the tribe.

Lao and the others arrived. There was a beautiful Seminole and black woman with them, who was to be Cougar's wife. She was the granddaughter of the Seminole Chief, her name was Conchita. Most of the Seminole's had a Spanish name.

She was 5' 4", weighed 125 pounds and her skin was dark with a reddish tinge.

Wilber O'Gilvey came to Raven and wrapped him up in his bear like arms. Wilber was bigger than Raven, he stood 6' 6", and weighed 300 pounds at the age of thirty. He and Raven stood to the side as the clan settled in around the post. Wilber looked deep into Raven's eyes and asked. "What's going on here son?"

"We had trouble with the previous owners and a small squad of Calvary. So we killed them all and took over the post. We know the merchants won't do business with us if they think the post is ran by the people or blacks. If they do then they are sure to charge us more than they would a white man or give us inferior goods. So I need you to be the front man for the post, you'll be an equal partner with me and the others."

"What about the clan?" asked Wilber.

"They will be taken care of, me and my brothers will take care of them from our share of the profits."

Wilber nodded his head, then said. "I agree on the condition we sell no spirits to the Braves."

"That has already been established," said Raven. "You must teach the women to plant and grow, as well as livestock. Times are changing and the old ways are dying so we must look to the future and use the white man's method to prosper. Our survival depends on us being able to change with the times."

"You see far for one so young , but there is more we must do to insure the survival of our clan. We have to stake claim to as much of this land as possible before the homesteaders move in." said Wilber.

Raven nodded, then said. "You take care of that. I want to ride up to the Spanish settlement and see how they are doing things."

"Has anyone come looking for the soldiers or the owners since the trouble?" asked Wilber.

"No. We haven't had any whites come since the trouble." said Raven.

"They'll come, It's just a matter of time. We'll be prepared, but what we can't do is get into a shooting war with the U.S army. You've seen some of the results of the so called Indian Wars. The tribes have been decimated and we have no where near the amount of Braves to fight a war." said Wilber.

"I understand," said Raven. "Believe me that's the last thing I want, but I want to see the clan prosper in the ways of the white man."

"The only way you'll be able to do that is with gold or money. Enough of either and your color will be over looked. The first thing we need to do is build a settlement around the post. No Teepee's, but log cabins for each branch of the clan, then a hotel and saloon separate from the post. The post will serve as the general store." said Wilber.

"You'll have to teach us how to do these things and the sooner the better." said Raven.

"We'll start tomorrow, it will be work for men. The women as well, but we need to have everything done before winter. Most of the things we'll need are readily available, but the Braves will balk at the work unless you explain it to them." Wilber said.

"It's done. I'll talk with my father first." said Raven.

*   *   *   *

After the women had set up camp, they all sat in the

trading post. Raven sat with Lao Tzu and explained to him the plans he had for the clan. Lao agreed that the plans were good and should be put into action soon.

Lao called the clan together and told them what they would do.

All of the men were his sons so they didn't complain.

Night fell and Lao was in the Teepee with Sparrow and Mandy. He looked at the women, and said. "Our son Raven is destined for great things. He has come up with a plan to insure the future of the clan. It involves learning the ways of the white man and employing them to our benefit. It will take much effort on all our behalves to make it work."

"What about the customs of the people?" asked Sparrow.

"They will be passed on to the young ones as always." replied Lao. "It is a good thing to have knowledge of the old ways. As time passes I find myself remembering less and less of the ways of my people. And that will not happen to my sons or the sons of my sons, as long as life is within us. We are the elders, it is our responsibility to make sure they don't forget."

Mandy looked from Lao to Sparrow, then asked. "What of the ways of my people? I have no knowledge of them, only of the whites and the people."

Lao moved to her and pulled her into his arms, then said. "History will teach our sons and their sons the way of your people. These are strange times and your people are from a far away land. In time they will learn, rest assured of that."

Mandy had long ago learned to have confidence in Lao Tzu. She held him tight as Sparrow moved over to them. They were still dressed in traditional clothing.

Lao looked at the women, then said. "You two will have to curb the warrior spirit within you in the times to come. The discipline you've learned will help you. When the time to fight comes, you will as always follow me into battle. We have much work to do, but you will have even more. You will teach the daughters each day, all of them. We are alone now and no longer have the strength that comes with numbers. Each member of the clan must be ready to do battle, if we are to survive the times to come."

Lao and the women undressed, then made love and went to sleep.

Early the next morning the entire clan was hard at work, with Wilber overseeing. They cut trees in ten plots that they would build their homes on.

The men planed the logs, as the women cleared land for the crops they would plant. The work was hard, but they were persistent and in two months they had built all the cabins.

Progress was swift and each day they accomplished more. It had been nearly three months since they had taken over the post. Because of their fair dealings with everyone, they had amassed a great deal of trade goods and even a good bit of gold.

They had to build extra storage space for the goods, as they were getting customers from far and wide. They were expecting the suppliers to come thru at any time.

No one had come inquiring about the missing soldiers, but Wilber knew that soon they would. By Wilber being the sole white man in the settlement, they named it after him. "OGILVEY" There was a big sign with the name at each end of the settlement.

Word began to spread about the new town and homesteaders started moving into the area; black, white and Native Americans. Soon the population increased and there were nearly 200 people in Ogilvey. As with any large gathering there was bound to be some trouble.

* CHAPTER # 6 *

The white settlers had built on one side, the blacks and natives on the other. There was close to 100 whites and the town would soon be in need of someone to uphold the law. Due to the times, it could only be a white man.

The supplies came and soon others built their businesses around the trading post.

The U.S department had sent a detachment of soldiers in search of the missing troopers, but it was to no avail. In nine months Ogilvey had close to 350 people and had become segregated.

A bad element moved into town and the black and native townsfolk were being harshly treated, despite Wilber doing all he could to keep down racial incidents.

The Bird Clan had increased their land holdings. They had 2,000 head of cattle and 500 horses. They had acres of crops and most of the black and natives worked for them. They had moved about ten miles from town, since large numbers of whites had moved there. And they were still partners with Wilber in five or six businesses.

A man by the name of Willis Grimsley had moved to town and brought five hard cases with him. All of the blacks and natives feared Willis, except for the Bird Clan. Willis Grimsley was a small, sallow skinned, pinched face man. Simmie Lukes was his right hand man. A big blond man.

Willis had opened his own saloon and soon Wilber's only catered to the social outcast. Willis wouldn't serve the blacks at all, though he had a shed out back that he served the assorted Braves rot gut whisky from. The town had grown so large that it was a true need for law enforcement.

It was only natural that Wilber was the Mayor, as the whites had established a town council. The town council was influenced by Willis and soon two of his men served as Sheriff and deputy.

Wilber knew there would be trouble and there was little he could do to prevent it. He had seen similar scenarios and could prophecy what the outcome would be. Inwardly he quaked, for he knew that death was in the forecast. A few of

Wilber's trapper friends had moved into the area on the outskirt with their Indian and black wives. They had heard that the small town of Ogilvey was tolerant to their domestic situations, children's lives and futures were in the balance.

*   *   *   *

  Jerry Vine was the sheriff of Ogilvey. Vine was a tall rangy man, slim but with corded muscles that bulged thru his too tight clothes. He thought of himself as a Dandy and dressed the part. Off white low crown Stetson, crème colored broadcloth jacket and tan riding breeches that fit almost like a second skin. A beige waistcoat, off white shirt with brown string tie and a thick gold chain that swung between the two pockets of the waistcoat. He wore highly glossed nut brown cowboy boots, with big, shiny, silver Mexican rowel spurs. On his hips hung a beautifully constructed holster. In them were two blue black Colt 45's with oiled walnut grips. He was a gunfighter of renown. He had killed eight men and had developed a taste for death.

  Lester Whitted was his long time companion and partner, an equally dangerous man. Where Vine was a sharp, clean man, Lester was dirty, vicious and sadistic. He was a small, dark haired, weasel faced man with buck teeth and a ragged beard. His clothes were so dusty and dirty that you couldn't tell what color they actually were. The only way to describe them, was earth toned. Vine was the only one who could control Lester.

  Willis, Vine, Lukes, Lester and two more of their men sat with Clem Hartfield and Alex Mews in the back of Willis's saloon. Clem was a big mountain man from the hills of Kentucky. Alex was a short rotund man, he had huge hands and was exceptionally strong.

  Willis looked at the men gathered, then said. "Fellows we've got a golden opportunity here. Word has spread that Ogilvey is a very good town, prosperous and growing. The railroad is planning to bring a spur thru, going straight up to New York. What we need is to be able to get all the land we can in Nigger Town. We can sell it back to the railroad and get rich in the process."

  "I like the sound of that," said Vine. "But what do we do after we sell the railroad the land?"

  "If they put a depot here that means we get all of the

business. We sell the railroad water, coal, wood and anything else they need. It will keep the money coming and we can live like Barons." said Willis.

"So what's the plan?" asked Lukes.

"We need an excuse to kill off some niggers and some Indians." His eye's twinkling with pleasure.

"You know the Mayor is a nigger and a Injun lover." said Axel.

"That's true," Clem chanted.

"Well that means if he gets in the way he'll meet with a nasty accident." Willis said laughing.

The other men laughed too.

A few day's later Gantry Smith was in the Blacksmith shop with his son Lijah. Gantry was huge, 6'5", and a muscled 350 pounds. His son Lijah at 17 was nearly as big, 6'2", 240 pounds, he too was a blacksmith. They stood next to the forge as Gentry pumped the bellows to fan the fire.

"Pa, we need to talk." said Lijah.

"Son, I know what it's about and I've had my say. Can't no good come of you seein that white woman. This world ain't ready for that yet, hell may never be ready for it. They can do what they want to us, but the ground ain't nowhere near level boy."

"Pa, I love Bess." said Lijah pleadingly.

"Forget her boy, I ain't asking you I'm telling you. Find a woman among your own, there are plenty of pretty girls."

"I want Bess Pa, none of the others. She feel's the same way." said Lijah.

"What you know bout love? Not a damn thing, but let me tell you this boy. That women ain't worth the grief she'll bring you. All they need is an excuse and you're dead. Don't you see that, the way they treat us?"

"My mind's made up Pa, and I'm gonna be with Bess." said Lijah firmly.

"In that case, I guess I better go see the carpenter." said Gantry.

"What for Pa?" asked Lijah.

"To get three coffins built, for you, me and your Ma." Gantry replied hollowly.

"It ain't that bad Pa. Look at the white men that got black wives or Indian wives. Look at the Indian men with black wives." said Lijah.

"Yeah, look at them. You don't see a single Blackman with a white woman, no Indian with a white woman. What does that tell you?" Gantry asked.

"You don't understand." said Lijah storming from the shop.

Gantry shook his head and released the handles of the bellow, washed his hands, put on his hat and headed to see Chany Woods the carpenter. He was resigned to the fate that he knew was ahead. If they killed his boy, they would have to kill him too.

   *   *   *   *

Lijah stood in the empty shed at the back of the Melman's property. The floor was spread with blankets. As he stood in the darkness, he heard a soft rustling sound and stood even stiller.

"Lij," whispered Bess Melman.

"I'm here." Lijah whispered.

Bessie Melman was a big corn feed white girl of 15. Her breast were full, her hips wide and well rounded. He took her into his arms and they tumbled to the blankets, where they frantically undressed. In no time she had guided him in and they were thrusting and bucking wildly. So deep were they into their love making that they never heard the door open. Only the moon light shining thru the door on their thrashing bodies and the roar Dan Melman made when he spied them, alerted them to his presence.

"My god!" he roared.

"Pappa," Bess moaned in the throes of her orgasm.

Lijah's head spun around at the sound and he saw Dan standing there with the lamp in one hand and the pistol in the other.

Dan Melman screamed , "you bastard!" then pointed the pistol and fired.

Lijah had started to roll from between Bess's legs and the bullet missed him and slammed right into Bess, between the milky white twin mounds of her breast.

Blood spurted upward as she moaned out, "OH" then slumped back to the floor. A trickle of blood spilled from the corner of her mouth, and her glazed green eyes locked on her father.

Lijah sprung up from the floor and attacked Dan.

Dan was momentarily stunned, but he had heard the rumor his daughter was seeing a nigger. He vowed to kill them both if it was true, so he wasn't completely out of it. He spun, his gun still pointing at the ground, and fired it. The big slug smashed into Lijah's knee, and blew it apart. Bone splinters and blood splashed the night, as Lijah crashed to the floor at Dan Melman's feet.

"Oh no nigger, it ain't gone be that easy. You gonna be an example to the other nigger's and redskins. We ain't tolerating this shit." Then he swung his gun down viciously and clubbed Lijah in the head.

Lijah slumped and tried to shake the ringing in his skull out.

Dan clubbed him again and again, until Lijah was unconscious. His head was a bloody mess.

Dan Melman looked quickly around trying to fix a scenario that would protect his daughter's image. He spotted a big knife sheathed to Lijah's belt. He pulled the big knife and walked to where Bess lay. He lifted her to see did his bullet penetrate and saw that it didn't. Gently he laid her back, then plunged the big knife in the gunshot wound. He found rope, and tied Lijah, then walked back to the house and woke his wife Verna.

"Honey, Bess is dead. That nigger raped and killed her."

Verna screamed, "NOOOO…. My baby!"

"Calm down honey, that nigger is going to pay. I got him tied up in the shed, and I'm gonna get Terry to go get the Sheriff."

Verna buried her head in his chest and sobbed uncontrollable.

"Terry…Terry," shouted Dan loudly.

A big boned young man of 16, Terry Melman, was the spitting image of his father.

"Go get the Sheriff right away son." said Dan

"What's wrong Pa?" asked Terry.

"Get the Sheriff son, I'll tell you when you come back."

Terry looked at his father, and hurried from the room.

*　　　　　　*　　　　　　*　　　　　　*

Vine and Lester, left Clem and Axel in town as they rode with Terry to the Melman's place. When they arrived they were met by Dan, who led them to the shed.

"My Lord!" shouted Terry as he saw his sister lying on the floor of the shed, with a big knife plunged between her naked breast. Breast he had fondled. His gaze moved down and he saw the light glisten on the silky hairs of her cunt. He had personally deflowered her a year earlier. Of lately she wouldn't let him so much as see it. He looked at the still, bloody figure, that lay trussed on the floor and knew the man hadn't killed Bess.

"Is that piece of shit alive?" Vine asked Dan.

"I hope so," Dan answered. "I want him to take a long time dying."

"I think that can be arranged, but if you want to send a message to the other niggers we need to take him into town." said Vine.

"I agree," said Dan. "Go get us a horse for this sack of shit. Then stay here with your Ma and get your sister ready for burying."

"Alright Pa," said Terry with tears threatening to fall from his eyes as he walked away.

They had Lijah in the small log cabin that served as the jail. It was connected to a bigger log cabin that served as the Sheriff's office. Vine, Willis, and the others were in the office.

"This could be just what we needed." said Willis. "All we need now is to get this nigger hung and it won't be hard once news gets around."

"You got that right." said Vine.

"I'm gonna go to the saloon and light the fuse." said Willis heading for the door.

"I'm with you Boss." said Clem who rose to follow Willis.

Axel got up, and said. "Let's strike terror into all the niggers!"

*   *   *   *

Around noon, Gantry rushed into Wilber's place looking around desperately. He spotted Wilber and rushed over.

"They got my boy in the lock up, Mr. Wilber. Say he killed Bess Melman. He didn't kill her Mr. Wilber. I need your help."

Wilber had heard the rumors that Lijah and Bess were messing around. He shook his head because even though he knew what was going to happen, he didn't think it would be so soon.

"Let's go over to the jail and see what's going on." said Wilber walking from behind the desk.
As the two men stepped outside, they could hear the noise coming from Willis's place. They hurried to the Sheriff's office.

Vine looked up as the door swung open and saw that it was Wilber and a big black man with a rifle.

"What can I do for you Mayor?" Vine asked.

"I want to know what's going on here?" Wilber said.

"We've got a nigger locked up for killing young Bessie Melman. Her father caught him in the act." said Vine. "We're going to give him a fair trial then hang his ass."

"My boy didn't kill that girl, Mr. Vine. He was in love with her." Gantry said.

"Nigger, did I ask you a question or in any way indicate I wanted you to speak?" asked Vine disrespectfully.

Gantry bristled and the rifle he carried swung in Vine's direction.

With uncanny speed and cat like agility, Vine had quickly launched himself from the chair and drew his pistols. His speed surprised both Wilber and Gantry.

"Put the rifle down or you're a dead man." he hissed at Gentry.

Gantry looked down the twin barrels of the 45's and gently lay his rifle on the hard dirt floor.

"Wilber I suggest you get the nigger's rifle and you both leave my office." said Vine.

Wilber looked Vine in the eyes, then said. "You're a dead man. I know what will happen and I'll try my damndest to stop it, but I know I won't be able to. You've been warned, I'm gonna be justice of the peace in the case. It's going to be a fair trial." Then he picked up Gantry's rifle and the two men left.

*   *   *   *

Raven and Eagle walked into the post and greeted Wilber and Gantry, who were in a heated conversation. Wilber raised his hand to silence Gantry as the two men approached.

"Raven, we've got a big problem. Gantry's boy is in the lock up for rape and murder. " said Wilber.

"Rape and murder," echoed Raven puzzled.

"Yep, rape and murder. Lijah supposedly raped and killed young Bess Melman last night, but half of the town if not the whole town knows the two were seeing each other." Wilber replied.

"My boy loved that girl, he wouldn't hurt her." said Gantry.

"So what are we going to do about it?" asked Raven.

"I don't know," answered Wilber. "But I ain't gonna sit and just let them hang the boy."

"Were going out to the ranch." said Raven. "If you need us anytime in the next few hours send word. We're going to take some cattle to St. Augustine today and we'll probably be gone for a couple of weeks.

"I think things can hold until then." said Wilber.

Raven and Eagle turned and walked from the post. "Do you think it wise we deliver the cattle now considering Wilber might need us?" asked Eagle.

"We gave our word and wise or not we'll abide by it." said Raven as they mounted their horses and rode off

*   *   *   *

"I'm telling you boys, if we let this nigger go to trial with that nigger loving Mayor as Justice of the Peace he'll walk. What would that say to the white women in this town? They wouldn't be safe." said Willis to the drunken crowd.

"I say we take that nigger and string his ass up from the highest tree." said Clem.

"I second that motion." said Axel.

The men in Willis' saloon roared their approval and soon the drunken crowd surged toward the door. One man grabbed a rope from the saddle horn of a horse and quickly fashioned a noose. The men trooped to the Sheriff's office and a big man named Wiley Edwards called out to the Sheriff.

"Vine, bring the nigger out so he can face justice or we'll come in and take him!"

Vine stepped from the office with Lester on his heels. "You men head on back to the saloon. We're not turning our prisoner over." said Vine.

"Hang the nigger, hang the nigger," the crowd chanted! They moved in mass toward Vine and Lester, who seemed to grudgingly give way to the mob. Soon the men were flooding into the Sheriff's office.

*   *   *   *

"I think there will be trouble in town." Raven said to Lao Tzu.

"No doubt," Lao replied. "I knew from the start that it would not be easy living like the whites. They have destroyed this once beautiful land and it's inhabitants, both human and animal."

"Be careful father and keep the clan close until we return. If you think I should leave Hawk or one of the others I will." said Raven.

"No need my son, we will be here until you return unless Wilber needs us."

Raven and his band said their good bye's, and headed the cattle north. Dove was pregnant with Raven's child and was due in the next month or so.

*   *   *   *

"Wilber, I think we better get our gun's. They're about to lynch that kid!" shouted a trapper called Beaver.

Wilber and the other men in the saloon, his trapper friends, equaled five men. All big men, plus Gantry. The men all grabbed their rifle's and filed out quickly, running towards the screaming crowd at the Sheriff's office.

Clem and Axel dragged a bruised and bleeding Lijah from the lock up into the street. Dan Melman stepped forward and kicked the battered man viciously in the face. Lijah's head snapped back. Wiley Edwards took the noosed rope that was passed to him and looped it around Lijah's neck. A loud rifle shot rang out and the crowd grew quiet.

"Take that rope off the boy's neck!" shouted Wilber his rifle pointed at Wiley. The trappers had their guns lazily trained on the crowd.

Wiley looked at Wilber, and said. "You'd defend this piece of shit, instead of a white woman this animal raped and killed?"

"How do you know he did it?" asked Wilber.

"He was caught in the act man!" Wiley shouted.

"Her Pa killed her when he caught us together!" shouted Lijah in the silence.

"Lying sack of shit!" screamed Dan Melman pulling his pistol as he aimed at Lijah and fired.

"NOOOO!" screamed Gantry swinging his rifle to bear on Dan Melman and firing an instant after Dan.

Dan Melman's round slammed into Lijah's forehead which seemed to implode and then cave in on itself. Then the back of his head exploded in a geyser of blood, bone and pinkish grey brain matter.

Gantry's 30-30 round smashed into the side of Dan Melman's neck and severed his artery. Blood sprayed into the faces of the men closest to him, then he crashed to the ground.

Everybody started shooting at that point. It was nearly a massacre. Gantry was shoot several times by Vine and his big hulking mass tumbled tree like to the ground. Two of his trapper buddies fell to the gun fire from the crowd. Ten of them were down, dead or dying. Wilber was hit in the left shoulder and in the side. The round went straight thru. He had crawled behind a watering trough and continued to fire at the fleeing men.

* CHAPTER # 7 *

In less than 24 hours, 15 people had died violently in Ogilvey. The town was in an uproar, and Wilber and the remaining trappers had disappeared. Willis and his men were in the back room at his place.

"That's just the beginning for us. You see how all the niggers in town are armed and being bold. Lookin white people in the eye like they are equal. Disarm them all Vine." said Willis.

"Gonna take more killing to do it." Vine said.

"The more dead niggers, the less we have to deal with later." said Willis.

"When do we start?" asked Vine.

"You'll need to deputize Clem and Axel." Willis said. "Make it look legal like."

Clem and Axel pulled badges from their vest pockets. "We kind of anticipated this." said Axel.

The four men stood and headed to the door with Vine in the lead.

"Better them than us!" shouted Willis to the retreating men.

The men looked across the street. Standing in front of the post was a slim black man with a rifle cradled in his arms, staring intently at them. The four men crossed the street and stood a few feet away from the man. "What's your name boy?" asked Vine.

"Ain't no boy, but my name Tom Rivers." said the black man.

"Give me that rifle boy." said Vine. "It's against the law for niggers to tote firearms in the city limits."

"Ain't givin up my gun." Tom Rivers said stubbornly.

"Drop the rifle or die, nigger boy." said Lester venomously.

Before Tom Rivers could reply Lester drew his gun and fired three quick rounds that punched into his chest. Tom's arms were flung skyward, the rifle hurtled thru the air. He stumbled backward then crashed to the ground in a cloud of dust. People stepped outside and peered at the bloody body that lay in the street.

"Shit is about to bust at the seams around here Lao." said Wilber from the big bed at the clan's ranch. "If I were you, I'd get the people and head back to the swamps."

"Look around you Wilber, the white way is killing out the old ways. To run would only prolong what is inevitable, I will fight while I can. They are only men, white men I grant you, but men nonetheless. They too can die in battle." said Lao Tzu. "We built this place. It is what it is, because of us, we can't just abandon it. My son will return."

"People are gonna die if you stay." said Wilber.

"They will die if we go. Death is an eventuality, we must all face it." said Lao.

"You are a true warrior brother." said Wilber with respect.

"As are you and it would be an honor to fight by your side." said Lao.

         *   *   *   *

A group of white men gathered around the body of Tom Rivers, gloating. Tom's brother Tobias Rivers came around the corner at a run, with his rifle in his arms. When he saw his brother's body sprawled in the street he came to a sliding halt, brought his rifle up and opened fire on the crowd of men. Three men fell before the others broke and ran in different directions, returning fire. It seemed that gunfire came from everywhere and riddled Tobias. Rounds tossed him into the air and against the front wall of the post, where he slid down. Tobias had killed three men and wounded several more before he died.

"The niggers done gone crazy!" shouted one man who trained his rifle on a black woman who was trying to make it into the post. He fired. And the woman, shot in the back collapsed into the building.

The whites filed into the street in mass and began firing randomly at any black or native in sight.

Soon the streets were filled with armed white men, heading towards the part of town where blacks and natives live. They shot, beat and burned down an entire section of town. The blacks and natives fled, scattered in the woods. Some pockets of resistance existed, but soon they too were cut out. By night fall 25 people were dead and twice that number wounded. Ogilvey was turned into a killing field and the whites were running in packs. They had spread out, killing and torching the black owned ranchers. Chaos reigned, as the whites approached the ranch of the Bird Clan.

*　　　　　*　　　　　*　　　　　*

A man named Lenny Shakes had rode to the ranch and warned the Bird clan of the roving bands of whites. They were raping, killing and burning out the blacks and Indians in and around Ogilvey.

The Bird clan had built a hidden root cellar and that's where Lao sent Dove with Crow and Little Bird to hide. The other members of the clan dressed for war. Lao looked at the seven women and four men gathered in the cabin, then said. "Me, Mandy, Sparrow, Willow and swallow will go out and take the fight to them. Wilber you and the others will fight from the inside."

Wilber, two trappers, Lenny Shakes, Fern, Violet and Conchita were all armed with rifles. They moved to the firing ports built into the cabin, as Lao and the others bristling with arms left the cabin.

*　　　　　*　　　　　*　　　　　*

Clem, Axel and eight men from the town met up with six other men, who were led by a skinny, bucktoothed man name Virgil Haskins. The 16 men banded together and closed in on the Bird clan ranch.

Lao Tzu, his wives and two daughters were spread out in a horseshoe formation in the woods that lead to their ranch. Before they had spread out, Lao had warned them to let the men show their intentions before attacking.

The men from town were packed in a bunch, many carried torches so the group was well lighted. Lao and the others watched silently as the men closed in on the big log cabin and then spread out around it.

"Alright niggers and redskins, toss out your weapons and come out with your hands up. And you might live to see daylight!" shouted Virgil Haskins.

"This is private property and you're trespassing!" Wilber shouted to the men.

"That's that nigger loving Mayor." said Clem to Axel. One of the men raised his gun and fired at the cabin.

Lao did a bird call which was the signal to attack. Mandy quickly notched an arrow and aimed at a man on horseback, who was perfectly lit by one of the torches. There was a light twang as the arrow was launched. The arrow struck the man between the shoulder blades. His back arched as the arrow ripped into him and he tumbled from his horse. When Mandy let loose her arrow, four more arrows streaked into the group of men. Death on feathered shafts silently streaked into the men, who fell from their mounts dead or seriously wounded.

The cries of the men who were hit by the arrows, threw the group into panic. They unleashed a deadly hail of rifle fire into the cabin and surrounding woods.

Lao and his group quickly returned fire with their bows. The gunmen couldn't see where the attack was coming from, as the people inside the cabin opened fire on them too. A man on horseback threw a torch on the roof of the cabin and the dry shakes quickly caught on fire. Lao saw the roof catch fire and knew that they had to get rid of the men soon, if they were to save the people in the house. They had either killed or wounded seven or eight of them so the odds were not as lopsided.

"AIEEEEE!" screamed Lao Tzu as he rushed from the woods with his rifle blazing. Soon he was joined by his wife and daughters, all screaming their war cry.

Clem and Axel spurred their horses and galloped away from the scene as Lao and the women attacked the men. Sparrow fired her rifle and a man fell to the ground. It was only a flesh wound. The man had dropped his rifle and was clawing for his pistol. The gun came free and he fired two shots at the figure running towards him from the dark. His first round smashed into Sparrow's shoulder and spun her around. The next slammed into her ribs, shattering them as it punched thru her lungs and heart. She fell to the ground silently.

The man leaped from the ground and rushed to his horse to mount it, when a big dark figure swooped in on him with upraised tomahawk. He opened his mouth to scream as the tomahawk slashed into the center of his face and cleaved his head almost in two. As Mandy struggled to free the tomahawk from the man's face, another rider drew close to her, pointed his weapon down and squeezed off a round. The big 30-30 slug punched into her breastbone and catapulted her backward, where she crashed to the ground. Her big dark eyes staring up blindly into the starry sky.

Swallow seeing her mother tossed backward by the gunshot, pulled her knife from her waist and tossed it underhand at the rider. The big blade spinning and flashing glints of light, cut into the man's throat. He dropped his rifle and his hands shot to the hilt of the big knife embedded in his throat as he fell from his horse.

Lao was unaware that his wives had fell in battle. He raced for the cabin door after killing two men. As he reached the door, a gunshot from a heavy caliber rifle sounded. The big slug from the Buffalo rifle smashed into Lao Tzu's back and pulverized his spinal column, pinning him to the cabin door. Slowly he slid down and lay slumped on the door.

Clem Hartfield sat on his horse almost 200 yards away, looking for another target in the well lit area. There were none so he sheathed his rifle and they rode off.

Swallow and Willow had made quick work of the men that remained, then sprinted for the door of the cabin. They saw that Lao was dead and dragged him away from the burning cabin. The door of the cabin burst open and Fern, Violet and Conchita stumbled from the cabin coughing. As Wilber and the three men struggled to the door the roof of the cabin caved in and the four men were engulfed in the blaze. The five young women could do nothing for the men and their screams didn't last long at any rate.

The women went to the hidden root cellar where Dove and the children hid safely. After they had got the bodies of Lao Tzu and his wives, they placed them in a smoke house. The six women preformed the death rights for their parents, then danced for them until exhaustion caught up with them at sunrise.

*   *   *   *

Willis and his group met in the back of his saloon the next day. "It was a lot easier than I thought it would be, faster too." said Willis.

"So what's our next move?" asked Vine.

"We wait. The railroad or one of their

representatives will come thru before long. What we need to do in the mean time is lock this town up tight and bury as much of what has gone on in the last few days as deep as possible." said Willis. "And oh yeah, the new name of the town is Grimsley."

They all started laughing.

* CHAPTER # 8 *

Raven and his band had sold the cattle and had been on the trail for ten days. They came across a family who were the worst for wear. Raven knew the man as he had worked for the Bird Clan from time to time. His name was Albert Silvers and he had an Indian wife, and six half-breed children.

"What's going on Al?" asked Raven.

Albert told Raven and the others what had taken place and told them about the death of their parents. Raven and his brothers fed the Silvers and gave them some gold to get started. Then the brothers pushed their horses to the brink of death, in their haste to get back to their family.

When the six men rode to the ranch, they saw that the big cabin had been burned to the ground. It was plain to see that most of their cattle and horses had been stolen as well. The six men fanned out and went in search of survivors. Raven came across three mounds of earth and knew that he was looking at the graves of his parents. Rage washed over him and he was filled with hatred for the white man and his ways. He came to the root cellar and from the tracks he knew that some of the women had survived. He went to the opening, and gave the Bird call that was familiar to the entire clan. The door burst open and Dove rushed out into his arms.

Automatically he noticed she was no longer big with child. He looked into her eyes and she smiled, then said. "You have another son."

Raven nodded then made the Bird call again. The sound echoed thru the woods and soon the other men rushed to the root cellar where they were reunited with their wives.

"What happened?" Raven asked.

"The whole thing was engineered by Willis Grimsley. Willis found out that the railroad was gonna have a depot in town and they needed land for the right of way. So Grimsley came up with a scheme to drive the blacks and the people off the land." said Dove.

"We must get ready to travel." said Raven. "I want to round up a good sized herd of the cattle and horses that are left. I want you women to pack as much as you can and be ready to ride at a moments notice."

"How long do you think it will take us to gather a herd?" asked Eagle.

"A day or two at the most. Once that is done we will send the women and children north. Then we will avenge the deaths of our parents." said Raven.

     *   *   *   *

"You've got a nice little set up here Mr. Grimsley." said Cyrus Walcott, the agent for southern railway. "I thought the name of the town was Ogilvey?"

"Oh, it was, but the Mayor decided to abandon the town and get back to trapping. He didn't want to face the scrutiny of the public, for having a heathen wife." said Willis.

"I guess that would cause a problem for the upstanding white citizens of this fine town." said Cyrus.

"That it would," said Willis laughing. "Now have you thought about the matter of land?"

"Yes I have and we'll deal directly with you as far as purchase is concerned. I also have conditions that are strictly between you and I." said Cyrus with greed in his eyes.

Having dealt with immoral men and being one himself, Willis smiled at Cyrus then asked. "And what might those conditions be?"

Cyrus cleared his throat, and said. "I'll pay you the maximum price for the land and you kick me back 20% of the total."

Willis laughed. "That's a little steep don't you think?"

"Not at all." Cyrus said.

"15% no more." said Willis with a dangerous glint in his eyes.

"Done," Cyrus said with a smile.

"Well I guess that calls for a celebration. I'd like to show you some of the hidden pleasures of our lovely town. I hope you have a taste for dark meat, if you know what I mean." said Willis

"It has been a while since I last enjoyed it, but if memory serves me correct it was a very good experience." said Cyrus laughing.

The two men left Willis's office thru the back door and walked to the post that now served as his general store and whore house.

*   *   *   *

In two days, Raven and his brothers had rounded up 300 head of cattle and 50 horses. The women had packed up all the goods they had in the root cellar and awaited Raven's orders.

"In the morning we'll load the goods on the wagon. Dove you'll drive one, Conchita will drive the other. The children will ride in the wagons. Willow, Fern, Swallow and Violet, you all will spread out and drive the herds north. There will be no need for haste, because we'll help you the first part of the day. When we're what I estimate is a day's ride from the town we'll turn back. We must avenge the deaths of our parents." said Raven.

"They were our parents too and our blades want to taste the blood of the enemy." said Dove.

"In time to come there will be a need for you to do battle, but now the survival of the clan is at stake and you are the guardian of the seed. We all have a role to play and right now this is yours." said Raven.

"I understand husband." replied Dove.

The next day they loaded the wagons and took off. The men taught the women how to move the herd in mass and keep them together. They pushed hard until noon, took a break, then pushed until nearly sundown. Raven halted them and they made camp, then he and the men headed back to town. Each of the six men had two horses and they rode in relays until they were on the outskirts of town.

"Were gonna raze the town." Raven told his brothers. "We can't burn out the settlers because we lack the numbers, but not a building is to be left standing."

The five men nodded their heads, checked their weapons, mounted up and rode into town.

*   *   *   *

Willis' saloon was jumping. Whores were sprinkled throughout the crowd, black, white and Indian. The drinks were flowing profusely. Willis, Cyrus and Vine sat at a table drinking and laughing.

"That was quick." said Willis to Cyrus who had

50,000 dollars in gold in Willis' back office.

"Actually it wasn't," said Cyrus. "I already had the gold. I just wanted to see if the man I had been dealing with was of the same mind as me."

"Well you sure found out." replied Vine laughing.

"That I did." replied Cyrus.

The sounds of laughter and the tinkling of the piano came to a sudden halt. Every eye in the place turned to the door.

Raven, Eagle, Hawk, Falcon, Cougar and Wolf had stepped thru the bat winged doors and fanned out. Raven approached the table where Willis and the others sat and Vine jumped up and shouted.

"Niggers carrying guns in the city has been outlawed for your kind, so I suggest you unlatch the gun belt and let the pistols hit the floor!"

Raven looked in the man eyes and laughed. "I didn't know dead men could talk."

"We'll just see who's the dead man here." said Vine his hands streaking to the guns on his hips. His two guns were just clearing leather when four rapid shots sounded.

Raven's hands had shot to his guns with lightening like quickness when Vine made his move. Raven's hands moved so quick, they looked like a blur. No sooner than the barrels came clear of the holsters did they belch fire and smoke. The four rounds crashed into the star pinned over Vine's heart and knocked him backward. He was dead on his feet, as his two pistols discharged their rounds into his thighs. Blood spouted from his mouth as he crashed to the floor.

"NOOOO," Lester shouted from the table he was sitting at with a black whore in his lap. He rose to his feet dumping the whore to the floor and reaching for his gun. He never made it as a round from Falcon's rifle struck him in the bridge of his nose and exploded from the back of his head in a shower of blood and gore.

Hawk, Eagle, Wolf and Cougar fired their rifles into the throng of men sitting and standing in the big room. They used withering fire to kill as many men as they could. There was little return fire as Raven and Falcon joined the fray.

Clem and Axel were gunned down at the bar where they stood, neither touching the guns holstered at their waist. For the whores who had witnessed this same type of thing months ago it was like déjà vu and they hit the floor looking

61

for cover.

In a matter of minutes the floor of the saloon was covered with rivers of blood and floating saw dust. Willis and Cyrus were beneath their table screaming, for neither had witnessed such carnage. After the gunfire all that could be heard was the moaning of the dying and the prayers of those who had survived the deadly fusillade.

Raven emptied the cartridges from his pistols, then quickly reloaded. His brothers did the same, as he walked to the table that Willis cowered beneath. He kicked the table over and Willis looked up at him with pleading eyes, then said.

"There's $50,000.00 dollars in gold in the back room. It's yours if you let me live."

"Now wait a minute there, that gold's not yours to give away!" shouted Cyrus.

Raven looked over at Cyrus, raised one of his pistols and shot Cyrus in the face. Cyrus's head snapped back, as the big slug drilled thru and exited in a shower of blood and brain. Raven holstered his left hand gun then grabbed Willis by the collar and drug him to the back office. Willis opened the safe and gave Raven a strong box. Raven looked in the safe and saw bundles of paper money and stacks of gold. He looked around the office and spotted a pair of saddle bags. He made Willis load them with the gold in the safe, then what paper would fit. He put the saddle bags over his shoulder and the strong box under his arm, then led Willis back to the saloon proper.

There were several men who were not wounded seriously and some not wounded at all. They were crowded at the back of the saloon unarmed and held at gun point.

Raven looked to where the whores all stood, then said. "Get what money you find from the dead men, then get out."

"What about them?" Cougar asked pointing his weapon at the group of men standing in the corner.

"Fuck them." Raven replied.

Cougar, Wolf and Hawk opened fire on the men and gunned them down.

"Get a rope!" Raven said to Eagle.

Falcon walked over and butt stroked Willis in the face with his rifle. Willis crumpled to the floor and Falcon reached down and drug him outside.

The whores had got all the money and valuables from the dead, then moved to the corner where the others had just been shot. They went thru their pockets, then left the saloon. All of the men weren't dead, but most were.

Raven and the others grabbed lanterns and set the place on fire, then walked outside where Eagle and Falcon held Willis with a noose around his neck. They walked him to a tree that stood in the middle of town. Raven threw the rope around a low lying limb, then pulled it until Willis was on the tip of his toes and tied it off.

"Your death will not be sudden." said Raven as he moved to bind Willis's hands behind his back. As long as Willis stayed on his toes he would live, but should he leave them he would strangle.

Raven looked at his brothers, then said. "Not a building will be left standing!"

The six men got torches, mounted their horses and systematically set every building and house on fire. Those occupied by Indians and Blacks were left alone.

When the town was blazing they rode back to the tree where Willis stood red faced, sweating in the flickering light on the tips of his toes. The men sat on their horses and watched as the man's legs trembled, then finally his heels hit the ground. He started strangling and raised back up on his toes, stood there for a moment then dropped back to his heels. This time he didn't raise back up on his toes. His body thrashed, his eyes bulged, then he pissed in his pants. There was the sound of a loud fart, then he voided his bowels and went still. The men sat there for a few minutes, then Raven wheeled his horse and they rode off into the fire illuminated night.

* CHAPTER # 9 *

Raven and the remaining members of the Bird Clan set off north the next day. They encountered a few bandits and cattle rustlers, but they easily dispatched them. Three months after they had set off, they came to a small town that was started by black union troops after the Civil War. The town was called LaVilla, and it sat on the outskirts of a bigger town called Cowford. It would in the future be given the name of a Confederate General, Andrew Jackson. Jacksonville would become the biggest city in the U.S, land wise, in the future. The Bird Clan settled around LaVilla and soon became upstanding citizens.

Raven's second son was named Ransom, by his father. The other wives all bore children and it seemed the clan would flourish. By the turn of the century, Raven was forty years old and Dove had bore him several more children both sons and daughters. Crow had been killed in a gunfight ten days after his twentieth birthday. Ransom at twenty four was the spitting image of his father and had married a beautiful woman named Emma Jean who had given birth to two sons; Marcellus and Brooks.

The Kanes prospered in LaVilla. Ransom fought in France during World War I, and was highly decorated when he came back from the war. In 1920 he got involved in the underworld. Raven at sixty was still a robust man. Dove had died a few years earlier, and he had taken up with a young woman named Celia Mace. She was thirty years old and was the daughter of the biggest bootlegger in town.

Brandford Mace was a big light skinned man, who was the product of a slave woman and her master. He was sixty five years old, and had five sons and one daughter that he doted on. He didn't like the idea that Celia had moved in with Raven, but he couldn't do a thing about it. Raven was a powerful man and had a large family.

Raven's two youngest sons, Turk and Prince were terrors and Ransom was even worse. Crow had been the meanest of Raven's sons and the man who had shot him in the back faced the wrath of the whole clan. He was killed by

Falcon's son Lao Tzu Kane, who hunted the man down. The Kanes then hunted the male members of the man's family down and killed them all.

Brandford Mace, was called Mace by all of his friends and enemies. His sons were, Brandford jr. called Ford, Louis called Lefty, Drake, Vernon and Preston. Their mother was a big light skinned woman named Lola. The Maces had the bootlegging locked down.

If Mace had had his way he would have killed Raven, but it was too much trouble and he didn't want to go thru it if he didn't have to.

Ransom came home to his family and started up his own business, he stopped in to see his father and brothers. They sat in the parlor of Raven's big house, and he told his father his plans.

"Pa, I'm thinking we should get in on the bootlegging." said Ransom.

Raven looked at him, then said. "You know that could cause us some problems."

"I've got a plan Pa." said Ransom.

"Does this plan move us in competition with Mace and his boys?" asked Raven.

"No it doesn't. My plan is to sell to the blacks in Cowford which Mace doesn't do. They have to come here to get their liquor." said Ransom.

"That's not a bad idea son, but I heard the bootleg business over there is ran by a group of crackers named the Bellamys." said Raven.

"I know that, but I still think we should do it." said Ransom.

"Let me get with the others and see how they feel about it first." said Raven.

"I don't think we should let them crackers sell that rot gut to our folks, Pa." said Ransom.

"He's got a point Pa." said Turk who was twenty two years old.

All of the men and women had married and had children, and the family grew. Wolf and Swallow's son Timothy, could have passed for Raven's boy and he was proud of the fact that he resembled his uncle.

Raven looked at his sons, then said. "I wish you boys could have known your grand parents, they would be proud of you. I can't see why we should prolong this. I want you to go get your uncles and cousins and let's sit down and see how we can do this."

After his sons left, Celia came into the parlor and sat in his lap. "Raven I got some news for you."

"What's that woman?" he asked gruffly.

"I'm pregnant." she answered.

Raven laughed then said, "You sure it's mine, I'm an old man."

She slapped playfully at him, then said. "If it ain't, then the good Lord done did another miracle."

"So I guess we got to go and get married like we white folk now, huh?" asked Raven.

"Honey I'm alright with the way things are, but it would be nice to get married in a church like other folk do." she said wistfully.

"Woman if that's what you want we can do that. I ain't much for that God and Jesus stuff. I believe a little different as far as religion is concerned, but if it'll make you happy I'm all for it." Raven said.

"How do you think the others will feel?" she asked.

"I'm head of the clan and if I choose to marry you in a church they'll all be there. They will abide by the customs, because I will." said Raven.

"I don't know if my folks will come." she said.

"I'll go talk to your folks. Me and your Ma has always gotten alone fairly well, but your Pa has always seen me as competition. It's been that way since we come here. All I want is the best for mine and I'll fight for it. I don't look for opportunity to try and bring the next man down and as long as he brings no harm to me or mine he won't have a problem from us. If trouble comes we don't run from it, we run to it, to head it off. We've all lived thru some troubled times, so trouble ain't no stranger to us. I'll talk to your folks tomorrow."

She hugged him close, and said. "I love you old man."

  *   *   *   *

All of the adult men in the Kane Clan were seated in the parlor of Raven's house. Raven looked at his brothers, nephews and sons, and noticed for the first time that his brothers were getting old. Yet they all still looked to be in fighting shape. He was 60, so Cougar and wolf had to be 63 or 64 .

"I know you have an idea as to why you're all here. The big war hero Ransom, has an idea about taking over the crackers bootlegging operation."

"That would open up a can of worms." Eagle said.

"I know that and I told the young buck that, but he had all the answers." said Raven.

"How do you justify stirring up the shit, Ransom?" asked Falcon.

Ransom looked to his father then to his uncles and said. "Why should them crackers get rich off of our people? It's always been that way and if we don't draw the line somewhere it will always be. I fought in France and I can tell you from first hand experience. Crackers look the same all over the world and they treat us like shit all over the world too. Prohibition is making them rich and it could do the same for us. That's the only justification I need."

All of the young Kanes murmured their agreement.

"Believe me, I know how crackers are. We're where we are today, because of their conniving ways. There's nothing I'd like to do better than to hit them where it hurts, but think of the danger and death it could bring. The law, or what law there is, is made for them and will surely be used against us." said Raven.

"It's gonna always be that way, so we've got to carve out our place in this world. It's ours, as much as it is theirs." said Prince.

"I see this boy been listening to Ransom." said Hawk smiling.

"He's right though Pa." said Trace. "We got to walk on tiptoes when white folks come around afraid to make eye contact for fear we'll offend them."

"I'll look at them eye to eye, because I'm a man." said Lao. "If they're looking for trouble, here it stands."

Falcon looked at his eldest son and smiled with pride, then said. "If it comes to it brother we can raze the town."

Raven made eye contact with his brothers after Falcon made the statement and they were each taken back to 1876. Each man nodded imperceptibly.

"The first thing we need is to set up several stills, get a fleet of trucks, stock up on weapons and find someone that can supply us with top quality whiskey." said Raven. "If were going to do it, let's go all out."

Ransom looked at Raven and his uncles, and said. "I got a supplier for weapons and whiskey, but not the money to purchase them.

All of the old men laughed, then hawk said. "We've got the money, you just set it up."

"I'll get the trucks and the supplies to build the stills." said Falcon.

"I'll get what we need to brew the liquor." said Cougar.

"Do any of you know how to build the stills, or brew liquor?" asked Raven.

All of the men looked at each other and shook their heads.

Raven laughed, then said. "I thought so. We've got to find someone to teach us then."

"Tigger Wells use to do that for Mace, until they had a falling out." said Wolf. "He does odd jobs at my place from time to time. As a matter of fact he's in my barn sleeping off a drunk now."

"Sober him up and see if he wants to work for us." Raven said.

"I'll do that." Wolf said.

*   *   *   *

Brandford Mace looked at his sons and thought. "Drake is the best one of the bunch." All of his sons were big, red men. Lefty was the meanest, and most dangerous physically. Drake could accomplish the same feats, but was much more shrewd and could almost match Mace in intelligence and cunning. He alone of the Mace clan saw the good in Celia being with Raven Kane. He knew that once the family bond was solidified, Raven and his clan would be duty bound to assist them if trouble came. And he knew that the Kanes were merciless, when it came to enemies.

Mace shouted. "I don't like the idea of Celia shacking up with that black ass nigga!"

"I think them Kanes need to be taught a lesson anyway." said Ford. "They been lording it around town every since Lex Clanton killed Crow. Just because they massacred the Clanton males it seems a big cloud of fear has come over certain people, but I ain't scared."

"Then you're a damn fool." said Drake. "I've sat and listened at you Pa, and you Ford. Let me tell you what I see. If you fuck with the Kanes you can kiss our asses goodbye. They won't leave a threat, and that thing with the Clantons should've showed you that. The young ones are trouble, but the old men are the ones that scare me. If you sit back and think about it, there are benefits to Celia being with that old black ass nigga as you called him, Pa."

"Benefits my ass!" shouted Mace. "We ain't did too bad protecting ourselves or defending what's ours. What the hell are the benefits?"

"Pa, you may not be looking at it from the same perspective, but think about it like this. It's better that were friends with the Kanes, than the other way around. This alliance could be valuable in the future."

"Damn it boy, the future is now!" shouted Mace.

"Pa, could you just cut out the screaming. Celia done made her choice. She won't have nobody but him so we might as well get use to it." said Drake.

"So you're grown enough to make decisions for the family now?" asked Mace.

"I am if it seems the survival of the family is at stake." said Drake.

"And how many of you boys think Drake is right?" asked Mace.

Lefty, Vernon and Preston generally agreed with Drake, while Ford was just the one to agree with Mace. As the elder, Ford was an ass kisser and Mace secretly despised him for it.

"So now I ain't smart enough to head my own family?" asked Mace softly.

"Pa it ain't that. It's just that Drake makes sense, is all." said Lefty.

"So I don't make no sense then?" asked Mace.

"That ain't what he means Pa." said Vernon.

"What the hell does he mean Vern, you tell me?" Mace said.

"Drake doesn't see the point in hunting trouble with the Kanes. It ain't about fear. What do we gain by teaching the Kanes a lesson? It could end with some of us dead for no good reason. We don't stand to benefit from it, at least not as far as I can see." said Vernon.

"In all of your twenty five years that might have been

the smartest observation you've ever made." said Mace. "So
what do you suggest?"

"I suggest you be more amenable to Raven, he could
be useful. They're a big powerful family." said Drake.

"Well I guess I could do that, since I got a plan." said
Mace.

"Tell them the plan Pa." Ford said excitedly.

"Shut up Ford!" said Mace. "I been thinking we
should provide liquor to the blacks in town as well."

"You know the Bellamy's got that end tied up, Pa."
said Drake.

"That's because we let them." Mace said.

"Bull Parsons lets them you mean. I bet he gets a cut
off it, plus he keeps the niggas in line. If we go against the
Bellamys, we'll have Bull to deal with too." Drake said.

"So what. Bull's a man too, and all men can die."
Lefty said.

"I'd wait and think it all out first." said Drake.

"We'll do that then. Now get the hell out of my
house."

     *   *   *   *

Sheriff Early "Bull" Parsons was a big, over weight,
red faced man. He had at least three rolls of fat hanging from
his neck, that made it seem like he had three chins. He wore
Khaki uniform, as did all of his men. A big dingy, once white,
straw cowboy hat and it seemed that he was born with a chew
in his mouth. He was a sloppy man and tobacco stains were
always on his shirt front. Bull was also the Imperial Wizard of
the, Duval County order of the Klu Klux Klan.

His chief deputy was his younger brother Shelby
"Shel" Parsons, who was a short, rat faced man. Shel's face
was always screwed into a frown and he was a mean spirited
man that suffered from a Napoleonic complex. He felt the
need to prove he was as tough as men bigger than he.

The other Deputies were Conner "Con" Majors, who
was a big muscular man. He had straw colored hair, and pale
washed out blue eyes. He wasn't the sharpest knife in the
drawer, but he was fearless and idolized Bull.

Then there was Anton Billings, an olive skinned man
who the others often jokingly called nigger, because of his
skin complexion. Anton was a man of medium build , but he

took particular pleasure in putting blacks in their place as he called it.

Lastly there was Carlton "Cad" Lowe, who was considered the ladies man. Cad kept his jet black hair slicked back and he had vivid blue eyes. He was an ex cowboy and never let anyone forget it. He was tall and rangy with corded muscles.

All of the men were members of the Klan as were the Bellamys. They had an old house out on the outskirts of town, where they held their meetings. The Duval order of the Royal Knights of Klan were better known in the south as Klavern 9. A large number of townsmen were members, almost all of them influential men. The town leaders were at the top of the order. The only man with clout that wasn't a member, was Prescott Snidely Wellington. A one time English aristocrat, who sympathized with the down trodden. He did fair business practice with the Black, Asian and Indian community. A fair price for goods was his motto and he lived it.

On a Wednesday night the Klavern held a meeting, and Prescott Willington was the topic of discussion. "Pres, isn't a bad man, he just has different ideas." said Mayor Wally Cronin.

"Yeah the type of ideas that could run us all out of business, while he grows rich." said Big Oscar Bellamys.

Oscar Bellamys, was the head of the Bellamys Clan. Because the Bellamys were once dirt poor and looked down on, Bull Parsons decided that they would run the Klan's illegal activities. What they didn't know at first, was how lucrative it would be. When they found out, it was way too late. For the Bellamys, through murder and mayhem, had a tight grip on the underworld. Oscar Bellamys brother, Simon, was his right hand man. He and Oscar both at 50 & 51, looked like Lumber Jacks. Big muscular men, with dark brown hair and beards.

Oscar's sons, Thomas, Bernie, and Ronnie were in the mold of their father, just smaller versions. Simon's sons were both tall, Slim men, but the Bellamys all bore an uncanny resemblance to each other.

"What do you suggest we do to Wellington." asked Bull Parsons.

"I don't really think it's him we need to do something to. " said Bubba Stanley.

Bubba Stanley, was in the Bellamys clique. He was a

mean man, small in stature, but not in reputation. He had red hair and big ears, freckles over the bridge of his nose and both cheeks. He looked like a man child, with emerald green eyes. He was the smartest man in the room, but few knew it. He was very manipulative and could make the men think it was their idea if he came up with something. It was because of him, that the Bellamys prospered. He knew his success was linked to them so he made sure they did well.

His twin brother Randy Stanley, though bearing the same face was like a deaf mute. He could speak and hear, but you'd never know it. He spoke rarely and only in whispers to his brother. Randy was nearly as smart as his brother, but he was a psycho-path. A cold, emotionless killer. Only Bubba could control him and most of the time he just turned him loose.

"Who should we do it to, to hurt his business?" asked Oscar. "His customers. I think it's time the nightriders put a little fear in the niggers." said Bubba.

"No killing, none. Whip a few asses, bust a few heads, but no killing." said Wally Cronin.

"Niggers got hard heads in these parts. We may need to hang one or two to get the message across." said Bull Parson.

"I don't think so. " said Wally Cronin. "You can only push a person so far before he strikes back."

"Niggers ain't struck back in all this time, I don't believe they will." said Simon Bellamys.

" I wouldn't bank on it." said Wally Cronin.

"The real question is, when do we ride?" asked Bull Parson. "Lets wait til next week," said Wally Cronin.

All of the men agreed. Drinks were passed around and the men waited while Cad Lowe went in search of some whores.

* CHAPTER # 10 *

Raven and Celia stood on the porch of Mace's House and waited for someone to open the door. It was 8:00 in the morning and most people hadn't got up yet. Lola Mace came to the door in a housecoat. She saw Raven standing there with Celia and thought to herself. "I sure would have liked to met that big black nigga when I was younger. Hell, even now".

Raven wore a black broadcloth jacket, a snow white, starched, wing collared shirt and a white silk waistcoat with pearl buttons. A thick gold chain swung between the pockets, at the end of which was a gold pocket watch. He wore black tweed trousers that hugged his still muscular legs. Black highly polished boots, and as always on this hips hung blue black colt .45 pistols. He still wore his hair in twin braids, that looked like big ropes of sliver hanging from underneath the short crowned Stetson he wore.

Celia was dressed to the nines too. She wore a white summer frock with lace trimming. The dress was daringly cut for the times, as it revealed the twin mounds of her voluptuous, honey colored breast.

Raven, loved the way men stopped to stare as Celia walked by. He made sure she was fabulously attired everyday. Raven was some what of a dandy himself and flaunted convention. He had suits made from a variety of different cloths and in many colors. From greens, yellows and all the colors of the rainbow.

"What brings you young ones here at this ungodly hour?" asked Lola as she opened the door.

"I'd like to speak with you and Mace about an important issue and I'd like to say it just once." said Raven flashing Lola a white smile.

They walked in and Lola lead them to the parlor. "Y'all ate breakfast yet?" asked Lola.

"Yes we have, but coffee would be fine." said Raven.

"Give me a minute to wake Mace and I'll bring the coffee right in." Lola said walking from the room.

Raven looked over to Celia, and said. "I see where you got all that ass from."

She swatted at him playfully with her white parasol. Lola came back with two cups and saucers. "Mace will be here in a minute."

Mace walked into the parlor in pants, shirt and suspenders, he was barefoot. "Raven, Celly. How are ya'll?" asked Mace eyeing Raven.

"We fine Mace." said Raven.

"Mace, I know you ain't pleased that Celia's my woman. I can see your point of view, I'm twice her age. You probably think she should be with a man her age or at least one younger than me. Too late for all that, cause we getting married."

Mace just shook his big head.

"It was my idea Pa." said Celia. "I'm having his baby and I wanna be his wife."

"So what do ya'll want from us?" asked Mace sourly.

"Your blessing." said Raven. "If we gonna be family, we might as well get along."

"And if you don't have our blessings?" Asked Mace.

"Then we don't have them. My Celia wants a wedding and she's gonna have one." Raven said with steel in his voice his eyes baring in on Mace.

"I guess it couldn't hurt." said Lola.

"Ain't nobody asked you shit." said Mace angrily.

"I'd watch my tone of voice if I was you." said Raven ominously. "I don't take kindly to abusing women."

Mace jumped up and shouted. "Nigga you in my house, this my wife and I'll say or do what I damn well please you got that?"

You're right in most of what you've said, but if I'm here you'll show Lola and my wife the respect due to women of their caliber." said Raven raising to his feet. His hands sweeping his jacket aside, so he could reach his pistols.

Mace looked in Raven's eyes and knew that the wrong words would seal his fate, because here was a man who wouldn't be trifled with. "I can see your point." Mace said shakily. Just the thought that Raven would gun him down in his own home had a sobering affect on him. He knew right then that Drake was right. If the others had half the balls of this one, starting trouble with the Kanes would be extremely costly.

"You got our blessing on one condition." Mace said.

"That is?" Raven asked.

"That I throw an engagement party for you Saturday night." said Mace.

"Oh Pappa," cried Celia jumping up and running into her father's arms.

"Make my baby happy is all I ask." said Mace.

"I will. You can count on that." said Raven.

They sat around for a while talking, then Raven and Celia left.

"I ain't never seen that girl so happy." Mace said to Lola.

"That's cause she got a real man honey." said Lola wistfully.

     *   *   *   *

Wolf walked out to his barn, then into the back room where Tigger Wells lay asleep on the cot. He walked over and gently shook Tigger.

"Wha....What?" Tigger sputtered as he slowly regained consciousness. Groggily, he shook his big head. Tigger was a massive man in his early 40's, that stood at least 6'8". He weighed 350 pounds, if he wore an ounce. His big body smothered the small cot, to the point that it almost appeared he was levitating. He struggled up to a sitting position and placed his head in his huge hands.

"Go wash up and come on to the house and get you some breakfast." said Wolf. "I'll be waiting for you, I got a proposition I think you'll like."

"I'll be there shortly." said Tigger rising from the cot and stretching.

Wolf walked back to the house and Swallow met him at the door. She was 53 years old and still beautiful. Swallow was 6' feet tall, and still had a fantastic figure. From looking at her, you wouldn't think she was her age.

"What were you men up to last night, I heard there was a meeting at Ravens?" she asked Wolf.

"Don't be so nosy woman." Wolf said with mock sternness.

Swallow laughed, and said. "I'll just ask Fern or one of the daughters. They know since you wanna be so tight lipped about it."

"It was just business. You'll hear all you need to know when Tigger comes in." Wolf said.

She held out her arms and he came into them. "You know Lyle and Greg Jenson, been courting the girls. They been hinting about marriage." she said.

"Can they pay the bride price?" asked Wolf.

"You know them boys ain't got much, but they are respectable, hard working men. They got a small piece of land and I think they're up and comers." said Swallow.

" I was just joking." he said. "Hell, I'll be glad to get rid of them."

"You waited long enough don't you think?" she asked.

"What I didn't want was some no good man who wanted them because we're Kanes. The family holds weight and I'd rather see them as old maids, than with a man not suited for them." said Wolf.

Swallow shook her head just when Tigger Wells rumbled up.

"Good morning Ms. Kane."

"It is that, Mr. Wells." Swallow said. "Come on, I'll get you some breakfast."

"No need to go thru that trouble Ms. Kane." said Tigger.

"Nonsense, we haven't had breakfast so you might as well join us." said Swallow.

"Don't mind if I do." said Tigger smiling.

They went thru the same thing each morning, both knowing what the outcome would be. Wolf smiled, as Tigger was lead to the big dinning room. When they walked in Timothy, Mandy and Sparrow were all seated. Timothy had taken to dressing like Raven, so he was finely turned out in a black frock coat and pants. Yellow waistcoat, white on white shirt with string tie, thick twin braids, short crowned Stetson and two guns strapped to his hips.

"Boy do you have to wear arms at the tables?" asked Swallow.

"I wear them naked Ma." said Timothy.

Wolf laughed. They ate breakfast, then Wolf lead Tigger to the sitting room. "Tigger, me and my brothers want you to build some stills for us and show us how to brew liquor and maintain the stills. The job is yours and we'll pay you a percentage of the profits." said Wolf.

"How much of a percentage are we talking about here?" Tigger asked.

"I'm thinking two percent. Now mind you, two percent of the profits will be plenty if this goes how we plan." Wolf said.

"Hell if you had said 1 percent I was in. I done been around you Kanes long enough to know that y'all think big." said Tigger smiling . "So when do we start?"

"Right now. The first thing we do is get you with Falc, so you can get the supplies to build the stills. Then we'll get with Cougar, and get the stuff we need to brew the corn." said Wolf.

They stood up to leave and Swallow who had stood quietly through the conversation looked at Wolf, who stopped and let Tim and Tigger go out.

She walked over, and asked. "What's going on here with this talk of stills and such?"

He looked in her eyes, and said. "It's always been our way to follow the head of the clan and as long as we're alive that's how it will be."

"So Raven the one behind this?" she asked.

"No, it's Ransom, but we're all behind him." said Wolf.

"You know there's gonna be trouble." she said.

"We done dealt with trouble before when the odds were against us and we came out on top. Now we have the benefit of numbers and we'll come out on top again." Wolf said.

Swallow smiled and hugged her husband. "Keep a tight rein on Tim, the boy idolizes Raven."

"He hardly a boy woman, he's a man!" Wolf said.

"You said something different about the girls." she said.

"I told you my concerns too." he replied. "I'd better get on they're waiting for me." He said as he broke the embrace and walked for the door.

*   *   *   *

Wolf, Tim and Tigger drove to Falcon's place. The Kanes, Maces, and a few other blacks in town had cars. The three men got out of Wolf's ford sedan, and Falcon stepped out on the porch followed by his sons Lao, Eddie and Lonnie who was called Lon for short.

"Y'all boys rolling pretty early ain't you?" asked

Falcon. "Obviously not as early as you brother." Wolf replied.

The two men embraced, then Wolf said. "This here is Tigger Wells, master corn maker!

"I done heard about the great man, but I've never had the pleasure of meeting him." Falcon said with a smile. "He's a big nigga too."

The men laughed. "Tell me Falc, do you know what you need to build a still?" asked Wolf.

Falcon raised a brow and smiled, then stuck out his hands to Tigger, and said. "Pleasure to meet you, Mr. Wells."

"Plain Tigger will do, Mr. Kane." said Tigger with a big smile that seemed to show off all of his big white teeth. "It could get hectic saying Mr. Kane, as all of you boys are Mr. Kane's."

The men laughed, then Falcon said. "Just call me Falc, like the rest do."

"I guess we better try to get us some trucks." Wolf said.

"Trace and Ransom, done beat you to the punch there." said Lao. "They got with Elliot Weanberg at Duval Ford and brought five pickups and they should be here shortly.

" Are Marcellus and Brooks, coming too?" asked Eddie.

"They should be." said Lonnie. "I still can't believe them boys are Kanes Them some lazy ass niggas. All they wanna do is cat around."

"That's bout to change, but we ain't the type of folk to bad mouth kin." Falcon said sternly.

"He didn't mean nothing by it Pa, but truth is light or so you say." said Lao.

Falcon looked at his son, and in a hard voice said. "I done had my say and don't think you're so grown that I won't bust you in your chops for taking a condescending tone with me."

"Rest easy brother, the man didn't mean anything." said Wolf staring hard at Falcon.

"I'm sorry if I offended you Pa." said Lao sincerely.

"I'm the one should be sorry son." said Falcon. "I taught you to be your own man, and you should, even if it means you disagree with me."

Just then, five brand new ford pickups pulled in. Ransom and Trace jumped out of the first one. Turk, Prince,

Marcellus, Brooks, Blake, Jose, Juan and Hawk got out of the others. Trace walked over and embraced Wolf and Falcon, and said. "Come see what I got."

All of the men walked over to the truck and Ransom threw aside a tarp.

"Holy shit," said Lao loudly.

"Hush boy, your Ma might hear." whispered Falcon.

In the bed of the truck were crates and they could see the open ones contained Thompson Submachine Guns. Another contained drum magazines, another Dynamite, another smaller box, grenades.

"How many are there?" asked Falcon.

"24 to a crate, 4 crates. 10,000 rounds of .45 caliber, 50 Grenades and plenty of Dynamite." answered Ransom.

"We won't be lacking fire power, that's for sure." said Turk.

"These ain't like regular rifles, these are full automatic and I'm gonna teach y'all to use them." said Ransom. "Where my daddy?"

"He had some personal business, but knowing him he can probably feel we're here and will be by." said Falcon.

Before he had finished speaking two big sedans pulled behind the trucks. Raven, Eagle, and Cougar got out of one. Pat and Pauly out of the other.

"Damn if you weren't right, Falc." said Hawk.

Raven walked over and the men embraced. "You boys having a party and we wasn't invited?" asked Raven.

"Well brother, there are these who knew you'd be along." said Wolf.

Raven looked at the crates, and said. "Starting a war Ransom?"

"Might be Pa," Ransom said smiling. "I think we need to hide the hardware and get busy. Pa you gonna need some work clothes, or you're gonna mess that pretty suit up, you too Tim."

All of the men laughed, then Ransom and Trace assigned the men to tasks. They would only use blood in the operation and each man was given an area of responsibility.

Both Marcellus and Brook were to work with Tigger, which would be the hardest work. The two Young men knew their father and grandfather wouldn't put up with laziness.

*　　　　　*　　　　　*　　　　　*

"I don't know what them Kanes are up to, but if they're buying all the stuff I hear they're buying, then it means Ravens spittin in my eye. It's like he's saying, fuck you Mace." said Mace angrily. "That black ass nigga was just in my house this morning, talking that we might as well get along if we're family shit."

"So what do we do Pa?" asked Ford.

"Kill that motherfucker." Mace replied.

"Now hold up there Pa." said Drake cautiously. "Just cause the man's buying the stuff, don't mean he's disrespecting us. I think you ought to go talk to him."

"Damn right I should." said Mace. Y'all boys get your guns, cause we're about to pay that nigga a surprise visit."

Mace and his sons all got their guns. Drake shook his head, because he knew if his father approached Raven wrong they'd all end up dead.

* CHAPTER # 11 *

Raven had a store that did good business and most days he or one of his daughters ran it. Celia had taken to working there too and Raven paid them all. Raven, Hawk, Falcon, Eagle, Wolf and Cougar sat at a table in the store just talking.

"I saw us, for seemed like the first time last night," said Raven. "Brothers we're getting old."

"That we are," said Eagle.

"I think we should just provide support for our sons on this." said Hawk. "Let this be their thing."

"I think Hawk is right." said Cougar. "We've made a name for ourselves and built a foundation for them. Let them do the rest."

Hawk seldom spoke much, but when he did it usually made sense.

"So you're saying we should miss the action?" said Wolf. "At heart I'm still a warrior and I want to choose my day to die."

"Time will choose it for you brother." said Raven. "There will be enough action to go around, besides what we need to do is try to make sure we all come out alive.

Falcon looked towards the door, then said. "Here comes Mace and all his boys and they're toting iron."

The door swung open and Mace walked in, his sons trailing him. "Raven we need to talk." said Mace menacingly.

Raven looked out from under the brim of his hat, and asked. "Is there a problem Mace?"

"Damn right there is, if you think you're gonna just muscle in on my business." Mace replied.

"Let's talk about this in the back Mace, just you and me." Raven said and rose from his seat.

Mace watched as Raven slid the two .45's back in their Holsters, then looked at the other men and saw they all had guns in their hands. He shivered and knew someone had just walked over his grave. He knew if he and his sons had so much as flinched wrong, they would've all been gunned down. He followed Raven into the back office and they sat down. Raven raised his hand to silence Mace before he could speak.

"I know what it looks like, but it isn't that Mace. You don't need to know our business, but it won't take a dime out of your pocket. We're about to be family and I wouldn't compete with family."

"So, you mean to tell me you and yours ain't getting into boot legging?" asked Mace.

"I didn't say that. What I said was, it ain't what it looks like. We getting into it, but we gonna do it somewhere else. Trust me on that." said Raven.

"Well, alright," Mace said.

The two men walked back out front. "I got some cold beer if you boys want some." Raven said.

They all sat down, drank and talked. Drake eyed the old men secretly. He could hardly wait to leave, because he wanted to know what Raven had told his father. He listened closely as the Kanes spoke and watched how they interacted with one another.

Soon Mace rose, and said. "We been a little busy and I haven't had a chance to break the news to them yet."

"Well I'll leave that to you then." said Raven.

"Come on, boy's." said Mace as his sons rose from their seats.

After the Maces left, the men looked at Raven. "Me and Celia gonna get married soon." Raven said.

"And you just decided to tell us?" asked Eagle.

"Well bro, we have been busy and I had forgotten." said Raven.

"Don't let Celia hear you say that." Falcon said with a smile.

"So, y'all ain't got no problem with me marrying a woman half my age?" Raven asked.

The five men looked at him in amazement. "Why would we have a problem with that brother?" asked Hawk. "You're happy and Celia's a fine woman. I mean that in both ways."

The men laughed and got up to embrace Raven.

"She gonna have my baby too." Raven said.

"Go on, old man." said Cougar laughing. "I wanna know how you got the energy to love up that young girl."

"It ain't hard, I'll tell you that." Raven said grinning from ear to ear.

"So what's up with the party?" asked Wolf.

"Mace and his folks, are gonna have us an engagement party Saturday night." Raven said. "You're all invited.

"Now you tell us." said Falcon laughing.

*　　　　　*　　　　　*　　　　　*

Mace and his sons went to a house on the outskirt of town that they used as a headquarters. "The nigga said they wouldn't be competing with us. So, I wonder who they'll be competing with?" said Mace.

"The only place to do business besides here, is in town." said Drake. "If they're going into business, that's the only place that makes sense. One thing is for sure though. If they do that, then they'll be going up against the Bellamy's and their crew. If that's the truth, then we may not have to worry about the Kanes."

"You're right about that." said Preston.

"Well, I can tell you this. If they need our help, then we hem and haw, but stay out of it." said Mace. "I just can't see no nigga winning in a war against them white boys."

"I feel different about that Pa." said Drake. "If I had to put my money on it, I'd bet on the Kanes."

"Damn it Drake," said Mace. "It seems to me you done placed the niggas on a pedestal!"

"Nah Pa, it ain't like that." said Drake. "I been watching them for years and they ain't nothing like the average niggas or Indians. They operate differently than us all. Far as family goes we're tight, but they're even tighter."

"How can you say some shit like that?" shouted Ford angrily.

"Ford, now ain't the time for that shit. I didn't mean it as disrespect to us, it's just a fact." said Drake.

"Enough of that. We got a business to run, so let's get." said Mace.

The men rose and left the house.

*　　　　　*　　　　　*　　　　　*

Prescott Snidely Wellington and his wife Elisabeth, stood behind the counter in their store talking to a big black woman named Eula.

83

"I'm telling you Ms. Eula that these bolts of cloth are the rage in New York. All of the women are making dresses from it." said Mrs. Wellington.

"I would like to make a dress or two, so you can give me a bolt." Eula said with a big smile.

Just then, Wally Cronin walked in. The Wellington's looked up in surprise, since Wally had never visited before.

"Mayor, how can I be of service?" asked Mr. Wellington.

"We need to talk Pres." said Cronin.

Prescott led him to the back office and showed him to a seat. Then he sat behind his big desk, steepled his hands, rested his chin on them and just stared at Wally. Prescott Wellington was a big, strapping man in excellent shape. He had dark brown hair and piercing blue eyes.

"Well Pres it's like this. People think you've gotten a little too close to the niggers, treating them like white folks are the exact words they used." said Wally.

Prescott raised his head, then cracked his knuckles loudly, raised a hand to cut Wally off, then said. "I don't see but one color and that's the color of a man's money. I'm a businessman and the principle behind business is to generate income. That's what I do. A fair price for all goods, regardless to a man's skin color."

"Now look here Pres, ain't no need to take that tone with me. You don't talk to your nigger customers that way."

"The key word in your statement is customer, of which you're not one. I've gone so far as to do business with everyone in town, but not a single white man has done business with me. Should I let my family starve or suffer for ideals in which I disagree?"

"It ain't like that Pres. You're a stranger here." said Wally.

"I've been here for twenty years, a member of the town council and I'm still a stranger?" asked Pres.

"You're takin this wrong, Pres." stammered Wally.

"Yeah, you're probably right. There's no way you, a pillar of the community would ask me to lie, steal and cheat from your constituents." said Pres sarcastically.

"Damn it man, I'm trying to save your life here." shouted Wally.

"I beg to differ." said Pres. "It seems to me, as if you're trying to deny me my lively hood."

"Fuck it, you deal with it when it comes." said Wally rising from his chair and storming out.

Elisabeth stepped into the office and looked at him.

"It's nothing. Who's watching the store?" he asked.

"Lucy Pearl," she answered. "I know something's wrong Pres, I have a right to know."

"Some people want us to use questionable business practices with our customers." Prescott said.

"Wally had the nerve to come ask you something like that?" she asked.

"Not in plain words luv, he hinted at it. I do know something is going to happen. Tell Lucy Pearl to spread the word for the blacks to be careful. You know Wally's with the Klan." Pres said.

"Are we in danger Pres?" asked Elisabeth.

"I hope not luv. We ran from our homeland, because of how they felt about our point of view. No more running luv. If you feel you need to get away for a while, please feel free because I'd like nothing better than to see you some place safe." he said.

"We came here in the wilderness to escape the confines of the small mined and it seems they've come to enforce their rules even here. There is no safe place, when a man can get hung for simply looking a white person in the eyes." she said firmly. "If there is one place I could be in the whole world, it would be by your side."

"I know, that's why I didn't send you away. I knew where you would choose to be." said Pres with a smile.

"Let me go talk to Lucy Pearl." she said.

He rose from behind his desk and followed her from the room.

Lucy Pearl was a beautiful, high yellow girl, of 16. She was a big girl, fully developed, big breast, wide hips and big legs. Many of the men in town were trying to court her. Prescott gave her a job in the store. The Wellingtons were childless and Lucy Pearl was Prescott's daughter. Prescott had been seeing Lucy Pearl's mother Ella Mae for 18 or 19 years. Even Lucy Pearl didn't know. They stood in the front of the store and Elisabeth said.

"Honey I want you to go home early today, because you need to tell your people to be careful. The Klan might be up to something."

"Yes mam I will do that." Lucy Pearl said.

85

"You be careful too, you hear me?" asked Pres.

"I will Mr. Prescott," she replied.

*   *   *   *

The Kanes stood in a wooded area on Hawk's property, with ten Sub Thompson's. "I want y'all to gather around and see how these weapons work." said Ransom.

The men all got in a circle with Ransom in the center. He showed them how to charge the weapon, load it and clean it. The men practiced that for several hours, until each man could break the weapons down and reassemble it. Ransom chose a group that consisted of Trace, Lao, Patrick, Jose, Juan, Tim, Eddie, Turk and Prince. They were the first Kanes to fire the Sub Thompson's. The others laughed, as the weapons climbed to the sky when the trigger was pulled.

"Damn this gun got some kick." shouted Trace taking his finger off the trigger.

"A man could do some damage with one of those." said Raven.

"Yes he can." Ransom said. "That's why I got them. See them crackers ain't armed this good. It ain't gonna be no cake walk, but these will get the job done. When we make our move, everybody will ride with one from then on."

Ransom walked over to a stump that had a small crate on it. He opened the crate and pulled out a big flat pistol, and said. "Army issue colt .45, 1911 model." He showed them how to clean and assemble the pistol, then showed them how to shoot it.

"That's a nice piece of workmanship, but I'll stick with mine on this one." Raven said.

The men laughed as Ransom gave them to those who wanted them. The men sat around and Raven looked at them then turned to Ransom, and asked.

"We've got all of the stuff we need now, do you have the connections to get the corn sold in town?"

"Yes, I do Pa." answered Ransom. "An old army buddy name Tyrus Biggers is setting it up right now. So by the time we get our first shipment cooked off he should have everything set up."

"I see you've thought this thing thru. Now what we've got to do is be prepared for the repercussions that are sure to come when we start. I want to find out what we're faced with, because we're gonna have to kill white men. And if the sheriff gets in the cross hairs and we kill him, then some federal agency is gonna come in. Years ago it was told to me that I couldn't start a shooting war with the army. Well, we can't start a shooting war with the government." said Raven.

"How do we do it then brother?" asked Eagle.

"We make sure we cover our tracks and also that we don't leave any trails that lead back to us." Raven answered.

"That's easier said than done, Pa." Ransom said.

"Not really," Trace replied. "We use the same tactics they use."

Raven looked at Trace, then asked. "What do you mean?"

"Night Riders," Trace answered. "They hide under hoods so we'll do the same thing, only our hoods and robes will be black. They terrorize us, we do the same to them."

"That's my boy there." said Hawk laughing.

"It wouldn't hurt you to be a little more modest brother." said Raven with a smile. Raven looked at his brothers, their sons and his, and knew they were all able men. The clan would survive and thrive in the hands of their sons.

"I think we need to get busy on the stills in the morning. There's plenty of work to go around. Cellus, I expect you and Brooks to pull your own load. There'll be plenty of time for that other stuff. It's gonna get sticky in a short while and you'll need to prove you're up to the task. You're Kanes damn it, and its time to stop riding on the coat tales of your father and the rest of us. Understand?" asked Raven.   "We ain't never had to do much Grandpa." replied Brooks.

"I suppose that's my fault as well as anyone's, but that's over now and it's time to stand on your own. You both will be needed in the times to come and we need to know we can depend on you." Raven said.

"You can depend on us, Grandpa," Marcellus said sincerely.

"There's still some light out." said Ransom. "Let's get some work done.

     *   *   *   *

"I'm telling you Bull, I don't want killings." said Wally.

"Don't tell me you've all of a sudden become a champion of the niggers Wally?" said Bull sarcastically.

"Now Bull it ain't like that." Wally whined. " I just don't want to rile the niggers more than we have to. We want their money and the more you kill the more animosity it's gonna cause."

"What are they gonna do Wally? They ain't gonna fight back."

"You can beat a dog and beat him and sooner or later he gonna bite you. Niggers is almost human, they're a lot smarter than dogs." stated Wally.

"And I'll do them just like I'd do a dog that bite me. I'd shoot the motherfucker." said Bull with an evil glint in his eyes. "Further more, I'd shoot the dogs owner or anyone else that tried to protect it." He looked into Wally's eyes, then said. "Do you get me?"

Wally swallowed and nodded his head. Just then, Oscar and Simon walked into Wally's office.

"What's going on Wally, you look like you just seen a ghost?" said Oscar.

"Hey Bull" Oscar and Simon snickered.

"I talked to Pres, and tried"….

"You what!" screamed Bull.

"Talked to Prescott Wellington and tried to get him to see our point of view." Wally stated sharply.

"Damn fool," said Oscar. "Don't you know he'll warn the spooks!"

"Don't that beat all." said Bull. "How can we trust someone who would go warn a nigger lover about what we plan to do."

"I didn't even get that far." said Wally. "We just talked, that's all."

"Anybody ever tell you, you talk too much." said Simon menacingly. "I think we need to get the Klanvern together and see if this sympathizer should remain in the order."

Bull and Oscar nodded in agreement.

"Now hold up there fellas. You got this wrong." Wally said pleadingly. Wally knew that if he was kicked out, he wouldn't be long for this world.

"I think we'll just keep this to ourselves for now, if there is any indication that he's helping Wellington or the Niggers, we'll ride on his ass!" said Bull.

"Well that's settled, so when do we ride?" asked Oscar.

"Tomorrow night's as good as any." said Bull. "You boys go spread the word."

* CHAPTER # 12 *

The Kanes met Tigger Wells at the place where they would build their first still. Raven looked at the gathering of men and had to smile. He though back to the times when he and his brothers went on forays with his father. Now he would go out with his sons and grandsons. He wished his mothers and father could see them. He was gripped momentarily by sadness, but the warrior spirit that survived across the seas and time rose within him.

"Ransom, I think you and some of the boys should ride into town and check on the whiskey. If it's there, then you know where to store it. Anything else you think needs doing, do it." Raven said.

"Alright Pa," said Ransom. "Come on Lao, Trace, Turk, Tim, and Pat, we're taking three trucks."

The six men got in the trucks and pulled out.

"You know shit is gonna get thick brother." said Falcon.

"Yeah, I do." Raven replied. "To tell you the truth I'm kind of looking forward to it."

"Me too," said Hawk.

All of the older Kanes nodded their agreement.

"It's been way to quiet for my taste these last few years anyway." said Eagle.

"You got that right brother." said Cougar. "In the old days we didn't have to wait for action, it was all around us. The land was wide open, but now look around. All you see is so called civilization and damn if it ain't more barbaric than the old days."

"No need to harp on changing times brother." said Wolf. "It is what it is."

"Good thing our Pa looked ahead though." said Raven. "He prepared us for the times, that's why it was so easy for us to make the change."

"There's work to be done." said Blake smiling.

    *   *   *   *

Ransom and the others drove thru town, then pulled up to Tyrus Biggers place. Tyrus and his sons, along with Sonny and Bart Lumpkin, were standing in the front yard. Tyrus Biggers was a small man, maybe 5'3", and 140 pounds. He was jet black with close cropped hair. His voice was deep, it sounded like it came form a well. His sons Price and Elmore, looked just like him, except they were both at least 6'2", and nearly 200 pounds. Tyrus looked like their little brother. The Lumpkin's were high yellow men, both rail thin and rangy.

"How's it going boys?" asked Tyrus.

"It's alright Ty." said Ransom. "Let me introduce you to my kin. This here is Trace, my cousin, Lao my cousin, Tim my cousin, Turk my brother and Pat my cousin."

Ty shook hands with all of them, then he introduced his group. The men walked to the back of the house and sat on the porch.

"Any word on the whiskey?" Ransom asked.

"We got to pick it up from the dock." said Ty. "It's gonna cost $8,000.

"We made an agreement for six." said Ransom. "What happened?"

"I don't know, the man said he'd talk to you only." said Tyrus.

"Let's get it done then." Ransom said.

The men all piled into trucks and drove toward the docks. As they drove thru town a police car pulled in behind them and turned on the siren. Ransom and the others pulled over and Cad Lowe, got out of the police car followed by Con Majors.

"All of you niggers get out of the trucks." shouted Cad.

"That's Cad Lowe and Cad Majors." whispered Tyrus to Ransom. "Just be cool bro."

The men got out of the trucks and stood there, as the two deputies approached.

"Where you niggers headed?" asked Cad

"We're going down to the docks, Mr. Cad." said Tyrus timidly.

Ransom knew it was just an act. He had seen Tyrus in action and knew the man was a fierce man if need be.

"Some of you nigger ain't from round here, where bouts y'all from?" asked Cad.

"They from LaVilla sir." Tyrus said.

"You the spokesman for these niggers or something? They can't talk for themselves?" Cad asked.

He walked up to Tim and looked at him closely. He noticed the nice brown suit, white shirt with brown string tie, beige waist coat, highly glossed Brown Wellington boots and the brown derby cocked at the rakish angle. "What's your name boy?" He asked Tim.

Tim stood there staring in the man's eyes not answering.

"Can't you hear boy?" Cad asked menacingly.

"Tim." Ransom said softly.

"I'm Timothy Kane." Tim replied.

Cad looked at Ransom then back to Tim, and asked. "You niggers brothers?"

Ransom nodded. "Yes we are!"

"These some silent ass niggers Cad." said Con.

"I don't like to see too many strange niggers in my town, so you boys be careful or you could find yourself in deep shit." said Cad. "Now get on bout your business?"

The men got back in the trucks and pulled off.

"I didn't know they had that much work at the docks." said Cad.

"They don't for white men, but there's plenty of shit work for the Jigs." said Con. The two men laughed as they walked back to their car.

Ransom and the others got to the docks and were directed to a warehouse. They stopped outside the warehouse and Ransom, Trace, Tyrus and Lao walked to the office. A weasel faced white man named Grady Spates, who introduced them to Lomas Tappen met them . The men were seated in the office.

"I thought we made a deal for $6,000." said Ransom. "I wanna know when that changed!"

"I can understand how you feel, but please let me explain." said Grady.

"Go on," said Ransom.

"What happened is this. Some people had ordered more than they could pay for, so I thought you'd wanna go on and buy the excess." said Grady.

"As long as that's all it is, we can deal with that." said Ransom. "I don't know how regularly we'll need shipments, but try to keep the same amount on hand and we'll take care of it."

"It's in plain crates. Get your trucks in and we can get you loaded." said Grady smiling.

The men walked to two big bay doors. Lomas Tappen pulled a long chain and the big doors swung open. Ransom motioned for the men in the trucks to drive in. They drove into the big warehouse and to an area that Grady pointed out. The men jumped form the trucks. No introductions were made. The men loaded the trucks, then covered the crates with tarps and drove off.

"Did you notice they didn't even check the merchandise?" asked Lomas.

"I don't think it would be a good idea to cross these boys." said Grady. "I sense something dangerous in those men and I wanna be on their side."

*   *   *   *

"Turn down there." said Tyrus pointing to a dirt road. Ransom turned onto the road.

"We'll use the back roads until we get in your neck of the woods." said Tyrus. "We don't wanna get caught with this shipment. The crackers would probably try to steal most of it and leave just enough to hide us in prison."

"Ain't gonna be no prison." Ransom said forcefully. "It's either we stop them from taking it or we go to prison. Them or me, too bad for them!"

"I know how serious you are about this, but we can't be killing police." Tyrus said.

"They'd kill us." Ransom said with conviction. "It's all or nothing bro. You in all the way or out?"

Tyrus looked at the big handsome man as he navigated down the bumpy dirt road that was little more than a trail. "I'm all in and things are gonna get hot."

"I'll be there just like in France." Ransom said.

Automatically both men minds went back to 1917, and the Argonne Forest, where they were under heavy enemy mortar fire for two days and nights. The trees that were once festooned with the beautiful colors of fall had looked like skeletal fingers reaching up into the smoky sky. After the bombardment, then came the enemy troops and shortly after that close combat. Who could count the number of times they had saved each other's lives. Their bond was deep, as only the closeness of death can force.

"We'll get you some arms for your people and you can teach them to use them." Ransom said.

"How soon can you get them, cause we're gonna need them?" said Tyrus.

"If you want, we can Load a truck with it and bring it back when we unload the shipment !" said Ransom.

"That would be good, but make sure to leave me some liquor. We can start on that right away. We'll water it down, then rebottle it." said Tyrus.

"No, we sell it like we bought it. We didn't get cheated, we ain't cheatin nobody and if somebody cheats us that's their ass." said Ransom.

"Man you're serious, I say again!" said Tyrus smiling.

"Them crackers gonna get rich off our people, why should they? I answer, they shouldn't." said Ransom.

The men drove to the house where they stored the majority of their weapons. Each of the Kanes had choppers and were prepared to use them. The elder Kanes arrived with the young men. Raven watched as they stacked the liquor, then went to a crate and opened it. He pulled out several bottles, then called out.

"Turk, Price, Cellus, Brooks. Y'all get two bottles a piece and crate up these for me." He passed them the bottles he held. "That's for my engagement party!" Raven said.

"I don't know what the Maces have in mind, but I'm going top shelf. They can serve shine, I'm serving good scotch whiskey."

The men laughed, then Raven said. "Hold on, I got a surprise for y'all."

He walked to his car and came back with a big cardboard box. He sat the box down and opened it. He pulled out two black garments and turned to the other men, and said. "I gave this some thought. And I had Mamie the seamstress, to make these for us." In his hands he had a black conical hood and a black cape.

"They were easy to make and there's enough for everybody. We can just ride around with them in our cars. I talked to Wiggens, the welder too, and he's gonna make us false beds for the trucks. And compartments for our cars so we can get by a cursory search." said Raven.

All of the men gathered around and the hoods and

capes were passed out. Tyrus looked around at the men assembled and knew he was with real men. He didn't get a hood or cape. The Kanes would be the enforcement arm, as well as the managerial staff and distributors. They loaded up a truck with choppers, grenades, and dynamite. They had left several crates of whiskey. They loaded into the trucks, except this time Brooks drove and Tyrus directed. They were headed to Tyrus' headquarters.

    *   *   *   *

"Lucy Pearl, it's getting late. I think you should be heading on home before it gets dark." said Prescott.

"I'm almost finished, Mr. Pres." said Lucy Pearl.

"You can finish tomorrow. Whatever you're doing can wait, now go on and get home." said Prescott firmly.

Lucy Pearl walked from a back room, followed by Elisabeth. Elisabeth hugged her, then said. "We can finish tomorrow. It'll give us something to do."

Lucy Pearl walked to Prescott and he threw his arms around her. He hugged her tight, then whispered. "Don't tarry. Go on home."

Alright," she said as he held her at arms length. Lucy Pearl walked to the door, waved, then walked out into the rapidly fading sunlight.

Prescott watched her and thought, there goes my heir. As Lucy Pearl walked swiftly down the sidewalk, she heard her name called. So she stopped and turned toward the sound. She saw Bobby Rodgers leaning against a building.

As always he was dressed nicely. A navy blue double breasted suit with chalk white pin stripes. A freshly starched, snow white shirt. Black shiny brogues and a black fedora cocked at a jaunty angel. When he smiled, the gold caps on his teeth flashed in the waning light.

"Hello beautiful!" he said in a silky smooth voice.

"Hey Bobby." she replied batting her eyes flirtatiously.

Bobby Rodgers was about 6" feet tall and well built. He had a coco skin complexion and long glistening hair, that he kept pressed and greased. "Pearl, you know I been wanting us to get together. I know you been busy, but make time for me." said Bobby.

Bobby was a hustler and well known womanizer.

Lucy Pearl had been warned about him and others like him by both her mother and Elisabeth, but still she found him exciting and attractive.

"Let me drive you home sweet heart." said Bobby.

"No my mother would kill me. I can just walk, it won't take but a minute." she said smiling and waiting to see what his next move was.

He walked towards her, his eyes eating her up. He stopped, stared down in her lovely eyes and whispered. "You were made for me."

Lucy Pearl shuddered and felt herself getting wet just being close to him. She was a long way from being a virgin and it had been a while since she last had sex.

"I got to go." she said tearing her eyes from his, turning on her heel and walking off.

Bobby watched her as she walked away, thinking. "For that, I could stop chasing all the others."

Lucy Pearl hurried down the street then turned a corner. It would take her at least twenty minutes to get home, if she went the long way. So she decided to take the short cut through the woods, which would cut as much as seven or eight minutes off her walk.

She veered off and walked onto a well defined path. It was getting dark quicker than she thought it was and she saw danger in every flickering shadow. She picked up the pace, then tripped over a root, twisted her ankle, and crashed to the ground.

She reached down and gripped her ankle, then slowly rose to her feet. She winced, as the pain jolted thru her ankle. Limping, she tried to Hurry from the copse of trees.

*   *   *   *

The Klan had chosen their time to ride and made all of the preparations. When they rode, they used horses to ride thru and spread their reign of terror. They had split up in two groups and were heading towards their victims.

Deputy Anton Billings, Thomas Bellamys, his brother Ron, and their cousins Chester and Manley, along with the Stanley brothers, rode their horses down a back road. Their robe's glowing a ghostly white. There were 3 more members of the Klavern with them.

As the men slowly padded down the road, there was a

loud rustling in the bushes. The men halted their horses and sat silently. A figure tumbled from the bushes into the road, then stood and gingerly placed weight on one leg that appeared to be injured.

"Well, well, what have we got here?" asked Anton.

Lucy Pearl looked up, saw the Klansmen and turned to run. hobbled by her twisted ankle, she didn't get far.

The men spurred their horses forward and crowded in on her. Randy Stanley bumped her with his horse and she fell to the ground. Quickly he dismounted and snatched her up. All of the men got off their horses and surrounded her. Randy Stanley grabbed her dress by the neck and in a powerful motion tore her dress open exposing her full young breast to the darkening night. She fought and kicked, until one of the men smashed his fist into her jaw stunning her. Randy ripped the dress from her body, then tore at her frilly bloomers until she lay naked and exposed before the men.

She shook her head form side to side to clear the grogginess. She thought she saw lights, but she was still dazed and unsure. She felt her legs being held, then spread apart. Automatically her hands went to her mound. Her arms were grabbed and she found herself spread eagle to the night sky. Frantically she looked around at the men, who had started to unbuckle their pants and pull out their flaccid penis'.

"This looks like some young stuff here." said Ron from behind his mask. "It ought to be good too."

The men laughed, as one of the townsmen got on his knees between her legs. His penis was pink and seemed to glow in the dim light of the night. She wiggled from side to side, as he tried to penetrate her.

"Be still damn it!" the man said and slapped her viciously across the face.

She saw the lights again and heard the rumble of what sounded like a motor. She didn't know if it was the effects of the blows or reality. She felt the man's rigid penis pierce her and she screamed out in anger. "NOOOOO....!"

He thrust into her hard and fast and she wiggled to buck him off which only made it good for him. The men were so engrossed in what was before them, that they never heard the trucks that pulled up or the sounds as the men got out of the trucks.

Turk had been turning the lights on from time to time, to navigate on the bumpy road. That was the light Lucy

Pearl saw. The men quickly came up on the Klan and Price turned on the truck lights. All of the Klansmen froze, except the one that was thrusting wildly in Lucy Pearl.

"Get off of her right now, you red neck motherfucker!" shouted Ransom.

The Klansmen looked and saw there were several heavily armed black men. The Klansmen couldn't see the men's faces, but they knew now was not the time to reach for their guns. Ransom held a .45 in his hand, so did the others, but it was the menacing look that did the trick. The man that was raping Lucy Pearl had stopped and the ones holding her had all froze.

"Cracker, get off her right now." Ransom said his voice filled with fury.

The man crawled from between her legs, then stood and attempted to put his penis in his pants. There was the loud report of two quick gunshot and the man screamed. Ransom fired the big .45 twice. The slugs smashed thru the man's hands and shredded his penis and testicles. His hands shattered, the man fell to his knees, as blood spurted form his various wounds.

"Get a rope." said Ransom in a deadly tone. "I'm sure they got one!"

Brooks, Turk, Price and Tim all got ropes from the milling horses.

"This one is dead." Ransom said pointing at the wounded man. "This is what we'll do to any cracker, that dares to molest our women!

The men formed a noose and tossed it over a tree branch, then secured it to the man's neck. The other end they secured to a saddle horn, then walked the horse until the man was struggling and spasming in his death throes. They tied the end off on the tree and left the man hanging there in full Klan regalia.

"I want the rest of these asshole stripped naked except for the hood and robe, then tie their asses up." Ransom said.

The men quickly finished the task, then they blindfolded them, which was fairly easy since all they had to do was turn their hoods around. They loaded the men in the trucks, then gathered the horses. They drove to town and tied the men behind the horses, then fired a hail of gunfire from the machine guns. The horses bolted in panic dragging the

Klansmen behind them

Tyrus took Lucy Pearl home and the men dropped off their goods and quickly drove back to LaVilla.

     *   *   *   *

Oscar Bellamys, Simon, Bernie, Bull Parsons, Con Majors, Cad Lowe and Shel Parsons rode to their destination. The men kicked in doors, drug people form their homes and generally busted heads. Always with the message that, if they kept doing business with Wellington someone would end up dead. They rode to the stables, got in their cars, and headed for town.

When they arrived the town was in an uproar and several members were in the hospital and one had been mutilated and hung.

"Who did this shit?" Bull roared. "I wanna know who's responsible for this!"

Everyone just stared around, looking at each other.

"Let's go to the hospital, maybe we can get some answers there." Bull said.

The men drove to the hospital and went directly to see Anton Billings.

"What the hell happened out there Ant?' asked Bull. "I want it all, from a to z!"

Anton, looked up at Bull from where he lay in the bed. Gauze was all over his lower body and you could see blood seeping thru in several spots. "Well Bull, we were on the way to do what you told us, when this nigger girl came stumbling out of the woods. We rode down on her and figured we'd have a little fun before we went on. I think the woman was bait, cause them niggers came out of nowhere, all armed with machine guns. There wasn't much we could do. Tom Curry, was fucking the girl when they came up. They shot off his dick and balls, then hung him. Said that's what would happen to anyone that molested their women."

Bull looked at the man, but felt that something didn't ring true with his statement. Just what, he couldn't put his finger on. "Did you recognize any of them?" Bull asked.

"It was dark and you know if niggers ain't smiling you can't see them in the dark." said Anton. "I won't forget that niggers voice, I can tell you that!"

Wally came rushing in, whispering. "I told you what

would happen if you kept pushing the niggers!"

"There's more to it than that, I bet." said Bull thoughtfully. Bull felt it inside that something was looming. Intuitively, he just knew it wasn't what it looked like on the surface.

"Ain't much we can do until we find who's responsible, so let's get on that right away. I wanna know everything!" said Bull.

The men followed him as he walked from the room.

* CHAPTER # 13 *

"Pa, I couldn't very well have just walked away and let them crackers rape the girl." said Ransom.

"I'm not saying you should have." said Raven in reply. "All I'm saying is you could have been a little more subtle, is all. You've humiliated them, hung one and left a sign for the rest of them. How do you think they'll respond?"

"I hope by hanging the one, the others will see that it can happen to them too." answered Ransom.

"It won't," Raven said firmly. "What it will do, is cause them to tighten down. Everywhere they see blacks gathered, they'll go in busting heads. Whites have a different mentality than us. They feel threatened, they attack viciously never thinking to retreat. It's worked for them so many times before, that they think it will work always." "In that case, we'll do the same thing. Never retreat, always attack. If we put them on the defensive, they'll change their tactics!" said Ransom.

"I don't know if they will or not, but I personally like the idea of giving them a taste of their own medicine." said Falcon.

"They don't ride over here, because of our strength, but they'll get bolder if the blacks in town let them run over them." said Hawk. "We've seen it before so it shouldn't be a surprise."

"So, I guess you want to ride on the whites every time they ride against the blacks then?" asked Raven.

"The men all nodded their heads.

"I don't think so.' Raven said. "I think what we should do is, show them they're not safe in any capacity first. I want stolen cars to drive thru town and if they're stopped I want the passengers to open fire on the deputies. They don't have enough men to stop every car, but I want fear in them so they'll let more go by. That way, insuring we get our shipments out."

"When do we start grandpa?" asked Brooks.

"Soon as you get the cars." said Raven.

*   *   *   *

Tyrus sat around with his people and they talked about the Klansmen and how they had rode and about the Klansman that had been killed.

"I'm telling you, them Kanes are some mean motherfuckers." said Tyrus. "They didn't take no time stringing that cracker up. If the rednecks know like I do, they'd pack their bags now!

"So where does that leave us Pa?" asked Price. "What do we do?"

"What we do is go to all the speakeasies in town and sell the whiskey. They ain't gonna tell the crackers where they're getting the stuff from. And whites only frequent certain ones. I don't give a damn if they get the watered down stuff." said Tyrus. "Hell it would serve them right if you let me tell it."

*　　　　　*　　　　　*　　　　　*

Raven and Celia, lay naked in bed. She had one leg tossed over him and her hand tenderly massaged his semi-erect member.

"You been like a randy young boy lately." she said with a satisfied smile. "Was it the news about the baby?"

"That and a combination of other things." he said pinching at the pinky sized nipple of her left breast. "I guess it's been a while since I've had anything to really get excited about."

"Are you saying I haven't excited you?" she asked.

"Woman don't start that, you know perfectly well what I'm talking bout, so don't play that game." he said smiling.

She knew perfectly well that she excited him. To prove the point, she pulled herself on top of him and guided him into her warmth.

"Think you should be up there, with the baby coming and all?" he asked concerned, as she bounced energetically on his stiff rod.

"Yesss…Yes….I… should." she moaned.

After they had made love, she lay there in his arms. "I'd like you to make me a promise!" she said.

"And what's that?" he asked.

"I want you to promise me that you'll at least tolerate

my folks Saturday night." she said.

He laughed and hugged her tighter, then said. "Woman I was feeling pretty down on myself before you came into my life. You've made life more worth living. You've made me happy, how could I do less for you?" he asked her.

She snuggled deeper into his embrace, smiled to herself, then said. "Thank you honey."

"You're my princess, I'd give half my kingdom for you. Plus all of my love and my life!" he said softly.

"I haven't seen Lucy Pearl for at least a week." said Elisabeth.

Prescott thought long and hard, then said. "Beth we need to talk."

She looked in his eyes and knew the matter was serious. She reached for his arm, as he turned to lock the front door. They walked to the back office and he helped her to a seat. Then kneeled in front of her and clasped her hand tightly. He looked up at her, then said. "Lucy Pearl, was beaten and raped the night the Klansmen was killed. The men that killed them came up on the Klan Raping her, and did justice. The Klan doesn't know who she was and she knows who the men are that killed the Klansman and hurt the others."

Elisabeth sat with awe, hand held to her mouth. Tears flowing from her eyes, she muttered. "Poor darling."

"There's more," he said solemnly. "I'm Lucy Pearl's father!" He felt her hands squeeze his tighter.

She looked in his eyes, and said. "I figured as much, since she looks so much like your sister Nellie."

Now that he thought about it, she did look like Nellie. So where do we go from here?" he asked her.

"Just like we've done, except since we know she's our child, then we give her the benefits that go with being our daughter!" she said.

"Do you understand why I told you this?" he asked.

"I could assume, but I'd prefer if you told me." she said.

"I've been trying to help the less fortunate all of my life and I met one who stirs something inside of me. I love you, truly I do, but Eula has something that draws. That one inner quality that I can't find words for. I was practicing being elite without knowing it. Here I am, a wealthy white man, with a mistress."

"I can see where that could be hypocritical, but it doesn't have to be that way." she said.

"What do you mean?" he asked puzzled.

"I love you Prescott. More than life itself and I'd do anything to make you happy. I never bore you an heir and that has weighed heavily on me. I would prefer it if you bought both Eula and Lucy to live with us. There's plenty of room."

"Are you sure? People will talk."

"We've always fought against convention, why should it be different now?"

He leaned forward and kissed her lips lightly, then said. "Lucy is in danger as long as she's here, because she can identify the men that rescued her."

"Get them here safely and we'll figure what to do from there." she said.

He nodded his head, then rose to is feet and strode purposely from the store.

*   *   *   *

Prescott arrived at the little cottage, he had given Eula the money to purchase. He walked to the door, took out his keys and went inside. Eula and Lucy sat on the sofa drinking tea. Lucy wasn't too traumatized by the incident, as she had saw her attacker die.

"Lucy Pearl, I think there's something you need to know." said Prescott. "I'm your father!"

Both of the women dropped the tea cups and saucers they held, as their mouths dropped open.

"I want you both to pack some things, you're moving in with me and Elisabeth.

Eula looked at him with wide doe like eyes, questions screamed at him from their depths.

"It's alright Eula. Beth knows and understands. She wants us to be together, as a family." said Prescott.

The two women moved to their rooms and packed a small valise, then returned to the front room where he still stood. They walked to him and he took their bags and led them to the car. They drove to his house, which was behind the big store. Elisabeth, came onto the porch when she heard the car pull up.

The women stepped cautiously from the car and looked at Beth. Their eyes asking her to forgive them.

104

She walked to them and hugged them, then said. "Your home. Welcome."

They went inside and Elisabeth showed them their rooms. Prescott dropped their bags off, then they all went to the sitting room. "Eula, you'll work in the store from now on. I'll get to our domestic arrangements later, because right now Lucy is in danger, as are the men who helped her. Lucy, can you get in touch with those men?" asked Prescott.

Lucy Pearl nodded her head. "I know one of them, but the one that shot the man ordered him hung. Told me that if I ever needed him, to contact Tyrus Biggers."

"Can we go see him now?" asked Prescott. "We've got to hide you away, until this blows over."

Lucy Pearl looked at Eula and Eula nodded her head. Lucy Pearl stood up, and said. "Let's go meet him then, Mr. Pres."

"Honey you can call me Daddy, Pa, or Father." said Prescott. " Things are forever changed now."

    *   *   *   *

"You're telling me, that you need to see the man who saved Lucy?" asked Tyrus.

"Yes that's what I'm saying." Prescott replied.

"I'll tell you what I'll do, because you feel the girl is in danger. You leave her here and I'll get her to him. She won't be away too long, because soon the law around here is gonna be plenty busy!" said Tyrus.

Prescott looked into his eyes, then said. "Tell him I said take care of my daughter."

Tyrus looked from Prescott to Lucy and noticed their resemblance. If you didn't know, you wouldn't be looking for it, but Lucy did resemble her father. Prescott left and drove back home.

    *   *   *   *

"How could you just leave her there, with a man you don't know?" asked Beth.

"She gonna be alright, Mrs. Beth." said Eula. "They saved her from harm, they won't hurt her."

"Eula, I don't know the words to describe what we are to each other, so let's just say we're sisters. I don't want you to call me Mrs. Beth, Beth will do just fine. This is your home now and you won't be treated like a servant. We'll share all of the wifely duties, love making included. We'll raise Lucy together, do you understand?"

Eula nodded her head, then said. "All of this is new to me, Mrs...." she caught herself, then continued. "Beth. All my life I've been told how to act towards white folk. My folk told me, what theirs told them. Except for getting with Pres, I followed it. Cause I don't need the grief. I ain't use to bein treated like a white woman and don't know that I ever will be. In this house one set of rules apply, but out yonder in the world they get different notions. And I don't wanna bring shame down on you."

"Prescott moved to her and held her tight. Beth watched how they interacted with each other and thought to herself. "I want to see them make love."

"Don't worry about what people will say, what's most important is the love we share and what we think, nothing else." said Prescott.

"It's easy to see from the outside looking in, but you can't know what it's like being a nigger woman in these days and times. You think you could really know? I can answer that for you. No you don't. Beth, I love Pres like I ain't never loved a man before and I've always respected you and your home. When Pres wanted Lucy to work the store, I didn't really want her to. Anybody could see him in her, if they looked. Y'all done took me and Lucy in, so we gonna do you proud!"

Beth walked over and the three hugged each other tightly.

*   *   *   *

"Somebody's knockin on the door, Ran." said his wife Emma Jean shaking him.

Ransom rolled over, grabbed his .45 automatic, slipped on his robe, then he silently padded to the front room. He peeped out of the side of the curtain and saw Tyrus standing their with a valise. And behind him, the young girl they had rescued from the Klan.

He opened the door, and said. "Y'all come on in."

Tyrus and Lucy came inside and Ransom shut the door. He looked from Tyrus to Lucy, then back to Tyrus, and said. "So what gives Ty?"

"Well Ran, it's like this. The girl's pa brought her to me. He wanted to meet with you, but I didn't think that was wise. He wants you to hide her out, until this thing blows over with the Klan. They don't know who she is just yet, but in time they'd find out. Then they would know who you are. Ain't no sense thinking she would hold up to what they'd do to her." said Tyrus.

"Good thinking Ty." said Ransom. "You can head on back home or stay til morning, which ever suits you."

"I better get on back then. Merly, might think I done started back cattin around." said Ty laughing. He turned to the door, and walked out.

Ransom locked the door, picked up Lucy's valise, and said. "Follow me, this where you'll sleep. You can stay as long as you like."

Emma Jean walked out tying her robe. She looked at Lucy, then to Ransom. Emma Jean was a big woman in every way. She was nearly 6" feet tall, well muscled, big pillowy breast, wide hips and thick sturdy legs. She had the classic hour glass figure. Her face told the tail of her mixed ancestry. The lips big and full, the nose flared and wide, the eyes slightly slanted with a hazel color. Her skin a sun kissed, honey complexion.

"This the girl I told you bout." said Ransom. "She gonna keep you company for a while. She's a daughter and I expect for word of that to get around, you hear?"

Emma Jean nodded and walked over to Lucy, and asked. "You got a name sugar?"

"Yes mam, my name is Lucy Pearl Shores." she said timidly.

Emma Jean hugged her, and said. "Call me Emma, or Mamma like everybody else."

"Okay," Lucy said with a small smile.

"Ran, you know the party for pappa is tomorrow night. I just know Lucy ain't got nothing to wear. So, I'm gonna go to Mamie in the morning and get her a pretty dress. Plus some shoes and other stuff."

"You need money?" Ransoms asked.

"I got plenty." Emma said. "We gonna have to get one of the boys to escort her. I think Timmy should be the one, since he ain't got no steady woman."

"It's done," Ransom said. "I'll tell Pa, and he'll get it

done."

"I want you to do it." Emma said firmly. "It's time you took your rightful place, at the head of the family. Pappa and the elders, ain't gonna live forever Ran!"

"Em, why you always pushin so? I know my place in the family and in this house. So, I suggest you remember yours!" said Ransom.

"I didn't mean nothing bad baby." said Emma apologetically. "You got the family movin in a different direction and you'll have to lead."

"We been doing pretty good doing things the old way. I don't see no need to upset the apple cart." said Ransom.

"That's just it honey." said Emma passionately. "These ain't the old times. These are new times and gonna get newer, mark my words. You got to change with the times. And if all the stories I've heard are true, then they did it like their people before them. Different times call for different methods!"

"You might be right." Ransom said. "I just don't wanna be the one to seem pushy. Let the elders fade and in the mean time I'll add small changes."

"I guess that will be good for now, but I'm gonna talk to pa about it and see how he feels." said Emma with a smile.

Ransom shook his head and smiled. "I got one hell of a woman there." he said to himself.

They walked Lucy to a room and Emma said. "You can come and go as you please, but be sure you never go out alone. You were sent here for us to protect you and we take that serious chile!"

"What about my folks, who gonna keep them safe?" Lucy asked.

"I'll do what I can to make sure they're alright." said Ransom.
They left her and went to their room.

"Ain't but a little while til sunrise." Ransom said. "I thought we might stay awake til then."

Emma slapped him on the arm playfully, then whispered. " We got company Ran."

"I won't scream too loud." he said laughing.

"In that case, I guess I can go on and give you a little bit." she said removing her robe.

He watched, as she shrugged the robe from her

shoulders. He could see that her nipples were stiff. She looked good in the white, silk gown, he had imported from France. He watched as she pulled the gown over her head, and her magnificent breast came into view.

He looked downward and saw the matching silk drawers that hugged her mound. He could see the slit plainly out lined, and he felt his penis fill with blood. He watched as she hooked her thumbs in the waistband of her drawers and slowly shimmied out of them. By then, he was rock hard.

She walked backward and lay on the bed with her legs spread wide. He saw her puffy nether lips, were coated with dew. It looked so erotic, surrounded by silky black hair. He watched as her hands came down and spread the lips open so he could see the beautiful pink walls. A trickle of her juices leaked from her hole and his robe had a great tent at the groin. He slowly removed his robe, as he watched her fingers dance between her legs.

He gripped his staff and walked between her legs and positioned himself. She reached for him, held him and guided him in. She raised her hips, as he gently slid in her.

"Oh baby," she moaned softly, as he stroked deep into her.

* CHAPTER # 14 *

"I'm telling you Bull, we need to stir shit up around here." said Oscar sternly.

"And just why should we do that Oscar?" asked Bull.

"Because the niggers might get the wrong idea and think we done got vulnerable. Ain't no telling what kind of notions they'll get then." Oscar said.

"You know he's right Bull." said Simon. "We know that girl was from around here. She knows the niggers that killed Tom!"

"The question is this, how do we find her?" Bull asked.

"We got to bust some nigger ass, that's how!" said Oscar.

"So you're suggesting we ride again soon?" Bull asked.

Bubba Stanley spoke up. "I think we need to put the pressure on, all around. What you do Bull, is you deputize all of us, that gives you more man power. All of the members of the Klavern are in the militia so it shouldn't be a big problem. A white man lynched, is as good a reason as any."

"Damn it, I think that's the answer." said Bull. "We'll really put the pressure on. Stop cars and wagons. Beat a few niggers, kick down some doors. Yeah, that ought to do the trick!"

*   *   *   *

Emma and Lucy, walked into Mamie's Dress Shop.

"How are you Emma?" asked Cilla.

"I'm fine girl." said Emma. "Is your Ma around?"

"She's in back." Cilla replied.

Mamie Waters and her daughter both, were big dark skin women. Their faces had a somewhat Egyptian look. Hooded eyes, high cheekbones, thin noses and full luscious lips. Mamie came from the back, saw Emma, and asked. "Girl what you need?"

"I need some dresses for my daughter here." said

Emma pointing at Lucy. "She new in town and I want her to always put her best foot forward. She gonna need everything, price is no object. I need her a beautiful dress for Raven's engagement party tonight. By the way, did y'all get the invitation?"

"Yeah honey we got them." Mamie said. "I ain't got but one problem with the whole thing."

"What's that?" asked Emma.

"That I ain't the one he engaged to!" said Mamie laughing. All of the women laughed with her.

"Mama ain't you a little old for that?" asked Cilla playfully.

"Might be some snow on the roof, but there's still fire in the fire place." Mamie said sassily. "Raven is a fine figure of a man. I been knowing him more than 30 years, your Ransom looks like he did years ago. And that Timmy, looks like him the first time I saw him. We done had a little thing, but he was loyal to his wife. A real man. I suspect Ran and Timmy are the same way.

Emma shook her head. As long as she had been a part of this family, still there were things she didn't know. "Let's get busy." Emma said to Mamie.

They walked thru the shop looking at dresses. Emma picked several and several pairs of shoes. She brought Lucy everything she thought she'd need. She had watched the young girl's eyes beaming with pleasure, as she touched and tried on the dresses. Emma watched her eyes keep going back to a canary yellow dress, that hung in a corner by itself.

"That yellow dress, is it sold?" asked Emma.

"No, I just threw that together. It's suppose to be the latest fashion, but girl it's a little too daring for these parts."

"I want to see her in it." Emma said.

They walked to the dress and Mamie got it and passed it to Lucy who clasped it tightly to her chest. She went into the small changing room and put the dress on, then stepped out.

"Good Lord," said Mamie. "That dress was made for this chile!"

Emma eyed the dress critically. She walked around Lucy and saw how the yellow dress hugged the young woman's voluptuous body.

"Look at her breast, the way that dress got them spilling out at the top. Could you put a sheer lace over that?"

asked Emma

"Hmmm.... I could do it, but I think it would affect the drape of the dress." said Mamie.

"Tack it on and let's see what we got." Emma said.

Mamie walked and got a piece of sheer lace and some pins. She tacked the lace over the twin swells of Lucy's breast and stood back. You could still see the swollen mounds of her breast, but it was like looking through fog.

"That's it," Emma said. "I want you to do that one right away. Them white shoes we just picked, is what the doctor ordered. As Lucy went to take off the dress, Emma saw a pearl cameo brooch.

"I want that, but attach it to a white silk ribbon. She can wear it as a choker." Emma said.

Lucy and Emma hung out in the dress shop until the dress was finished. They got their packages and left.

      *   *   *   *

"Tim, you remember the girl from the other night?" asked Ransom.

"What other night, Ran?" asked Tim.

"The one we saved from the Klan?" Ransom said.

"Yeah I remember her." Tim said. "What about her?"

"Well, I want you to escort her to my pa's party tonight." Ransom said. "Treat her with respect Tim, she's in my care!"

"I'd do it even if she wasn't cousin." Tim said. "How'd she find you?"

"She didn't, her pa sent her. He felt she was in danger so he wanted her out of town until things blow over." Ransom said. "Tyrus brought her last night and she's gonna be staying with us til then."

"I hate to be the bearer of bad news, but them crackers ain't gonna forget one of theirs got hung." Tim said.

"Well it's done now and we can't undo it. Shit, if I had to, I'd do it again." Ransom said forcefully.

"Me too cousin. I would make it last a little longer though." said Tim laughing.

"How are things going getting the stolen cars like we wanted?" asked Ransom.

"Well we got two and we stole them from Baldwin.

The boys went to white house so they might have something."
Tim answered. "When we gonna start with that?"

"I'd say Monday, but we'll check with the elders
first.

* CHAPTER # 15 *

Emma and Lucy stopped by Raven's House on the way home and Celia opened the door. "Hey Em how are you? And who is this pretty thing?" she asked Emma as she pulled Lucy into her arms.

"This is Lucy Shores and she's living with us for a while." said Emma. "I need to see pappa."

"Pappa...!" Celia screamed.

"Damn it woman. I done told you about screaming and hollering in this house." Raven said as he stepped into the room. "Oh, we got guest?"

"Pappa we need to talk." Emma said seriously.

Raven looked at Emma and knew it was an important matter. "What is it?"

He knew Emma loved him and she was one of the few family members who would be straight with him. She was a smart woman and Raven couldn't understand where Cellus and Brooks got their habits from.

"Let's go in the sitting room." Celia said. "Ain't no need to stand in the door!"

They walked back to the sitting room. After they were all seated, Celia said. "I'm gonna get us girls some tea and pappa some coffee. Don't say a word till I get back, Em."

"Go on and get the refreshments, old nosy heifer." said Raven smiling as Celia hurried from the room.

"You know I'm glad you feel like you can talk to me, cause Tracy and Cissy don't. It's like, I'm from another planet to them." said Raven with a smile.

"What do you expect pappa? You got a woman their age." said Emma. "It's hard for them because they loved their Momma. They see Celia as someone replacing her!"

"It ain't bout them though, it's about me. And Celia has made me happy as I've been in the last few years. I wish Dove could be here, but she ain't. So much has changed, things can't stay the same as much as we'd like them to. I can't say things are getting better, but we all must adjust to the times or we will fall by the way side!" Raven said.

Celia walked back into the room, and said. "Heifer I

told you to wait until I got back."

"Aw hush woman." Raven said smiling. "So what is it Em?"

"You touched on it pappa, with what you just said. Times are forever changing and either we change by choice or by force. I think it's time you let Ransom lead the family. We're going in a different direction and Ran is better qualified to lead than any of the others, except for maybe Trace." Emma said. "It's time pappa and you know it."

Raven looked at her and laughed, then said. "I'm not laughing at you so don't think that. I can see your point, but it's not like that in the family. There isn't a leader, per say. They come to me, because they always have. True, in a sense I'm the leader, but it's not quite so cut and clear. If Ran is to be the head of the family he will prove it by action. I'll know when the time is because the young ones will go to him instead of me. If he asserts himself he will eventually be the head. Had my first boy Crow still lived, Ran would still be my choice cause he wasn't as smart and thoughtful as Ran. That's what got his ass killed. But I can't make Ran the leader, the family has to do that and in time they will. Kane men are unique, in that there is no jealously or envy. One of them will emerge as leader, but that's off a ways. I'll help him because I think he's worthy."

"So I wasted a trip then?" she asked.

"Hell no you didn't." he said. "Plus you brought me a sweet young morsel."

Celia slapped at him playfully.

"This is Lucy Shores, the girl Ran and the others saved from the Klan." Emma stated proudly. "Her pa sent her here for her protection."

"Who's your pa?" Raven asked Lucy.

"Mr. Prescott Wellington, sir" Lucy replied.

"Prescott Wellington the businessman ?" asked Raven.

"Yes sir," Lucy Answered.

"I've heard good things about your pa. He's my kind of man.." Raven said. "I'd like to meet him. Meant to, but never got around to riding over that way."

They sat around talking for a while, then Emma and Lucy rose to leave.

"Don't be late now hear me?" Raven asked. "Go on home and start getting ready, cause this a special night for us!"

Emma and Lucy hugged Raven and Celia, then they got in the car and drove home.

"That Em is a special woman." Raven said. "Ain't no any kind of man could have her. I hope Ran knows how special she is."

"He does," said Celia. "Em was the first woman in the family to accept me or rather to accept us being together. All the others thought I was after your money, cause they don't see you like I do. They see father, uncle or brother. Not lover, friend and confidant."

"That's because at the time, that's all I was." Raven said. "My wife was sickly for a number of years before she passed. I did my little catting, but nothing serious. Dove told me to find a wife or a companion. I didn't really want to, cause it was kind of fun to be single. Then I met you. Girl you sure did change things. See, all of my life I've had a wife and responsibilities, that's the way I was raised. You filled a hole, an empty space in my life and heart. I love you for that!"

"I love you too." she said. "It ain't like I didn't know no other men, but you were different. And all of the older women wanted you for themselves. I told myself that if you were half the man they made you out to be, I would have you for myself. Yeah baby, I found out that you're not half the man they said, but that and much more. I've never felt so loved or so safe, not even at home with my family. You're a man and that's what made the difference for me!"

*   *   *   *

"We got three cars." Blake said to Ransom. "They're all pieces of shit though. Gonna need a little work if we plan to get away in them."

"Get the work done and get it done quick. Cause Monday, we're gonna start our reign of terror on them crackers!" Ransom said. "Take the cars to Hootie Carson and tell him I said put a rush on it. We got two cars that are ready to go so we'll need them by Wednesday at the latest."

"Who's gonna go the first time?" Pat asked. "I'd like to."

"Me too," Juan said. " I Want them to feel like they've made our folks feel. I want them crackers to panic every time they see a strange car!"

"Y'all two can go, but somebody else gonna be with you. I want two gunners in every car. All the driver does is drive. If you kill crackers it's alright, cause that's what we want.

"I want in on this too pa." said Brooks.

"You got it son." Ransom said smiling. "All of y'all are gonna have a part in it, cause we gonna send at least two cars every time."

Lonnie looked at Ransom, and said. "What about me Ran?"

You're family Lon so you got to take part. See, we gonna need every able bodied man if this is gonna work. Ain't a one of us, better than any other. Each of us has his place and I expect everyone to tote his load. Ain't no room for slacking, cause our lives gonna be on the line. We've got to be extra careful and if it goes like I think it will, we won't have to do too much killin. So stay on your toes and ain't no drinking while we're working, cause we'll need to be in full control. I think y'all better head on home and get ready for the party. Don't be late or my pa will have your asses." Ransom said. "Tigger you coming to the party?"

"Wouldn't miss it for the world Ran. I wanna see Mace's face when I show up." said Tigger laughing

"What really happened between you and Mace?" asked Ransom.

"I'm married to his sister Margie and I guess that made Mace think I was under his rule. I work by my own rules and no man treats me like I'm some stupid kid, which is some of what Mace did. The rest is to try and cheat me out of what's mine. See I ain't had much book learning and some men take that to mean I'm dumb. I can cipher some if I take my time, but I can figure real good. Have to in my line of business, cause it takes exact measures. He tried to cheat me and I got a little rough with him. Now Mace is a fighter, but he ain't young as he once was. He gave it a good go, but I put him down, then the boys decided to jump in. I gave them some lumps, but in the end they put me down. Would've killed me if Mace hadn't stopped them. He didn't kick me while I was down and I'm thankful cause I would've killed him. After that, I caught them boys of his one by one, and whipped them soundly. I ain't had much to do with them since, but I got along well with Lola, she comes by the house regularly. When I do my drinkin I stay away from the house, cause Margie ain't havin none of that around the little ones." said Tigger smiling

"You ain't got to worry about that type of things with us." Ransom said.

"Hell I know that. Y'all two different kinds of people. I ain't heard nothing but good bout y'all. And I done worked for your uncle and he's been more than fair. Shit he done lent me money and wouldn't let me give him no extra or anything, so I know y'all are good folk!" Tigger said seriously.

The men hurried and put away their tools, then each headed home.

*   *   *   *

Mace struggled, as Lola finished tying his tie. "You tryin to strangle me before we get to the party, Lo?"

"Mace! Please zip it shut. I want you to be on your best behavior. Look at the benefits of being affiliated with them. It would open doors that thus far have been closed!"

"Don't start acting like them Kanes are, the be all and end' all." said Mace sternly. "I ain't gonna start nothing Lo, but if something gets started with me I plan to end it!

"Mace honey you can't always just rush in. At times, it calls for more subtle tactics. Just be a gracious host. You ain't got to kiss ass, so don't even think I'm saying that, but I am saying be smart. Them Kanes are hard men.

"All right baby, I can see your point." said Mace as Lola stepped back at arms length and looked him over.

He raised his hand up and stuck one of his big fingers between his neck and collar and ran it around his throat.

"Leave that tie alone!" said Lola sternly, but with a smile.

"Lo, I ain't use to no tie and you know that." Mace said sadly.

"Get used to them, cause you're about to be a big man round here!" Lola said laughing.

He pulled her into his arms and kissed her with a gentleness you wouldn't expect from a man with so gruff an exterior.

"Stop it," she giggled as his hands glided down to the twin globes of her ass. "We're the host baby, that means we got to be there first to greet the guest, so none of that alright?"

"So what, let's be late." he said snuggling up with her.

"No! We're gonna be the first there and last to leave, so save your energy. If you got anything left we can do this later." she said firmly breaking his embrace.

"Is this that important to you, pleasing them Kanes?" he asked angrily.

"You keep on with them Kanes this and them Kanes that, but not once have you mentioned Celia. That's our only daughter and she's marrying a fine man and upstanding citizen. We ain't about to ruin it for her. It's special, past important and we'll do our duty to Celia, cause she don't deserve anything less!" she said.

His face melted, as it dawned on him that he had clean counted Celia out of the equation. "I'm sorry Lo!" he said apologetically.

"That's alright, let's go, we got an engagement party to oversee!" Lola said taking his hand.

   *   *   *   *

By 8:00 that night, everyone was on their way to the meeting hall where the party was to be held. Lola and Mace stood by the front door waiting for the first guest to arrive.

"I forgot to tell you how beautiful you look tonight Lo!" said Mace.

"You cut a pretty dashing figure yourself honey." said Lola pulling him closer. Mace preened like a man half his age.

Blake was the first to arrive. He had as his date, Laine Brown. A pretty brown skin woman, who was tall and sort of on the slim side. She had a fantastic body, plus she was slightly bowlegged.

Blake wore a black suit, white shirt, tie and highly glossed walking boots. Laine wore a blue dress that fit her perfectly. It showed her every curve.

Soon cars were pulling in and the place was filled to the walls with dancing couples.

   *   *   *   *

There was a knock at the door and Celia looked out and saw Tim standing there. He wore a tan two piece suit of

Twill, a white silk waist coat, with tan, white and red cravat, and tan boots. In his hands, he held a white straw boater. He looked dapper as he tapped his foot, waiting. "Go on in the back for a minute Lucy." said Celia.

Lucy walked back to her room, as Celia opened the door. Tim walked in, tipped his head, and said. "Aunt Celia."

"My, my, Timmy, you're looking sharp!" said Celia. "Lucy come on, your escort has arrived!"

Lucy walked form the hall into the front room and Tim just stared at the way the bright yellow dress clung to her young voluptuous figure. He squinted, to see what it was that covered the thrusting mounds of her breast. He looked at her big red legs, or what he could see of them. She wore white strap heel shoes and held a small white purse underneath her breast.

"Timmy, this is Lucy, Lucy this is Timmy." Celia said making the introductions.

Tim took Lucy's hand in his, brought it to his lips and kissed it gently, then looked in her eyes, and said. "I'm pleased to meet you, Ms. Lucy!"

Lucy giggled, then said. "You can just call me Lucy."

"I'd like that." he said.

Celia watched, as the two young people were lost in each others eyes.

Raven walked into the room in a hunter green, velvet double-breasted jacket, hunter green Calvary twill trousers, a white on white starched linen shirt, with a hunter green string tie and highly polished wing tips.

Celia wore a hunter green velvet dress that stopped at her knees and a pair of emerald colored shoes.

"Y'all kids can go on." Raven said. "We're the guest of honor and it wouldn't do for us to come in before y'all!"

Tim took Lucy's hand and they headed for the door. Lucy turned her head and looked at Celia, who winked, and said. "Have a good time, we'll see y'all later!"

After they had left, Celia looked at Raven, and asked. "Are you sure you wanna go thru with this marriage honey?"

He walked to her and pulled her into his arms, then said. "Celia I ain't sure about much ,but I'm sure I love you. I wanna do whatever it takes to make you happy. I was alright with things as they were, but if it's your desire to wed then that's my desire too. I'd do what I have to, to make you happy!"

She hugged him tight, then asked. "Think it's time we headed to the party?"

"Why not, no need to keep them waiting to see the most beautiful woman in the world!" Raven said smiling.

They walked to the door and headed out.

*   *   *   *

When Raven and Celia stepped into the hall with Mace and Lola, it seemed that even the music stopped to stare. All eyes were on them. Raven looked over at Turk and his wife Rosita, and asked. "Did you bring the stuff for us?"

"Yes sir, I did." Turk said smiling. "Come on Blake, Pat, Prince. Let's go to my car."

The four men left their women and walked outside. Pat had come with his long time girlfriend Loren, a small beautiful dark skinned woman. Price was with his wife Consuela.

"Congratulation Kane." said Mace holding his hand out.

Raven took his hand, then said. "Thanks Mace. Kind of you to honor me and Celia this way. I hope you'll let me repay you some day."

"No need to repay me son." said Mace acidly.

"Mace don't you dare." Lola whispered fiercely.

Raven laughed and clapped Mace on the back, then said. "We won't have to use verbal digs every time were at a function together, will we dad?"

Mace's jaws blew up as he set himself up to respond, but Lola stopped him with an ice cold voice. "If you do, I will never speak to you again. I'll be damned if you're gonna ruin my baby's day, damn it!"

"I'm sorry Lo, I couldn't help it." Mace said guiltily.

Hawk, Fern and their beautiful daughter Lisa, walked up to the two older couples.

"Congratulations brother." Hawk said punching Raven in the shoulders lightly.

Drake, who was always in the role of observer watched, but what really had his attention now was Lisa. She wore a pale orange colored dress, her hair was plastered to her head in jet black silken waves. Her legs were bare from mild thigh and his gaze locked on her dimpled knees and the curve of her calves. He looked up at her face and it seemed he fell in the deep pools that were her dark slanted eyes.

Her gaze had traveled around the room, then she saw him. She knew he was Mace, because he had the look. He was a big, light skinned man, in a well tailored brown suit. He was slowly inching his way to where she stood frozen, her eyes locked on his.

Trace, on the other side of the room, had been watching Drake. He had come in contact with him from time to time and he seemed like an alright guy. There was something about him that Trace liked, but he couldn't put his finger on it. He looked to see what the man was staring so intently at, and saw his sister Lisa. He watched, as they held each others gaze and Trace moved in. "Come on Myra." he said to the beautiful red woman, who was built like a sex fiends dream whore. They walked toward where Lisa stood on the edge of the circle of older people.

Drake beat them there and he stood two feet away and just stared.

Lisa, lost in the big handsome man's eyes, also stood there mute. It seemed that nothing existed for them but each other. The crowd was oblivious to what was taking place in their midst.

Trace walked up with Myra, and said. "Drake, this is my sister Lisa. Lisa, this is Aunt Celia's brother Drake.

"How do you do?" Drake asked reaching out his hand.

"I... I'm fine," Lisa stammered as she took his hand in hers. It seemed the two were jolted by electricity, as they touched. Lisa blinked her eyes from the shock of the attraction.

"Would you like to dance?" Drake asked.

Lisa turned towards her parents who were engrossed in the conversation they were involved with. "Oh alright," she replied tentatively.

Blake walked up, as Drake and Lisa took to the dance floor. "Look like Lisa done got one sprung." he said to Trace laughing.

"Yeah, if looks are any indication, I believe you're right brother." said Trace laughing. "Hey Laine, how you be?"

"Hey Trace. I been doing alright, just waitin on this rotten nigga to have a big shin dig for me!" Laine said pouting.

"Don't start in on that again, Laine." Blake said pleadingly.

Trace decided to stir the pot a little. "That sounds like a good idea Laine. Why don't you just do that brother."

Myra cut in then and Trace froze at her words.

"Yeah Trace y'all can give us one together." she said eyeing Trace who she knew would run.

"I'm just joking around." he said. "When the time is right we'll get hitched in high style!"

The group laughed, as Ransom and Emma Jean walked over.

"What up cousins?" Ransom said gaily. "Y'all enjoying yourselves?"

They all spoke to Ransom and his wife, then Ransom asked. "Isn't that Drake Mace dancing with Lisa?"

"Yep, that's Drake." said Trace. "I think Lisa got him sprung!

"No shit?" Ransom asked.

"I shit you not." Trace said. "If you had seen it, you would have thought it was one of them dramas I been hearing so much about."

"So, how y'all feel about Lisa seeing a Mace?" Ransom asked.

"Drake the best man in the bunch. I ain't really had no dealings with the man, but I believe he got sand!" Trace said. "He's got a good reputation and despite what folks say about the others, he's seen as a fair man. And a dangerous man if crossed. I'd ride with him!"

"Yeah so would I, cause I've heard the same things, and I've seen him around. Besides, Celia's a Mace, so they ain't all bad." Ransom said. "Lola's alright too, if you get to know her.

"I'm gonna encourage the relationship, Blake will too. I see it as a way of the two families having a working relationship." said Trace.

"I could see it as a good will offering. It can't hurt to let them see one of theirs, with one of ours." Ransom said.

"Damn, I thought we came to have fun and not be on the job." Blake said as Tim approached them with a beautiful young lady on his arm.

"Hey cousins." Tim said smiling from ear to ear.

"Be careful Timmy, or you're going to swallow your

ears, that smile so big."

"I'd like to introduce you all to Ms. Lucy Shores." said Tim drawing her forward gently and gallantly presenting her to the group.

Ransom leaned into Emma and whispered. "That joker is something else. We better keep our eye on young Lucy, cause Tim's gonna pluck that chicken. Look at her face, see how she's hanging on his every word? She's smitten."

"Yeah that's true, but look at his face, see the admiration there? This isn't a conquest. I think the boy's serious about her. He's not introducing her as the girl y'all rescued, but by her name. The man is smooth, but he won't hit that one and run. The girl ain't never went far, but she's smart, resourceful and to top that off she's resilient. She's bouncing back and strong!" Emma said smiling.

Ransom stepped thru the crowd tenderly pulling Emma with him, as he navigated to where his father and Mace stood laughing.

"Hey boy, where you been? I would've thought you would be the first one to find me and congratulate me." said Raven smiling.

"Damn pa, what kind of jacket is that?" Ransom asked.

"This is velvet son and no you can't have it. Do like Tim does and have Mamie make you some suits. That's who does all of mine." said Raven sternly.

Hawk looked at Raven, and asked. "Brother do you ever long for the old days? You know when we use to ride far and wide, sleeping under the stars?"

Raven smiled, then said. "Brother, I still see mamma's smile. I see pa's face and hear the words he spoke as he taught us. But those days are long gone, never to return except in dreams and memories. I see mamma's smile when I took at Swallow. I hear poppa's voice and see his face in you and yours. So there is no need to long for what has been. Look around you brother, for there lies our future." said Raven. His eyes locked on Drake and Lisa, who stood to the side of the dance floor talking. "There is a need to forge ahead to the future. Always we've looked ahead and that we must continue to do if the clan is to survive!

Mace had listened at Raven's words and knew that they were the words from his heart as well. If Raven was a part of his family, then he would look to the future for the survival of his clan, as Raven put it.

"Aw brother, your tongue still flows as smooth as a deep flowing stream! said Eagle laughing. "I've been letting you two circulate a little before I intruded."

Raven laughed, then reached for willow and hugged her. "Sister, are you well?" he asked.

"I'm well brother." said Willow. "Celia, I thought you were gonna stop by earlier."

"Sister I was." said Celia. "I got so tied up with this one here, that I couldn't get away.

Falcon and Violet came up and soon Wolf, Swallow, Cougar and Conchita were all there.

Raven looked at the weathered faces of his brothers and sisters and was momentarily whisked back to the past. In a flash he saw the raiding parties they had went on and the many coup they had counted on their enemies. He saw it all in a flash, then he looked at his future. There was Tim and Lucy. Young Brook, who was turning out to be a Kane after the first breed. He looked at Celia's stomach and there he saw his future.

Mace and Lola stood there and watched the Kanes, and the genuine love they had and showed for each other. They got along without force and Mace saw the ideal. He could learn from these people how to make his family strong.

They danced, drank and a good time was being had by all.

* CHAPTER # 16 *

Bull Parsons and the other members of the Klan were poised to attack the blacks this Saturday night. "I want havoc!" Bull shouted. "We got to show these coons who's the boss. We don't tolerate no niggers hangin a white man. Let's go boys, we got some nigger ass to beat!"

The men broke their horses into a gallop and in less than 5 minutes they were kicking in doors and dragging black men into the street and beating them. The Klan attacked them viciously and violently. They left broken and battered bodies in their wake. It was pure carnage. To fight back, was to get drug over the hard cobble-stoned street.

Bull and his men rode back to their staging area and loaded the horses up in trailers.

"That was a damn good piece of work there men." Bull said. "I think that will get us the information that we need!"

"I do believe you're right." said Simon. "I think we should harass them all day and every three days or so, we can ride and bash some heads. These jigs would learn then, I bet."

"I like that Simon." said Oscar. "We can stomp the life out of these niggers. Kill thier spirits!"

"You boys got a plan, that's for damn sure. I think we can give these niggers hell, while they're coming and going to nigger church. See niggers got a different God than white folks, but they see the white man represented as God. They worship us and don't know it.

All of the men laughed.

"What if them niggers were serious about striking back?" asked Anton.

"Them niggers ain't gonna do shit. We whipped every able bodied man among them. Trust me, they ain't in no shape to strike back." said Shelby Parsons.

"You got that right Shel." said Ronnie Bellamys. "I had a ball bustin nigger ass, so I know they ain't gonna be strikin nothing!"

They all laughed, then started heading to their homes. Bull had deputized the entire Klavern and the men were drunk with the power they possessed.

* * * *

The party was breaking up, when a Ford Sedan screeched to a halt in the front. Tyrus Biggers jumped out of the car, followed by Sonny Lumpkin. They rushed to the front of the club and Tyrus said. "I need to see Ransom Kane, it's an emergency!"

"Come on in." said Lefty Mace. He lead Tyrus to the crowd that stood in the corner.

Ransom looked up at the sudden hush and saw Tyrus trailing Lefty. He knew something was wrong when he saw the man's face. Ransom turned back to the crowd, and said. "Ladies excuse us please."

The other men looked at him and he said. "Gentlemen we'll need to talk out of the women's earshot, please, this way!"

Ransom lead them from where the ladies stood and over to where the band had been.

"What's going on Ty?" asked Ransom.

"The Klan rode tonight and they did some real damage Ran." Tyrus said. "It's better if they kill, cause then the community pulls together to help the bereaved. This way damn near all of the men suffered serious injuries and won't work for at least four weeks and that means some hungry bellies!"

"We told them if they rode, so would we." said Ransom angrily.

"Tell me you ain't talking bout night riding on white folks." Mace said.

"They'd ride on us Mace. They been stomping on our people for years and it ain't bout to change unless we change it!" said Ransom

"I just can't see where it would have a positive effect on black and white relationships." Mace said.

"But it will," Raven said. "Think about it. They'd feel like our people have felt and they'll know fear. We're invisible to them, unless we're the victim of their wrath. They won't know if the black man that's been raking their yard, the maid cooking their food, or any other black they see, is the one behind the mask. Damn right I'd ride on them!"

"I'll ride with you Ran." said Drake.

Mace looked at him, and said. "Think about what this could start. Their next move might be to just kill some poor unfortunate son of a bitch, that's in the wrong place at the wrong time. It could start a back and forth thing and if too many whites are killed, we'll have all kind of government agencies down on us!"

"Mace is right!" Raven said. "The back lash could be more than we bargained for, so tread careful. Think before you make your move because lives will depend on it!"

"Pa, I don't need to think. I've thought this out. I understand your and Mace's point of view, but look at it from this point of view. They gonna ride, beat and kill us anyway. They was raping our women and lynching us, before we decided to do something. And they gonna keep on doing it unless we show them that if it's good for the goose, it's good for the gander! Ransom said firmly. "It's done pa. I told them if they did it, we'd do it. They expect us to wait, or not to do it at all, but we do it and we do it tonight. Ty, do you know who the big men are in the Klan?"

" I got an idea, but I know who does." Tyrus answered.

"Who's that?" Ransom asked.

"Lucy's pa!" Tyrus said. "He's a good man, but he's alone and if they find out he's involved he's a dead man."

"Let's get the equipment and find out who these men are. Then we'll see if they can take, as well as they give!" Ransom said. "Lao, Tim, Trace, Drake, Brook, Pat, Pauly, Turk, Prince, Juan, Jose, Cellus, Ed, Lonnie, Blake, y'all going with me."

"I'd like to go too, Ran. If I could, that is." said Lefty. "I always wanted to beat a cracker!"

"So where does that leave us?" Hawk asked.

"To watch the women as always, old man." Raven said laughing.

Hawk clapped him on the shoulder and said to Raven. "The family is in god hands brother. The other elders nodded and it was then that Raven knew the torch had been passed.

"Let's get the women home safely, Mace." Raven said.

Mace looked in Raven's eyes and knew that the survival of their families and their future would depend on Ransoms' judgment. The men had knocked down the wall of dislike and banded together.

"Alright Raven." Mace said smiling. "You ain't half bad." Mace threw his arm over Raven's shoulder and they headed to where the women milled around.

"We got some pressing matters that we need to take care of." Ransom said to the women. "I hope you won't hate me for taking your men, but they're needed. The family's honor is at stake!

Emma looked at Ransom and saw a change. She turned to Raven and looked in his eyes. He nodded his head slightly, and she knew Ransom was selected to head the family.

"Em, you and Lucy head on home. I'll bring Tim by before he goes in, no matter what time it is." Ransom said to the women.

All of the men had women there and there was a flurry of activities as they arranged transportation and reservations for later. None of the young men even thought that he could very well die this night.

"Be careful son." Raven said to Ransom with Mace by his side.

Ransom looked at Mace, then said. "We'll be back, it shouldn't take long!"

Mace looked at him and nodded his head. Two of his boys were going to terrorize the whites. That was a chance he had to admit. These Kanes got balls, that's for sure Mace thought. Then he smiled, as he thought he'd get a kick out of some action.

*   *   *   *

Ransom and the men he had chose stood in the barn like structure preparing for the coming raid. "How did your people fair in the raid by the Klan?" Ransom asked Tyrus.

"We come out good Ran." Tyrus answered. "We live outside of the town and we'll shoot, so they basically keep their activities in the city."

"Do you know where they keep their horses?" Ransom asked.

"Yeah, they got a lively stable bout two miles out on this side of town." Tyrus answered.

"Well that's good." Ransom said. "We'll use their horses to ride on them!"

The men laughed, as they gathered all of the things they figured they'd need. Ransom knew the Klan would never expect them to attack tonight, but they would be on their toes from here on in. The men gathered their things, loaded up in the cars, and headed toward their destination.

$$* \qquad * \qquad * \qquad *$$

Prescott heard the tapping sound at the back door. He had been in the process of having one of the most memorable nights of his life. That is before the Klan rampaged thru town and spread their peculiar brand of confusion and fear. From that point on, he had sat guard over the women with his pistol held tightly in his hand.

"What is it Pres?" Eula asked, afraid it was the Klan at their door.

"Shhhh…" Prescott hissed. "Let me go check. Don't leave the room." He eased quietly down the stairs and padded silently to a window that looked out on the back yard. He saw several dark figures huddled near his back door. He peered into the dim light trying to see a face, or something that would indicate who the men were. Just as he was about to give a warning, he heard one of the voices loudly whisper his name.

"Mr. Wellington, it's me, Ty Biggers!"

Prescott recognized the man's name and voice, he went to the door, opened it and whispered. "Get in here!"

The men filed past him into the kitchen. All of the men wore dark capes and had what looked like hoods held in their hands.

"Sorry to bother you Mr. Wellington." Tyrus said. "It's important and I thought you'd like to meet the men that helped your Lucy."

Prescott eyed the three men that stood there and assumed that two were brothers. One was a big light skinned man, who's face was tightly screwed into a frown.

"I'm Ransom Kane!" said Ransom extending his hand to Prescott. "This is my cousin Trace and my uncle, Drake Mace."

"Prescott Wellington," said Prescott shaking hands with the men. "I want to thank you for coming to the aid of my child, her mother thanks you as well!"

"Mr. Wellington," Ransom said smiling. "I want to know who the heads of the Klan are!"

130

"I'm not sure who the head is, but the Sheriff is high in the order. As are the Mayor, Lucas Blackstone, Archie Ransom, Percy Chambers. I'm sure Oscar and Simon Bellamys are big men too, probably Bubba Stanley and Shel Parsons. Why do you ask?" asked Prescott puzzled.

Ransom looked in his eyes, and said. "We're gonna give them a taste of their own medicine!

"You're gonna ride on the Klan?" Prescott asked incredulously.

"Exactly," Ransom replied. "The difference being, we won't attack the innocent, only the guilty!"

"Do you realize what that could do? It could very well blow this town apart!" Prescott said desperately.

"Pres, I'm sure you've had your share of persecutions, but we've been persecuted for what to us seems like forever. If we strike against them, it could well mean they'll stop. If all they do is ride again, so what? They rode unopposed for years and will do it for years to come if someone doesn't take a stand now. They've lynched us, barged into our homes and dragged us into the streets like we're trash. Then they beat and bruise us, plant fear into our women, and thru them to our seeds. The number of their injustices are uncountable and who has raised a voice for us? I will!" Ransom said.

Prescott stood there gazing into the big dark skinned man eyes and knew that this man was hard and unyielding when he chose to be. But there was also compassion for those who suffered the same fate.

"I see your point Ransom and pray that it works. Before you leave I'd like to introduce you to the ladies. Beth, Eula, please come down." Pres shouted.

The two women came cautiously down the stairs, then saw the strange black men and came forward.

"These are my wives, Elisabeth and Eula!" Prescott said.

Ransom's mind flashed to the stories his father had told him about his Grandfather, Lao Tzu and his wives Sparrow and Mandy. Ransom greeted them, as did Trace and Drake, then the men stepped out into the shadows.

"Things are gonna get pretty hectic around here, but they just might get safer," said Prescott.

131

* CHAPTER # 17 *

Tyrus knew where each of the men named lived, so he was the point man. They rode to the livery stable and stole the Klan's horses. They mounted up and galloped into town.

As they pulled the hoods on, Ransom said. "We can't get them all, so we'll just get the ones in town. Drake I want you, Lon, Pat and Lao to go to the jail and down any guards that are out. They're probably Klan, so make sure to abuse them soundly. Trace you got Tim, Pauly and Brooks, y'all get the Mayor. Jose, you, Cellus, Blake and Juan get Blackstone. Me, Ty, Turk, Lefty and Prince gonna get the sheriff. They all live close, so we wanna get them together. Each one has to know how the other held up under our assault. We'll start dissension in the ranks. Let's ride!"

*

The men all got in position and there was the loud cry of a bird screeching into a dark, clear, silent night. The men attacked as one. Ransom rode the horse thru the big French doors, at the side of Bull Parsons big house. Turk leaped from his horse cradling a Sub Thompson, with which he sprayed a shower of .45 slugs into the wall and ceiling.

Ransom leaped from the horse and pulled the twin .45 automatics from the shoulder holster he wore and charged up the stairs with Prince hot on his heels, holding his Thompson to his chest.

Tyrus raced thru the lower portion of the house, his Thompson leading the charge. Lefty was pulling up his rear.

Ransom kicked open a door and there was Bull Parsons struggling from between the thighs of his young wife Maybelle. Ransom rushed to the bed and clubbed the man viciously across the head. Bull slumped on his wife stunned. Ransom slammed the pistol into the man's head again and this time he lost consciousness.

Lefty had come to the door and he helped Ransom pull Bull off of his wife. As Bull was pulled away, the men saw the golden bush of Maybelle, who made no move to cover

132

herself. The men saw the swollen pink nipples, the full alabaster white breast, the expanse of her stomach and the pouting lips of her vagina open and inviting. Lefty looked at Ransom, and said. "It would be just deserved for this cracker."

"Yeah it would, but look at this bitch. It's what she wants, and I'll be damned if I'll be fuel for her fantasies. If she wants some black dick, let her go beg for it!" Ransom said.

They roughly dragged Bull from the room and rolled him down the stairs where he landed in a untidy head. They raced down behind him and drug him naked and bleeding from the house.

*

Drake, Pat, Lao, and Lon had tied the horses a block from the jail and closed in silently. The men heard the bird call and Lon pulled the door open. Drake and Lao, stepped thru with machine guns blazing. They fired high to instill fear and the rounds crashing into the walls and ceiling of the jail did the job. The three men in the sheriff's office all hit the deck, covered their heads and prayed. Pat and Lon rushed to the men and clubbed them into unconsciousness. They dragged the men from the jail and saw other dark robed figures doing the same thing.

*

Trace, Tim, Pauly and Brooks crashed into Wally Cronin's home and wreaked havoc. They shot his house up and dragged him into the street, after beating him senseless.

*

Jose, Cellus, Blake and Juan brought Lucas Blackstone to the spot where the others held their men.

Ransom stood over the dazed, beaten and bleeding group of men. He ordered his men to get each man and plunge his head into the watering trough. They brought each man back sputtering. The frightened men, looked at the men in the black hoods and capes.

"What the fuck is this, a goddamn joke?" shouted Bull.

Ransom walked over to him and lashed a wicked kick to his mouth that dislodged several of his front teeth.

"Don't speak unless you're spoken to!" Ransom said with authority. "Get me a rope somebody. Make a noose too."

"Just a minute here mister." Wally pleaded.

Ransom kicked Wally viciously in the mouth, then asked. "Anymore of you crackers got something you wanna say?"

The men all looked up fearfully except Bull, who's eyes blazed with anger.

"You men rode thru town tonight and you beat and humiliated us. We told you that if you ride, so do we. If you kill one of ours from this day forth, we'll kill two of yours. Molest our women, we'll molest yours. Harm our offspring and yours wont be safe. One of you will provide a message to the others. The same message your lynching send, we are going to send." said Ransom.

Drake walked to him with the rope and Ransom walked to where Bull sat glaring.

"Well, sheriff, your lucky today. You'll be the one. If we string you up they'll know how serious we are!" said Ransom walking to Bull Parsons and dropping the noose over his head.

Bull's hands shot up to the noose and Drake and Lad moved in and grabbed his arms. Bull struggled mightily, but the two strong young men were too much for him.

Trace came over with a short length of rope and they tied Bull's hands behind him.

"You niggers are all dead!" Bull shouted thru his mangled lips, as blood flecks flew thru the air.

Ransom slapped him across the face, with a blow that sounded like a pistol shot. Bull's head snapped back and his eyes took on a glazed look, because the blow from Ransom's callused hand had stunned him. He shook his head and blood from his head and mouth was flung into the night.

"Maybe we all should rape your wife in front of you first." Ransom said to Bull. "But, we want you to know what happened to your friends. Beat them.!"

The men fell on the stunned Klansmen with barely restrained ferocity. They beat them with quirts, boots, fist and short lengths of rope. When they backed off, the men were bruised and battered masses of quivering flesh.

Ransom tightened the noose on Bull's neck, then asked. "Anything you want to say before we hang your dog ass?"

"Fuck you, your ma and your pa, nigger!" Bull said with hatred.

Ransom laughed in his face, then said." You got balls boy. I admire that in a man!"

He lead Bull to a lamp post, where he tossed the loose end of the rope. He caught it, then pulled it tight, and said. "Somebody come help me hang this heavy bag of shit!"

Drake and Lao stepped up and the three men took the rope, and looked at the beaten men, to be sure they watched.

"Oh God," a voice moaned out softly.

The men pulled and Bull's feet left the ground. He kicked and jerked wildly. He farted, then his bowels voided.

"Enough!" shouted Ransom as they let Bull down. Ransom ran to him and loosened the noose. Bull's face was purple, as he choked and sputtered. When he caught his breath he looked up and met the dark, dead eyes of Ransom, who said. "Next time you die!"

Ransom's fist crashed into his eye and he rocked backward. Drake, Ransom and Lao beat Bull, broke his ribs and knocked several of his teeth out. They left him curled in his own shit, vomit and blood. "Mount up!" Ransom shouted.

The men got on the horses and Ransom pulled out his pistol and fired into the night sky. Soon the sound was echoed, by the staccato burst of the Sub Thompson's. The men spurred the horses and raced away into the dark night in which they emerged.

*   *   *   *

Drake rode in the car with Trace and Blake. He spoke from the back seat. "Do you think Lisa really likes me?"

"Man whatever you do, don't get love sick on me. Here you, just met the woman!" Trace said.

"Lisa ain't just any woman, Trace." said Drake.

"I've known her for her whole life and I know that the question is this, what are your plans?" Trace said.

"It's like you just said. I just met her, so how would I know. I just wanna see where this goes." Drake said.

"Well you'll see her again tonight. She's at Myra's.

That's Myra's way of making sure I come back. You can take Lisa home and come pick me up in the morning. I think we got a place for a man of your caliber!" Trace said reaching back to pat Drake's shoulder.

  *   *   *   *

Tim and Ransom, pulled up to Ransom's house. "Tim, if Lucy's awake you can set with her for a spell. I want you to respect her Tim, cause she's been thru a lot!" Ransom said.

"I like her Ran and I ain't worried about the past. I'd like to spend some time with her." Tim said earnestly.

Ransom nodded and the two men got out of the car and walked to the house. The door opened and Emma stood there with relief in her eyes. Lucy stood at her back, gazing out of the door expectantly. The women still wore their party dresses.

"Em, put your shoes on, we got to go over to poppa's house?" Ransom said.

"He ain't there. He's at Mace's place." she said.

"Well get your shoes and we'll head over there! Tim, look after Lucy til we get back. It's late and if you wanna sleep over, Lucy can get you some stuff to make a pallet." Ransom and Emma got in the car and drove off.

"Like a drink Tim?" Lucy asked coyly.

"Yes I would, if you'll have one with me." he said.

"I don't know if I should." she said. "I ain't much for that sort of thing."

"Get us some coffee." he said.

She smiled and left the room. Tim watched her walk away, her ass swaying hypnotically. "Damn," he muttered under his breath.

She came back with a small tray that held two cups, two saucers and a small pot with steam coming from the spout. She made two cups of coffee, gave him one, then sat next to him on the sofa.

"I did have a fine time tonight. I ain't never felt so beautiful and safe." she said sliding closer to him. "You just introduced me and didn't mention that incident."

"No need to girl. That's behind us, the future is my concern." said Tim. "I think you're a special woman and I'd enjoy it if you allow me to stop by to see you from time to time!"

I'd like that Tim." said Lucy as he eased his arm around her shoulder. They snuggled close together and she lay her head on his shoulder.

*

Ransom and Emma, pulled up to Mace's house. They got out and walked to the door and knocked. They stood and waited, then Ransom knocked again. He heard someone coming, then Celia's muffled voice floated out to them. "Who is it?"

"Ran and Em!" Ransom shouted. "I need to see my pa!"

Celia opened the door, and asked. "Do y'all know what time it is?"

"Yeah we do and it don't look like you were sleeping girl." said Emma giggling.

"Nosy heifer," Celia said with mock anger. "Raven, Ran is here to see you!" she shouted.

"Damn it woman!" shouted Mace sleepily, as he walked into the room. "I thought I had heard the last of that when you moved out."

Raven walked into the room and soon Lola was there too.

"It went well." Ransom said to Raven and Mace.

The old men nodded. "Is that it?" Raven asked.

"I just wanted to let you know." Ransom replied.

"Hell, all of you come out alright, you could've waited til morning." Raven said gruffly. "Disturbing folk for nothing." Inside, he was pleased that his son had gone out of the way to find him. "Y'all go on home, me and Celia got to get some sleep."

"That's what you call it now?" Lola asked smiling.

"Mind your own business Lo." Raven said sheepishly.

Ransom and Emma drove back home, where they found Lucy and Tim cuddled up on the sofa. They looked at them, then Ransom said. "Don't be up all night Tim, we got work to do come morning."

Tim just looked up and smiled.

Trace dropped Blake off at Lane's place, then he and

137

Drake drove to Myra's. When the men got inside, they saw that the women had fell asleep in the front room. Trace walked over to Lisa and gently shook her awake. She looked up at him with questioning eyes.

"Time to go home sleepy head." Trace said smiling.

Lisa stretched like a big cat and Drake saw her dress contour to her womanly curves. She sat up and rubbed her eyes as Trace woke Myra.

Myra stood, stretched, then said. "It's nearly morning now, so let her sleep in the kids room. They're still at my folks house, though Trace Jr. was ready to come home. That boy is getting a little too big for his brothers."

"He's 13 Myra and at his age my pa was married and all."

"Well, you need to talk with him." she said.

"I'll do that." Trace said reluctantly. "Drake you can sleep on the sofa, Lisa you know where the kids room is."

Trace and Myra walked to their room and closed the door. Myra turned to him, and said. "I was serious about what I said at the party."

He knew she was back on the marriage trip. He looked at her, then said. "My folks ain't never marry the white folks way and it was good for them and us. Why you got to do it this way, when we been doing just fine?"

"Yeah, it's fine for you. We got two growing kids and we live in different houses and you call that getting on just fine? Let me tell you how it affects me and the children." she said.

He raised his hand to stop her. He pulled her into his arms and said. "Uncle Raven's doing it, so it must be the right thing for these times. If it means that much to you, then I'm obligated to do it, because of the love I have for you. Tomorrow you can go bring all of my stuff and the stuff you and the kids got at the other house on here. We'll rent the other house. I'll talk to Blake and see how he feels about it. And if he says yeah, we can have the big party. If he doesn't we'll still have it. I love you Myra and I'll do all I can to honor any wish you have!"

Myra squeezed her body against him, then asked. "You tired yet, I know you've had a hard day."

"I'm tired sugar, but just what did you have in mind?" he asked.

"I thought you would give me a little lovin, before

you get some rest. I'll do all of the work, so you can just relax.'" said Myra rubbing at his crotch.

He pinched her erect nipples between his big fingers, as she tenderly cupped his balls and stroked his swollen shaft. His hands danced over her stomach, fluttering softly like the gentle touch of butterfly wings. His hands came to her waist, glided over her flaring hips, and around to the full, firm globes of her ass. He squeezed and caressed them and slowly drew her closer. She released him and guided him to the big four poster bed. She lay him down, then kneeled beside him and resumed stroking him. He reached around and parted her fleshy lips. Up and down, he massaged the lips until his fingers came to the hard nub of her clit. He stroked the button, until she swung her hips to his hand. He plunged his fingers in her and her juices flowed freely. She breathed deeply, as his fingers brought her close to the edge. She stroked him erratically and finally she stopped all together and bucked rapidly against his insistent fingers.

With his free hand he guided her to him, she spread her legs so she was straddling him, holding on tightly to his stiff penis. As soon as she felt him enter her, she swung her hips rapidly down to him. He felt her warmth envelope him and he thrust up into her. She placed her hands on his chest and rode him swiftly. Her head tossed from side to side. She had her bottom lip trapped between her teeth, as she drew closer to an orgasm. Her body shuddered and she grinded down on him as her orgasm washed over her. He held her hips and pistoned in and out of her spasming box until he exploded in her.

She slumped forward dazedly and laid her head on his chest. He could still feel her clinching and unclenching, as she sighed contentedly. They had long ago learned to make love with minimal noise, so Drake and Lisa couldn't have heard them all the way up front. What they didn't know was, that Drake and Lisa were in the kids room.

They were so aware of each other, because the sexual tension was thick. They both knew what the sounds coming from Trace and Myra's room meant, but they had not so much as kissed. Both lay there burning with desire and each knew that if the other made a move they wouldn't deny themselves.

"Lisa, do you think we should be here alone in bed?" he asked.

"No we shouldn't, we just met. I ain't no virgin

Drake and I don't want to give you that impression. I know you ain't neither, cause I done heard about you. I don't want to be one of your little conquest. I ain't the kind of woman to run around and I respect a man's wish to be a man, but I expect my man to respect me above all else." she said.

"It sounds like you're laying the ground rules here, Lisa." Drake aid softly. "I understand your point of view on both relationships and the distorted vision of me. I've had my escapades with the fairer sex, but I've always been honest in my intentions. You know I feel physical attraction to you, definitely sexual attractions, but I also feel something I've never felt before. I don't have a name for it. I feel comfortable in your presence, I feel I've always known you. How long I'll feel this way I can't say, because I've never felt this way before."

She rolled over on her side and looked at him. He rolled over, so they were face to face.

"I want to know you." he said softly, as their lips grazed.

Her head moved closer, and she kissed him lightly. His tongue flicked into her mouth and she sucked greedily at it. Never did their bodies touch.

She broke the kiss and looked in his eyes and pleaded. "No more Drake. Let's give it some time!"

He nodded, then leaned in and kissed her passionately. She didn't resist and he knew he could take her then, but instead he broke the kiss. Then he reached out and caressed the silky smooth skin of her cheek. "No pressure!" he said softly against her lips. They lay there, lips touching, just staring into each others eyes. They both had thoughts. He, "This is the one."

She, "It feels so right, I think he's the one."

They feel asleep and before long she lay curled in his arms in the manner of old lovers.

* CHAPTER # 18 *

Amy White, came into the Wellington's store and walked to the counter where Beth and Eula stood smiling. "Did y'all hear about the black night riders that beat hell out of Bull Parsons and his crew last night?" Amy asked.

Prescott stepped from the back and caught the last part of the question. "What was that Amy?" he asked.

"A group of black night riders, busted up Bull Parsons and his goons last night." Amy said gleefully. "They beat Wally's ass too, them boys left their mark that's for sure!"

"How do you feel about that Amy. Don't you think that will just make it worse?" he asked.

"How much worse can it get? What they gonna do now, lynch us? Hell, they do that already. Beat us? They do that too. I say it's about time, that's how I feel. Hell, I wish I could've seen it. They say Bull shitted on himself." she said laughing.

All that day, until they closed at noon, the news came floating in. Prescott, said to himself. "They really did it. I'll be damned." he chuckled and his two women looked at him.

"What's so funny darling?" asked Beth.

He waved her off, and Eula asked. "Them men from last night, they're the ones aren't they?"

He looked at her, then said. "You never saw them, if you see them again, act like you don' know them. Lucy's life is in the balance here, as well as ours!"

"I didn't mean no harm Pres. I'm glad they did it." Eula said.

"So am I, to a degree, but no one besides us is to know. Those are hard men, Eula. I doubt if either of us has met men of their caliber, the entire system is against them, but they choose to fight. And they use the same tactics their enemies use, fear and terror!" he said. "Since today is Sunday, what would you ladies like to do?"

Elisabeth looked at him lustfully and said. "I'd like to practice that stuff we did yesterday, or should I say last night, or was that this morning?"

They both laughed, as Beth headed up the stairs to their room. She halted and looked at them, then asked. "What are we gonna do when Lucy comes back?"

"Sit her down and spell it out for her." Eula said. "In the mean time let's get that practice in!"

*   *   *   *

"I don't give a damn what them niggers said!" Bull roared from his swollen mouth. "Them sons of bitches humiliated me and they're gonna pay!"

"Now Bull, I know you want revenge, but think about it. Them niggers done rampaged thru town and to top it off, they stole our fuckin horses. They serious and before we make our next move we got to be ready for them." said Oscar.

"I'm ready now." Bull said angrily. "Them niggers barged into my house and scared the shit out of my wife. They threatened to rape her in my face, man!"

Bubba just sat there and listened to Bull rant. He knew Bull was a headstrong man and a powerful enemy. But, if they let Bull have his way, he'd turn the town into a slaughter house.

"If it was me, I'd give it some thought. See them niggers ain't all the way dumb. They know that as night riders we're outside the law, but as deputies we can bust their asses. So, I suggest we put the pressure on tomorrow during the day. We'll stop every nigger, male, female, or child that's driving or in any kind of vehicle and we'll rough them up. Go easy on the women and children or all of the niggers might revolt!" said Bubba softly.

"That's it," said Bull. "I'll personally take part in this."

"Oh no!" said Simon. "You get well and let the boys handle this. There'll be plenty of niggers left to feel your wrath!"

*   *   *   *

"I think we should be operating fully by week after next." Tigger said. "All of you boys have been a big help, as far as building the stills. If y'all prove to be as useful during the brewing process, we may be ready even sooner!"

All of the Kanes were present at the location where

the last still would be built.

"I'd like to bring Drake Mace in with us on this." said Trace. "I like the man personally."

"I think that would be a good thing, but he works for his father. Why would he leave to do the same thing for us?" Raven asked.

"He'd be better suited for working with us. I don't think Mace's thing is big enough to continuously provide wealth for all of them." Trace said. "It would benefit him financially to work with us."

"So, your saying he'll choose money over family?" Raven asked.

"No he won't. I sense he's loyal to his family. If you recall last night, he said we were family. Mace knows his operation can ill afford to support six men, their wives and children." Trace said.

"I think Drake's a fine man, but I think we ought to wait and see if Mace's operation can support them all." Raven said. "It's much to soon to start taking away from Mace. He and I are getting along better than we have in the thirty years I've known him and I'd hate him to think I had an ulterior motive for being with Celia."

"I see your point." Trace said. "I'll hint around and feel Drake out on the issue."

"Do that and I'll toss Mace a bone and see if he naws on it or what." Raven said.

The men stood around talking, then Ransom stepped in the middle and motioned the men forward.

"This is the way the operation is going to be set up and each of our places in it. Tigger is going to brew and keep the stills running. Pa, you and the elders will be under him. I expect each of you to learn the process. Lon, Cellus, Brooks, y'all gonna be the drivers. It will be your job to make sure the liquor gets to the people. Tim, you'll be the point man, you go in first and set things up. The rest of us will provide protection for our merchandise. Everyone is important, so no one, I mean no one gets too big for their britches. Tim you need to get with Ty and have him introduce you to all his people. This is going to be very profitable. The areas we want are far and wide, at least ten or twelve times what Mace is dealing with and that means plenty of money for us!"

"Gonna be plenty of trouble too!" said Raven. "White folks been in charge so long, that they done forgot that things could be reversed. We lived thru a similar situation in the old days. This was way before you was born. We stumbled up on change and from that point on we been looking ahead. Our major concern has never been riches. What it's been is the survival of the clan!"

Ransom cut in, "That's not our sole goal, pa. In order for us to make it in the future we'll need riches, we'll need to be people of substance."

Raven looked at his son and knew that Ransom's words touched on truth. "Son I can see your point of view and I don't disagree fully. See, we are people of substance. We're Kanes and we set a certain standard by which we live. I'll back any idea or plan, that in the long run will benefit us as a whole."

"I know you will pa." Ransom said. "This is for the good of the clan. If we lay docile and let the powers that be remain, then we'll suffer the fate of the down trodden. We've got to make a stand here! If this goes in our favor, then we can practically control the reins of power."

"Ogilvey!" said Eagle loudly. "Remember Wilber?"

"How can we forget?" asked Cougar.

"Ran sees it from Raven's point of view." said Falcon. "When we took the trading post, Raven knew that we wouldn't be able to run the post, cause whites wouldn't deal with us. So he got Wilber Ogilvey to front for us and we gave him a percentage of the profits. We can't run the town, but we can run who runs the town!"

"Falc's right," said Hawk. "Different scenario, same situation!

"Y'all are right about that much, but the bottom line is this. Those were different times, the land seemed to be much larger then and the only law was the one we made and enforced. Times are different now, things can't be settled the old ways, at least not everything. Pa, provided us with the tools to survive in the new age. How many blacks or Indians you know can read, write and comprehend as well as we do? None I'd bet. The key to our survival lies in the knowledge we have and pass on to our offspring. That's true riches! Raven said.

* CHAPTER # 19 *

Monday at around noon, the town was crawling with deputized Klansmen. They stopped every car that rode thru and beat the men who were bold enough to stand.

Bull, Shel and Oscar sat in the jail drinking whiskey. Bull looked at the others, and said. "What we really need to do, is set them niggers up. They said every time we ride, so would they. Now they know where we live and I got to give it to them even though I don't want to, they got balls. What we do is, we put men in each of the houses they attacked last time. Then we ride and each of us go to the houses and wait until they show up. Then we kill the sons of bitches!"

"That would be a lot of killin Bull." said Oscar. "It could well draw unwanted attention."

"Damn attention!" Bull shouted. "You ain't felt a single blow, or had a fuckin noose around your neck and shitted yourself!"

"Aw Bull, come on now. Any of us would've probably done the same thing." said Shel.

"I don't give a fuck what y'all probably would have done!" Bull screamed hoarsely. "I felt it, I was damn near hung! I shitted, not y'all! How the hell can I hold my head up in this town? Them black fuckers saw my wife naked!"

"What can we say Bull?" Oscar asked.

"What the hell!" Shel shouted, as the still day was shattered by the staccato chatter of automatic weapons.

"What the fuck is that?" asked Oscar jumping up from his chair.

The other two men rose as well and they hobbled to the door.

Wesley Pipes and Drew Caffy were at the intersection on main street, when a big sedan with four black men stopped at the corner. They raised their hand to the driver of the sedan, to stop him. As the men drew near the car, two men in the car swung up until they were sitting in the passenger side windows with their Sub Thompson's on the roof.

"Holy shit!" Wesley screamed, as he saw the man in

the back seat put his gun out of the window.

The two deputies, both went for their side arms. It was too little too late, as the men in the sedan opened fire. The deputies were riddled with automatic slugs. Their bodies danced a macabre jig, as blood, cloth and pulverized tissue sprayed mist like into the air. There were screams of horror, as the townspeople ran for cover.

"Get in!" Brooks shouted to Lonnie and Tim who sat in the windows. They hurried and slid back into the car.

Brooks pressed the gas peddle to the floor and the big car accelerated, the tires screaming as they burned rubber.

"Make sure you swing by the jail!" Tim said from the back seat.

Brooks nodded and swung the car in a tight right turn. Blake behind the driver, had his weapon pointed towards the sheriff's office on their left. When Brooks drove by, Blake opened fire, spraying the front of the squat brick building.

Brooks did a u-turn, then Tim and Lonnie unleashed a hail of gunfire into the sheriff's office. Then they raced away.

*

"Son of a bitch!" Shel screamed as the automatic rounds punched thru the door and windows.

The three men scrambled to the floor and all tried to crawl behind the big desk. As sudden as the gunfire begin, it stopped. The silence was enveloping, as the men lay jumbled together with hands covering their heads.

"Go take a look." Bull said, nudging Oscar.

"Fuck that!" Oscar said. "I ain't about to go to that door!"

Bull looked at the door and saw that it was damn near shot off. It hung lopsided by one hinge. He struggled to his knees and winced, as the pain from his broken ribs lanced thru him. "I'll go since you fucks are afraid." he lisped thru his missing teeth angrily.

Cautiously he peered out of the shattered window and saw people on the street slowly climbing to their feet. He walked quickly to the door and looked out. Just then, one of the three patrol cars they had came careening around the corner and slid to a skidding halt in front of the jail.

Cad and Anton, leaped from the car with their pistols

in hand. Bull looked at the two men and screamed. "It's a day late and a dollar short for you two assholes to come racing to the rescue!"

The men holstered their weapons and looked at Bull sheepishly.

"What the fuck is going on here?" Bull asked angrily.

"Wes and Drew been killed!" Cad said.

"They been what?" Bull said incredulously.

"They were shot down!" said Anton. "The witnesses said, a big Sedan that they stopped, was filled with niggers that opened fire on them. They're tore the fuck up Bull. I mean they don't even resemble nothing that was once human!"

"So, you asshole's left them lying in the street I guess?" Bull asked.

"Con, and Archie Newsom are at the scene. They covered them up." Cad said. "We just got here fast as we could."

"Wasn't fast enough!" said Oscar walking outside, followed by Shel.

A battered and bruised, Wally Cronin rushed up to the scene. "Bull, we got to put a stop to our actions until we find out who these niggers are." Wally said fearfully. "How many more good men got to die, for you to see that we got to change our method? If we keep on at the rate we're going, the government is gonna step in and that means we'll have to shut down a lot more than harassing niggers!"

"Will you shut the fuck up!" Bull shouted. "If we let you have your way, the niggers would be running the whole damn town!"

"Now Bull, ain't no call for you to talk to me that way." said Wally, nervously eyeing the assembled men.

"I want y'all to get the word out that we're having a meeting tonight, as soon as the sun sets. We got to come up with something to put a halt to these renegade niggers!" Bull demanded.

*   *   *   *

Ransom sat with the elders and told them about the shooting. They all sat silently and listened at the report.

Raven looked at his brothers, then asked. "What do you think we should do next?"

"I think we should curb the killings for now and wait

to see what their next move is." said Eagle.

"That's the way I see it too." said Hawk. "Them rednecks ain't that bright, but they ain't fools either. See, sooner or later they'll come up with a plan to counter the stuff like that. When they do, it could turn into a massacre!"

"Yeah you're right about that." Raven said. "Ran I want you to focus on what we set out to do. We stumbled into this with Klan, I believe we should get back to our objective, which was to run liquor. Ain't no telling how long this is gonna be contained in town. It could get out and bring real grief on our people and we don't want that. They ain't gonna do much right now I'd bet, because they're running scared, so we can get down to business.

Just then, there was a persistent knocking at the door. Ransom went to see who it was. It was Tyrus and he looked to be excited. Ransom let him in, then said, "Damn it Ty, you grinnin like the cat that ate the canary. What's going on?"

"They done called a meeting for sundown tonight." Tyrus said.

"They who?" Ransom asked.

"The Klan!" Tyrus said. "After what went down, they sent word out for the members to meet at the city hall near the Mayor's Office."

Ransom looked at the elders with a perverse gleam in his eyes, and Raven said. "No...!" He shook his head decisively. "We can't kill them all, or the federal government gonna step in. We don't want to get into a shooting war, that could endanger the entire clan!"

"We ain't got to kill them all, pa." Ransom said. "What we do is spread terror. We already done showed them they ain't safe in their homes, or the street. Now, we show them they ain't safe nowhere!"

"The boy has a good point." Falcon said. "If you attack them in mass, then they'll know that even in large numbers there is no safety."

Raven looked at the other elders and each nodded. "How do you know this isn't a set up? he asked.

"We don't know and it doesn't matter if it is. We ain't going in blind and we got the firepower to do more to them, than they can do to us. Besides, we'll be in our element. The dark!"

"Get your men ready then and we'll all meet here three hours before sundown. That should give us time to check the area out before we strike!" Raven said. "By the way, we're going too!"

"Hold on there pa." Ransom said. "Don't you think, y'all a little too old for that kind of stuff?"

"I could kick your ass now!" Raven said. "So could any of them. We're going and that's that!"

Ransom shook his head, as Tyrus laughed out loud.

      *   *   *   *

Ransom and all of the Kane men. Along with Mace and his sons, met at the warehouse behind Raven's store. The men were silent, as Ransom stood in the center of the floor.

"The Klan are meeting in city hall at sundown and we're gonna crash the meeting!" Ransom said.

There was a loud roar of approval from the assembled men. Ransom raised his hands for silence. The men all went silent.

"We'll go there, but there won't be any killing unless it's absolutely necessary. What we want to do, is put the fear of God into those ass holes. We'll bomb the Mayor's office and the outside of city hall, then disappear. After that, we'll get back to our agenda, which is to take over the bootlegging operation. I know we may eventually have to get back to the Klan, but after tonight we'll put them on the back burner, unless they ride, or continue to make their stops. Does anyone have a problem with that?"

All of the men remained silent, so Ransom dropped the bomb. "The old men want to take part. I told them no, but they out voted me."

"Pa are you serious?" asked Turk.

"Damn right we're serious!" Raven said. "How do you think we got in the position we're in today? Sure it was happenstance, but we got it done and we've been better off for it. There's not a man among you, that could beat us in combat right now. Sure, some of our physical skills have diminished, but what we lack in youth we make up for with wisdom and intelligence!"

"I guess that settles that then." said Lao.

"Mace, I know your operation is profitable, but I doubt it's successful enough to support all of you. I'd like to bring Drake and Lefty, in with us. We're family and it would do us all good to have a working relationship. They can still

149

do what you need them to do, but we're gonna need them to be on our security detail."

Mace looked at Ransom, then to Raven, and said. "The choice is theirs to make, not mine."

"I know that." Ransom said. "But they won't, unless you give them the okay. They're loyal to family and that's why you've been so successful."

Mace talked in a low voice, and said. "They're the best of the bunch. Vern and Prescott are alright. Ford, I don't know, he's my first born, but damn if he doesn't act like the last. I could make do without them, but keep your eye on Lefty, cause he's a dangerous man. I'll give them the word, on the condition that I go with the others tonight."

"That was a given." Ransom said. "You're family and that's why you're here. You won't be losing two sons, you'll be gaining the strength of our clan!"

* CHAPTER # 20 *

That night at sundown, all of the members of the Klan were gathered at city hall. The Klan was worried about the recent turn of events. They were use to dishing out terror, not being on the receiving end.

"What are we gonna do about niggers that are going around killing decent white men?" one man asked from the back. "Next it'll be our women and children!"

Bull raised his hands to silence the men, who then started to talk at the same time.

"Listen up brothers." Bull said. "That's exactly why we're here, to address that problem. I been giving it a lot of thought and I can't seem to figure out why the niggers would act like this now. They've never given us any indication that they'd fight back, but now not only are they fighting back, they're striking at us first. I don't believe the ones responsible are from here, you never can tell though with niggers. I want all of you to keep your ears open and try to find out what gave the niggers the heart to strike at us."

"I'll tell you what gives them the heart!" Wally shouted. "It's the night riding and all of the rest. I done told you that you can only push them so far and they'd try to fight back. Give them time to calm down and we can go back to doing things like we always have."

"I don't think it will be that easy." Bubba said from the front of the room. "The way I see it, is like this. If we let the niggers get away with beating and killin white folks. They'll think, there's nothing they can't do!"

"Bubba's right," Percy Chambers said. "We got to find out who's behind this shit and put a stop to it. Now, we don't know how, when, or where they'll strike next, but we do know that if we ride so will they. All we've got to do is be ready for them next time!"

"That sounds good, but what if they don't ride the next time we do? Do we stay alert and for how long?" asked Simon.

"For as long as it takes!" Bull said forcefully. "Them niggers can't be as strong as we are, eventually them other niggers gonna get tired of us bashing their heads in. And then they'll tell us who's attacking us!"

    *   *   *   *

Raven, Hawk, Falcon, Mace, Eagle, Cougar and Wolf had broken into the Mayor's office and were placing bundles of dynamite at the foundation and in each corner. They joined all of the fuses, and hurried out back where Prince, Lefty, Drake and Marcellus stood guard. Lonnie, Jose, Juan and Ed were in front. Raven looked at the others, then loudly made the call of a night bird. His voice echoed thru the silent night. It seemed no one was on the street. It was like they knew there was something in the air.

    *

Ransom, Pauly, Pat, Blake and Vern were all outside of city hall. Turk, Lao and Trace were covering their flanks. Each of the men had four grenades and were waiting on the show to begin.

    *

Brooks, Tim, Ford, Preston and Tyrus were covering the front and back of the jail. They too awaited the signal.

    *

Raven depressed the plunger on the box that the fuses were wired to and seconds later there was a bright flash and loud explosion. The Mayor's office seemed to swell outward, upward and come crashing down in a shower of brick, glass and wood debris.

"What the fuck!" shouted Lucas Blackstone, as the windows of the town hall exploded inward from the concussing force of the explosion and showered the men inside with glass shards.

Then suddenly there was the sound of multiple explosions outside of city hall, that rocked the building on it's foundation and caused several of the walls to collapse. You could hear the men crowded inside screaming and praying, as portions of the walls were flung into the crowd with devastating force. The men broke for the exits in mass, only to see the doors explode and hurdle huge wooden splinters like shrapnel.

When the Mayor's office exploded, Ransom and the others started lobbing the grenades at the building. Soon the night was torn apart, by the mini explosions.

Brooks and the others, opened fire on the jail to pin the men inside down.

The explosions and gunfire lasted less than two minutes, then the night was again silent except for the groaning, as what was once the Mayor's office settled.

*

"What was that?" Prescott asked. "It sounded like an explosion!"

The women shrugged their shoulders, then came the small explosion and the distant popping of automatic weapon's fire.

"It's them again!" said Eula excited. "They some how found out about the meeting at city hall."

"Damn!" Prescott exclaimed. "I hope they haven't killed them all. If they have, then that's bad news for the blacks in the area."

"Why?" asked Eula. "I can only see good in it!"

"That's because you're not looking at the whole picture." Prescott said. "If they kill them all, then the government will get involved. And if you think it was rough before, then imagine hundreds of armed men just like the few that were killed.

"It couldn't be that bad Pres." said Beth. "The government will protect the people."

"I'd like to believe that Luv, but this country is not like that. They've been lynching blacks for years and the government has yet to step in and put a stop to it. Since we've been here they've hung at least 30, or 40 men and women for little or nothing and no voice has been raised in protest. Put the shoe on the other foot and they'll come charging in. That's just the way it is."

"Does it always have to be that way?" asked Eula.

"No Luv, it doesn't and in time it may well change, but for now that's how it is!" said Prescott.

The women dropped their heads, as he walked over

to them. "Time has a way of changing things." he said softly.
"I just pray that it does in this instance!"

*   *   *   *

The Klansmen stumbled from the smoking city hall
coughing and gagging, as the dust choked them. They
stumbled into the street gasping for breath. They drug the
wounded men from the damaged building into the street.
None were dead, but many were seriously wounded. There
were broken bones and various wounds from flying debris.

"They could have killed everyone of us." shouted
Wally hysterically. "It's time we stopped. They sent us a
message damn it!"

Randy Stanley pulled a pistol from his holster,
pointed it at Wally and squeezed off a round. The bullet
slammed into Wally's knee and shattered it.

Wally screamed out in pain. "Arrghh.....!" as he
crashed to the ground.

Randy walked over to him and pointed the gun in his
face. And Bubba shouted, "No... Randy don't shoot him!"

Randy looked in Wally's eyes and slowly lowered the
hammer of his gun, then turned and walked over to his
brother.

"You should've let him kill the son of a bitch!" Bull
shouted.

"What purpose would it serve?" Bubba asked. "We
need every man, even him!"

"Damn it, that asshole is planting seeds of cowardice
in the men, and soon there'll be others expressing the same
shit." Bull said emphatically.

"That may well be the truth." Bubba said. "We know
one thing for sure though, asshole he might be, but he has a
point. Wally sees this for what it is. If they had wanted to,
they could've killed a lot of us, maybe all of us. I don't think
they wanna keep on killing. They're up to something, they
have an agenda and I'd stake my life on it. What it is I don't
know, but I believe we'll find out soon!"

*   *   *   *

"Well, all we can do now is wait and see what the
outcome is." Raven said. "Ran it's your show and you can get

on the ball starting tomorrow. If I were in charge of this operation, the first thing I would do is hire some loyal foot soldiers to drive the merchandise, and use the family to protect the shipments. I'd put distance between us and the actual product. What I mean is, I'd get someone I could trust to be the front man. Trace can do all the contacts, as well as pay and collect profits. Let Drake go with him and always send at least three heavily armed men on their tail. I'd suggest Lao, Lefty and Turk. All of the others including you, would ride shotgun on the shipments. I wouldn't do a lot of small drops, I'd do them all at once and make sure I kept my ass covered all the way. We'll provide you with the necessary funds to get it off the ground, but keep a good account of the money, cause you'll be paying it back. Mace, I've got a proposition for you since we're talking business."

"Oh yeah?" Mace asked his brows raised. "I'm listening son."

The men laughed.

"This is it. I want us to go over the river and see if we can do the same thing." Raven said, "We've got the man power and the finances to get it done!"

"If Ran uses all of the men to protect his shipments, just who are all of these men we have?" Mace asked puzzled.

"The same ones." Raven said smiling. "If Ran was of the same mind as me, he would only make a couple of drops a week, And we can do the same, using the same men and keeping it in the family!"

"I kind of like the sound of that, but we'd have to know somebody across the river that had all the contacts." Mace said.

"Pa, excuse me!" said Preston. "Jeanie's folks are from over there and they're in the know."

"Not our Jeanie? Mace asked.

"Our Jeanie," Preston said.

"Burk Laws and Nelly are Jeanie's folks and they've lived here long as we have!" Mace said.

"We got folks elsewhere too pa." said Preston. "Nelly's sister Vivian, lives over there with Dave Sumner, who is kin to big Larry Sumner, who has his hands in every pie over there."

"Bull Parsons and his crew, run the liquor over there too." Tyrus said. "The river ain't stop him from spreading his greedy, grasping hands, over there!"

"Well that settles it for me." Mace said. "We done already put a crimp in their operation, so we might as well go all in!"

"What's in this for us?" Ransom asked. "I'm not talking monetary pa."

"What's in it for every man in this room, is security. We're family and will secure our future by branching out and getting as much as we can. We'll make the community safer and provide jobs for those that wanna work. We'll make this benefit our people too. We're building up, instead of tearing down!"

All of the men nodded in agreement, then they sat around talking and planning for the next day.

* CHAPTER # 21 *

Everything was quiet for the next few weeks, as the Klan licked their wounds and planned their next course of action. The whites in town started to notice that the blacks had added pep in their stride and openly carried themselves with pride and confidence.

The Kanes had started selling their liquor to all the blacks and even to some whites that had speak easies. The trade was lucrative and it wouldn't be long before Bull and his group felt the crunch. The Kanes provided a better grade of liquor, than the bath tub gin that the Bellamys sold. People were getting a lot more confident when dealing with them, since they now saw that even the Klan could be hurt. The dark cloud of fear and terror, had almost disappeared.

Raven and Mace, accompanied by Trace and Drake, had met with big Larry Sumner to find out the lay of the land. They were in negotiations with the bootleggers in the area. They used diplomacy where ever they could, but they were sure to leave the impression that they were men not to be trifled with.

Trace and Drake proved to be an excellent pairing, as both men were intelligent, persuasive and innovative. They played off of their weaknesses and strengths. They were extremely successful and the entire family benefited.

Ransom was proving to be a solid leader, though he was basically relying on the counsel of the elders. He was somewhat prone to use violence to settle problems, but slowly he was moving towards other methods. He was sure to consult with the elders before he made a move that involved the entire clan and that was just about everything. Sometimes he followed their advice and some times he didn't, but never were the results detrimental.

*　　　　　*　　　　　*　　　　　*

10 months after the attack on city hall, Raven, Mace, Lola and Celia sat in the living room of Mace's house. Mace was bouncing his new grandson, (Raven and Celia's boy)

Baron on his knee.

"Mace, what say we take the women out tonight?" Raven asked. "Been a while since me and Celia been dancin!"

"Old ass nigga, what you know about dancin?" Mace said laughing.

"A lot more than you, old man." Raven replied.

"Where did you have in mind?" Mace asked. "Don't say the Bucket of Blood, cause I wouldn't be caught dead in that joint."

"I was thinking along the lines of the Velvet Club, over the river." Raven said.

Mace stopped bouncing the baby and looked at Raven. "We need to talk son." Mace said seriously, as he passed the baby to Lola.   Raven stood and the men walked into the den and closed the door.

"Are you sure you wanna go over the river?" Mace asked.

"Why not?" Raven asked.

"You know Lefty killed Strom Stevens over there and the Stevens are a bad lot." Mace said. "That Pip Stevens is a bad man and the twins ain't far behind. There's a lot of them and I can't see taking our women folk into it!"

"Mace, I was thinking about that earlier, that's why I suggested the Velvet Club." Raven said. "See I ain't one for waiting on them to kill one of ours, then we retaliate. I'm for getting it done and let the chips fall where they may!"

"But taking the women, I can't see it Raven." Mace said. "Why can't we just go?"

"Because Celia and Lola wanna go to the Velvet. If it's what they want, I want it for them!" Raven said. "Since Celia and I got married, things done changed. You know how stubborn she can be, hell she got it from you!"

" No hell she didn't, she got it from her ma!" Mace said. "If Lola wants to go we're going and if we don't there'll be hell to pay around here. Shit, they might do me a favor and kill her."

The men laughed, then Mace asked. "How will we do it?"

"We'll take Drake, Trace, Tim, Lao, Ransom and Blake with us. We'll get them to bring their girls. We'll get Lefty to go alone and hang at the bar. Lon, Pat, Ed, Pauly, Brooks, Cellus and Preston will be outside spread around the building. If Pip and his folks show up, we'll reel them right on into the net!" Raven said.

"What about Obie Reed?" Mace asked. "You know he's the law over there, endorsed by Bull. That nigger thinks he's God!"

"Obie Reed, is Bull's Lackey and if he and his boys are ever in my sights, I'm shooting them down like the dogs they are!" Raven said defiantly.

"Well I guess we better spread the word then." Mace said, as they headed back to the women.

    *   *   *   *

Raven and Celia were seated at a table with Mace and Lola, the others were spread throughout the room with their women. Drake sat with Lisa, Trace and Myra.

Trace and Myra had gotten married, as had Blake and Laine. Drake, Lisa, Tim and Lucy were planning a double wedding, that would take place in two months.

Tim, had virtually moved into Ransom's house with Lucy. It was nearly safe for Lucy to return home to her parents, but she decided that she would stay, so she could be close to Tim. Who had asked Prescott, for Lucy's hand in marriage.

Lefty stood at the bar nursing a drink. All of the men were armed to the teeth. They waited for the Stevens' to make their appearance.

They sat and enjoyed the entertainment, which was really good. A big band and a glamorous female singer named Bess Waters, who had performed as far away as New York, but was a local girl.

Big Larry Sumner and his wife Trish, walked over to the table where Raven sat with Mace. "Mr. Kane, Mr. Mace, ladies!" he said respectfully as a greeting. "I hope you're enjoying the show, because it's not often that Bess is in town. I think she wore out her welcome up north!"

Raven raised his brows questioningly.

"It's a delicate matter, that I wouldn't feel comfortable discussing in front of the women." Big Larry said. "I do need to talk with you gentle men about a possible business venture, if I might?"

"Now?" Raven asked.

"It's just a preliminary to the actual discussion." Big Larry said smiling.

Raven looked at Mace, who nodded his head imperceptibly and they excused themselves and rose.

Trish Sumner, sat with Lola and Celia as the men walked towards the back office. Big Larry owned the Velvet Club.

"Girls, that hooker Bess Waters is a dope addict!" Trish whispered to the women, who looked at her puzzled. Lola and Celia were familiar with drunks, but didn't know what a drug addict was. Trish was a street wise woman, who had clawed and scratched her way to the top. She ran a big whore house. She and Big Larry were made for each other, as they were born hustlers.

"Yeah, the bitch got a monkey on her back." Trish said.

Lola's pride wouldn't allow her to ask what a drug addict was, but Celia had no qualms about asking. "What's a drug addict?"

"Baby, a drug addict is somebody that is hooked on drugs. It's just like a wine, except they on skag, instead of wine." Trish said knowledgably. "Skag is heroin, that's a drug made form opium. That shit is bad girl!"

*

In the back room, Big Larry seated Raven and Mace, then sat behind his big desk. He looked at the men, and asked. "Are you fellows familiar with junk, or skag, as it's called?"

The men looked at him and shook their heads.

"It's a drug made from opium, it's the trash, that's why it's called junk. It's highly addictive and it's popular among the in-crowd up north. It has slowly drifted down south and is gaining a big following in La Villa and over here. I'm sure you guys know Slim Beals, over in La Villa?" asked Big Larry.

"Yeah we know Slim, he's one of our best customers." Mace said.

"Well, Slim has the skag on y'all end and Pip Stevens and his group, are the skag dealers on this end. I see a big future in the junk business." said Big Larry. "I'd like us to go into the business together!"

Both Mace and Raven shook their heads no, then Raven spoke.

"That sounds like a young man's game, and we're not

interested, but we can put you in touch with our boys. You know them, Trace and Drake. They might be interested, but I for one ain't!"

"Neither am I!" said Mace firmly. "I been riding on this nigga coat tails for nearly a year and things been real good. So I'm apt to agree with him."

*　　　　　*　　　　　*　　　　　*

Lucky James, rushed into the black cat, a speak easy that was owned by Pip Stevens and his twin brothers Donald and Ronald. "Where Pip?" he asked a big, dark skinned woman, named Joann.

"He in the back with Ronnie and Donnie. They got Tip back there and they're talkin business." she said.

Lucky hurried to the back, knocked on the door and shouted. "Pip, it's Lucky, I need to talk to you!"

The door was snatched open and Pip stood there scowling. "Nigga you got my money?" Pip asked.

Lucky was a junkie. He dropped his head, then said. "I'm gonna have it for you later Pip, but I got some information for you!"

"Come on in, this better be good!" Pip said menacingly. Pip was a medium sized, brown skin man, with hazel eyes. It was a Stevens family trait. They all had the same cat like eyes.

"Alright nigga, spill it." Pip said.

"That nigga what shot Strom, is in the Velvet!" Lucky blurted out.

The twins jumped up from their seats so swiftly, that the chairs toppled over. "Who is he with?" asked Ronnie.

"He was alone, but I seen some of them niggas he runs with too." said Lucky.

"How many?" Pip asked.

" I ain't see but two." Lucky said. "I was outside the club, tryin to see what I could come up with. You know I got Ether Myers on the stroll. I was tryin to get your money, so I could pay you off and see about getting fixed up!"

"How long ago was this, that you saw the nigga?" Pip asked.

"He been inside for an hour or more. I didn't wanna leave, so I hung around for a few. Bess is performing, so I don't think they'll be leaving anytime soon."

"Ronnie go call Obie Reed and have him and Iron Head meet us in back of the Velvet in 15 minutes. We gonna kill that nigga and whoever is with him!" Pip declared.

     *   *   *   *

When Raven, Mace and Big Larry walked out of the office, Raven's eyes danced over the crowded room. He locked eyes with Eagle, who nodded his head towards the restroom. Raven tugged Mace's sleeve and headed to the restroom. The big red man followed. Soon Eagle, Hawk and Falcon joined them. Cougar and Wolf had stayed home.

"What is it?" Raven asked Eagle.

"Let's get the ladies loaded up brother." Eagle said. " I got the feeling things bout to get hairy!"

Raven looked in his brother eyes and nodded his head. He had long ago learned to trust his elder brother's hunches. The men walked from the restroom and gathered their women. They loaded them into cars and sent them on their way. The men then spread out around the big room. Mace and Raven, watched the front door, while Trace and Drake, watched the back. The men outside had been alerted and told to let the Stevens come on into the trap.

                         *

Obie Reed and Iron Head Waters, pulled up behind the Velvet Club and got out of the car. Both men carried shotguns. They leaned on the car and waited for Pip. Pip had Obie and Iron Head in his pocket.

Brooks spotted the men and keeping to the shadows made his way quickly to the front of the club. He spread the word as he went, then rushed inside to Raven.

"Granpa, there are two men outback leaning on a car and both of them totin shotguns?" Brooks said.

"What do they look like?" Raven asked.

"I can't rightly see one of them, but one is a big wide nigga with a big, bald head." Brooks replied.

"Obie and Iron Head." Raven said. "Hurry back out and tell the others to follow them in when they get here, now hurry!"

Brooks rushed from the club and told the others, as Raven warned the men inside. They all pulled the compact military issue .45 automatics from their shoulders holsters and covered them with the big napkins the club provided.

Pip, the twins, Lucky and Tommy Perkins or T.P. as he was called, pulled up behind the Velvet Club.

"That's the niggas car right there." Lucky said pointing at a black coupe.

"T.P give that nigga a bundle of skag and wipe out his debt." Pip said. "I figure this information just about covers it."

Pauly, watching from the shadows, saw Lucky point out Lefty's car. He whispered to Preston, who was behind him. "That nigga ratted Lefty out, he's mine!"

Preston looked at him and saw the anger in his eyes even in the dark, and whispered. "He's yours!"

Pip and the others, walked over to where Obie and Iron Head, leaned on the car. "Let's go. I want that nigga personally!" Pip said as the men headed for the back door.

Lucky watched the men as they walked to the back door, then he turned on his heels and hurried across the lot. He never saw the large group of armed men silently emerge from the shadows, nor the one that detached himself from the group to hurry after him. Lucky was thinking only of the fat bundle of dope, that he had in his inside jacket pocket.

As Lucky turned the corner to go to the front of the club, Pauly caught up with him. "Hey man, got a light?" Pauly asked.

Lucky was startled and he froze in his tracks at the sound of the voice. He swiftly turned and saw a slight man with slanted eyes, and a big smile.

"What was that?" Lucky asked.

"Got a light!" Pauly asked holding a cigar in his left hand where Lucky could see it.

"I ain't got no light." Lucky said angrily. "You on the wrong side of town ain't you boy?"

"So are you." Pauly said softly, as Lucky turned to walk away.

Pauly dropped the cigar and a big knife miraculously appeared in his right hand. The big silvery blade, glinted in the moon light as Pauly's left hand shot out and gripped Lucky's forehead and jerked it back. The blade flashed, as it streaked towards Lucky's throat. In one wicked stroke, Pauly slit the man's throat from ear to ear. Blood gushed in the night air, from the man's severed arteries. Pauly held him upright for a few seconds, then released him. Lucky crashed to the ground, his unseeing eyes wide and filled with horror.

*

As Pip and the others, barged thru the back door they were met by Big Larry, who shouted. "What the hell is this?"

"Nigga step aside!" Pip said pointing a big revolver in Big Larry' face. "That nigga what killed my brother is in here and he's a dead man!"

"You're making a big mistake Pip." Big Larry said.

"The man said move!" Obie Reed said loudly. "Now get your ass out of the way!"

"Ain't gonna be no killin in my place!" said Big Larry sternly.

Iron Head Walters stepped forward and clubbed Big Larry in the head with his shotgun and Big Larry dropped to one knee shaking his bloody head. Iron Head struck him again and the big man slumped forward barely conscious.

The men stepped over his prone body and hurried into the club proper. As they stepped into the big room, Pip was in the lead. His eyes scanned the room and he saw Lefty leaning on the bar smiling, but didn't know who he was. He fired his pistol into the ceiling, then shouted. "Which one of you niggas is Lefty Mace?"

Lefty's gun hand was hidden behind his left leg. He spoke softly. "I'm Lefty Mace and who might I ask are you?"

Pip's head swung back to Lefty, and he said. "I'm Pip Stevens, the man who's gonna kill your ass!"

Pip and his men, didn't see the armed men who had stepped behind them with the Thompson sub machine guns.

Lefty saw them and burst into laughter. "That's a mighty big order there son!"

Before Lefty finished speaking, the other Kanes and Maces stepped forward, each pointing a gun at the six men.

Pip and his men saw that they were out numbered and Obie spoke up. "I'm Obie Reed, the law over here. You men drop those guns, he's under arrest for murder!"

"That's a damn lie!" Vernon Mace said from behind them.

The six men looked behind them and saw that there were five men armed with machine guns. Pip and the others, holstered their guns, and Pip said. "This ain't over!"

"You got that right." said Lefty, who swung his guns up and fired four quick rounds that smashed into Pip's chest. They catapulted him backward where he crashed to the ground.

"That was cold blooded murder!" shouted Obie. "You won't get away with this one!"

"Who says he won't?" Raven asked raising his pistol and firing one round that struck Obie between the eyes and exited in a spray of blood and brain, that splashed on Iron Head.

Big Larry stumbled from the back, blood had drenched his shirt front. He kneeled and picked up Obie's shotgun, raised it and shot Iron Head in the face. Iron Head's face was erased in a shower of blood and gore.

"Ain't no need in looking over our shoulders." Mace said as he fired his weapon. Eagle, Hawk and Falcon fired with him and the other three men were cut down in a hail of lead.

Raven looked around the room at the terror stricken crowd and proclaimed in a loud voice. "If anyone entertains the thought of harming us in any way, know that you'll receive the same. We won't stop until every adult male in your clan is dead!"

The men looked over the crowd. Then Raven holstered his gun and pulled out his bill fold. He took a large wad of bills out, then passed them to Big Larry, and said. "For any inconvenience we've caused!"

Raven made the call of the night bird, turned on his heels and left, followed by his clan.

* CHAPTER # 22 *

The years passed and the Kanes and Maces became intermingled. Falcon's daughter Beth, married Lefty shortly after Lisa and Drake married. Tim married Lucy and the families bloomed. They never got involved in the heroin trade, but their bootlegging business took off. Ransom had followed Raven's advice and hired drivers for their shipments.

Bull and his group, killed several of their men and so started what was called the Whiskey Wars of Duval County. The killings went back and forth for several years.

By 1926 the Kanes and Maces, were firmly entrenched in liquor running and in the community. Ransom, Drake and Trace convinced most of the family to invest in the stock market as the economy seemed to be flourishing. They had large investments in various stocks and bonds.

Then came what was called Black Thursday, Oct 24, 1929. The market crashed and the once rich found themselves suddenly poor and destitute. The depression struck with a vengeance and the entire country was thrown into turmoil. Bankers jumped from windows and committed suicide in every form known to man.

Raven, who had never trusted the whites and most of the elders carried the family through the lean times. But, still there was a tightening of belts. Times were tough for everyone. It seemed all of the elders started dying at once. First Cougar, then Wolf, Swallow, Eagle, Falcon, Violet, Willow, Conchita, Hawk, Mace, Lola and Fern.

Raven was the last of the elders living and Celia stood by his side. Ransom had taken firm control of the clan, with his brothers Turk and Prince by his side.

In 1938, there were rumbles of America getting involved in the war that Germany had begun. They were supplying arms and munitions to the British, who were hard pressed by the Germans.

Baron was 18 years old and he was set to marry the daughter of Big Larry Sumner. Baron had the Kane build. He was a big man, at least 6'2", and well muscled. He was a combination of his parents. He wasn't as dark as his father, nor as light as his mother. He had a co-co brown complexion and was quite the ladies man until he met young Lois Sumner. A petite, brown skinned beauty, who had the body of a goddess.

Baron and his cousins were basically running things, while Ransom and the other old men sat back and pulled the strings. Bootlegging was still profitable, even though prohibition had been repealed in 1933.

Drake and Lisa's oldest son, Will Mace, was his right hand man. His crew consisted of Tim and Lucy's first born son, Chance. Lao and Esmeralda's son, John. Blake and Laine's son, Bobby. Trace and Myra's son, Ausha. Juan and Tracy's son, Dennis. Cissy and Jose's son, Roger. Turk and Rosita's son, Roy. Prince and Consuela's son, Charles. Lyle and Mandy's son, Ben. Greg and Sparrow's son, Samuel. And Preston and Jeanie Mae's son, Brandford, named after Big Mace.

The Kane, Mace, and Jenson's boys were a rough lot and they believed in an eye for an eye. If you wronged one, you wronged them all.

*   *   *   *

"Baron, I think I'm pregnant." Lois said happily.

"Are you sure?" Baron asked.

"About as sure as I can be!" she replied. "I done already told my ma about it."

"Well, I guess we better set the date up for the marriage!" Baron said. "I'm gonna need to talk to your folks and tell them our plans. My folks need to know too, so let's swing on over to their place, then we'll go see your folks."

"I don't want you to start nothing with L.J. either." she said firmly.

L.J, was Larry Jr., her oldest brother. He was 23 years old, and involved in the heroin trade. He had made a name for himself and was backed by his brothers Leonard, called Nard and Leon. Jack Lee Evans, and his brother Spencer, were their enforcers.

Lois was 16 and had moved in with Baron, who had his own place. Raven had managed his money fairly well, but they were nowhere near as wealthy as they once were. Raven had started a small trucking company, called Kanes moving and storage. He had two large warehouses and did decent business even though the old boy network was still in affect.

Baron and all of the younger Kane men, were all employed as drivers. None would get rich, but the family ate and that was Raven's main concern.

Raven, by this time was a mere shadow of his former self. His mind was still agile as ever, but physically he was wearing down. At 78, he was still spry, but his once powerful frame was now frail.

Baron and Lois drove to the store that Raven still owned. He had taken a major hit with the store, but refused to close it even though it barely broke even. He gave credit, even when he knew he wouldn't be likely to get paid. He refused to see his people starve or go hungry. And if he could provide for them with no real loss to him and his family, then he did.

"Hey boy!" Celia said surprised to see Baron. "Lois how you doing chile?"

"I'm fine Ms. Celia!" Lois said smiling.

Lois, genuinely liked Baron's family, especially his father and mother. They took to her from the start and treated her like a daughter.

"Where Pa?" Baron asked his Mother.

"That any way to greet your momma boy?" Celia asked. "Ma, don't you start up with me now." Baron said jokingly as he walked to his mother and wrapped her in his strong arms. He lifted her and spun her around.

Celia squealed and screamed. "Put me down boy!"

Baron set her down and kissed her lightly on the cheek. "I need to talk to you and pa." he said seriously holding her by her shoulders.

Raven walked in followed by Brooks son, Nelson, who was constantly at his side. Nelson was 15 and he adored his great grandfather, couldn't get enough of the stories that Raven told him. Nelson was huge and his size promised he could get even bigger.

"Why ain't you workin boy?" Raven asked Baron.

"The same reason you ain't." Baron said light heartedly, as Raven approached.

"Lois, I don't see what you see in that lazy nigga. If I was a few years younger, I'd take you from him!" Raven said laughing. "Nigga don't deserve you no how. I got to ask your daddy what the hell he was thinking tellin that joker he could marry you."

They all laughed, as Raven pulled Lois into his arms

and kissed her cheek.

Nelson hugged Baron and Lois, then assumed his place next to Raven. Nelson had moved in with Raven and Celia when Baron moved out.

"Ma, Pa, Lois is pregnant and I don't want my child born out of wedlock. So we gonna marry soon!" Baron said happily.

"I don't have a problem with that and I'm sure your mother doesn't either." Raven said. "I suppose I got to pay for the wedding."

"Nah, you ain't got to do that pa. I been saving for it and I got a few buck set aside." Baron said.

"Just how much, is a few bucks?" Celia asked.

"I got almost $300 saved!" Baron said proudly. "I do hope that's enough."

"Oh it's enough," Raven said. "I guess you can go on and pay for it, hell that'll save me some money."

"Nel, you watch the store while we ride across the river." Celia said. "If anybody comes asking after us you tell them we went to see the Sumners about Baron's wedding!"

Nelson nodded, as the four people left.

*   *   *   *

Lucy, Tim, Prescott and Eula sat in the parlor all saddened by Beth's sickness. The doctor was in the room tending to her. They were all silent just waiting to see how she was. Beth had been sick for nearly a year and lately her health had really deteriorated.

"Y'all need to get in here now!" the doctor shouted.

The four people hurried up the stairs to Beth's room.

"She wants to speak to y'all." the doctor said.

They crowded around the bed where a pale, and washed out Beth lay. Weakly she lifted her head and looked at them, then asked. "Lucy, where my grandbabies?"

"They ain't hardly babies no more, Ma Beth." Lucy said.

"I wanted to tell them bye, but I don't guess I'll be able to now." Beth said, then her body was wracked by coughs.

"Don't say that Beth!" Prescott said firmly. "You can't leave us!"

"Pres," she reached for his hand. "My darling man.

It's not that I wanna leave, but I can't bear up under the pain. You been the world to me darling and I don't regret a minute of the life and love we've shared. You opened my eyes to so many wonders and took me halfway around the world. Even though we had our tough times, things always worked out for us. You brought two wonderful people into my life and I never got the chance to properly thank you. I love you all.

Eula, I got to go sister, so take care of our husband like you always have. Lucy, look after your father and mother, cause they're gonna miss me. Timmy, you got to carry the load now. Pres don't realize yet, that he's old. Comfort him like the good son you've proved to be!" Beth said and doubled over with another coughing spell.

"Ma Beth!" Lucy said leaning down onto Beth's chest.

Suddenly the coughing stopped and Beth looked up, and said. "I love you all!" She slumped back in the bed, closed her eyes and expelled a big breath. Then her body went still.

"Ahhhhh..!" Eula screamed and kneeled beside the bed holding Beth's limp hand.

Tears flowed freely from four sets of eyes, as it dawned on each of them that Beth had died.

    *   *   *   *

Baron arrived at the Velvet Club and parked. The two couples left the car and walked inside. The Velvet Club was still the place to be. Heroin use was increasing in the black community, passed down form the entertainers, whores, pimps and musicians. Big Larry had entered the trade and did well.

"Hey Raven, how you been?" Big Larry asked, genuinely glad to see him.

"I'm holding alright Larry!" Raven said, approaching with his hand extended.

The men shook hands and Big Larry looked at Celia, and said. "Damn it woman, you still lookin good!"

"Go on now Larry, I'm gonna tell Trish you been getting fresh." Celia said giggling.

"Baron, Lois," Big Larry said.

"Hey pa!" Lois said smiling.

"Larry," Baron said. "I come by and brought my

folks along to tell you we're moving the wedding date up!"

Big Larry looked from Baron to Lois, then back to
Baron. He raised one of his brows and Baron smiled. Big
Larry clapped him on the shoulder, and said. "So y'all bout to
have a baby."

"Yeah we bout to have one." Lois said.

"Well, I guess you gonna need your mamma then."
Larry said. "Celia, why don't you and Lois use my car and go
to the house and get with Trish, so y'all can make the
arrangements. Ain't no need to take these two. I got
something I wanna talk to them about!" He reached in his
pocket and gave Celia the keys to his big Caddilac.

Celia took the keys and they left. Larry lead Raven
and Baron to his office where they had a seat. Larry offered
the men a drink. Raven declined because of the hour. Baron
because his father did. He tried to follow the examples his
father set for him. Loyalty to the family was the philosophy.

"I want you to know that things are looking kind of
bad for us now." Larry said solemnly. "I don't mean
financially, I'm set there. But you know I'm involved in the
drug trade and I got a situation that's close to blowing up!"

"Just what kind of situation is this?" Raven asked
inquisitively.

"My boy L.J, shot a man uptown three nights ago. It
had been brewing longer, but it came to a head in the Hi Hat
the other night!"

"Who'd he shoot? Baron asked. "Did he kill him?"

"No he didn't and it was Tab Williams!" Larry said.

"He should've killed him!" Baron said. "If it was me,
I would've. Tab ain't gonna take it laying down and he ain't
the roughest one in that bunch. Ace and Son Kellam are the
ones you'll have trouble with!"

"That's why I'm letting you know now, I ain't trying
to get y'all involved in a shooting war. We can hold the
wedding until after this is resolved. It ain't your fight!" Larry
said decisively.

"Raven looked at Baron, to see how he would react.
Baron, unaware of his father's scrutiny turned to face Larry,
then said. "When me and Lois got together, you didn't have
this problem. We gonna get married soon. You family, you
treated me like a man, judged me on my on merits. That made
you family in my eyes. Me and Lois marrying just seals it.
I'm with you and that means the Kanes, Maces, and Jensens

with you too!"

Raven smiled inwardly, as he thought to himself. "This boy's a Kane! "Welcome to the clan!" Raven said.

"We need to get Ran and the others over here. He's head of the clan now."

"Larry, let me use your phone." asked Baron.

"Go on and use it. It's behind the bar out front!"

After Baron left, the older men were alone in the office. Larry looked at Raven, and asked. "How do you really feel about this whole matter?"

"Does it make a difference?" Raven asked.

"It does to me." Larry replied. "I've known you for nearly 20 years and you've always been an honorable man, I trust your judgment!"

"If that be the case, then you already know the answer to your question. If Baron says you have the clan behind you, that's truth. You and yours, are now ours, and we'll do what we have to, to insure the survival of the entire clan!"

"You said Ran was the head, but you are the true Patriarch of the Kanes!" Larry said firmly.

"That may well be the case, but my time is gonna come someday and they'll need to learn how to get by without my counsel. I'm there, should the need arise, but Ran is an extremely capable man. So is Baron for one so young, but Nelson may be more my son than any of them!"

Just then, Baron walked back into the room. "I got bad news pa!"

"What is it?" Raven asked curious.

"Aunt Beth just died!" Baron said.

"Beth Mace?" asked Raven.

"No, Beth Wellington!" Baron said. "She died today. Tim and Lucy been tryin to contact you for an hour!"

"I got to go get Celia then. Pres, Eula and Lucy gonna need us." Raven said.

"You ain't gonna stay until Ran and the others get here?" Baron asked.

"Ain't no need to." Raven said. "Y'all boys can do what needs to be done."

"Call Trish and she'll get back here with Lois and Celia." Larry said. "Being honest, all you can do for the others is provide comfort, so a few more minutes ain't gonna make too much difference!"

"You got a point there Larry." Raven said. "Baron, go call your ma!"

Baron left the room and went back to the phone.

"You remember years ago, I asked you about getting in the drug trade?" Larry asked Raven.

"Yeah I do and my answer then is the same one now. Talk to Ran!"

Larry laughed and the men sat and waited. In less than 15 minutes Trish, Lois and Celia returned.

"I'm gonna go with Raven and Celia." Trish announced. "Lois goin too!"

Larry nodded his head, as Raven and the women left. He and Baron sat in the office talking. They heard footsteps approaching, and voices speaking in hushed tones.

L.J, stepped thru the door speaking. "Pa, was that old man Kane that just left here with ma?"

Leonard, Larry's son, who was called Nard, was behind L.J, followed by Larry's youngest son Leon, who was called Leo. The three Sumner boys, were followed by Spencer and Jack Lee Evans.

"What the hell did he want?" L.J asked sarcastically. He didn't see Baron seated in the corner.

"Whatever he wanted it ain't none of your damn business!" Larry said firmly.

"I don't like them Kanes!" L.J said. "They're up to something."

"Yeah they are," Larry said. "Protecting your ass!"

"I can protect myself." said L.J vehemently. "I ain't needed the Kanes before and I don't need them now!"

"It ain't about your needs or wants." Baron said softly.

L.J's head whipped around to the sound of the voice and he saw Baron sitting there.

"I don't know what the problem is between us." Baron said. "I can't ever recall us having a run in, but I'm about at the end of my rope where you're concerned. I've bent over backward to be civil with you and that ends today. If you ever set yourself against me again, I'm gonna take you down a peg!"

"You and what army?" L.J said bristling for a showdown.

"This army!" a cold voice said from behind L.J and his group.

The men spun around and there stood Ransom, Drake, Trace, Lefty and Will.

"What's the problem here?" asked Ransom.

"Ain't no problem here yet!" Baron said calmly. "This is a family matter."

Larry knew the older men were not to be trifled with, he had seen them in action. And though he wasn't a coward, he didn't want any part of the trouble that was brewing. So, he decided to try and dispose the problem.

"Ran we need to talk." he said. "I know you probably heard about the shooting earlier this week uptown!"

"Yeah, I heard one of your boys shot Tab Williams." Ransom said. "He should've killed that skunk!"

"Baron, said the same thing. Anyway this is the thing, you know Baron and Lois had planned to get married. I just found out that they got a baby on the way and Baron wants to marry sooner. I told him to wait until this thing with Tab blows over because I didn't want to get him involved." Larry said.

Baron cut him off. "Excuse me Larry, but I'm already involved. It doesn't matter if we marry next year. I'm obligated to family and as of now you're family. By virtue of being your son, L,J's family too. That won't stop me from busting his ass, but I'll see to it that no one outside of the family harms him!"

"So will we!" Ransom said. "So what are you gonna do about Tab and the others. I don't think Chauncey and his group are gonna take this layin down. They're a ruthless lot, them Spires."

"I haven't really had the chance to give it much thought." Larry said. "I don't want things to get out of line, and that's what could happen."

"I heard that Pike and his boys were looking for L.J." Will said. "I don't know if there's truth to it, but you know Pike and his boys got their hands in almost every piece of pie."

"I don't think Carl Lee knows Pike is on the take. Carl Lee is a hateful man where blacks are concerned, but he's for damn sure honest!" Ransom said.

"Y'all gonna talk about me like I ain't here and ain't got no say in this?" L.J asked angrily. "Fuck Pike, fuck Tab and the whole bunch!"

Baron chuckled and L.J spun toward him, and said

174

venomously. "Nigga you think something's funny?"

"Damn right I do." Baron replied. I find it amusing that you're not taking them boys serious."

"I should kick that smirk off your face, you son of a bitch!" L.J shouted.

"L.J damn it!" shouted Larry. "I don't know what you got against Baron, but cease that bullshit this minute!"

"He done stepped over the line one time too many now, Larry." Baron said softly. "I told you, if you came against me I'd take you down a peg. Now we can do this the easy way, or the hard way. You're family, so I won't kill you, but I'm gonna beat your ass. No knives or guns, just feet and fist!"

L.J was a big strong man and was a rough and tumble fighter. He had engaged in his share of fights, but he had never fought a Kane.

"Pa, he's talking shit. So, I'm gonna teach him a lesson he won't soon forget!" L.J said menacingly.

"Hold on now boys." Larry said, trying to stop them before it got out of hand. "Ain't no need for us to be at each others throat, we're family!"

"Still gonna be family when it's over." said Baron. "We need to get this issue resolved in order to go forward!"

Baron stood up, looked in L.J eyes and pointed to the door. L.J turned on his heel and headed to the back lot with Baron behind him.

The other men followed them out back. The men formed a circle, as Baron and L.J removed their jackets and squared off.

"When this is over, it's over!" Ransom said with authority. "You boys hear me?"

Both men nodded as they stepped into the circle.

"I'm gonna prove you ain't man enough for Lois." L.J said.

Baron just looked at him and raised his fist. L.J rushed him and threw a looping right that Baron ducked under. When Baron ducked, he fired a right, left combination to L.J's midsection. L.J took the two hard blows and stepped back his face screwed tight with pain.

Baron pressed the advantage and moved forward. He threw a left jab, that L.J easily dodged. And a right cross, that L.J blocked. L.J fired a straight right, that glanced across Baron's left cheek. Then a left cross, that Baron weaved. The two men went around and around with no one landing a telling blow.

L.J rushed forward as Baron shot out a left jab. He slipped the jab and ran into the vicious right uppercut that Baron threw. Baron's rock hard fist smashed into his chin with jarring force and L.J's head snapped back. He stumbled and Baron's left cross grazed the top of his head.

L.J, dazed, threw an over hand right, that smashed into Baron's neck with numbing force. Baron's head was cocked to the side, his left arm nearly dead.

The men backed off, warily circling each other. Baron looked in L.J's eyes and saw new respect there.

"I think the point's been made L.J, what say we end this here, no winners?" Baron said.

Though L.J had new respect for Baron, still he was driven to beat him, and he replied. "Oh no, you ain't gonna weasel your way out of this ass whipping!

"I gave you your only chance!" Baron said. Baron closed the distance and feinted with his right.

L.J bit and he launched a vicious front thrust kick to L.J's midsection that caught him completely off guard. L.J folded forward and baron's hand slashed down in a wicked chop to the back of his neck. L.J, fell to his hands and knees dazed. He shook his big head to clear it and Baron stepped back.

"I'm giving you quarter, cause you're family!" Baron said firmly. "Anyone else, I'd destroy!"

L.J struggled to his feet and rushed Baron, who side stepped him, and fired a right to the back of his head. L.J stumbled forward and Will caught him and held him upright until he regained his balance.

"Enough damn it!" Larry said.

L.J looked at his father, his eyes blazing with anger, and said. "Not yet Pa!" Then he turned back to the fight and Baron gave him a sound whipping.

Baron didn't mess up his face, except for a few lumps. Ransom looked at the young men, and said firmly. "That's the end of that. No more, ever! If you two disobey, the family will discipline you. And I promise, you won't like it!"

The men filed back into the club and sat in a big circle in the main area.

"I'm gonna go talk to Chauncy Spires and see if I can

stop this before it turns into a shooting war. If it comes to us having to make some concessions to prevent bloodshed, then we'll concede. If he dishonors us, then we'll deal with it. Anyone disagree?" Ransom asked.

"Why do we have to seek peace with them?" L.J asked. "It seems kind of cowardly to me!"

"Watch your mouth there boy!" Larry said angrily. "Respect your elders!"

"I didn't mean any disrespect Ran. I'm just saying that it seems that way to me." L.J said.

"He's got a point Ran." Baron chimed in.

"And well he may." Ransom said. "But what are the rules of engagement?"

"I know Chauncy and his crew and they are men without morals or scruples. They may ambush you, or attack you while you're with the women. So what I want to do is prevent that. If I can't, then like I said, we'll deal with it!"

"I agree with Ran." Larry said. "Let him talk to them before we take any other action."

All of the men looked at Larry and Ransom and nodded.

"Ran, remember I asked you to come in with me on the heroin thing?" Larry asked.

Ransom nodded his head, and Larry said. "It's still open and there's money to be made!"

"What would we have to do?" Ran asked.

Before Larry could answer, the front windows of the club exploded inward. Bullets and shards of glass showered the room. Luckily the men were seated, and the rounds buzzed over their heads. The men all fell to the floor and most pulled guns from their jackets.

Lefty, Drake, Trace and Will, crab walked swiftly to the shattered windows. Carefully they peered out. Two cars were parked and men outside of them were firing round after round into the building. Jack Lee rushed to the front door and nudged the door open and fired at the cars.

Lefty and the others opened fire and the men hurried into their cars and sped away.

"Brant and Elmore were in that group. I think I saw Son Kellum." Jack Lee said angrily.

"Ain't no need for talk now." Ransom said. "Will, Baron, take L.J, and a couple of the others and pay them Spires boys a visit. I'm gonna call the others and get some more of our people over here."

Baron nodded, then looked at L.J, who looked to Jack Lee. The young men cautiously left and loaded up.

"Chauncy got to go down." Ransom said.

"That's gonna leave a void in the heroin trade. One you can fill." Larry said.

Before the two men were finished, they heard the sound of sirens approaching.

Put the weapons away. "Ransom said. "Ain't no need to kill Pike and his men, at this point!"

The men put their weapons away, as they heard two cars squeal to a halt outside. Pike Richards rushed thru the door, followed by Haney Burch, Slocum Lewis and Step Harvey. The men all held their service revolver in hand.

"What the hell is goin on here Larry?" shouted Pike.

"Some assholes decided to redecorate the place." said Larry sarcastically. "What the hell do you think happened?"

"Nigga don't get smart with me!" Pike said. Pike wasn't a real big man, but he was well put together and fast on the draw. He was a medium brown complexioned man with piercing eyes and a big voice.

Haney Burch was a giant of a man, 6'5" and at least 350 pounds, of which very little was fat. Step Harvey was a tall thin man, that resembled a living scarecrow.

Slocum Lewis was a round man, whose appearance always appeared jovial, but underneath, just below the surface, was a sadistic streak that was barely detected.

"This got anything to do with the shooting that took place uptown the other night?" Pike asked.

"What shooting?" Larry asked feigning surprise.

"Don't play with me nigga, if you don't want no problems!" Pike said menacingly.

"You're a police officer and you expect us to do your job for you?" Ransom asked.

Pike finally took a good look around and saw the Kanes. "Well I'll be. If it ain't Ransom Kane himself. The man who thinks he and his, are above the law!"

"If you're the best example of law in this town, you're damn right we're above your brand of justice." Ransom said.

Slocum moved close to Ransom and looked at Pike.

"Come a step closer Slo and I'll bust your ass!" Ransom said softly.

Slocum stopped a few feet away.

"I don't want you niggas takin the law in your own hands." Pike said. "You can only make this worse."

"Choose your side Pike." Ransom said authoritatively. "Choose wrong and we'll ride thru you, or over you!"

"You got a big mouth for a nigga that ain't armed!" Pike said smiling.

"Touch me and I promise you'll regret the day you were born!" Ransom said sternly.

"I just wanna do my job and if you niggas get in my way. I'm gonna come down on y'all like a pallet of bricks!" Pike said. "Come on boys, let's go before I shoot one of these smart mouth niggas!"

Pike and the others, walked from the club, got in their cars and left.

* CHAPTER # 23 *

"Did you kill any of the Sumners?" Chauncy asked his eldest son Brant."

"I don't know pa." Brant replied.

Chauncy Spires was medium sized, maybe 5'10" and 185 pounds. He was a high yellow man with silky black hair, that was plastered to his head. He had sharp grey eyes that spoke of his mixed ancestry.

Brant and his younger brother Elmore were high yellow men too, but both were much larger than their father. The family resemblance was strong, except both of the sons had red hair.

Sonny Kellum was a cocoa brown skinned man, that stood about 5'6", and weighed 140 pounds, but was mean as an agitated rattlesnake.

Ace Washington, was Son Kellum's cousin. He was a tall well built man, who ran Chauncy's whore houses with Brant and Elmore's mother Big Maggie. Ace mostly provided security along with Tab Williams, who was Maggie's cousin.

Tab was a big dark skinned man who stayed getting into scrapes because he was a bully. Maggie was a big boned, red woman, with a freckled face and red hair.

The men sat in the office of the Tip Top Bar and Grill, which served as Chauncy's head quarters. "I think them Sumners gonna be running scared after that incident." said Elmore.

"I don't think so." Chauncy said. "It takes guts for them to even have shot Tab in the first place!"

"Wasn't nothing but a flesh wound Chauncy." Tab said. "L.J gonna be dealt a much worse hand when I catch up with him!"

"You boys stick around for a few days I want y'all here. I can get Rollie and Punch to watch the front of the place and Lex and Mac to keep watch on the back. I just wanna see what they do. If they don't come at us, we'll hit them Friday night when the club is in full swing!" Chauncy said.

*　　　　　*　　　　　*　　　　　*

Baron had gathered all of his cousins and told them what had happened and they were in the process of loading their gear.

"This is what we're gonna do." Baron said. "We'll hit the Tip Top when night falls. L.J, Will, Chance, Bobby, Sha, we'll go inside. The rest of y'all split up and get the front and back."

"What about me?" Nard asked. "I wanna go in too!"

"Me too," said Leo.

"Alright then, y'all can go with us, but follow my lead. They're gonna be in the back of the place like always and we'll rush in and take them out!" Baron said.

*　　　　　*　　　　　*　　　　　*

Pike and his brother Bill Lee walked into the Tip Top, and stopped just inside the door. They let their eyes adjust to the dim light in the room. They spotted Chauncy and his group at the back of the club in their customary spot. They walked quickly over to where the men sat. Pike looked down at Chauncy, and asked. "What the hell was that shit you boys pulled across the river?"

"I don't pay you to ask questions Pike. I pay you to smooth the way for me and to knock out my competitors. So far you've proved you're worth the investment, let's keep it like that." Chauncy said.

"Nigga, what the hell do you think I am, a trick pony?" Pike asked angrily. "I'm the only thing between you and a stiff prison sentence!"

"Calm down man." Chauncy said. "Don't take it personal."

"Personal my ass, do you know who was in the Velvet Club when they attacked?" Pike asked. "No you don't, so I'll tell you. Ransom and some of the other Kanes and Maces. Those boys are real trouble, if you believe some of the stories!"

"Fuck the stories Pike." Chauncy said. "If they stick their noses in my business they can get some of the same!"

"I'm just warning you." Pike said. "Be on your toes!"

"Already am," Chauncy said. "I got Rollie, Punch, Mac and Lex on the front and back. They'll warn us if trouble comes."

"They'd better cause if the Kanes get involved, that's what it's gonna be. Trouble and plenty of it!"

"If I didn't know you better Pike, I'd think you were afraid of them Kanes!" Chauncy said.

"If you had any sense, you would be too!" Pike said turning and walking back towards the front door with Bill Lee behind him.

*   *   *   *

"Well Celia, it's that time again." Raven said. "It's almost like a replay of nearly 20 years ago. What's a man to do honey?"

"All we can do is like we always have!" Celia said. "We gonna keep on going forward. The boys learned from some of the best and they still have the benefit of your knowledge!"

"Yeah, but for how long?" Raven asked. "All of the others have passed, but not me. I see them sometimes Celia just like it use to be. This isn't meant to cast a bad refection on you honey, but I miss them!"

"Baby don't talk like that, you know I need you!" she said. "It ain't like Ran and Baron don't need you. We all need you, you're the tie that binds us to the old ways, you're the symbol of the clans longevity!"

"Can't you see I don't wanna be a symbol, I wanna live out my last few years in peace." he said. "That's all we really ever wanted from the start. Baby so much has changed and it seems like my mind is getting clearer rather than dim. I see and smell the familiar sights of my youth!"

"Honey, you're scaring me." Celia said seriously. "Are you alright? Think you need to see the doctor?"

"Doctor can't cure what ails me woman!" He replied.

"I got something that might bring you back to the present." she said seductively.

"What you got in mind?" he asked.

"What say we go to bed early tonight, I got a surprise for you!" she said smiling impishly. Celia was still fine and good looking and Raven though being elderly still desired her after all these years.

"I think I can manage to do that." Raven said as he reached out gently and caressed her cheek.

182

*   *   *   *

"Yeah Ran, we're a block away now and we've been by the Tip Top several times. They got a dude watching the front, and another the back!" Baron said into the phone.

Ransom's voice floated thru the line. "Listen brother, you've got to be decisive and ruthless. If you don't get them all it could come back to haunt us!"

"I got it Ran." said Baron. "We're about to move now, so I'm hanging up!"

"Be careful Baron!" Ransom said and hung up the phone.

"Well fellas this is it!" Baron said. "Y'all be careful and shoot who we came here to shoot and not innocent bystanders. Remember we got to live here too!"

The young men all wore long dark car coats. They looked at Baron and nodded.

"Let's go!" Baron said, and lead the way to the Tip Top.

When Dennis and Roger Kane saw Baron and the others headed in their direction, they immediately went into action.

Punch and Lex were leaning against the side of the building. Their eyes glancing back and forth down the road. Dennis and Roger drunkenly stumbled across the street and stopped several feet away from the two men. Neither was a trained observer, but still they didn't pick up the tell tale signs that the long car coats sent. They never thought that the two young men looked too clean for the role they were playing.

Dennis and Roger grappled with each other. And Roger managed to spin Dennis toward the men who chuckled at what appeared to be the men's drunken antics. The two men managed to conceal their right arms. And when they stumbled into the two laughing men there were two flashes, as the silver of the long blades slid from their sleeves.

With cat like agility and speed they turned ferociously on the men. Dennis 's forearm slammed into Lex's neck and pinned him to the wall. Dennis's blade streaked in and slid between his ribs and punctured his heart. Lex's eyes glazed over slowly as they starred into the night sky.

Punch had spun to try and push Dennis away from Lex. But in doing so, he took his eyes off of Roger.

183

Roger looped his arm around Punch's neck and jerked him backwards. Punch's feet flew upward as Roger pulled him deeper into his embrace. Roger's blade slashed out and severed the man's throat. A gush of air hissed from the gaping wound soon to be followed by a geyser of blood from his severed artery. Roger shoved him forward as Dennis let Lex's body slump to the ground.

Roger made the call of the night bird and Baron and the others quickly made their approach. The men never doubted that the back was taken care of, so they hurried into the club.

Baron stepped thru the door closely followed by Will and L.J. The patron's were all into their own things when Chance, Bobby and Sha stepped into the club and spread out. Nard and Leo stepped inside and hurried to catch up with Baron and the others. Baron spotted Chauncy, his two sons, and Tab sitting at a big table in back of the club.

The club was dimly lit and smoke was in layers. The men at the table never saw Baron and Will, when they pulled the four colt .45 automatics from their coat pockets. They never even perceived the threat until it was too late.

Chauncy looked up from his conversation with Tab, just as Baron stepped up and raised both of his pistols. Will at his side did the same, then they both fired in unison. Before Chauncy could speak a round smashed into his forehead and shattered his skull. Exiting in a spray of blood that painted the wall behind him in grisly still life.

The four men were pinned in and Will fired round after round into their jerking bodies.

Pandemonium reigned in the club as people rushed for doors, or hit the floor.

Son Kellum had just stepped out of the men's room when Baron and Will opened fire. He pulled the big revolver from his shoulder holster and sought a target. He fired a round that smashed into the meaty part of Nard's left shoulder. The force spun Nard around and Son fired again. L.J crashed to the floor, as the big slug slammed into his thigh breaking the bone.

Bobby and Sha both raised their pistols and fired a hail of rounds at Son Kellum. One slug hit Son in the chest and punched him backward. Three more rounds hit him and he dropped to his knees, where wearily he tried to raise his pistol. The two men took aim and fired. Son's head seemed to explode, as the big slugs impacted. He reeled around one time then crashed sideways to the floor.

Ace, looked up from under the table where he hid then quickly looked around. He locked eyes with L.J, who sat on the floor grimacing. One hand held his thigh and the other his pistol.

Ace raised his pistol with lightning speed and swung it toward L.J. Who just raised the barrel of his pistol, braced his hand against the floor and pulled the trigger twice in rapid succession. The rounds punched upward and pulverized his intestines, heart and lungs. The force caused him to lunge upward and launch the table into the air.

"Any more of them left?" Baron asked. "If you fuck with a Sumner, you're fuckin with us!"

The men looked around the Tip-Top, then hurried and filed out.

    *   *   *   *

"Pike can't you control them niggers?" Sheriff Carl Lee Eggers asked. "I know you got your hand in everything that's illegal over there. You niggers are a greedy, grasping lot, if ever I seen one!"

Pike looked at the white man with hatred in his eyes, and said. "You'd be greedy and grasping too, if you had to scrape by on the crumbs white folks give!"

"Damn all that revolutionary talk!" Carl Lee shouted. "You're supposed to be keeping the niggers towing the line and that's what I expect. If you can't do it, then I'll find a man that can!"

"Carl Lee, you ain't gonna find another nigga to do what I do. You'd have to send your boys in bustin heads, to get done what I do!" said Pike. "Some shit is brewing between the Spires and Sumners. If that Kane bunch gets involved, you might as well round up the militia, cause there's gonna be big trouble!"

"I know about them Kanes, and I've heard the stories, but I'll be damned if I'll be cowed by legend. You just get things calm over there. With niggers on the rampage, it ain't safe for decent white folks to walk the streets!" Carl Lee said seriously.

"I'll do what I can, but I need help, I'm gonna call on you." Pike said.

*   *   *   *

As Baron and Will, stepped out of the Tip-Top. Haney, Slocum, Bill Lee and Step pulled up in two police cruisers and leaped out with their weapons drawn. Baron still held the twin .45's and he raised them and fired. The big rounds smashed into the patrol car and a round hit Haney in the shoulder. It drove him backward into the car, where he sprawled across the seat, his legs kicking in the air. A round smashed into the sole of his shoe, smashing his foot in the process. Haney fainted from the excruciating pain.

Will fired and a round punched thru step Harvey's waist, blowing out a chunk of flesh and fatty tissues. Though it was only a flesh wound, the force knocked him against the car. He dropped his pistol and clawed at his bleeding side. The other deputies quickly hit the ground and covered their heads with their hands, as the rounds smashed into the cars. Baron and the others, quickly disappeared into the dark night.

"Them was Kanes!" Slo Lewis said, after they got up off the ground.

Haney lay unconscious in the car, while Step Harvey moaned in pain. Bill Lee looked at the bullet holes that scared the patrol cars and knew that when Pike saw it he would go nuts. "Let's see what we got inside. Make sure you get help for Step and Haney."

Bill Lee walked into the Tip-Top and knew shit was gonna be hectic when he saw the bodies on the floor. "What the hell happened here?" Bill Lee shouted.

He was met with silence. He looked into the fearful eyes of the many witnesses and knew he'd get the story sooner or later, but not tonight. It was all too fresh in their minds for them to talk. They had witnessed cold blooded murder and most knew of the Kanes and their wrath. So, mouths were tightly shut.

"Ain't nobody leaving until I find out what the hell went on here!" Bill Lee shouted.

* CHAPTER # 24 *

The next day at about 11:00 a.m., two big Caddilacs pulled up outside of Raven's store. Ransom and Raven were standing by the windows looking out and talking when the cars pulled up. They watched as three hard looking, olive skinned men got out of the first car. All of the men were well dressed. One of them walked to the other car and held the back door open. Out stepped a big, silver haired man, in a beautifully tailored suit. Two more men got out of the car and they flanked the man. One took the lead and they walked to the store.

The first man opened the door and stepped in. He panned the room, as the other men came in. Raven looked at Ransom, who hunched his shoulders in the universal I don't know sign. They turned their attention back to the men.

A crowd had started to gather, because this was an uncommon sight. Whites rarely if ever, did business with the Kanes.

Raven and Ransom walked over to the men, as Nelson slipped from the backroom and flanked the men. He held a Thompson Sub machine gun with a drum magazine.

"Good morning gentlemen, how can I help you?" Raven asked cordially. He looked at them closely and could see that these men were true warriors. They had an almost Spanish look about them, but taller and broader than any he had seen. The silver haired, big man stepped forward, he looked to be in his early 40's or even younger.

"Yes you can help me, if you're Mr. Raven Kane." the man said. "I'm Giancarlo Torronelli and we need to talk!"

"About what?" Ransom cut in.

"Aww, you must be Mr. Ransom. I've heard a great deal about you." Giancarlo said smiling. "Please allow me to introduce my associates. This is my brother Salvator."

Salvator was a big man like his brother, but he was a little soft around the edges.

"This is Paolo Castellano or Paul Castle."

Paolo Castellano was a man of average height and size, with thick jet black hair plastered to his head like a skull cap.

"Joseppe Verda or Joe Green. Vincente Deleon or Vinnie Dee."

Vinnie was a tall thin man, with acne scarred cheeks and a mean disposition.

"Guido LoCasa or Gus Lowes.

Guido was a round bowling ball shaped man. He was always at the edge.

Raven and Ransom greeted the men, then Raven said. "This way gentlemen please." as he lead the men into his small cramped office.

Giancarlo raised his hand and stopped his men when they had come to the door. "Just me and Sal." he said to the others, who stood at the door.

Raven gave the men a seat, then asked. "Would you men care for a drink? It's a little too early for me."

Both men declined, so Raven and Ransom took a seat.

"Mr. Kane, it has come to my attention that you had a dispute with some of my business associates." Giancarlo said. "It seems your people terminated our contract with prejudice last night."

"I'm not sure which business associates you're referring to." Raven said.

"The Spires." Giancarlo replied. "From the reports, your son Baron and his group, hit the Spire's last night and left not a man standing. I don't have a problem with that, but I'd like to propose a business venture we can both engage in. I assure you it will be beneficial to us both, financially!"

Raven looked over at Ransom and raised his brows. Ransom nodded his head slightly, as Raven turned back to Giancarlo.

"Just what is this venture and how might we be instrumental in making it a success?" Raven asked.

"You have a small trucking business and I can throw a great deal of work your way. But, I would want you to move certain products from New York, to Miami and several points in between." Giancarlo said. "There's gonna be a vacuum in the spot left open, because of Chauncy's untimely demise. I'll need it filled."

"Just what product do you want us to move and what about storage space?" Raven asked.

"We'll take care of the storage and handling. All I

need you to do, is move it!" Giancarlo said. "I'm talking about heroin, horse, junk, skag. That's the product. I'll pay to have hidden compartments built into the trucks, so there won't be an immediate concern if they're stopped."

"What kind of money are we talking here?" Ransom asked.

"$40,000 a trip, fifty if you drive it straight thru!" Giancarlo said smiling.

Ransom looked to Raven for confirmation. Raven just stared ahead, in his mind he was calculating how much the $50,000 could do for the clan.

"If you step in and take Chauncy's place, I'll even give you a discount on product. I'll sell it to you for twice what I pay. Trust me, it cost a lot more on the open market." Giancarlo said.

Ransom looked at Raven again, then said. "We'll make the runs straight thru as often as you like, but we want $60,000 a run. As for taking Chauncy's place, count it done. I believe we have a deal Mr. Torronelli!"

Giancarlo chuckled, then said. "I would've went as high as $80,000!"

The men shook hands, then Raven asked. "Where does Carl Lee and Pike fit in here?"

"They don't!" Giancarlo said. "A man that won't uphold his duties to the public for money, is not to be trusted!"

"When will we make the first run?" Ransom asked.

"I'll make the arrangement, then Pauly Castle will bring you half the money. The other half you get when the shipment is delivered!" Giancarlo said. "I know me and my people couldn't win a war against you if we fought on your turf. So, I decided to see if peace could be established. You're a powerful group and I would rather us be friend than foe!"

"Thank you Mr. Torronelli." Raven said. "As long as we are honest in our dealings with each other and crush the greed that may arise, we will prosper. But, should we come at odds it would be a battle to remember!"

*   *   *   *

Several hours later, Ransom had called all of the men in the clan. They were gathered at a farm that Raven had way out on the west side.

"This is the deal," Ransom said. "We're getting into

the heroin trade! We got an offer that was hard to refuse and it's worth $60,000 to the family a trip. Chauncy's dead, so that leaves a vacancy in the trade here in town. We will fill that vacancy. Baron it's your show here in town. You've got full control, but you can't tie up all of the men!"

"I do get to choose the men I'd like with me right?" Baron asked. "No reflection on those that I pass over. I know you're all capable men!"

"You might as well go on and pick your men. Will, you might as well stand with him!" Ransom said.

Will Mace walked over to where Baron sat, they were like brothers. They had been raised together.

"I want Bobby, Sha, Dennis, Roger, Ben and Sam!" Baron said. "I think we can hold this end, and provide security if needed!"

"Alright, Baron has his men. Now I'm gonna call out the men who will drive the trucks! Prime."

Prime, was Turk Kane's son. Turk and Rosita had three children, Prime the oldest, then Roy and Betty.

"Jeff," Jeff, was the son of Drake and Lisa Mace, who had four children. Chaney, Greta, Will the oldest and Posey the baby boy.

"John," John, was Lao and Esmeralda's son. They had two daughters, Pearl and Susan.

"Chance," Chance, was the son of Tim and Lucy and they had four children. Chance, Rose, Phillip and Lucretia.

"George," George, was the oldest son of Lefty and Beth Mace. They had three children, George and two daughters, Lisa and Raylene.

"T.J" T.J, was Trace Jr. the oldest son of Trace and Myra. They had four children, Trace Jr., Ausha, Drew and Louise.

"Charles," Charles was the oldest son of Prince and Consuela. They had four children, Charles, Matty, Princeton and Sharon.

"Larry," Larry, was the oldest son of Blake and Laine. They had three children, Larry, Bobby and Connie.

"Joe," Joe, was the oldest son of Juan and Tracy. They had three children, Joseph, Dennis and Jack.

Ben, who Baron chose, was the oldest son of Lyle and Mandy. They had two children, Ben and Josephine. Sam was the oldest son of Greg and Sparrow Jenson. They had two kids, Samuel and Prissy.

"I don't know what us old men will do, but I'm sure some of us will tackle some of the driving too. Hell, I've always wanted to go up there!" Ransom said. "If y'all got a problem with who you'll work with, speak up now!"

"How will we be paid cousin?" Drew Kane asked.

"Trace, you ain't taught that boy no manners yet?" Ransom asked laughing. "Good question son. Times been tight for us, but everybody ate. That's how it's got to be. If we prosper, so do those around us. The first thing we do is take care of the family, then we make sure to keep some pocket change in everybody's pocket. If you fellas would have heard this man talk, he's talking about us being rich! The continued survival of our family, could well depend on our success or failure in this. I say we go full speed ahead!"

The men looked up to Ransom, and said. "We gonna win!"

Ransom smiled, because he saw the future in Baron and the other youths. Plus his grandson Nelson, who was constantly by Raven's side. He knew that come hell or high water, they'd be alright. The family was the most important thing, Raven had instilled in his generation and they in turn passed it to their sons and daughters.

*　　　　*　　　　*　　　　*

"Celia, I don't think we should've got involved in this heroin business!" Raven said distastefully. "I can't see me profiting from my own folks misery. I just can't."

"Why didn't you say something then?" She asked.

"I wanted to, but I knew that would cause a big problem. See, Giancarlo Torronelli is a mobster and he has pretty big pull. He exudes warmth and charm, but the man is as vicious as a fox in a hen house. If I had interfered, it would have changed the outcome. We cut off their money and to them Italians that's like cutting off one of their nuts!"

"So what do you do now?" she asked.

"What I've always done sugar, if you want peace you have to prepare for war!" he said.

*

"Carlo do you think we can trust those dinges?" asked Joe Green.

"Let me tell you guys a thing or two here. You've never in your life met a man like Raven Kane and probably never will again. That old many is sharp as a razor and not to be taken lightly. We could maybe beat them in a fight. Only reason is, because we're closer to being white. That man is a fighter. It wouldn't surprise me if he gave either one of us a run for it. Even now, look at how organized they are, almost like this thing of ours. But, with one big difference, they're all blood ties. Raven is like a feudal Lord, he controls them. If he said no, they wouldn't have done it no matter what the cost in money or lives. Trust me, these are some dangerous men. Their loyalty for each other is fierce. Personally I plan to pick this man's mind, I can learn a lot from a man like him once I get him to trust me!"

"Speaking mighty high of a nigger ain't you?" asked Sal sarcastically.

"I don't wanna hear that word again from any of you, even in privacy, nor any other word that they could take as disrespect. They're men, so we'll treat them like men in every way!" Carlo said authoritatively. He made eye contact with each of the men and with his vivid blue eyes he drilled his point home.

Giancarlo Torronelli was indeed a mobster and so was his father Gianni, before him. He was married to an Italian woman named Sophia and they had two small children. Rose Marie and Fransisco Luigi, who was called Frankie. Frankie, bore a striking resemblance to his father at 1 year old. Carlo hoped to have more children and he worked at it with Sophia who was a lusty woman.

"This is about honor, so don't forget that!" Carlo said seriously. "These are men who will suspect us from the start. They've never got a fair shake from whites, so they'll look at us thru their past dealings, because we're white to them. They don't know our culture or history, but we'll show by our actions that we're men of honor!"

"I'm not trying to cause no problems Carlo, but why are you so intent on impressing them?" Pauly Castle asked.

"I told you from the start that we may never have the chance to meet a man like Raven and when he dies I want him to know he's met a man!"

The other men looked at Giancarlo and saw the intensity blazing from his vivid blue eyes.

*   *   *   *

A few weeks later Ransom, Baron, Big Larry, L.J and Turk sat in the back office of the Tip-Top.

"So you're saying we can get our product from your source, for cheaper than what we're paying the Mexican?" Larry asked.

"Yeah, I am!" Ransom said. "It's probably a better grade too!"

"I'm in!" Big Larry said smiling. "I just hope that there are profits enough for all of us!"

"We're family, so we won't go hungry. We don't have to put restrictions on this because we're not in competition." Ransom said. "Baron will handle the street level for us and he's your son in law, so it's all in the family!"

Before the men could go on there was a loud knocking on the thick door.

"Who's there?" Turk asked going to the door. He heard a voice shout out.

"This is Pike Richards, get out here now!"

Turk opened the door and Pike stood there with Bill Lee and both men were unarmed. Bobby and Sha held their .45's to the men's head. Dennis and Roger took the men's guns, while aiming their pistols at them too. You could almost feel the heat of his anger as he grimaced.

"Alright fellas, put the guns away." Turk said softly with the glint of laughter in his eyes. "Pike, Bill Lee, we gonna give you back your guns, so don't be a fool!"

Dennis and Roger both gave the men their guns and stood there waiting for the men to holster them. Reluctantly, the men slid the guns into their holsters. Turk stepped aside and the men moved inside. Turk looked at the four young men and flashed them a quick smile, then closed the door.

"What the fuck kind of welcome party do you think that was !" Pike screamed. "I ought to lock all of you niggas up. I know y'all killed Chauncy, and that son of bitch there damn near killed Bill Lee." he said pointing at Baron.

"First off, you ain't gonna lock up shit!" Ransom said viciously. "And you ain't gettin a dime of our money, so don't think you will. You're puffing up like you're in charge. Nigga, the only reason you ain't dead already is because I ain't said so! Them crackers ain't shit, they need you. This is how it goes from here. We'll make sure that trouble is taken care of and you just keep on pinching off your little pieces of the pie. But, if you oppose us in any way, you're dead, Bill Lee is dead. If your father's still alive he will die, so will your sons and nephews!"

"Nigga you threatening my family!" Pike roared.

"Your days are numbered Pike, so don't make us punch your ticket. The survival of your family depends on that!" Ransom said.

Pike looked around the room, then said. "You niggas got it all figured out, but your ass gonna fall. And when you do, I'll be there to pick up the pieces!"

"I told you once Pike, it's thru you, or over you. A smart man would know when to step aside!" Ransom said.

Pike looked at the men, then spun on his heel and headed for the door with Bill Lee behind him. After they had left Baron asked Ransom. "Do you think he'll be a problem?"

"He's a problem now Baron, but we can't really afford to get rid of him. Draw too much heat from Carl Lee."

The men sat and talked for a few more minutes, then they each rose to leave.

* CHAPTER # 25 *

Raven, Celia and Nelson were in the front of the store. It was only 9:00 in the morning and they had been there for two hours. They rose early.

Raven stood leaning on the counter, Celia stood behind it. Nelson was sweeping toward the front of the store. He stopped, lay the broom aside, and said. "Grandpa, that white man is back!"

Raven walked to the front door, as Nelson headed to the back. "Ain't no need for that son." Raven said, as he watched Giancarlo step from the back seat. He saw him say something to Joe Green and watched as Joe Green bent into the car and grabbed two packages. Pauly lead the way to the door and held it for Giancarlo.

"How are you Mr. Torronelli?" Raven asked, as Celia waved at Carlo. "To what do I owe this visit?"

I'd like to talk with you Mr. Kane, no business, just talk!" Giancarlo said.

Raven looked at him and raised his brows. "I've heard that somewhere before."

Carlo chuckled, then turned to Joe Green and took the packages. He walked to the counter and passed one of the packages to Celia, and said. "Cannoli, my wife prepared it. She would be honored if you took it!"

Celia took the package and opened it up and saw that Cannoli was an Italian dish. "Thank you sir, and please extend my thanks to your wife as well."

Carlo walked to Nelson and gave him the other package. ,"It's a few bottles of wine from my vineyard, outside of Naples."

"Thank you, Mr. Torronelli." Raven replied.

Carlo turned to Joe and Pauly, then said. "Go on and do what needs to be done. Come and pick me up at 5:00, or 5:30!"

"You're taking a lot for granted here Carlo!" said Pauly concerned.

Carlo looked deeply into Raven's eyes, and said.

"I'm in good hands Pauly. Mr. Kane would die protecting me, because I surrendered myself to his care. It would be an affront on his honor, if harm came to me while I was his guest!"

Raven laughed, then said. "I only hope to live up to the standard you've set for me!"

"You're sure?" Joe asked. "Sal, is gonna have our ass for this!"

"Sal might try to hit me himself, so forget about it. He'll pray I die before I get back." Carlo said seriously.

The two men nodded, then left.

Carlo turned to Raven, and said. "I hope I wasn't too presumptuous, in assuming you'd allow me to stay and talk with you."

`"Presumptuous, never. Bold, surely." Raven said warming to the big man. "Why would you want to waste a day with me?"

"First, I'd like you to call me Carlo, as do all of my friends and enemies."

Raven laughed and moved towards where four chairs and a card table sat. That one there is Nelson, he's my grand boy, actually he's my grandson's boy. He's a fine young man, but I just can't seem to get rid of him. Been that way since he was a baby. Took to me and Celia, like we were his parents. Couldn't live with his folks, so we raised him. Knows I ain't his pa, but acts like I am."

They sat down and Raven asked. "You know how to play checkers, Carlo?"

"Never even heard of it." Carlo said.

Raven reached back onto a low shelf and pulled a wooden case out, opened it and there was the board.

"You mean chess?" Carlo asked.

"I play chess, but I like checkers better." Raven said. "I'll teach you to play!"

The two men sat at the board and talked for several hours. They broke for lunch and Celia served them Cannoli with the meal she had prepared. They rode around and stopped at several business that Raven had a share of. Nelson was their driver and the two men talked all through the day. By 3:00 p.m. Raven knew what kind of man Carlo was and he wasn't much different than him as far as beliefs were concerned. Carlo had told Raven his life story and Raven told him about being raised with the Indians by a Chinese father.

The two men got along well and Raven found that he genuinely liked the man.

It was closely approaching 5:00 p.m. and Carlo showed no indication of wanting to leave Raven's side. It was a Friday night and Carlo didn't have any plans.

"What do you do on a night like this?" Carlo asked.

"Usually I take Celia out to one of the clubs and show her a good time." Raven replied. "She still likes to cut the rug!"

"Do you think me and Sophia could go out on the town with you?" Carlo asked. "I don't mean to impose."

"Son, do you know what it would mean if you went to a club with us?" Raven asked.

"I'm not sure I understand." Carlo said puzzled.

"It's segregated son. A black musician can perform for whites, but we aren't allowed to be in the audience unless it's at a black nightclub. Trust me, they can get pretty rowdy on a Friday night." Raven said chuckling.

"I've experienced a lot of things and most of what I've experienced as far as blacks are involved, is what I've learned about your people from word of mouth. We're not so different you know?" Carlo said.

"If you're determined to go, then it's alright by me. Nelson I want you to go to Ran and tell him that Carlo will be going to Club Havana with me tonight. He's our guest and I won't tolerate any disrespect!" Raven said firmly.

Nelson hurried from the building to do Raven's bidding.

"You won't need the others, unless they just want to tag along. No harm will come to you and yours, when you come to see me. I promise you that!" Raven said.

"Where will we meet?" Carlo asked.

"Right here at 9:00" Raven said with a smile. "You won't forget this night."

"He said what?" Ransom asked Nelson surprised.

"He said Carlo and his wife are going to the Havana and he wanted you to get the word out that he's under our protection!" Nelson responded.

"Fuck!" Ransom exclaimed. "Carlo has been there all day long?"

"Yep, from about 9:00 in the morning till now." Nelson said. "It seems like pa like him too!"

"Well I guess I better get the word out. Go tell Baron

that I want him to put four men on Carlo as soon as he meets
pa. They ain't got to get close, but stay close enough so if
anything happens they can protect him." Ransom said.

*   *   *   *

"Sophia, we're going out on the town with the old
man I told you about." Carlo said. "Just us, no one else!"
"That's just the break that Franco Lucca is looking
for!" Sal said angrily. "It's bad enough that you left yourself
open all day. Now you wanna do the same at night? That's
crazy Carlo!"
"Franco has become a thorn in our side, but I don't
think he would try to strike while I'm with the Kanes. Unless,
he thinks as little of them as you and the others!" Carlo said
smiling. "Raven takes my safety personal and I do believe
that if an attempt was made on my life, he would die trying to
protect me!"
"'What do these people know of honor?" Sal shouted
angrily. "Much more than you obviously." Carlo said
sarcastically.
All the while the men talked Diego Prizzi, Carlo's
butler, listened. He was being paid by Franco, for just this
type of information. Sophia sat and listened at the men go
back and forth. She knew Sal wasn't as concerned for Carlo's
safety, as he appeared to be.
Sophia was a beautiful, full bodied Italian woman.
She had beautiful, big round eyes, a lush and inviting figure
and a sharp mind. She knew that if Carlo felt so strongly about
this man Raven, then he must indeed be a special man. She
could hardly wait to meet him.
"I want to go." Sophia said softly. "I think it will be
fun. None of the same day to day monotony, that's for sure."
"That settles it for me!" Carlo said with finality!
Sal looked at him and threw his hands up. He just
knew in his heart, that these niggers would be Carlo's down
fall. "Well", he thought. "All I've got to do is protect myself
and the more Carlo stays with the blacks, the more confident
he would get. The time could well come when the family
needed a new leader."
Diego Prizzi made multiple excuses and hurried from
the Torronelli residence. He drove to a dive bar downtown
called Sharky's. He whispered in the Bartender's ear and was

lead to a back office. When he walked thru the door, Franco Lucca rose from behind the small desk and walked to him.

"Diego my friend, I can tell by the look on your face that you have something for me." Franco said smiling, with his hand extended.

Diego shook his hand and looked into Franco's laughing eyes. "Carlo is going to the Club Havana, in nigger town with no body guards or back up. He's gonna be in the company of a nigger named Raven Kane and his wife."

Franco Lucca was a medium build man with jet black hair, piercing black eyes and a disarming smile. He was a dapper dresser and had all of his suits and shoes hand tailored. He was a handsome man and new to this region. He had been here maybe six months, and saw the potential cash cow that this river city could be. He planned to stake his claim, since this was a free city. The Harlem of the south was what they called it, over in nigger town.

His right hand man Dominic Testoni, was a handsome, big bruiser. Dark hair, blue eyes, roman nose and dimpled chin. It always looked as if he had a five o'clock shadow, no matter when he shaved. "I've heard a few tales about that Kane nigger."

Franco turned to him and gave him a questioning look.

"They say the nigger was a real rough one, in his youth. Word is, his sons, grandsons and nephews are a hard group. Word is, they took Chauncy out. That's why I can't see Carlo in their company, Chauncy was Carlo's man. That cuts off his finances!" Dom said.

"Unless he's trying to get them to fill the void, left by Chauncy's hit!" Luka Pannelli said.

Luka was a small, thin man, who was quick with knives, guns, fist or feet.

"Luka could be right." said Primo Carni.
Primo Carni was a big man, that fit none of the stereotypes. He was fair skinned, with Nordic good looks and blonde hair cut in the latest fashion. He was fond of double breasted suits.

"If that's true, then we won't be able to put our nigger in over there." Franco said. "Where did you say they'd meet?"

"At Kane's store, 9:00 tonight!" Diego said.

"Primo get over there and find out where the meeting place is so we can be there waiting. I believe I can trust Sal

Torronelli to some degree, but Carlo is a different sort. Let's move on them tonight!" Franco said.

Baron looked at Will, and said. "My pa trust us to protect Carlo, so we're gonna do it right. If he has enemies, then they know that the best time to hit him would be at his home. Bobby, Sha, Ben, I want y'all to find out where the Torronelli's home is. Once you find it, call me here. Me, Will, Sam, Dennis and Roger will be there. Get on that now and be sure to get the Thompsons!"

The three men nodded and rose. "How many cars do we take?" asked Sha.

"Take three, so we won't be crowded." Baron answered.

*

At 8:00, Carlo and Sophia headed out of the house. It was going to be a beautiful night.

*

After Primo left to find Raven's store, Franco looked at Diego and asked. "Just how much do you think that information was worth?"

Luka Pannelli had moved behind Diego and stood close to him. Diego was unaware of the danger, as Franco's question rang in his ears. He licked dry lips and thought to ask for $1,000, but instead he asked. "How much was it worth to you?"

Franco looked in his eyes, and said. "We're gonna kill Carlo, you're aware of that. Repercussions are gonna come so we have to tie up all the loose ends. You my friend are a loose end. To answer your question, it was worth your life!"

Luka's arm streaked out and wrapped around Diego's neck and his right hand flashed forward burying his stiletto in Diego's kidney. Diego's body arched, as the sharp blade sliced into him. Luka eased the body to the floor and cleaned the little blood that clung to his blade on Diego's pant. He stood and before he could speak, Diego's body released a big fart, then he voided his bowls.

"Dom, you and Luka get this piece of shit out of here, before he stinks up the whole place!" Franco said.

200

Dom rolled Diego in the rug he lay on, there was little blood, as the hole from the stiletto had closed. All of the blood was trapped in the husk of the dead man.

*

Bobby was on the phone with Baron telling him how to get to the Torronelli estate in the quaint section called Avondale. Baron and the others got their weapons and loaded into a big sedan and drove to their meeting with Bobby and the others.

When they arrived at the gas station the men split up and got two men to a car. Baron had them drive to a secluded spot where he instructed them.

"Me and Will are gonna be right behind him. Ben, you and Sam will be up front. Bobby, you and Sha will tail me and Dennis and Roger will pull drag. We know where they are going, so we can tail them loosely. Not too loose, but keep your eyes open. If any vehicle appears to be a threat we'll take care of it and worry about the consequences later, got me?"

The men all nodded their heads, then got into their cars and kept up a roving patrol of the Torronelli estate. At 8:15, Baron spotted a Caddilac Coupe pull onto the street from the Torronelli's place. He caught a glimpse of Carlo and followed the car by about six car lengths. He saw Ben and Sam as their car accelerated to over take Carlo. He knew the others were behind him, so there was no need to check. The family took their duties seriously.

*

Franco and Luka sat slumped down in their car across the street from Raven's store. Primo and Dom sat in their car slumped down a block away.

Nelson had been watching the street all day. And from talking to several customers he knew that a big white man had been asking about the location of their store. That made Nelson suspicious, so he kept his eye on the street, especially since the man never came to the store. Nelson had an agile mind from studying at Raven's feet. Why all of a sudden was a white man interested in their store? Why would he find out its location and never show up? The only answer was that the man planned to harm Carlo and Nelson would do all he could to prevent that. The family's honor depended on it.

He had seen the two strange cars and had went so far, as to go out the back and walk past them. He saw the men trying to be invisible and one of them fit the description of the man trying to find their location. He watched them as they sat low in the cars and decided he should take this to Raven. He called Raven on the phone and told him of his suspicions. Raven told him to keep his eyes on the cars and he would be there shortly.

Raven called Ransom and laid it out for him. Ransom in turn called Trace, who called Drake. In a matter of minutes, most of the older Kanes met at Raven's house in the den.

"This is what I want done." Raven said. "I want the four men alive if it's possible, if not, so be it. When you get them, take them to the warehouse we got down on the dock and I'll be there shortly. Me and Celia got some partying to do tonight."

Ransom and the others walked out to the front yard and stopped.

"Drake, Trace, Tim, Blake, Lao, Prince, Turk, and me got this one." Ransom said. "Lefty, Jose, Juan, Brooks, Cellus, y'all boys gonna back us!"

The men got in their cars and drove off.

When they got in town, they drove by the two parked cars several times.

"Damn these niggers are out in force tonight." Franco said.

"It's Friday night and ain't but two things a nigger likes better than Friday night. And those are fried chicken and watermelon!" Luka said laughing.

Before their laughter died down a car swerved over and slammed into the side of their car with a thunderous crash that was echoed by another car slamming into Primo and Dom's car.

The four men were shook up and stunned so they were really surprised when they heard a voice scream. "Don't move a muscle!"

Dazedly the men looked up into the barrels of a small army of Thompson submachine guns.

"Holy Mother of Christ!" Franco shouted. "Hold on

there guys."

"Get out of the car with your hands in plain view or buy the farm!" Ransom said menacingly.

The men got out of the cars and were hustled into the trunks of the cars. Ransom and the others drove down to the docks and into the big warehouse. There the four men were taken from the trunk and frisked. Their pistols were removed and they were tied up and roughly shoved into a corner where the group of fearsome black men stood and stared at them.

*

Carlo pulled up in front of the store and Nelson was down the steps in a flash. He opened the door for Sophia, and said. "Good evening Ms. Torronelli!"

Sophia stepped from the car and looked at the big handsome young man blessed him with a smile, then asked. "And who is the gallant young man that opens doors for strange women?"

Nelson blushed and introduced himself, then lead them inside. It was 8:40.

When the Torronelli's walked in they were met by a sharply dressed Raven and Celia.

"So, this is the lovely Sophia?" Raven said impressed. "I've heard good things about you, but I must commend Carlo on his modesty because all of the things he told me about your beauty and character, dim in the light of your smile!"

"Alright, you rogue." Celia said with mock seriousness.

Raven took Sophia's hand and lightly grazed it with his lips.

"He's a smoothie too." Sophia giggled and blushed.

Celia came and embraced Sophia, and said. "You must teach me to make Cannoli."

Sophia nodded and Celia looked at Raven and winked. She had answered the phone from Nelson earlier and the one from Ransom about 14 or 15 minutes ago, so she knew something was up. In her years as Raven's wife she never really got into his business because he told her all he wanted her to know. She knew there had been killings, but never any of the specifics of the incidents. She waited a minute for Raven to give her a sign.

"Ladies, I fear we will be a few minutes later than I had intended. A very important business matter has come up and I'm the only one that can handle it. Sophia, can I borrow Carlo for say, 45 minutes to an hour?" Raven asked.

"Oh you men!" Celia pouted. "It's always business. If you're not back in an hour we're going alone and will meet you there!"

"Nelson, keep your eye on the women." said Raven as he grabbed Carlo by the elbow and guided him outside.

"I don't know if we've got a problem or not, but a man was mighty interested in finding out where my place of business is. A white man. After he found out, he got 3 more men and they were laying in wait. I don't know what their plans were, but they had high powered rifles in their cars, as well as side arms. We didn't think they were your people, because your people already know where my place is!"

As they got into Carlo's car, Raven said. "Drive to the docks. We picked them up and took them there. I'll ask all the questions Carlo. If they're your people we'll let them go. If they're not, then we'll see what threat they pose to us and do what we have to, to extinguish the threat!"

*

Raven and Carlo walked inside of the warehouse. "Where are they?" Raven asked. "Come on Carlo see if these are your people."

Ransom pointed to the corner where the four men sat huddled together. Raven and Carlo walked over to the men and looked at them.

"How are you, Franco?" Carlo asked.

"These your folks?" Raven asked.

"No, but I do know them! Carlo said. "As a matter of fact, Franco is a competitor in our new business venture."

Raven looked at Franco, and said. "Listen to me closely because your life hangs in the balance. I'm gonna ask you one question and one question only. If you lie, you're dead. If the answer is not to my liking, you're dead. I give no quarter to competitors and the only mercy I show is a quick death instead of a painful drawn out one!"

The four men looked up at the old man, who stood before them impeccably dressed.

"What were you doing outside of my place of

business?"

"We were just waiting on some..." Dom began.

Raven pulled a small .38 snub nosed pistol from his waist holster and fired a round into Dom's open mouth. The slug tunneled thru the roof of his mouth and exited from the back of his neck in a spray of blood. Dom slumped over on his side, dead. "He was lying!" Raven said coldly.

"Wait, wait!" Franco pleaded. "I've got $40,000 for my life. It's in a safe at my house. All I need is enough to leave town and I swear on my mother you'll never see me again!"

"Number one, you still haven't answered my question and two, you're a snake. But answer the question before you start putting a price on your life."

Franco looked up at the black man, and said. "We were waiting on..." and Luka cut him off angrily.

"These niggers just killed Dom and you're ratting on us to them?"

"Are you finished with your lecture young man?" Raven asked.

"Fuck you, black ass nigger!" Luka shouted.

Raven calmly pointed the pistol at the man and fired. The .38 slug crashed into Luka's forehead, blew a hole from the back of his head that showered brain and blood on Franco and Primo.

"Kill these assholes." Raven said calmly, then turned and headed for the door.

Carlo behind Raven was shocked by Raven's violent display. He was a violent man and had encountered his share of murders, but never had he seen it done so merciless and remorseless. He thought of the things that Raven had shared with him earlier and knew that the same warrior who went out on raiding parties in days past, still lived inside of him.

"By the way, find out where he was staying and get the money he said he has!" Raven said to Ransom, as he and Carlo stepped out into the dark night.

*

After they had gone to Club Havana and the 2 couples had returned home. Carlo and Sophia lay awake in bed both too excited to sleep.

"I had a really great time." Sophia said. "I didn't

think the blacks had times like that!"

"All of our dealings with blacks have been controlled and in environments where they have to wear masks when dealing with whites, so they're restrained. But, in their own environment they can let go with no fear of being persecuted." he said.

Sophia leaned into him and rubbed his hairy chest, then said. "I'd like to do that again some time."

"Oh, we will sweetheart, trust me!" He said pulling her into his arms. He kissed her and caressed her back, then gently guided her over onto her back. He moved above her and she spread her legs wide. He slid between them and she reached for him.

"My, my, you're so hard." she whispered, as she guided him in her damp opening. "Ummm...." she moaned, as she felt his stiffness penetrate her.

*   *   *   *

Sal, was sitting in Carlo's den the next morning with Pauly when Carlo walked in wearing silk pajamas and a robe.

"What the hell are you guys doing here this early?" he asked.

"I was dying to find out what happened last night!" Sal said. "I just know it was terrible."

"Well, you're wrong!" Carlo said. "I had the best time of my life! By the way, Franco is finito."

"Franco is finished?" asked Pauly. "Did he leave town?"

"Oh yeah, he left this world!" Carlo said remembering how ruthlessly Raven had dispatched Franco. "He tried to hit me last night, but the Kanes somehow learned of his plans and stopped him. Not a thing goes on in La Villa, that they don't know about. They know how to execute plans, plus they got Tommy Guns and plenty of them!"

"So they killed Franco?" Sal asked.

"Not just him, but his whole crew! The old man did two of them himself. You should've seen it. Those men are not to be trifled with on their own turf and they'd be hell on anyone elses. Blacks are our cooks, gardeners, butlers, maids, drivers and nannies. They could be anyone and you'd never suspect them. There's a large group of them and they are all honorable men!" Carlo said. "The question I have is, how did

Franco know I'd be going to Raven's?" He looked over at Sal.

"How the hell would I know? I damn sure didn't tell him." Sal said defensively.

It was at that point, that Carlo knew he would more than likely have to kill his brother some day.

"I never said you told him." Carlo responded. "I wanna know who did!"

"Who was in the area when we discussed it?" Pauly asked.

"Hmm, let's see. We were all here. Sophia was here and so was Diego, but he left." Carlo said. "As a matter of fact he was acting kind of strange and hurried off. He told Franco, I bet. Find him and kill that piece of shit!"

"Right now?" Sal asked.

"No you idiot, tomorrow!" Carlo shouted angrily.

The men leaped to their feet and rushed from the room, just as Sophia stepped thru the door. The men greeted her and left. She looked at Carlo, a question in her eyes.

"It's nothing love, Diego has been terminated. He has proved to be an enemy, understand?"

Sophia nodded her head, then said. "Come on your breakfast is getting cold."

The phone rang and Cita their maid picked it up. Cita was a pretty, light skinned woman, who had worked for the Torronelli's for two years. She was married to James Lewis, who was a heroin dealer that worked for the Sumners. She often brought her young son Jimmy to play with young Frankie Torronelli. Though Jimmy was a year older he doted on Frankie and was very protective of him.

Frankie would raise hell until Jimmy came around. Carlo was in the process of seeing if Cita and James would move onto the estate.

"Mr. Torronelli, Mr. Raven Kane is on the phone and he'd like to speak with you." Cita called out.

Carlo touched Sophia's arm, and said. "Go on start without me."

He walked to where Cita held the phone for him. She could be no more than 30, he thought as he looked at her ever smiling face. Cita had big pillowy breast, wide hips and a perfectly round ass. He took the phone and held up one hand to tell her to stay where she was. "Hello Raven, you're up early aren't you?"

"Hell no! I'm up earlier than this. I ain't got bankers

hours son." Raven said laughing. "We're having a cook out today and I wondered if you and your people would like to come?"

"Sure we would." Carlo said. "Can I bring them all?"

"That's what I said son." Raven replied. "We got 60,000 reasons to have a cook out!"

"I take it you found the safe then?"

"Yeah we found it and there was 60 in it, not 40. Plus some product!" Raven answered.

"How much product?" Carlo asked.

"I don't rightly know, but they were the size of red bricks.

"Probably two kilograms or more. Which is plenty." Carlo said.

"Where and what time do we meet?"

"At my place, as soon as you get here." Raven said, then hung up the phone.

Carlo turned to Cita, and said. "Call James and have him get over here. I need to talk to him!" Cita nodded and he walked to the kitchen where Sophia sat daintily eating her breakfast.

"I hope you don't have any plans for today." he said smiling. "The Kanes invited us all to a cook out!"

"Oh goodie," she said happily. "Can we take Cita and Jimmy too?"

"Sure, why not." he said. "I'm gonna try to get James as my driver. Since we'll be doing business with the blacks, I think it would serve me well to have him as my go-between. A bridge that spans the present, past and racial lines.

Sophia hugged him and they finished their breakfast.

*   *   *   *

Big Larry, Baron, L.J and James Lewis sat in the office at the Velvet Club.

"Don Torronelli has been tryin to get me and Cita to move onto his estate." said James. "I don't think it's such a good idea. I don't mind bein his driver, but livin with white folk in the same house. I don't think I could."

Baron looked at the men, then said. "My pa genuinely likes Carlo. Says he doesn't act like the rednecks we're used to dealing with. My pa said Carlo is a man to ride with and I trust his judgment."

"You're sayin if it was you, that you'd do it?" L.J asked.

"Damn right I would!" Baron said firmly. "Hell, the only way you can go is up. The man is rich already and he stands to get richer. I'd go along for the ride. Another thing is this, you can be our eyes and ears since he doesn't know you're tied to us."

" I hate to say it, but Baron makes sense." Larry said. "It can't hurt and the man has been fair to you."

"Alright then. In that case, I'll do it!" James said. "He had Cita call me earlier and he wants to see me."

"So, how are the wedding plans going?" Larry asked Baron.

"I don't know, maybe you could ask Trish and she could tell you. And you let me know!" Baron said.

"In that case, I guess you won't know. My only concern is that it gets done next Friday, like we want."

"Mine too," Baron chimed in. "By the way, did anyone tell you about the cookout my pa's having today?"

"Ran called and invited us all and I'm going." Larry said. "So are my offspring."

"Well, I'd better get on out there and get this over with." James said rising from his seat and heading for the door.

    *   *   *   *

The cook out was a success. It was there that L.J met his future wife Rose Kane, the daughter of Tim and Lucy. Will came out of his shell and finally declared his affections for Lavern Sumner. She was Lois' sister, who he would one day marry. It was a momentous occasion because quite a few other significant pairings came about.

Leon and Greta Mace, Drake and Lisa's daughter. Prissy and Leonard, Prissy was Greg and Sparrows daughter. Spencer Evans and Liza Kane, Blake and Laine's daughter. Jack Lee and Pearl Kane, Lao and Esmeralda's daughter.

All of them would wed and the Kane line would increase in number, as the Sumners were soon drawn into the family. Baron and Lois's wedding went without a hitch and was the talk of the town, until the other's tried to upstage him.

The Kanes, Maces, Jensens, and Sumners ran the

drug, alcohol, and prostitution rings in Jacksonville. Them, and Giancarlo Torronelli prospered. They had some of their shipments hijacked and always they retaliated ferociously, as well as decisively.

On October 26, 1939, Lois gave birth to a cocoa brown skinned, ten pound baby boy, who Baron named Bishop. Baron and Carlo became close friends as did their wives. Young bishop grew up as play mates with Frankie and Jimmy.

After Bishop's second birthday, nearly two months later on December 7, 1941. The Japanese attacked Pearl Harbor and the U.S.A. was finally and officially in the war. Bishop adored his grandfather and Raven spoiled the boy.

In 1943, Raven's health declined and the family was praying that he would pull thru. Raven had Nelson call all of the men together. The only outsider was Carlo and he was considered family. Nelson and Baron helped Raven to the barn where all of the men were gathered. Though his body was weighed down by age his mind and voice were still the powerful force they had always been. Time had not dimmed his vision nor muted his ears. He looked over the men in them he saw the faces of his father, brothers and sisters. He saw Mace and knew that in time the Sumners would be seen in his descendants.

"I called y'all here today because my time is running out and it will be up to each of you to keep the family together. When I was a child it was drilled into me that the survival of the clan was to be the first concern, then my individual goals. I've done my best to drill it into you. Celia told me years ago, that I was the symbol of the family. I told her I didn't want to be a symbol. I understand what she meant. The family is all I've ever stood for. It has never been about amassing riches, but about making sure that no one in the clan went to bed with an empty stomach or worry about where their next meal was coming from. I took care of mine first, then if there was more, my neighbors. I've tried to do my best for my people and by my people, I mean the blacks and Indians. Now there is a gulf between the two people and I won't be around to bridge it. It's up to you men gathered here. Troubled times will come, as they always have and you'll do as your fathers before you did. You'll stand and be counted and they won't find any of us lacking. The family honor depends on it. Judge and discipline each other and never let anyone outside of the family settle a dispute between you. Don't ever let anything, money, pride, or a woman cause you to slander each other or kill each other. Remember you're family first, everything else takes a backseat to that. Family first! Teach your children and their children."

"No one man among you is to make the decisions for everyone, let it be by committee. One man's judgment can be faulty, but the chances of a group of men having a common fault in judgment is astronomical. Unless the group, thru respect, or fear, agrees with whoever leads. If the government gets a hold of you, take it like you did the good times, cause someone will do what needs to be done to get you free or make sure you live as comfortable as possible. Take care of that family until the man returns. We don't need to worry if the home is cared for, that should be a given. Accept your responsibilities, even if they come from an irresponsible act."

"I've lived thru several eras and these eyes have seen both horrors and joys. I remember a time when you could ride for days and never see another man. I've lived thru wars, ones that were no cause of mine and others I chose. I've seen us grow from few to many, seen the birth and death of a town and been instrumental in both. All I want is to know that when the day comes, the clan will continue to grow and prosper. I know that I won't be getting much rest since I'm here, but I want you all to know that I love you and am confident that you will do me proud!"

Each man approached and hugged him. They all had tears in their eyes. The last to come was Carlo.

Raven looked into the man's vivid blue eyes, and said. "It is difficult for you to hide your affection!"

Carlo sniffed, then said. "My father was killed when I was a small boy, so I never got to know him. I was raised by a succession of uncles and none really filled the void left by the passing of my father. I met you as an adult and though our relationship is in it's infancy, you've been a father as well as a dear friend. You've taught me through your actions what it really means to be a man honor. It is not that I find it difficult to mask my affection, but the thought that in the future I will be without your companionship, affection, wit and wise counsel!"

"You've got a silver tongue Carlo, you could talk a cat off the back of a fish truck!"

The men roared with laughter.

211

"What I want is to enjoy what is left of my life with the people I love. Carlo you have a special responsibility to the family, because you can walk in the white world unmolested. You are not bound by the same strictures of the blacks, so you and yours must serve as eyes and ears for the family, until the time when there is no need to do so. I firmly believe that time is coming. I may not see it, neither you men here, but your sons may, and it is you who will prepare them for that time. Make sure the children are educated like we did all of you. Carlo the continued success and survival of the clan, depends on your success and survival. Let it be known now that Carlo is a brother and to be accorded the respect, love, loyalty, honesty and support that goes with the role. If someone does him harm, they are doing us harm, and we will give no quarter or be a respecter of men! No mercy!"

* CHAPTER # 26 *

Sylvester "Silk" Mathis, was new in town. Silk was a pimp and had brought four whores with him from his hometown, Harlem New York. He drove a brand new Caddilac Sedan and was a flashy dresser. He was also a small time dope dealer with big time plans. He had rented a house in LaVilla and was making a name for himself. He had only been in town a couple of months and had killed two men already. He was paying Pike Richards, who had resorted to extorting from the black business owners. The Kanes were off limits, because they wouldn't pay in cash, but in the kind of trouble he shied away from.

Silk lay in bed with his bottom woman Bonnie Randle, who was a small perfectly proportioned woman. She had a single gold tooth on her canine. His other three women, Francine Shaw, a tall, dark skinned stunner, with fabulous breast and an apple shaped ass.

Angela Meyers, half white, half black woman with long red hair, a freckled face and luscious body. Lori Smith, a Mexican and black woman with the best of both sides. The skin complexion and hair of Mexico and the lips and body of Africa.

"I think we can make this burg home for a few." he lisped in his high pitched voice.

Silk was about 6'0" tall, and he weighed a thin 165 pounds. He was of mixed ancestry and it could be seen in his skin color and his demeanor. He wore his long dark hair in a pony tail, his mustache a thin line above his lip. He had striking green eyes

"I got y'all a wife in law on the line and she is just about ready for the stroll." he said confidently.

"Who is she?" Bonnie asked. "I hope it ain't one of them raggedy ass ho's from uptown!"

"Bitch, look around you." Silk shouted. "You know my taste, and raggedy ho's ain't it!" He leaned over and his hand flashed out swiftly and smashed into the side of her face.

It sounded like a pistol shot and her head snapped

back. Blood trickled from the corner of her mouth, as she mumbled. "I'm sorry daddy."

"You should've been sorry before you opened your damn mouth!" he said calmly. "Now get your ass on up and y'all hit the bricks. There's money out there to be made. Anyway, the woman's name is Josephine Jensen."

*

Josephine Jensen, was the ring leader of the young Kane women. She was called Josey and was hell on wheels. She had inherited her mother and grandmother's size. She was 6'0" tall, and a voluptuous 170 pounds. She had huge breast, wide hips, a round fat ass and slanted eyes. She was a dark skinned beauty and she loved the streets, as did her group.

You could always find Josey with Sharon Kane, Matty Kane, Jackie, Von, Marica, Charity, Lorraine, Betty and Raylene Mace.

The young women hit all of the night spots and usually left trouble in their wake. This Friday night they sat in the new Cougar Club, fending off the attention of would be suitors.

"I can't wait to meet this nigga you keep on talkin bout." Raylene said. "You make him sound like the best thing to hit planet earth since sunshine!"

All of the women laughed.

Raylene was called Ray by family and friends. She was a small woman who could damn near pass for white, her skin was so light.

"He is sister, and he's all mine." Josey said laughing. "He's supposed to pick me up at 11:00, then we're going to his place."

"I just know you ain't gave him none?" asked Von, who was a cute chubby woman with a beautiful smile.

"If I told y'all the details, y'all draws would get wet. Let me put it this way, he did shit to me, I didn't even know men did!"

The women all laughed again as Josey went on about her new man.

"Have the men met this guy yet?" Matty asked. Matty was a striking woman with beautiful reddish brown skin.

"I don't want them to meet him. He doesn't even know I'm a Kane!" Josey said. "I don't want him to know either!"

*   *   *   *

"I want y'all to go to the hotel and stay there tonight." said Silk. "I need a little time to pull this bird in the nest. Y'all gonna like her."

"What time do you want us to come home?" Bonnie asked.

"Get here early, say about 10:00."

The women went to him and kissed him, then headed for the door. They halted at the sound of his voice. "Just because I ain't watchin, don't mean slack up. Since y'all gonna have so much free time I wanna see plenty green when y'all step thru that door!"

*

Silk put on the powder blue zoot suit, white silk shirt, a beige tie, with white and powder blue accents. He put on a white straw fedora and cocked it at a rakish angle. He slipped into beige wingtip shoes that were highly glossed. A gold watch and four diamond rings glistened on his hands. He looked at himself in the mirror, then left.

*   *   *   *

"I think Tony Bates likes you, Josey." stated Raylene.

"Girl, when y'all see my man, you'll see why I don't like Tony!" Josey said.

A fine, red skinned woman named Doris Mack was an arch enemy of the Kane women. She was once the woman of L.J Sumner, that is until he met Rose Kane, Tim and Lucy's daughter. Rose stole her man or so she thought. She was in the Cougar Club with her sisters and cousins. Doris couldn't keep her eyes off of the table where Josey and the others sat. "Look at them ho's." Doris said. "They think they can just take what they want and fuck who's feelings get stepped on!"

"Dee I hope you ain't fixin to start no shit." said Doris's sister Linda.

"I'm just sayin, is all." Doris replied.

215

"I know how you is when you get on the subject, fuck L.J! He wasn't shit anyway besides them girls ain't the ones took him!" said Linda.

"All them ho's just alike, look at them." Doris said. "Them ho's would probably steal each other's men!"

"Oh girl look!" shouted Myrlie pointing to the front door of the club.

All of the women stared as Silk made his grand entrance. He paused at the door and panned the room, reached inside of his jacket, and pulled out a gold cigarette case. He moved purposely slow, his movement dramatic. He replaced the case, then pulled a gold lighter from his pocket and lit the long cigarette that dangled haughtily from his mouth. He replaced the lighter, then reached up and removed his hat as he again scanned the room. His entrance was a production designed to draw attention, and it had as always worked like a charm. He watched as Josey's eyes lit up.

"Tell me that ain't him?" said Betty.

"That's him," Josey said. "Ain't he gorgeous?"

"Leave that one alone Josey." Betty said seriously. "He's big trouble, with a capital B.I.G!"

The other women were looking at Silk, as he slowly approached their table with a pleasant smile.

"A man that good looking can't be good, trust me!" Betty said.

"You talkin like he too good for me." Josey said hotly. Josey had always been ridiculed because of the color of her skin. And she was sensitive to the racism that existed, even among her own kind. If you were darker than a paper bag, you fell in the nigger category.

"You know I don't think like that Josey!" said Betty as Silk grew nearer.

"That pretty nigga going to the table with them ho's!" Doris said angrily as she saw Silk stop in front of Josey.

"Hello beautiful." Silk said, taking Josey's hand and pulling her to her feet, where he embraced her and kissed her deeply. Silk worked his tongue in her mouth until she was dazed with lust, then he released her.

"My God man, you tryin to kill her!" Matty said laughing.

Josey stood there swooning, her panties growing increasingly wetter, as he gently squeezed her hand. She gathered her senses and introduced him to her cousins.

The name Kane kept ringing a bell in his head, but he couldn't remember from where. He sat down and ordered a round of drinks and they just sat and talked. Silk was an engaging conversationalist and had the women hanging on his every word. He looked at the crowd of women and saw a couple of other possibilities and smiled. The fox was in the hen house.

Doris looked at Linda, then rose form the table. Doris was fine, breast, hips, ass, the works. It was topped with her grey eyed beauty. She walked to where Silk sat with Josey, and said. "Excuse me sir, would you like to dance?"

Silk looked up into Doris beautiful face and went into pimp mode. He knew he could have her eating out of his hand, but now wasn't the time. He made a mental note to get with her later.

"The first thing you should do is apologize to my date, for being so rude and disrespectful!" Silk said sharply. "I know your manners are better than what you're displaying!"

Doris mouth dropped open at his retort and she frantically thought of a reply. Before she could speak, Silk rose elegantly from his chair and grasped her elbow.

He had noticed her eyeing the table enviously, so he knew where she was sitting. Quickly he escorted her back to her table and out of ear shot of the other women. He spoke smoothly. "There's a time and place for everything sweet heart and now is not the time or place. The last thing I'll allow, is for you to embarrass me or yourself. Leave your number and address with the bartender and I'll contact you later!"

She looked into his green eyes, and nodded. He turned and started walking back to Josey.

*

"Damn girl, did you see how he put her in her place just then?" Charity said loudly.

Josey just sat there, beaming with pride.

"Listen baby, I had hoped that we could go to this nice little restaurant for a late bite." Silk said to Josey softly. "Of course, I'd hate to take you away form your company!"

Josey looked at the others, then said. "I'll see y'all tomorrow.

Silk took her hand, bid the others goodnight and headed for the door. He stopped and walked over to the bar, slipped the Bartender a dollar and got Doris's address. He smiled inwardly at his ability to catch. He walked back to Josey and they went to his car and drove off.

"That nigga was smooth as butter!" Marcia said.

"A little too smooth for my taste." Betty said, knowingly. "Something about him just don't fit, but I can't put my finger on it. He just seems too contrived for me."

"I get the same feeling." Lorraine said.

Lorraine was a pretty cocoa brown skinned woman. She was at least 5'10" tall, with a nice shape and slightly slanted eyes. What made Lorraine stand out, was that she was bowlegged

"Y'all talkin like y'all don't trust the man and y'all don't even know him!" Von said defensively.

"That's just the point." Betty said. "She don't know him either. A nigga like that is not easily forgotten and he's too flamboyant to be a low key nigga. He's into something, what it is, I don't know!"

"I think you're right Betty." Lorraine said. "What kind of nigga don't want no girls folks to know him?"

"The kind that's up to something, if I got anything to say about it!" Betty replied.

"Y'all making me scared." said Jackie, a pretty dark skinned girl. She was tall and fine too. "We need to find them or put the word out before something bad happens!"

"Aw girl please," said her sister Von. "It ain't that bad. The nigga ain't gonna hurt her cause he know we all know what he looks like. Besides, how many pretty men in this town are named Sylvester?"

The woman all laughed and went back to partying. Betty joined in, but still she was bothered by the situation.

*

After they had eaten a light meal at the restaurant he told her about. They drove to his home where he gave her the royal treatment.

Josey had been having sex, but nothing like what she experienced with Silk. She had never had her cunt licked and Silk was a master. He licked, sucked, and nibbled on her until she lay quivering on the bed. Then he made passionate, long, gentle love to her with his 10 inch penis.

Josey had never felt the sensations he made her feel. It was like anywhere he touched her, set her off. He knew she was almost ready and he planned to start putting his game down when the others came home in the morning. He would make love to her off and on thru the night, to prime her.

* * * *

Bobby, Sha, Roger and Dennis came to the Cougar Club at about 1:30 that night looking for some action. They saw their cousins and walked to their table. "What's up girl?" asked Sha.

He and the others hugged the girls and got some chairs and sat down.

"Which one of you cheap niggas gonna buy the first round?" Bobby asked, sitting next to Betty. "Damn Betty, you look like somebody just killed your dog or some shit."

"I'm cool cuz, but I just been thinking about Josey and that nigga!"

"Josey and what nigga?" Bobby asked alertly.

"Some nigga named Sylvester. He from New York and that's all I know about him." she said.

"Any of y'all know that nigga Josey left here with?" Bobby asked.

"What nigga?" Sha, Roger and Dennis asked in unison. The conversation at the table turned to Josey and her new man.

"You mean to tell me, y'all let Josey leave here with a stranger?" Sha asked.

"It wasn't like that." Charity said. "She been knew him, from where I don't know."

"You say this nigga form New York? He a street nigga?" Roger asked.

"He don't dress like your average nigga off the street. That is one flashy cat!" Von said. "Good looking too!"

Roger looked at the other men, then said. "Red nigga, long hair in a ponytail?"

"Yeah that's him," Jackie said. "Y'all know him?"

"Nah, but we done heard bout him." Sha said.

"Come on boys we got to go!"

The four men rose and left the club.

Outside, Sha looked at the others, and said. "I bet it's

219

that nigga silk!"

"Yeah it sounds like him, but this time he picked the wrong prey!" Bobby said. "How we gonna find them?"

"It shouldn't be that hard. All we do is catch his ho's and they'll tell us where he is. We don't need but one of them." Dennis said. "You wanna bring in the others?"

"Nah, we can do it ourselves. Ain't no need in the girl being embarrassed in front of everybody." Bobby said.

The men jumped in two cars and went to find Silk's whores.

At about 5:00 that morning, Bobby and Sha spotted Bonnie getting out of a car and they drove over to her. She came to the car and leaned in the window.

"Hey babies," she said seductively. "It's gonna be extra for two of y'all. My little kitty kat been busy!"

"Get in," Sha said softly.

Bonnie got in the car and Bobby drove to the place where they agreed to meet, if they found one of the girls. When they pulled up Dennis and Roger were standing by the car with Lori. Bobby, Sha, and Bonnie got out of the car and walked over to the others.

"Hold on a minute fellas." Bonnie said. "That's my wife in- law, what have you boys got in mind? A little freaky tonight ain't we?"

"Nah girl, this ain't about trickin," Sha said. "We want some information and y'all gonna give it to us!"

"Information bout what?" Lori asked.

"Bout your nigga, " Bobby said. "We wanna know how to contact him!"

"I guess y'all got a reason?" Bonnie asked.

Sha stepped to her and slapped her viciously across the face, then said. "Bitch this ain't no time for questions, what we want is answers!"

"You ain't have to hit her!" Lori shouted angrily, her hand sliding surreptitiously into her purse. She moved closer to Bonnie, who stood cringing next to Sha. Her hand swiftly left her purse, in it was a gleaming straight Razor, that she slashed swiftly towards Sha's throat.

Only his quick reflexes saved him, as he leaned back. The razor made contact with his stiff collar, and his tie fluttered to the ground cleanly cut. She swung the razor back handed and he jumped back.

Bonnie had pulled her razor and was rearing back her

hand to strike, when Bobby's big fist crashed into her jaw. She fell to the ground limply, as Lori concentrated her attack on Sha. He stepped back and raised both hands out protectively. She moved in slashing with the razor.

He faked at her with his left and the razor followed. His right fist rocketed forward and smashed into her chin. Her head snapped back and she stumbled. He closed in and grabbed her wrist and twisted it viciously until the razor dropped from her numb fingers. He slapped her wickedly across both of her cheeks. The power of the two rapid blows, almost knocked her unconscious. She sagged and he pulled her back up to her feet. Her head lolled and bloody saliva leaked from her slack mouth.

Bobby picked Bonnie up and lay her on the back seat of the car. He shook her gently, until dazedly she shook her head from side to side. She sat up and looked confusedly around. "Where am I?" she asked.

"I need to see Silk." Bobby said softly.

Bonnie shook her head to clear it, trying to remember what had happened. She looked at the big, handsome, dark skinned man and her memory returned. Fear cloudy in her eyes, she asked. "Y'all ain't gonna hurt him are you?"

"I don't know." Bobby answered honestly. "You can take us to him and we'll see what needs to be done!"

Roger, looking over his shoulder said. "If you don't show us, all we got to do is find the other girls and follow them!"

"He's home," she said. "Promise me you won't kill him! Promise me!"

"We ain't promising you nothing. If he needs killin, he's a dead man!" Roger said.

Bonnie showed them where their house was. The women had keys and the four men eased in the house with the women. It was almost 6:00 in the morning and Lori lead them to the bedroom. They could hear the bed squeaking and the sounds of a woman deep in the throes of passion.

Sha walked to the door and gentle turned the knob, it moved in his hand and slowly he pushed it open. Bobby quickly stepped into the dimly lit room. The sight that greeted them, was Josey's legs thrown across Silk's shoulders, as he pistoned methodically in and out of her.

She screamed in pleasure as her orgasm hit, "Ohh baby...Yes....Yes!" her feet twitching.

"Watch out daddy!" Bonnie shouted.

Silk swiftly dropped Josey's legs and rolled over and dropped on the side of the bed. Bobby, Sha, Roger and Dennis had .45's in their hands. When Silk rolled from between Josey's legs and hit the floor, Roger was already there before he could recover. He brought the barrel of his pistol down in a wicked arch and clubbed Silk in the head. Silk slumped to the floor stunned, as blood flowed from his scalp wound.

Josey lay there in a sex induced daze, her legs spread wide, cunt gleaming with her juices. Dennis walked over, closed her legs, and slapped her sharply across the face. He pulled the covers up over her, and shouted. "Get dressed now!"

Slowly coming out of the fog of passion, she looked at him, and asked. "Dennis?"

"Get dressed." he said sternly, as Roger and Bobby dragged Silk naked from the room. They pulled him to the front room and tossed him unceremoniously to the floor. Lori and Bonnie rushed to the man's side.

There was the sound of a key in the door. Bobby and Dennis swiftly moved to each side of the door, as Sha and Roger moved from sight.

Francine and Angela walked in and paused. Bobby and Dennis shoved the two women to the floor, as Sha and Roger stepped out, their guns raised.

Silk looked up at the men, his green eyes flashing daggers at them. "What the fuck is this all about? Some bullshit robbery?"

"Nigga, we ain't no petty thieves!" Roger said.

"Yeah, y'all hoodlums!" Josey shouted as she walked in. "Sylvester ain't done nothing to y'all!"

"Yes hell he did!" Bobby said. "That punk nigga tryin to make you a ho!"

"Make me a ho? What the hell is that supposed to mean and who are them bitches all over my man?"

"That sorry ass nigga a pimp and that's his stable. Them his ho's!" Dennis said.

Josey never wondered if what was said was true because she knew her cousins wouldn't lie to her about something like this. She looked down at Silk and the four women draped on him and moved closer. "So, I was gonna be one of your ho's, huh?"

He looked up at her, and said. "Pimpin is what I do. Look at my women, beautiful aren't they? You should feel honored that I wanted you to be part of this!"

He watched the transformation in her eyes, saw the tears well up and knew he had misjudged her. She would've fought tooth and nail, not to sell herself. Her foot shot forward and crashed into his nose breaking it. She went wild, kicking and stomping the dazed man.

Bonnie and Lori jumped up from the floor to attack her, but Josey had gone berserk. Her hand clawed at Bonnie's face and gouged four bloody streaks above her right eye, across her nose and down to the left side of her face. Bonnie screamed in pain and reeled backward. She tripped over Silk's semi-limp body and crashed to the floor. Her head struck the polished wood floor with a resounding thud and she lapsed into unconsciousness.

Lori moved in on Josey's left and Josey turned to meet her. Josey's longer reach enabled her to punch Lori in the mouth before she got in striking distance. Lori's head snapped back and Josey hit her again. Lori stumbled and dropped to her knees and Josey kicked her in the stomach. Lori folded over and slumped to the floor with the wind knocked out of her.

Josey turned back to Silk and the other two women and launched a flurry of kicks, until she was breathing heavy and covered in a fine sheen of sweat. Exhausted she stopped.

The men had made no effort to help her and she had done considerable damage to them. They were all bruised and bloodied.

There was the sound of sirens, as a patrol car quickly slammed on brakes. A few seconds later, there was a loud knocking at the door.

"Open up police!" A voice shouted.

No one moved to open the door and suddenly it crashed open and Slo Lewis rushed in, followed by Tip Byers a new deputy. Both men had their service revolvers in hand. They looked up and saw four men pointing big .45 automatics at them. Slo and Tip froze.

"Just put the guns in their leather and you'll walk out of here alive!" Sha said sternly.

Tip looked to Slo for instructions and saw Slo ease his gun into the holster. Tip followed suit. Slo looked at the battered and bloody group on the floor and asked. "What going on here?"

"None of your business Slo." Bobby said. "Just go on and get in your car and leave. This a family matter!"

Slocum looked at the four men, then touched Tip on the arm and headed out the door. When they got in the car, Slo turned to Tip, and said. "We were never here, got it?"

Tip looked him in the eyes, and asked. "Are them Kanes above the law?

"You been living here all your life and you know about the Kanes, so how the hell could you ask me that?"

Tip just hunched his shoulders, crank the car and pulled off.

When the Kanes were sure that Silk was fully conscious, Sha walked over to him, and said. "Today is your lucky day. I like the fact that your girls got balls, so I'm gonna do you this favor. Remember, this one's on me, the next one's on you. You got one hour to pack what you can and get out of town. If you ever come back to this city, or county, you'll receive no quarter. You'll be killed on sight, so get your shit and disappear!"

Silk was a long way from being a coward and it just clicked where he knew the name Kane from. He had heard it frequently, and thought the Kanes were the stuff of legend. An urban myth that would give the niggas here something to look up to. Now he knew it was real, but that didn't lessen the pain and humiliation that he felt. He knew he couldn't win against them and he didn't have a death wish. He looked in Sha's eyes and knew the wrong decision would cost him his life.

"You better get on the ball nigga, your hour runnin out fast and if you're here when it does, your ass is dead!" Bobby stated emphatically.

Silk nodded and rose shakily to his feet. The four women rose as well. "Y'all hurry up and pack, cause we about to blow this burg!"

"We'll escort you to the city line. Come back thru here again and we could take that to mean you're seeking revenge. And if that is the case, you might as we'll get a pistol and eat it!" said Sha. "I wouldn't make St. Augustine home either if I were you, too tempting!"

* CHAPTER # 27 *

The Kanes prospered in the drug trade and in their relationship with the Torronelli's.

Raven died in his sleep after a lengthy illness on what was called D-Day. The day America stormed the shores of Normandy, June 6, 1944. His passing momentarily threw the family into chaos. Ransom, Drake, Trace, Tim, Lao, Turk, Prince, Lefty, Juan, Jose and Blake were the elders and they fought the younger men to keep the family together. Their only allies among the younger men were Baron, Will, Bobby, Nelson and Sha. All of the younger men wanted to branch out and each have his own operation.

Dennis and Roger were extremely vocal since they had already picked their spot. The city was growing and the population steadily increased. Times were difficult, not financially because the drug trade was profitable.

Carlo had got Baron involved in hijacking shipments. Not shipments of drugs, but anything that was in trailers. Kanes shipping and storage was now Kanes Trucking. Raven had left the company to Baron and Will, at Celia's insistence. Celia knew that when Raven died things would change and she knew that Baron's future was tied to Will and Carlo, so she made arrangement for the three men to work closely before Raven passed.

Celia had grown a great deal under Raven's hand. She had sat at his feet as he spoke of times gone by and their connection to times to come. She saw how he handled situations and always tried to think ahead. In 20 years or so she had learned to think as he did. And even though she was younger than many of the Kane women she was looked at as the matriarch. She was respected for her wisdom and her one thought was for the survival of the family.

Nelson was her constant companion, as he was Raven's. There was still time for him to engage in other pursuits. He met and married a beautiful dark skin girl named, Annette Ray.

Bobby Kane married Doris Mack and Sha married her sister Linda. Bobby and Doris had a stormy heated relationship. When they fought, they fought hard and when they loved, they loved hard. Sha and Linda weren't the perfect couple, but they knew how to keep their problems behind their doors.

Dennis and Roger had made a pick up for the Don, as Carlo was now called in Miami. They spotted two black men there and after they found out who the men were, they came to Miami with their brothers. They robbed and executed the men who they found out were drug dealers. When they came home they moved all of their families out of LaVilla into what at the time was called Sweet Water and set up shop. After their product ran out they brought product from Baron and Will because none of the other family would deal with them.

It was Celia, who convinced Baron, Will and Carlo to do business with them. She told them that if the family's future was what they wanted to insure, then doing business with them could only inrich the family. The more money they made, the more they'd spend. After the men thought it out, they saw that she was right.

When the other young men saw what happened they all wanted to branch out and do their own thing. But, unlike Dennis and Roger they didn't have the capital.

Baron called a meeting of all the Kane men. The farm was crowded with cars as the men met in the big barn like structure. Kanes, Maces, Jensens, Sumners, yet all under the Kane banner. Baron brought up what the young wanted to do and with the help of Will and Carlo convinced Ransom and the elders with Celia's philosophy. After the men thought it out and saw how large the family was and in time would be. They agreed to set aside funds for the young men to branch out.

Celia had told Baron, Will and Carlo, that things had to change for the family to grow and prosper. There would always be a first family and they were the ones Raven chose. She had told them time and time again how far ahead Raven thought. She pointed to the time he spent with them,(Nelson and young Bishop). She urged them to think back to the conversations and when they did, his words came to them. And they saw her words were true.

She explained their places in the scheme of things. Baron, youngest male son of King Raven and Queen Celia. Will, son of Prince Drake and Princess Lisa. Carlo, Crown King of the Torronelli's. She used archaic terms to describe the present, and Carlo was into history so he understood her perfectly. He explained to Baron and Will a monarchy. Showed them the co-relation between it, and their situation. It clicked and all three men looked at Celia with new respect. She became their counselor and they prospered.

In the years up until Raven's death, Baron had fathered three more children, Brandon, Celia and Lola.

Will Mace had fathered three more besides he and La Vern's first born, Lil Will. And they were Denise, Donna and Erik.

Carlo had fathered two more, Gianni and Ann Maria. As they grew, so did the others and soon a whole new generation of Kanes were coming.

America bombed Japan and soon the war was over in 1945. It seemed the economy picked up and suddenly the car companies were pushing out new models. It wasn't long before America got involved in the Korean Conflict. In 1950, the U.S. sent troops to assist the South Koreans. Congress never declared war on Korea, but American soldiers fought and died there.

* CHAPTER # 28 *

In December of 1958, Murphy and Esther Johnson moved to Jacksonville from Douglas, Georgia. They brought the whole family and it was a scene straight from the Beverly Hillbillies. Murphy drove a big truck with all of their worldly goods strapped to it. The truck looked like it shouldn't have made it that far and wouldn't go another mile. With Murphy and Esther came their brood of children, Junior, Bopete, Ulyssess, Merlie, Anna Mae and Tyrel.

Esther had been a child bride and was only 13 years older than her oldest son Junior who was 23. Her children were born almost a year a part. Bopete was 22, Ulysses was 21 and that's where it changed. Merlie was 17, Anna Mae 15 and Tyrel was 14. Anna Mae had just turned 15 on Dec. 22nd ,and hated the move.

Murphy had gotten a job at a paper plant in Jacksonville after the one he worked for in Douglas had closed. Being a good worker, his former boss had helped him secure work at the plant, since he was going to be managing it. It was a good paying job for the time and he moved his family into a nice two story house on Dellwood. They lived only three doors down from where Baron and Lois lived with their children.

Bishop at the time was 17 and he was a ladies man to the core. Bishop had dropped of out school in the 10th grade and was working for Baron and Will at the trucking company. He was also involved in the drug trade. Bishop was driving trucks and in on the hijacking of goods. He made good money, yet still lived with Baron and Lois in their big house.

One day when Bishop got off work his brother Brandon was standing in the yard waiting for him. Brandon was 15 and he idolized his big brother.

"Man, some people just moved in a few doors down. And the two girls I saw are out of sight." Brandon said excitedly.

"Oh yeah?" Bishop asked slightly interested.

"You got to see them bro." Brandon replied.

"I ain't got time to now." Bishop said. "Cat, is

waiting for me."

Cat, was Catherine Drew, a fine red bone, who was Bishop's off and on woman.

"Can I go out with you tonight?" Brandon asked hopefully. "It's Friday night, I don't think daddy would care."

"We'll do something tomorrow Bran, I promise." said Bishop.

Brandon knew Bishop would keep his word, so he reluctantly agreed. "Still, you got to see them broads man!"

"I will bro, but not right now." Bishop said as they walked into the house. "Is ma home?"

"Nah, she's at the store with Grandma Celia!"

Bishop playfully punched Bran on the shoulder, then went to his room to get dressed. Bishop thought of himself as a fashion plate, and he was meticulous in his dress. He had a full length mirror in his spacious room and he used it often. He put on a navy blue pinstripe suit, a robins egg blue shirt and to add a dash of color, a crimson tie and pocket square. He put on lace up cap-toed shoes, that were shined to the point that they almost looked like patent leather. Then he grabbed his fedora and put it on. He looked at himself in the mirror, then cocked his brim at a rakish angle, smiled at his reflection and stepped from the room.

His father's voice stopped him. "You looking pretty sharp Bish, got a hot date?"

Bishop turned to his father, and smiled. "Yeah, I got a hot one!"

"Know anything bout them folk just moved in down there?" Baron asked. "I hear the daughters are lookers."

"You see them yet?" Bishop asked.

"I asked you first nigga." Baron said laughing.

"I bet we getting our information form the same source." Bishop said laughing.

Baron laughed too, then said. "The boy a Kane, he got good taste so you might wanna check them out!"

"You got that right." Bishop said. " I got to go daddy, me and Cat just got back together. And I don't wanna have to put up with none of her mess!"

Baron laughed, as he watched Bishop walk out the door. Bishop wasn't as tall, or as big as most of the Kane and Sumner men. He only stood about 5'11, but he weighed about 215. He was built well and had played football and basketball in high school. He was quite an athlete.

As Bishop walked out onto the porch he saw two fine cocoa brown skinned girls coming towards him. They were dressed like it was still in the 1800's. Long dresses that fell well over their knees, stockings, hard buckled shoes and they were bundled in thick jackets to combat the cold. He looked at their faces and thought they must be twins because they looked so much alike. He bounded down the steps and stood next to his Ford Fairlane. He waited until they drew near, then he spoke. "Good evening ladies, enjoying the brisk weather?"

The girls stopped, looked at him and giggled. Anna Mae was bold where Merlie was shy, so she spoke to the handsome young man. "It ain't no colder than where we from."

Bishop looked into her dark eyes, and thought, "damn she's cute." So just where are you from?"

"You askin all them questions and ain't even asked us our name, nor told us yours." Anne Mae said haughtily.

Bishop smiled, then in an apologetic tone said. "Please forgive my rudeness and in no way let it reflect on my parents, they raised me better. There is never an excuse for being rude, but please let me offer an explanation. See, momentarily I was stunned by your beauty, and it stilled my tongue. Once I gathered my wits, I knew I had to say or do something that would make you stop, so I could see if what I saw was real, or just a figment of my imagination. Now I see it was reality and I feel it's my duty to feast visually on your beautiful face."

Anna Mae hung on his every word and Merlie fell in love with him then and there. But, Bishop only had eyes for young Anna Mae. He extended his hand and said. "I'm Bishop Kane!"

Anna Mae took his big hand in hers, and said. "I'm Anna Mae Johnson, this my sister Merlie and we from Douglas Georgia!"

"It is a pleasure to meet you Anna Mae, you too Merlie. I hope that we can get together sometime and maybe see a movie or something!" Bishop said still holding her hand.

"We'll see," she said making no effort to pull her hand free.

"Anna Mae, we better get on to the store, before mamma send somebody to check on us." Merlie said timidly.

Bishop reluctantly released her hand, and said. "I'll see you later!"

Anna Mae smiled and boldly stared in his eyes, then she and Merlie walked down the street. Bishop watched them walk away, then thought, "I wonder what she's built like." He got in his car and drove off.

*

When Bishop arrived at Tip-Top, he saw that all of his boys were there. He walked over to the table where Lil Will sat with Cat and his girl Lissa Jackson. Cat and Lissa were cousins and Lissa was a red bone too, but she was a tall, slim fine woman. He saw that Cat had rocks in her jaws.

She was 21 years old and she had been with Bishop off and on, since he was 15. He walked to the table and bent to give her a kiss and she turned her head. His lips landed on her cheek and she said. "You couldn't leave the ho in time to be here with me?"

Bishops eyes blazed and he clenched his teeth to keep from snapping on her. "Don't start girl." he said softly.

Bishop had his group of young men, all Kanes. There was Lil Will, Bobby Jr. who was called B.J. the son of Bobby and Doris. Adam, the son of Sha and Linda. Devon, the son of Dennis and Stacy. Robert, the son of Roger and Nona. They were all teenagers, but they were in the dope game, gambling and stealing. Ransom, Drake, Trace, Tim and Lefty still owned Tip-Top, so the younger Kanes had no problem getting in.

Bishop sat down next to Cat, and asked. "What y'all drinking?"

"If you would've been here on time, you'd know." she said scathingly.

Bishop looked at her, then stood, grabbed her by the arm and snatched her up. "Y'all have a good time, cause it's obvious I won't!" He said to Lil Will and Lissa. Then he roughly pulled Cat from the room.

"I left my purse." she said shakily, as Bishop walked silently and swiftly to his car.

He unlocked the passenger side door, opened it and shoved her in. Then, went back and got her purse. He came back to the car, got in, tossed her purse in her lap and pulled off. He never said a word.

"Where we going?" she asked.

He didn't even acknowledge her, he just drove. It

didn't take her long to see that he was taking her home. He pulled up in front of her house, got out and opened her door. He pulled her roughly from the car.

"Oh, you gonna bring me home, so you can go be with one of your ho's!" Cat shouted. "I ain't gonna stay home, I bet you that!"

Bishop's hand rose swiftly and he slapped her sharply on the cheek. Her shouting stopped when his hand impacted. He grabbed her arm and drug her to the door. He had his own key so he unlocked the door and took her in. She was still in shock because he had never struck her.

He knew she had every reason to say and do the things she did. Because everything she accused him of, he had done to her time and time again. But, he was fed up with her mouth, regardless to the wrong he had done.

"I don't wanna hear another whining word from you Cat! he said angrily. "I'm bending over backwards to try to please you, but you still given me shit. I did you wrong and that's done. I can't change it, but I damn sure don't need you throwin it in my face every time I'm late or you suspect me of doing something. Either let that shit go, or let me go!"

She looked in his eyes and knew she had pushed him to the edge. She had been on him constantly for the last few weeks. Badgering him to move in, marry her if he loved her and all sort of other things. She thought quickly and decided to use another tactic. She really loved him and for one so young, he was a hell of a lover and provider. She hadn't worked in two years.

She looked at him and her eyes filled with tears, and she said. "All I want is for you to love me baby!"

Her tears washed away his anger and he drew her into his arms. "Listen sugar. You want a lot of things I ain't willing to give right now, but that don't mean I don't love you. I just don't want the shit we been going thru to keep on. We won't make it like that. Shit, I don't know how we'll make it, if you don't learn to trust me!"

"I'm scared I'm gonna lose you baby." she said her voice breaking, as the tears flowed freely.

"You ain't gonna lose me, you gonna drive me away carrying on like you do." he said softly.

"You fixin to go?" she asked.

"Nah, I ain't going nowhere!

She moved back and looked up into his face, and

said. "I love you so much!" Then she took his hand and lead him to the bedroom.

She slowly undressed as he stood there watching. When she was naked, she moved back to the bed, lay on her back and spread her thick thighs for him.

He watched her as her hands slowly began to glide over her smooth red skin. He saw her lightly pinch her nipples until they were erect. He saw her hands as they slid downward and delved into her bushy pubic area. He began to undress and move closer.

By the time he was naked and standing over her. She had worked herself into a near frenzy. He saw two of her fingers plunging in and out of her wet, hairy hole as she stared at his swollen member. He moved closer and got on the bed between her legs. She reached for him with her free hand and pulled him closer. Her fingers came from her wet slot, and she guided him in. He felt her warmth envelope him and he trust forward slowly. Her hips rose to draw him in deeper, and he was fully engulfed in her treasure. He thrust with long, deep strokes and she rose to meet him. Her hips moved faster and faster as he drilled her with his rock hard shaft.

She moaned loudly, "Ummm....Hmm....Ohh....!" as she felt her orgasm flooding thru her. She bucked wildly beneath him as the flood gates burst. He felt her contracting on his rod and the squeezing motion sent him over the edge. As he exploded, Anna Mae's face flashed in his mind!

*   *   *   *

Anna Mae and Merlie sat on the porch looking up at the stars.

"Notice how the stars seems farther away here than back home Merl?"

"Yeah, they do don't they?" Merlie said wistfully. "You miss home Anna?"

"Sort of," Anna answered. "But I'm kind of curious too. I ain't seen all there is to see here and I want to!"

"I wanna go back home Anna!" Merlie said. "I'm missin Pete something fierce!"

"Aw girl, you'll forget him. Soon as one of these city boys start sniffin around!" Anna said laughing. "I know you and Pete use to do it, what it feel like Merl?"

"You is a nosy heifer, ain't you." Merlie said

laughing. "At first it hurt a little, but then it felt real good. I know you done played with it Anna, but let me tell you ain't nothing like a man bein in you. It makes you feel whole Anna!"

Anna giggled, and asked. "You think that Bishop Kane fella meant what he said, about the movie?"

"Girl, I just know you ain't thinking bout that rascal. I wouldn't place no bets on his word, if you ask me." Merlie said secretly wishing that Anna wouldn't take a liking to Bishop, because she wanted him.

"I believe him!" Anna said emphatically. "He don't look like the lying kind!"

"You ain't seen him but one time and you can tell what type of man he is?" Merlie asked incredulously. "I hope you ain't got your sights set on that boy!"

"One thing he ain't, is a boy!" Anna said defensively. "He a man if ever I saw one and he gonna be my man too, just watch!"

Merlie shook her head and threw away her thought of ever having Bishop as her own. Even though Anna Mae was younger, she was a strong willed woman and she got that from their mother. When they set their mind or sight on something, they wouldn't be denied.

"Y'all heifers get on in here!" Esther shouted.

They rose and looked a last time at the stars. Just then a shooting star blazed brilliantly across the inky, blue black night sky. Anna closed her eyes and quickly made a wish. She opened her eyes, and saw the star appear to burn out. Soon it lost it's radiance and disappeared. Anna's face broke into a big smile because she knew Bishop Kane would be hers.

*   *   *   *

On New Years Eve Bishop saw Anna and her younger brother Tyrel walking to the store. It was a warm day, not like winter at all. He stood on the porch and looked at them approach. Then he bounded down the steps and met them in front of his house.

"How are y'all doing?"

"We fine," Anna said blessing him with a smile. "I hope you're having a good day too!"

"It would be better if I could take you to the movies

later today." Bishop said smiling.

"You'd have to ask my folks for permission." Anna said.

"Hell, why don't we just do that then." he said taking her hand and turning her back towards their house.

She stopped, and asked. "Don't you think I ought to do my business first?"

He laughed, then let her hand go. "I'll go with you." he said smiling.

They walked to the store in silence. Once they were inside, he asked her and Tyrel if they wanted anything. They shook their heads and picked up the items they were told to purchase then left.

As they walked pass the Kanes house, Bishop's sister Celia came onto the porch. She was in the mold of Mandy, a big girl for 16. She stood nearly 6' feet, and was a dark skinned girl. "Watch out for that nigga girl, he ain't no good!" she said to Anna.

"I'm tellin ma, Celia." he said angrily.

"I'm just playing." Celia said quickly. She knew Lois would whip her ass for bad mouthing her brother to folks.

"Bish, I was just jokin for real!" she shouted.

Bishop looked at her and continued on to the Johnson's house.

They walked up on the porch and Bishop stopped, and said. "I'll stay here, tell your folks I'd like to talk to them!

Anna nodded, then walked thru the door shouting. "mamma, mamma, somebody wants to talk to you!"

"Girl, you better quit hollerin in my house!" Esther shouted as she walked from the kitchen. "Who is it that wants to talk to me?"

Merlie walked into the room, just as Anna said. "Bishop Kane!"

Esther looked at Anna, then said. "Don't you dare be rude chile, invite him in!"

Anna walked back outside and returned with him. Esther watched the finely built young man walk into her house and thought, he's a handsome lil devil.

"Good day mam, I'm Bishop Kane and I live a few doors down. Perhaps you've met my folks?"

"No baby, I ain't had time to meet nobody, what with getting settled and all. A few people done came over and give me the run down on what's what. And the Kanes were mentioned in the same sentence with being good people, so I take it your folks are popular around these parts.!" Esther said smiling.

Bishop was instantly at ease with her and he laughed at her off key brand of whit. "Mrs. Johnson, I'd like to take Anna to the movies if it's alright with you." Bishop said. "I'd get her home before nightfall!"

Esther looked at him closely, then said. "I ain't got no real problem with that, but her pa might have a fit."

"Is there a way I could get in touch with him?" Bishop asked.

"No not right now, he's working." Esther said. "I'll go on and let her go, but you respect her, hear me?"

"Yes ma'am, and I'll take good care of her." Bishop said. "If Mr. Johnson returns before we do, you can tell him we went to the Strand theater!"

Esther laughed, and said. "You're a smart one, I'll grant you that."

"Would y'all like to come bring the New Year in with us?" Bishop asked Esther.

"Let me ask Murphy when he gets in." Esther said. "Anna, go put on something presentable."

She ain't gotta change, Bishop said. "Her clothes look fine."

"Boy, you got a lot to learn about women. How old are you anyway?"

"I turned 17, in October." he said.

"Anna turned 15, this month." Ester said. "The 22nd."

"Well, I'll go home and wait for Anna to get dressed." he said. "Send Ty to get me when you're ready Anna. It was a pleasure meeting you Mrs. Johnson. Bishop walked home and sat on the porch, and soon Brandon joined him.

"I told you them girls were foxes, didn't I?" Brandon said. "Which one you gonna leave me?"

Bishop laughed and playfully slapped Brandon upside the head. "Anna is mine, so if you can catch Merlie, you can have her."

"So I got the old one then?" Brandon asked.

"I guess so," Bishop replied laughing. "I'm fixin to take Anna to the movies."

"Dang, why didn't you tell me and I would've asked Merlie to go?"

"Nah bro. I want Anna all to myself!" Bishop said.

"You slick Bish." Brandon said winking and punching him in the shoulder.

The young men sat there and talked for a few until Bishop saw Tyrel coming.

"Well I got to go." he told Brandon. "Tell ma, the Johnson's gonna bring in the New Year with us."

"You know Grandma Celia, Uncle Ran, Uncle Carlo and the other gonna be here!" Brandon said.

"That's good then, I'll introduce them."

Bishop met Tyrel, who told him that Anna was ready. He and Tyrel got in his car and drove to the Johnson's house.

"What you been up to Ty?" Bishop asked.

"Just getting ready for school." Tyrel answered.

"Must be hard leavin all your friends behind and moving to a new place?" Bishop asked.

"Not really," Tyrel said. "I don't miss much, maybe the girls, but that's it."

Tyrel was a light skinned, thin, handsome young man and Bishop knew the kid must be quite a hit with the young girls.

"You won't miss them long Ty, trust me." Bishop said smiling as they stopped in front of Ty's house. "If you want some part time work, I can get you a job for after school."

Tyrel's eyes lit up, as he asked. "Can you really?"

"Yeah I can do it. My daddy will get you some part time work."

They got out of the car and Bishop was stopped in his tracks when Anna stepped out of the door. Her hair was done up in the latest style and she wore an emerald green dress that complimented her cocoa brown skin. She smiled shyly and Bishop whistled. Gone was the young country girl and in her place stood a beautiful young woman.

He walked slowly towards her and asked in a questioning tone. "Anna?"

She smiled and stepped towards him. He took her hand and said. "Girl you clean up pretty good!"

Anna giggled and slapped playfully at his shoulder. He guided her to the car, opened her door and helped her in. Then hurried to his side, got in and drove off.

"That boy likes Anna." Esther said shaking her head.
"He don't know what he's in for."
"She don't know what she's in for, you mean."
Merlie said. "He a man ma!"
"That he is," Esther said.

*   *   *   *

Frankie Torronelli was almost as big as his father at
18. And was dating 16 year old, Donnatella LoCasa, who was
the daughter of Giancarlo's solider Guido.
 Donnatella was a beautiful girl. She had the classic
hour glass shape, olive complexion skin that made her look as
if she had a year round tan, beautiful dark eyes and full lips,
but her most startling feature was her hair. It was long and
glossy black, except for two small sections upfront that framed
her face. The hair there was snow white. The midwife that
delivered her said Donnatella was marked for greatness and
her mother Aria believed it. Donnatella was an only child and
was treated like a princess. What was amazing was the fact
that she wasn't spoiled.
 Frankie, was back from college for the holidays and
had just really paid attention to Donnatella, though he had
long ago knew her. They were an item and Guido was pleased
that Carlo's son had taken a liking to his princess.
 Frankie had decided to throw a party New Years Day
and Sophia had gone wild with the arrangements. She had
enlisted the aid of Lois, Lavern, Doris and Linda. As always,
Celia was involved and she worked to bring the Kane and
Torronelli families closer together.
 Sophia didn't ask Fiora her sister in-law to assist, as
Fiora was racist, as was her husband Salvator, Carlo's brother.
There was a division in the Torronelli family, as Sal was
greedy. He wanted to rule and it was impossible as long as
Carlo was alive.

*   *   *   *

Don Paschal Locata, had moved to Tampa from New
York. And thru murder and mayhem took over the mob scene
there. He was a man with grand vision and saw the South as
his. The only obstacle in his way was Carlo Torronelli and he
knew that a frontal attack against Carlo would be suicidal. So

he planned more subtle means.

It was New Years Eve and Don Paschal sat in the living room of the suite he had rented at the Hyatt Regency in Jacksonville. He had four bodyguards and was leery of dealing with Sal Torronelli, who was due at any minute. He knew he could never trust a man who would conspire to kill his own brother.

There was a knock at the door and one of the bodyguards went to the peep hole, turned to the Don, and said. "They're here!"

"Well let them in and stay on your toes, this could be a trap!" The body guard opened the door and Sal stepped in with Joe Green. The bodyguard frisked them and they came to the Don. "Have a seat." Don Paschal said.

The men sat and Don Paschal looked at Sal, and said. "Let's get the show on the road. You said you had a proposition for me?"

Sal nodded his head, then said. "That's true. You want to take over the South and I'm the man to give you what you want, on the condition that Jacksonville is mine!"

"I see," the Don said. "And what's to stop you from going back on your word once this is done?"

"A desire for a good working relationship with your family." Sal replied.

The Don laughed, then said. "Greed is one of my greatest fears. Not for me, but for those who work with me. You are a very ambitious man Sal and in time you may begin to eye my position. So far the South is open and you Torronellis control most of the eastern seaboard from here to Miami. You mean you're willing to relinquish all of that, for one city?"

"Damn right I am, if the one city is this one." Sal said.

"You know our alliance would signal the demise of Carlo?" "That's a sacrifice I'm willing to make." Sal said.

"Alright then. I guess we got a deal." the Don said. "Leave the details to me and I'll contact you after the deed is done!"

Sal and Joe Green rose, shook the Don's hand and left.

*

"It can't get back that we had our hands in this." Sal said to Joe. "Don't change anything, but whatever you do stay away from Carlo, since we don't know when Locata will strike."

Joe nodded his head and the men got in their car and drove off.

*

"You know why I sent you away to college, right?" Carlo asked Frankie.

"I've got an idea." Frankie answered.

"One day you will sit in my place." Carlo said. "The old way of doing things is over. Times change and this thing of ours has to change with the times. That's one thing I learned from Raven. The government is getting better at what they do, so we have to get better too. The way to do that is thru education and legit enterprises. You'll make your bones soon and then you'll officially be in. Being my son opens a lot of doors, but expectations will be high. Remember the only expectations you have to live up to are your own. Not mine, your mother's, or anyone else. I sent you out of state for a reason, but I expect you to transfer to a college in town to get your degree. I'll need you here with me!"

"Pappa, there something I wanted to say about the school issue."

"What is it?" Carlo asked.

"I already transferred to Jacksonville University for the spring semester.!"

"You what?" Carlo asked.

"Already transferred," Frankie said. "I anticipated you needing me, plus Jimmy was going thru a lot of changes up North."

"What kind of changes?" Carlo asked concerned.

"He was left with a lot of free time and you know how he is." Frankie said.

"Well, I guess the girls up there will miss you huh?" Carlo said. "We'll get to work after the New Year. No need to wait around."

"I'm glad you're not angry I made a decision of that magnitude without consulting you." said Frankie.

Carlo looked at his eldest son and was filled with pride. He knew Frankie would do him proud. "I respect your

wishes son. I've raised you to be a responsible man and you're a man now. It's time you made your own decisions!"
Frankie hugged his father. Carlo broke the embrace and reached for a decanter filled with an amber colored liquid. He grabbed two glass, gave one to Frankie, then filled them. He looked in his son's eyes, held up his glass to toast, and said. "To the future!"

    *   *   *   *

It was getting to be around dusk when Bishop pulled up in front of the Johnsons house, and blew his horn. The front door opened and Anna's brother Bopete, stepped out.
Bopete was a jet black man, with smooth shiny skin. He was classically handsome, his long black hair was processed and whipped up into a glistening duck tail. He wore a sharp silvery grey, silk and wool suit, shined cap-toe shoes and he held a black fedora clasped in his right hand. He smiled and there was a glint from the weak sunlight off of his gold tooth. He walked over to Bishop's side of the car, and asked. "You the nigga seein Anna Mae?"
Bishop pushed open his door and stepped out. "Is there a problem brother?" Bishop asked. "I'm Bishop Kane. I live a few doors down with my folks, ask around about us!"
"I did." Bopete said smiling and extending his hand. "Ty told me you gonna get him a part time job. I was wondering if you could get me some work. I'm down at the paper mill and I make good dough, but I ain't no nine to five type nigga, if you know what I mean!"
Bishop looked at him and knew he was a hustler. "Come to my house tonight at about 11:30. I got some family you should meet."
Bopete turned and walked back to the house. He stopped at the door, and said over his shoulder. "By the way, my pa wants to meet you!"
Bishop walked to the passenger side and helped Anna out. Anna wasn't used to the way Bishop treated her. It never occurred to her that a man could be so considerate. She had stars in her eyes and was hoping the day would never end.
He escorted her to the door and she walked thru. She reached back and grabbed his hand and pulled him inside. It seemed like her whole family was there.
He stopped, then said. "Hello, I'm Bishop Kane!"

Anna's father stepped forward and extended his hand, then said. "I've heard good things about your family. I've also heard that you're a fine young man, though a hell raiser. What are your intentions with my daughter?"

"I don't know yet, we've only just met. I won't disrespect her, you or your family and I'll protect her with my life. I'll try to show her things she's never seen. Take her to places I think she will like to go. Give her things I'd like to see her with and enjoy the time I'm allowed to be with her." Bishop said.

Bopete looked at Bishop from across the room and thought, "this is a smart young nigga. I got to get to know him."

Bishop's little speech had touched Anna deeply and she fought to contain the tears that welled in her eyes.

Esther looked at Merlie and saw the wishful look in her eyes and thought. "Poor Merlie." She done gave her heart to a man who she could never have. Anna would get Bishop, she could hear it in the tone of his voice, when he spoke about her.

Anna introduced Bishop to her brothers. It became a family joke to address him by his whole name, as if it were one name, Bishop Kane.

*   *   *   *

Carlo, Sophia, Frankie, Donnatella, Baron, Lois, Grandma Celia, as she was now called since Baron's daughter was also named Celia. Will and Lavern, Ransom and Emma, Blake and Laine, Trace and Myra, Drake and Lisa and several more Kanes. Bishop had invited the Johnsons and introduced them to the family.

Jimmy Lewis was there with a pretty light skinned woman named Irene, who he had met when they came back home.

At the stroke of midnight the champagne was popped, and the party began in Ernest. It was late when they stopped, but tomorrow Frankie was having a party at the Torronelli Estate.

* CHAPTER # 29 *

Frankie's party was a success and he worked closely with Carlo for the next few months. He was like a sponge, he absorbed all of the information his father gave him and even came up with a few solutions to on going problems.

Bishop and Anna started a heavy romance that could only end at the alter. He dropped Cat and the other women he messed around with to concentrate on Anna. He had never met anyone so innocent. He showered her with gifts and they grew together.

On New Years night Bishop introduced Bopete to his father. Bopete was soon selling and using heroin. He was a ladies man, and that's what killed him. He had hooked up with a young lady named Ida Mae Wells. She was a pretty red girl of 18 years. Bopete was also sleeping with Ida Mae's mother, Norma, who was fine herself. Ida Mae killed Bopete when she found out.

In July of 1959 Carlo, Frankie, James and Guido were at the docks. Carlo was there with Ransom and Baron.

"I don't know who it was that dropped a dime on the shipment, but I plan to find out!" Carlo said angrily. "It's never happened before, cause they're paid to see that it doesn't!"

"It's done now," Ransom said. "What we should do is find out who would alert the federal government. That could mean real trouble for us!"

"Yeah it could," Carlo admitted. "Get the word out to your people that we're paying for information!"

"That's already been done. So I'll give you a call as soon as I hear something or ride to see you!" Ransom said.

The men embraced then Carlo, Frankie, James and Guido left. As was their custom, the Kanes had four cars on Carlo, until he arrived at his next destination. James drove while Frankie and Carlo sat in the back and Guido up front. They were in the warehouse district by the docks when suddenly a big truck swerved in front of them. James spun the wheel to avoid a collision and the big car slewed sideways and came to a shuddering halt.

The truck was a big flatbed with canvass roof and sides. The canvas sides dropped down and four men appeared with Tommy guns and opened fire.

Carlo and Frankie had been tossed to the side and into the well of the backseat. The rounds ripped into the passenger side of the car.

Guido's head exploded and sprayed a pink and grayish foam of blood into the cramped space. The bullets striking Guido saved James, who opened his door and rolled out. He pulled the pistol from his shoulder Holster just as the back door opened. Carlo and Frankie scrambled out both with guns in their hands. James rose to fire and a flurry of rounds zipped thru the shattered window and smashed into his chest. He was thrown back, his weapon discharged and he crashed to the ground with blood spurting from multiple wounds.

Carlo hurried to the rear of the car, peeped over and saw the men paid him no mind. He rose and holding his pistol with two hands, rapidly squeezing off round after round.

One of the gunmen was punched sideways by his slug. Another doubled over, his gun firing harmlessly into the ground as the slug burrowed thru his stomach.

One of the gunmen spun toward Carlo and fired, just as Frankie stood and emptied his weapon in the two remaining gunners. Gunfire erupted from the other side of the truck as two cars squealed to a stop.

Soon automatic weapons fire filled the air. The whole incident lasted maybe a minute before complete silence reigned.

Frankie looked around frantically for his father, then he saw him sprawled on his back at the rear of the car. He rushed to him and dropped to his knees, then pulled his father to his chest oblivious to the blood that spurted from his father's chest. "Dad!....Dad!....,don't you die on me damn it!" He cried out.

Carlo's eyes fluttered open and he looked up at his son. He coughed and blood trickled from the corner of his mouth. "Don't bring Gianni in, make him go to law school. Take care of your mother and tell her I love her!"

His body was wracked by coughing and his mouth sputtered out bloody foam. He reached up and clasped Frankie's hand, his strength ebbing away. "Sal's, behind....this! Remember I love you, you're the future!"

He squeezed Frankie's hand a final time, shuddered,

exhaled a bloody mist, then was still.

Frankie looked into his father's wide staring eyes and saw them go dim.

Bobby and Sha, dragged a man from the back of the truck. It was the one Carlo shot in the gut. Frankie closed his father's eyes, gently laid him down, then rose and walked to where the man writhed in pain on the ground.

"Who sent you?" Frankie asked ominously.

The man never even looked up, as the pain rocketed thru him.

Frankie went down to one knee and thrust his hand into the man's wound and squeezed it viciously. The man screamed in agony as Frankie viciously probed in the wound.

"Who sent you damn it?" Frankie screamed.

"Don Paschal," the man whispered thru blood filled lips.

"Who?" Frankie asked again.

"Paschal Locata!" the man screamed as Frankie twisted his shredded stomach.

Frankie rose to his feet, and said. "Leave him!" He walked to where his father lay and gently lifted him and walked to where Sha stood next to a big Sedan. He lay his father gently on the back seat and stood there. L.J, Jack Lee and Spencer got James's body and placed it in the back of the car. Then they covered Guido's shattered head and put him in a car and drove off.

    *   *   *   *

Bobby drove to Ransom's place of business, rushed in and told Ransom what had happened. Ransom raced out as fast as his aged body would allow. He saw Carlo's body in the back seat and tears flowed from his eyes. He looked at Frankie and saw the anger simmering in his vivid blue eyes. Ransom made the necessary arrangements, then they took the three bodies to a mortuary that they knew and left them.

Ransom had all the men gather at a warehouse in town.

"We know who had Carlo hit. We got a name, but what we don't have is a location." Ransom said. "Find out where we can find this man. When we find him, his entire male line is to be cut off!"

Frankie stood up, looked at the men gathered, and

said. "My father told me that my uncle Sal was involved. He said it right before he died!"

"Let's go get him." Baron said. "I bet we'll find out where Locata is then!

"We got to plan this right, because we don't want it getting back to the mob that we're involved." Ransom said. "We've got to snatch Sal and get the information. Then we'll strike against Locata. We take Sal tonight before word of Carlo's death gets out.

"I want Sal!" Frankie said. "I know where he is now!"

Bishop stepped up beside Frankie, and said. "I'm gonna go with him!"

Baron looked at his son and saw Lil Will, B.J, Adam, Tre, who was L.J and Rose's son. Jacky, who was Jack Lee and Louise's son and Spence, who was Spencer and Liza's son. They moved beside the two young men.

Jimmy walked up, and said. "They killed my pa too!"

Ransom looked at the young men and knew that they were the future. "Go get him!" was all he said.

*   *   *   *

Sal, Joe Green, Paul Castle and Vinnie Deleoni were all at a warehouse they had on the eastside of town. They all sat in the office.

"When do you think Locata is gonna take care of his end?" Joe Green asked.

"I don't know!" Sal said. "It's been six months since we talked to him and I don't know if he's gonna do it!"

"Oh, he'll do it." said Paul Castle. "I've heard about him and his word is good!"

*

Sal had four foot soldiers as look outs and they were less than vigilant. They never saw the nine masked men until it was too late. The men didn't kill the lookouts, but they did render them unconscious and tied them up.

Bishop left Jacky, Spence, Tre and Adam in their place as they cautiously approached the warehouse. They easily gained entrance and moved toward the office where the four men sat talking.

Frankie crept silently to the door with Bishop and Jimmy at his side. They stopped at the door and could hear muffled voices inside. Frankie looked at the two men then signaled Lil Will and B.J to watch their backs. Both of the young men nodded and took up defensive positions.

Frankie looked at Bishop and nodded, then turned the door knob and flung the door open. Bishop and Jimmy rushed in, their Sub Thompson's panning the room.

Frankie stepped thru the door shouting, "Don't fuckin move! Not a muscle!"

"Holy shit!" Sal shouted almost tumbling backward in his chair.

The four men threw their hands into the air and Sal said. "You guys are making a big mistake here! Don't you know who we are?"

Frankie walked to where Sal sat and viciously clubbed him in the face with the .45 automatic he held, then he said. "Yeah we know who you are, a bunch of fuckin snakes!"

Bishop used his heel to close the door.

Sal shook his big head and tried to stop the blood that freely flowed from the gash in his cheek. "There's not much money here, but get what there is and make sure you hide good!"

"You think we want money, you shit?" Frankie said angrily. His body vibrating with controlled fury.

Sal's head snapped up and he squinted his eyes, because the voice sounded sort of like Carlo's.

Frankie snatched the mask from his face and the four men recoiled in shock.

"Frankie," Joe Green uttered.

"That's right, Frankie." said Frankie. "Papa dead, so is James, and Guido. Paschal Locata had them killed!"

Bishop and Jimmy removed their mask. And Vinnie Deleoni said. "You brought niggers in on this?"

Bishop swung his Tommy Gun toward Vinnie and squeezed off a quick burst. Vinnie was lifted from his chair as the big slugs impacted with his chest and face. Blood and gore sprayed in the small room as Vinnie's bullet riddled body crashed to the floor.

"Are you fuckin crazy?" shouted Joe Green. "Vinnie was a made man!"

Jimmy, who had maintained his composure. Lost it and hosed Joe with a burst from his gun that nearly decapitated him. Blood gushed from the severed arteries in his neck as his body was tossed sideways into the wall. Where he slowly slid down and lay in a crumpled heap at the base of the blood smeared wall.

"Madre De Deus," Paul Castle cried.

"My pappa told me you were involved." Frankie said calmly to Sal, who threw his hands up in defense.

"Hold on there Frankie." Sal pleaded. "We can do something to cover up their deaths, but stop and think son. Carlo was my brother, I wouldn't have him killed!"

"I won't lie to you uncle Sal." Frankie said sarcastically. "You both are dead men! The question is, will you die quick, or will it be a long drawn out painful death. Paul you get one chance and one chance only. Tell me how to find Locata and your seeds will survive. Lie or hold back and I'll erase your name and line from the face of the earth!"

Paul Castle looked into the eyes of the three young men and knew they would do as they said. "It was Sal's idea to have Carlo hit."

Sal cut in, "You lying sack of shit!"

Frankie smashed Sal in the mouth with the butt of his pistol, and Sal's front teeth snapped off, and bloody froth flowed from his mouth.

"Locata's from Tampa. He has the west coast of Florida and the gulf coast. He wants to take over the eastern seaboard, but his base is in Tampa. Promise me you won't touch my family!"

"I gave you my word from the start." Frankie said, then raised his pistol and fired one round that struck Paul in the forehead. It exploded from the back of his head in a shower of blood and brain. Paul's body flew from the chair and crashed to the floor.

Frankie turned to Sal, and said. "Your turn. How do you contact Locata. Do you have an address or phone number?"

Sal looked at his nephew and knew that he would never survive the night. "Fuck you Frankie. Do you know what it's like to live in the shadow of Carlo?" he spit. "Fuck no you don't and you never will!"

"So you're gonna make this hard then I guess!" Frankie stated. "Jimmy get me something so I can tie this

248

asshole up!"

Jimmy left the office and came back a few minutes later with a roll of packing tape. They taped Sal to the chair, then gagged him. Frankie picked up a box cutter that the manager was using as a letter opener. He walked over to Sal, and said. "You're family so I'm giving you one last chance!"

Sal looked up with hate blazing from his eyes. Frankie used the box cutter to cut out Sal's finger nails. Sal screamed into the gag, his eyes tearing from the excruciating pain. Frankie waited to let the full force of the pain wash over him, then he started in again. He stopped, after seven of Sal's nails were gone. Then he unbuckled Sal's pants and zipped them down, reached in and pulled Sal's dick and nuts out. Sal mumbled urgently and Frankie looked into his pleading eyes.

Frankie removed the gag and Sal blurted out the information. Bishop quickly wrote it down, then Frankie had Sal repeat it.

"You wielded the sword that slay my father and because we're blood I won't kill your sons. But, you on the other hand are a dead man!" Frankie grabbed his genitals and cut them off, then stuffed them into his screaming mouth.

Sal's privates effectively silenced his screams and Frankie taped them in place. Then he watched, as Sal choked on them. He looked at the puddle of blood that was forming between Sal's legs, then fired one round into his gut. Sal's eyes widened as the additional pain assaulted him.

"Let's go," Frankie said softly, as he replaced the mask and headed for the door.

*

"We know where to find the man who ordered the hit on my father." Frankie said to Ransom. "All we need to do is go to Tampa and get him!

"It's a little more complicated than that." Ransom said. "We'll be in uncharted territory so we'll need to be careful and survey the area well before we strike!"

Frankie nodded his head in agreement, then asked. "When will we set out?"

"As soon as we lay our dead to rest. Baron get Lois. Will, you get Lavern. And I'll get Em and Celia so we can let Sophia and Cita know what has happened. Drake, Trace, Tim, contact all of the men and tell them to meet us at the warehouse tomorrow at 10:00!"

The men started filing out and Ransom stopped Frankie, and said. "You'll be head of your family and it's important that you remember that we're family too. Always have a ace in the hole son. Never let the mob know of your true ties to us. You see the treachery displayed so always have a safe guard against it. We are that safe guard. Things will change as time moves forward and you'll need to change with them. I won't be around too much longer I'm afraid, but there will always be a Kane that you can rely on!"

Frankie looked in the old man's eyes and saw his love and concern. And the tears flowed freely.

Ransom pulled him into his arms and held him tight, then said. "As long as I have life in me, you can come to me day or night and I'll be there for you. So will Baron!"

*   *   *   *

The next morning, all of the Kane men met at the warehouse where Ransom sat on a crate.

"We've got to avenge the deaths of our family members!" Ransom said with authority. "Problem is, we got to leave our turf to do it. I want volunteers to speak up now, so we can get a plan of attack set up. I'm going so ain't no use trying to talk me out of it!"

Drake, Trace, L.J, Lao, Turk, Prince, Tim and Lefty all stepped forward. When Baron stepped up, Ransom waved him back. "You got to stay and keep business in order. When I asked for volunteers, I didn't mean for all of you to step forward. Drake, Trace, Prince, L.J. Baron gonna need help keeping things in order, so I can spare Tim, Lefty, Turk, Lao and Blake. All the other elders gonna stay. Ain't no telling how long we'll be there, but say two weeks, on the safe side. Since everybody wants to go, I see I got to choose who goes!"

Bishop stepped forward followed by a contingent of young men. Lil Will, B.J, Adam, Devon, Tre, Jacky, Spence and Jimmy. Frankie stepped up beside him, as Bishop spoke. "Uncle Ran, I can see where you're headed business wise. And never would I disrespect or dishonor you, or any of the elders. But a new era has arrived and we're the future. I think we should all go!"

Frankie spoke, as soon as Bishop finished. "Uncle Ran, the talk we had last night was a prelude to this moment.

You said there would always be a Kane I could rely on, well Bishop is that Kane!"

Ransom looked at the young men, smiled, and said. "A case of my own words comin back and bitin me in the ass!"

The men laughed, then Ransom raised his hands for silence, and said. "After the funeral, get with me and we'll outfit you. I'll give you the details then!"

* CHAPTER # 30 *

After the funeral, the men that were going to Tampa all left. They took five cars and when they arrived, they rented three more. They drove all over the city familiarizing themselves with the town.

They rented motel rooms in West Tampa and a warehouse that was close to Davis Island where Paschal Locata lived. The warehouse was their base and they planned their strike from there.

Lefty and Blake along with the others had been going to the night clubs and other hot spots trying to get a finger on the pulse of the town. They found a club called The Two Spot, that was popular on Spruce St. . And being street wise they saw that all of the illegal activities were concentrated in that area of West Tampa. Blake and Lefty, in the week they were in town, became regular fixtures in the club. The man who owned the club was a tall, slim, light skinned man, named Hudie Smit.

Hudie had watched the two men and knew from their dress that they were high rollers. He also knew from the way they carried themselves that they were dangerous men. He wondered what they were up to and after his curiosity got the best of him. He sent his two henchmen, to find out what their business was.

Blue Powers and Dodi Pickett were both big men, but so were Lefty and Blake. Blue and Dodi stepped to the table where Blake and Lefty sat. Blue looked down on the men, and asked. "Y'all cats ain't from around here, are you?"

Lefty lifted his drink, sipped, then looked up at Blue, and asked. "Who wants to know?"

"I wanna know." Blue said. "You cat's been in here every night this week just observing. Being nosy could get a man killed around here!"

Lefty and Blake with lightning like quickness, pulled their guns out from underneath the table. They had held them concealed when they spotted the two big men approaching. Blue and Dodi found themselves staring down the barrels of two, big .45 automatics.

"What was that you were sayin about being nosy?" Lefty asked his pistol held steady, pointing at Blue's face.

"Listen man," Blue pleaded. "We had orders, that's all!"

"Tell whoever sent you that he could've come and asked us what out business is." Blake said sternly. "He probably wouldn't have learned much, but nothing beats failure but a try!"

Blue and Dodi just stood there watching the guns that the men held steady. Hudie watched as his men just stood there. He couldn't see exactly what was going on, but he didn't like the idea that Blue and Dodi weren't bringing the men to him. So he rose and walked over to where they stood. As he came to where his men stood, he saw that the two men held big automatics to his men's faces.

"Hold on there a minute gents." Hudie said. "Ain't no need for that. These cats are working for me."

"You should teach your boys better manners!" Blake said. "We were mindin our business when these fellows come over makin subtle threats. And we don't take kindly to be in threatened!"

"It was just a misunderstanding boss." Dodi said. "We didn't mean these fellas no harm."

"Could've fooled me." Lefty said.

"Why don't we put the guns away and talk about this." said Hudie. "It ain't got to escalate to shootin."

"What you think Left?" asked Blake. "Think we can trust these boys?"

"Yeah, long as we got iron in our hands." Lefty said.

"Come on fellas." Hudie said. "Let's be reasonable here."

"We might as well give them a chance." Blake said. "If they try any monkey business we can always kill them later!"

"You got a good point Blake." Lefty said lowering his pistol and sliding it back into his shoulder holster. Blake did like wise and Hudie waved his two men off and sat down.

"I get the impression you fellas are players." said Hudie. "There's an outside chance that we might be able to do business together if you're into what I think you're into."

"And just what do you think we're into?" Blake asked.

Hudie looked at the two men, then said. "Let me

explain to you my reasoning. Y'all ain't users, I can see that from your dress and the way you carry yourself. Y'all done been around the action and I can see that in the way y'all observe the things around you. Y'all ain't no nickel and dime niggas and I know that from the size of your bankroll, and the quality drinks you buy. Y'all cautious and easy to rile. I'd say y'all was killers too, but I don't wanna offend you. This my spot and I'm sure y'all know this a front for something bigger!"

"You're dealing on a decent scale." said Lefty. "But I don't think you're capable of supplying us. But, you might be able to get us in with someone we know who can!"

"And who is this someone?" asked Hudie. "And if you know he's capable of supplying you, why don't you go to him?"

"We don't actually know him, we know of him." Blake said. "Since we're not from here, maybe you can introduce us."

Hudie looked at them, then said. "You still ain't told me who this someone is."

"Don Paschal Locata!" Blake stated.

Hudie couldn't hide his surprise, but he quickly recovered, then said. "I've heard of him, but I don't know the man personally. I'll see if I can contact him thru some mutual friends. If I do, I'll let y'all know. So, how can I reach you if I get in touch with him?"

"You can't." Blake said. "Either us or some of our associates will stop by and you can pass the message on then!"

"Alright, we can do it like that." Hudie said. "In the mean time, y'all enjoy yourselves. Drinks are on the house!"

*

"I don't know where the men are from, but I do know they're from the South." Hudie said to Don Locata. Hudie had waited until the next day to drive out to Davis Island to tell the Don about the men who wanted to meet him. Hudie fronted for Locata in the drug business.

"I believe them niggers are from Jacksonville, try to find out. If you don't find out, just hit them!" Locata said.

"Them some hard cats Mr. Locata!" Hudie said. "I can't see them goin down easy!"

"I don't give a fuck! Just take them out if you can't

find out where they're from!" Don Locata said forcefully. Hudie rose from his chair and left the room.

Locata turned to the three men that remained in the room, and said. "I believe the niggers are those Kanes, that Sal warned me about. I find it funny that all of a sudden some strange niggers are tossing my name around. Augie, I want you to beef up security here at the house. Angie, Vitto, you guys are to stick with me all day and night. Until we find out who these niggers are and how they know who I am!"

*

"I don't trust that nigga, Hudie Smit." Lefty said. "Something about him doesn't quite ring true. The nigga a snake!"

"Snake or not, he might be able to draw Locata out." Ransom said. "We want him and all the adult males associated with him!"

"We can always make that nigga do like we want." Tim said. "He won't expect us to come at him in force so we need to do that tonight!"

"This is what we'll do then." Ransom said. "Left, Blake, y'all gonna go in the Two Spot as usual, but Adam, Rob and Tre will back y'all up. Frankie, Bishop, Jimmy and Lil Will, y'all are gonna be outside. If y'all hear gunfire, I want y'all to hit the club hard. B.J, Jacky, Spence, Turk, Tim, y'all gonna be the drivers, don't leave the cars. Devon, Lao, y'all gonna be with me and we'll keep the law off if it comes to it. We wanna try to take that nigga Hudie alive, if it's possible. If not, then we'll put him down!"

*

That night as soon as it got dark, Hudie sat in his back office with Blue, Dodi and five other men that worked for him.

"I want at least one of them niggas alive!" Hudie said. "My major goal is to find out where these cats are from. I believe if we kill one, we'll have to kill the other one too! Y'all spread out in the club so we can get the drop on these niggas. They fast and sharp, so stay on your toes!"

*

255

Adam Kane, walked into the Two Spot and looked around. Then he headed for the end of the bar, that covered the back door. He sat on a stool and ordered a drink. His eyes scanned the club and he saw Rob Kane come in. He headed to an empty table in a corner, that covered the front entrance. Rob raised his hand and a waitress walked over and took his order. Tre Sumner walked to a table in the opposite corner, sat, called a waitress and ordered a drink.

The three young men were busy scanning the club for any sign of trouble, when Blake and Lefty came thru the front door. All five of the men were well armed. Each carried two automatics and were primed for trouble.

*

Hudie had been watching the club thru the two way mirror, that was installed in his office. Five of his men, were positioned throughout the club in strategic positions. They had pistols and sawed off shotguns underneath their tables. Hudie saw the two men step into the club and he turned to Blue and Dodi, and said. "It's show time! Be careful and make sure them niggas don't catch y'all like they did the last time!"

Dodi and Blue pulled their pistols out and put them in their jacket pockets. They stepped from the office into the club area. Both men were determined not to get caught like they were the last time. So, their hands were jammed into their pockets, wrapped tightly around their pistols.

*

"Here they come." Blake said. "They got their hands in their pockets, and from the looks of things, they got guns in there!"

"Yeah, I see." Lefty replied. "Look, Hudie's comin out now.

Blake and Lefty pulled their pistols and thumbed the safeties off.

Adam, Rob, and Tre had their eyes locked on the two big men. Tracking them, as they slowly approached Lefty and Blake's table. They pulled out their pistols and rose to their feet. "Let's drop them, then snatch Hudie!" Lefty said.

Blake nodded. And as soon as Blue and Dodi were within seven feet of their table, they raised their twin .45's and started firing.

Blue and Dodi, saw the two men rise and pulled their pistols. But it was too little, too late, as Lefty and Blake's rounds ripped into them. The club was thrown into chaos, as people screamed and ducked for cover.

Blue and Dodi danced a jig, as the .45 slugs riddled their bodies. Both men discharged their pistols, but the rounds were nowhere near Lefty and Blake. They harmlessly crashed into the floor and ceiling.

Adam, Tre and Rob opened fire on the two dead men. And their bodies were tossed to and fro, as the wave of slugs washed over them. The three young men were concentrating so hard on the two men, that they never saw the five men that were scattered throughout the club. They stood with various weapons and unleashed a deadly hail of gun fire. A man sitting at a table behind Adam, stood with a sawed off double barrel shotgun and fired point blank into Adams's lower back. Adam was cut nearly in half, by the twin blast that severed his spine and exited in a spray of shit, blood and guts. His body folded back on itself unnaturally as he crashed to the floor.

Tre saw the man shoot Adam and he trained his pistols in that direction. Before he could fire, a man rose from the floor next to him with a .45 revolver and fired three rapid rounds. They punched thru Tre's ribs, pulped his heart and lungs and exploded from his side in a shower of blood. Tre was thrown sideways, where he crashed into a table and tumbled to the floor.

A man stepped behind Rob, who was firing at the man who had shot Adam. He placed his pistol at the base of his skull and squeezed off one round. It turned Rob's brain to mush, before exiting thru his right eye in a mist of blood and pulped eye ball. Rob crashed to the floor face first.

Frankie, Bishop, Jimmy and Lil Will raced thru the door moments after the shooting started, all armed with Sub Thompson's. They quickly scanned the club and saw Blake and Lefty go down to gunfire that came from several areas. The four men opened fire, and hosed the club with automatic weapons fire. The five men were ripped to shreds by their slugs.

Hudie saw the tide turn and rose form where he cowered beneath a table and made a mad dash for his office.

He never mad it, as rounds from all four weapons ripped into him and catapulted him into the two way mirror. He crashed thru in a shower of blood and glass shards.

The four men turned their weapons on anything that moved. The floor had puddles of blood, as the men sifted thru the bodies for their dead. The club looked like a slaughter house. They got the bodies of Adam, Tre, and Rob, then helped Lefty and Drake, who were both wounded and left the club.

*

It seemed as if the police were there in no time. Three patrol cars raced to the scene and six officers leaped from the cars, as the wounded men and the others left the Two Spot.

The cops never stood a chance, as the drivers of the cars, along with Ransom, Lao and Devon, opened fire on them. Four fell immediately dead before they were out of the car good. The other two tried vainly to get back into their cars, which became their metal coffins.

*

The Kanes drove to a meat packing plant and stole a refrigerated flat bed truck. Then, they placed their dead in it to be transported back home. They found a doctors name in the phone book and drove to his home and forced him to work on Blake and Lefty. Ransom, Bishop, Frankie, Lil Will and Devon were in the waiting room at the doctors home office. Jimmy, B.J and Spence, stood in the room with the doctor. Turk and Tim were standing guard over the doctors family, Lao and Jacky stood guard outside.

"Uncle Ran, I think you should go back with the dead. We'll handle it form here." Bishop said.

"I'm stayin!" Ransom said sharply.

"No!" Bishop said firmly. "You will accompany the dead. Tim will drive the truck and Turk will ride shotgun. Lao and Jacky will ride drag and you'll drive Blake and Lefty back home. They'll need medical attention and you can see they get it!"

"So you're takin over?" Ransom asked.

"Of course not, but this once, I think you and the

258

others should let us take the lead." Bishop said.
        "You're right," Ransom said. "I'll do it. You've got
to go after Locata at first light, before he gets word that Hudie
Smit is dead!"
        "I know," Bishop said. "We should have enough
men to do the job. I got a plan and the sooner we can do it the
better!"
        "What's the plan?" Ransom asked.
        "We're gonna steal trucks from a lawn service I saw
on the way here." Bishop said. "A group of black men would
raise an alarm in that area. But, not if they're workers, so
we'll use the lawn service as a disguise!"
        "That's a good idea son." Ransom said. "Go on and
get your men and do what needs to be done!"
        Bishop, Frank, Jimmy and Lil Will, got Devon, B.J
and Spence and they went to steal the trucks.

            *   *   *   *

        The next morning the seven men drove up to the
fence that surrounded the Locata Estate and waited until the
man at the gate came out.
        Frankie stepped out of the lead truck and waited on
the man to come to him.
        "Yeah, can I help you?" the guard asked, as he
stepped thru the opening in the gate.
        Frankie smiled, then said. "Me and my boys just
coming to do the yard is all."
        The man wasn't regularly on the gate, so for a
moment he was puzzled, then he said. "I'd better make sure
it's alright with Mr. Locata first."
        Sure, no problem I'll just go with you." Frankie said.
"I need to talk to Mr. Locata before we start anyway. The
man lead Frankie thru the gate and stepped into the little gate
house. The man reached for the phone and Frankie's arm
snaked around his neck. The knife that was in his sleeve
dropped into his hand and he drove it into the mans kidney,
ripped it upward, then to the side. The guard died soundlessly
and Frankie quickly lowered him to the floor, then walked
back to the gate swiftly and opened it.
        The two trucks pulled onto the grounds and drove to
the big mansion. The men all quickly piled out and rushed the
big house.

*

"What was that!" Augie said aloud, bolting upright in the bed. He was in a small room on the bottom floor of the mansion. He got out of the bed, grabbed his pistol and barefoot stepped out into the hall. He saw a white man rapidly approaching the stairs with a Sub Thompson and a black man coming his way. He raised the pistol and fired, just as the man squeezed the trigger of his Thompson. The rounds slammed into Augie and tossed him like a bloodied rag doll back into the room. He was dead before his blood splattered corpse hit the floor.

*

As Frankie headed for the stairs, Lil Will raced down the hall. He saw the man step from the room, just as the man spotted him and raised his gun and fired. Lil Will fired at the same time and a micro second later the man's slug crashed into his chest, and pulverized his heart. Lil Will and Augie died at the exact same time.

*

Frankie raced up the spiral staircase with Bishop, Jimmy, Devon, B.J and Spence hot on his heels. They reached the top landing and split up.

Angelo Provalone, known as Angie. Heard the gun fire down stairs and leaped from the bed and grabbed the shot gun that leaned on the nightstand and hurried to the door. Before he got there, the door crashed open and he fired.

B.J had kicked the door open and was just stepping in when the shotgun blast ripped into his chest. He was knocked backward where he stumbled to the rail, flipped and fell to the floor below.

Spence saw him reel backward and he shoved his machine gun around the door frame and fired a long burst that he swung back and forth. He saturated the room with hot lead. Angie was cut down in his tracks as the bullets punched into him.

Vitto Carmani, was in the room across from Angie. He flung the door wide and leaped into the hall with his two

260

pistols blazing.

Spence was pinned to the wall and a bullet smashed into his shoulder and spun him around. The bullet saved his life, as another hit the wall where his head had been and rained plaster over him.

Devon had just kicked open a door and sprayed the room, when one of Vitto's slugs hit him in the thigh and knocked him to the ground. He dropped his weapon and was at Vitto's mercy. He looked up at the grinning face resigned to death. Then suddenly the man's face seemed to disintegrate before his eyes as Bishop's rounds nearly erased his entire head.

Frankie kicked open a door and saw Paschal Locata standing beside the bed frantically clawing at the nightstand drawer, while his wife Yvonne held the covers to her chest and screamed.

"Don't fuckin move!" Frankie shouted.

Don Locata froze and turned to the two men who stood just inside the threshold.

"I've got money if that's what you want!" Locata said pleadingly.

Bishop stepped thru the door, as Frankie said. "I'm Francisco Luigi Torronelli. This is Jimmy Lewis and you killed our fathers!"

"No wait! It wasn't me, it was Sal!" Locata screamed.

"Sal is dead too. He died by my hands, as you will!" Frankie said ominously.

"Please, it was a mistake!" Locata pleaded.

Frankie and Jimmy opened fire and sprayed the Don with a fusillade that literally ripped his body apart.

"We can't leave her." Bishop said pointing his gun at Yvonne.

"Yeah, I know." Frankie said.

Bishop opened fire on the woman and her body was tossed from the bed in a bloody heap.

Bishop, Frankie and Jimmy then went thru the house and methodically killed everyone there. Then they got their dead and wounded and left.

Little did they know, they had left Locata's son Antonio alive.

* CHAPTER # 31 *

By 1959, America had started sending what they called Military Advisors to Vietnam. The Kanes had become fragmented due to new ideas and dissatisfaction by several branches. Ransom in his old age was finding it difficult to rein in the younger men and Baron's strength of character wasn't as strong as his father's though his creed was the same: Family first!

On New Years night of 1960. Bishop and Anna were at the Tip-Top with family and friends celebrating the start of the New Year. Anna was still a virgin and Bishop hadn't pressed her to have sex. When the urge was upon him, he found a woman to satisfy his physical needs. It had been happening frequently of late and Anna was starting to notice that they spent less time together. She looked at him as he sat deep in thought and wondered what was on his mind. She had felt the erections he would get when they kissed and fondled and knew the heat she felt between her legs was connected.

Merlie had gotten involved with a man named Jesse Block and was pregnant. They were getting married in March. Anna asked her all kinds of questions about sex and she answered as best as she could.

Bishop saw her watching him from the corner of his eye, and asked. "What's on your mind Ann?"

"Us," she answered with a smile. "Let's go Bish. I want to spend some time with you like we used to."

"You sayin we don't spend no time together?" he asked.

"No, I ain't sayin that, but lately somebody else is always there." she replied.

He reached for her hand and helped her from her chair. They walked outside and got in his brand new Caddilac Eldorado.

"Baby, there's a reason why I spend time with you in the company of others." he said as he crank the car.

"And what reason is that?" she asked.

"I don't know quite how to put this Ann." he said. "But I don't trust myself being alone with you. I know you love me and I love you too. I want you so bad in a physical way, but I don't want you to feel like you're obligated to do something you may not wanna do yet. I'd never pressure you into making a decision you're not comfortable with."

"Bish, if you're talkin about sex, what makes you think I'd be uncomfortable with you?"

"I don't know Ann. I ain't never met nobody like you, you're special and I wanna keep the love you have for me!"

"I want to Bish. I got this mighty yearning inside and I think you're the only one that could end it!"

"Are you sure?" he asked as he pulled away form the Tip-Top.

"Hell yeah I'm sure. Let's go to your place."

Bishop had a small two bedroom apartment on Stone Wall St. When they got there they went straight to the bedroom where he slowly undressed her. He stood back admiring her perky upturned breast, the curve of her hips and the bushy triangle between her thighs. He undressed and she gasped as she saw his swollen member. He lead her to the bed and slowly he kissed and caressed her. He licked and sucked at her breast, until the nipples stood hard and erect. He fingered her tight, wet hole, until her hips were pumping up to meet his thrusting finger. He lightly stroked her clit and she shivered. She was wet and he moved between her thighs. He grasped his penis and rubbed it between her slit, over her clit, then slid slowly in her.

"Ummm....she moaned as she felt herself contract and grip him.

His finger moved to her clit as he slowly and tenderly drove his rod into her. She raised her hips up to him until he hit an obstruction. He pulled back and drove forward again, all the while he stroked her clit. Her breathing was heavy and she humped to him faster and faster and he knew she was about to explode. He pulled back and thrust forward just as her orgasm crested. Her cunt seemed to grip him tightly and he pistoned in and out of her until he exploded.

Their bodies thrashed wildly against each other as they reached the pinnacle of their passion. Their motions slowed as their ecstasy subsided. He looked down into her passion dazed eyes and she smiled up at him. Her hands held his waist tightly as he leaned down to kiss her.

He broke the kiss, then asked. "You alright Ann?"

"More than alright!" She replied with a smile. "That felt so good!"

He laughed, then asked. "Ready for round two?"

She swung her hips up to him, then said. "That should give you your answer.

He laughed and stroked into her slowly.

    *   *   *   *

1960 was a sad year for the Kanes. Grandma Celia died in March of that year. It seems all of the elders started passing one by one.

In March, Anna told Bishop she was pregnant. After New Year's she had moved in with him. They were set to marry the next month.

Frankie and Donnatella had married and she was pregnant with their first child. He had taken over his father's business with the help of his father's uncle, Luciano Torronelli. Jimmy Lewis as always was by his side.

The Kane and Torronellis were still bound by the oath that Raven and Carlo had made.

The Kane family splintered as the elders passed away. Some moved to various parts of Florida and others all over the U.S.

Baron tried his best to retain the old ways and keep the family united, but differences in opinions and the distribution of finances, as well as who should lead was the major cause of friction. So the family was torn apart. Ransom Nelson, Baron, Bishop and their brothers and sisters were the last of Raven's seed.

On October 2nd, 1960 ,at 1:30 a.m. a son was born to Bishop and Anna Kane. Bishop wanted to name him after him, but Anna persisted. And so, the child was christened Berean Kane. Anna had no idea what the name truly meant. Bishop was content with the name and slightly surprised at Anna's strength of will. So Berean it was.

The Beginning!

COMING SOON

"REDEMPTION"
THE LINEAGE STILL CONTINUES

A
KANE FAMILY SAGA
BY BOBBY DENNIS JR.

ALSO

"A THUG'S PASSION"

WRITING AS: BENYAHMIN DAVIS

CHAPTER # 3

Kane wasn't just a gangster or a thug, he was a man truly torn between two worlds. He held down a 9 to 5 as a machine operator and made decent money. Enough to take care of his family and enjoy a few of the finer things, but secretly he hated his square job and only kept it to please Leslie. Kane loved women, and had fucked just about every woman that worked at the plant. As a matter of fact, he was working on his latest conquest. An older woman that had the hots for him since he started working there. She was fine as hell, with a body of a woman nearly half her age.

Emma was 50 and frisky, about 5'3" and 130 pounds. She had apple sized breast, a nice trim waist, flat stomach, flaring hips and an ass that was shaped like a upside down Valentine. She wore her hair in the short cut that Toni Braxton and Halle Berry had popularized. She was cute, and from looking at her you'd never believe she was 50 years old. He had been playing hard to get with Emma because the dude's on the job had told him she was a black widow. She had sucked a few young guy's that had worked there dry and cast them to the side. They acted like fools and soon left to find employment else where.

Kane had no fear but he wanted total control where she was concerned, so he went thru the young freaks that worked there. He dicked them and dismissed them, yet there was never any animosity because they still got together every now and then for a lil fun and games.

For the next two days all he did was go to work, go home and hang out with his family. That Wednesday after work, he went home and ate dinner, bathed and kicked it with the kids. After he helped them with their homework he hung out with Leslie for a few then got ready to hit the streets.

He stayed strapped but kept most of his major arms

locked in a big red toolbox. He kept it in his trunk when he was in the street, and in his garage when he was home. He always kept a snub nosed .38 or a .380 on him, even at work he was armed. At home he would hide it but it was always at hand.

He got his toolbox and put it on the floor of the passenger side, got in and looked at the door where Leslie stood. He waved, blew her a kiss then pulled off.

*   *   *   *

Kane arrived on the set at around 9:30 p.m. He rode around to all the hot spots to see if Becky was on the scene. When he drove thru the hood he saw Tony with two young men that he vaguely knew, by the names of Sonny and Tracy. He knew they lived in Mixon and he also knew they got a lil money serving. They were up and coming dope men. They had the rides, the gear, and a lil rep. They went to school with kane's youngest brother Alvin, who was killed in a gun battle with the police a few years earlier at a jewelry store robbery.

Kane pulled over, got out of the car and walked over to where they stood. He hugged and kissed Tony then gave the other men some dap.

"Tee break bread."

Tony reached in his front pocket, pulled out a nice roll of bills and asked. "What you need Bro?"

"I just wanted to know if you had some cheese in your trap." Kane said smiling. "What y'all cats up to?"

"Actually we were waiting on you to show." Tony said.

"I got something I wanna run by you!" Sonny said excited.

"They came and got me and put me up on a lick." Tony said. "I know how you feel about me going on capers so I asked them to wait till you swung thru. That's why were standing here. If you hadn't come by 10:00 I was gonna call you."

"Alright, dig this. Let's go to my girl's room so we can talk in private." Kane said. "I don't want all these niggas round here in our business."

They walked to his car got in and he drove to Becky's room. They sat down and begin to talk.

"So what's the deal?" Kane asked Sonny and Tracy.

"This nigga we know name Jermaine is strapped," Tracy said. "He got west 21st street sewed up. He serve the whole area up to 45th street, but his main spot is an apartment right behind Pearl's Place. They usually keep a bird or so on hand. They serve both hard and soft plus they got boy. He usually ain't there, but he got two young broads servin. They ain't packing no heat so I guess the nigga feel like they can't be touched."

"I feel you," Kane said. "But I wanna know why y'all ain't knock them off yourself if it's so easy?"

"The ho's know me and Tracy." Sonny said. "They don't know you and Tee. It's an easy lick and you can throw us whatever once you take it off."

"The shit sounds sweet." Kane said interested. "Before I hit it I wanna check it for myself. If it looks straight I'll hit it, but if it looks fucked up I'm gonna back off. I ain't usin my car and Tee ain't going in with me."

"That's cool," Tracy said. "We can use the car I got, it's a rental."

"I'm cool with that but I'm going in solo. When we get there let Tee drive y'all stay in the car. If shit get flaky I don't need to be hesitating when I start cappin. Everything I see outside the car is fair game so stay in the ride. Y'all got gats?"

Sonny and Tracy nodded but Tony spoke up. "Naw I ain't packing."

"Y'all chill for a minute." Kane said and left the room.

He came back with a big red tool box and a tote bag. He opened the tote and pulled out a Dickie jumper and a Raiders cap, both black. He pulled the Dickie on over his clothes put the Raiders hat on, then slipped on a pair of black driving gloves. He opened the tool box and pulled out a sawed off pump shotgun. He took a lightly greased rag from the tool box and wiped the shotgun down. He pumped the shotgun five times and each time a bright red shell jumped out. He pumped it again to make sure it was empty then he wiped each shell and reloaded the gun. He sat the shotgun down and pulled out an Army issue .45 automatic. He racked the slide a couple of times then wiped it down. He dropped the clip, wiped it and the shells then reloaded it. He pulled out a 9mm, did the same thing and passed it to Tony.

Tony took the gun from Kane and smiled at him.

268

"Remember what I said Tee, stay in the car." Kane said.

"Damn Bro we done did this enough times for me to know what you always say by heart." Tony said smiling. "I got it Bro."

"Alright. And you can give me back my nine before I drop your ass back off."

"Nigga I ain't gone sell yo shit." Tony said laughing.

"You did it before." Kane said laughing.

"Aw man that shit dead."

"Don't sweat it Tee," Kane said rising to his feet. "Come on let's roll."

They walked out got in the rental and jumped on I-95 north. They got off on 20th st. expressway and drove down to Myrtle Ave. and made a right. They drove up two blocks and made a left on 21st st., Sonny pointed out the apartment and Kane said.

"It's looking good so far."

Tracy drove on down the block made a right and parked by the beauty salon that sat on the corner.

Kane pulled his cap down over his brows, zipped down the Dickie jumper and slid the .45 in his waist. He grabbed the shotgun and said, "One of you niggas give me twenty dollars."

"What you need twenty for?" Sonny asked.

"How am I gonna buy a dub rock without a dub?" Kane asked. "I ain't gonna use my money. I need to be able to see inside the crib. Plus when they see the money comin to them, more than likely that's all they'll watch."

Sonny gave Kane the money and he got out of the car. He walked quickly down the street with the shotgun riding close to the side of his right leg. He walked to the door and knocked. He had his body turned to shield the shotgun and the twenty dollar bill in his left hand.

A man's voice said. "Yeah who is it?"

"Yo it's Black." Kane answered.

The door cracked open and the man asked. "What's up Black?"

"Let me get a dub dog." Kane said passing the man the money. As the door begin to open Kane saw that the dude held a pistol in his hand and he sprang into action. He kicked the door with tremendous force and it crashed into the center of the man's face. It broke his nose and smashed his lips, knocking out several teeth. His head snapped back as blood gushed from his nose and mouth. As he fell back the pistol flew from his hand in his feeble attempt to break his fall. He landed hard on his ass then rolled on his back. The momentum forced his head back and it slammed into the floor with a sickening thud. He was dazed, and he raised his head up slowly as Kane quickly stepped thru the door. He glanced around the room swiftly his shotgun up panning the room. He saw two young women, one on the sofa, and one curled up on the love seat. They were smoking a blunt and drinking wine.

Kane lashed out with the heel of his boot and kicked the dazed man in the face. He grabbed the door and closed it. Kane aimed the shotgun in the area where the stunned young women sat with their mouths hanging open in shock.

"Don't scream! Don't make a fuckin sound! I want the dope and money now!" he shouted.

The women looked at him in shock as still as marble statues. The entire incident was over in a matter of seconds. He talked to the women in his normal tone of voice.

"I ain't got all night so don't trip and start all that screaming and shit. Just give me the shit I asked for."

One of the women got up and got a big bag that sat on the table and brought it to him. He looked in the bag and saw that it was filled with small ziplock bags of rocks.

"There's some powder and boy under the seat cushion with the money we done made today." The woman said her voice trembling.

"Let's go get it." He said as the woman turned and walked back to the sofa. She moved the cushion and pulled two more big bags and a small bag out. He looked in the three bags and saw that everything she said was there.

The other woman just sat on the love seat watching him. The fear that was once in her eyes gone and replaced by anger. Her eyes shot daggers at him. He walked to her dropped the bags on the table, and viciously back hand slapped her. Before she could recover his palm lashed into the other side of her face. Her head snapped to the side and blood trickled from the corner of her mouth.

He gripped her chin, turned her face to his and looked in her fear filled eyes and said.

"You tryin to memorize my face, don't? If I ever suspect you of pointing me out to anyone I'll find you and I'll kill you. Understand?"

Tears streamed down her face as she nodded her head.

"Now where is the rest of it?" he asked.

"I'll show you." she said in a tremulous voice.

The woman that cooperated was stunned by the sudden outburst of violence. She had stumbled back and fell on the sofa crying. He released the woman's chin and walked to where the man's pistol lay. He picked it up and slid it in his waist near the .45 .

"Let's get the rest." he said.

The woman he slapped said. "It's in the back." and pointed down the hall.

Kane pointed to the unconscious man and said. "Get your partner. Y'all grab an arm apiece and drag dude to where the rest of the shit at."

The women followed his instructions and drug the man into a room in the back.

As soon as the women grabbed the man Kane locked the door. He slid the security chain on then rushed to catch up with them.

"Y'all sit on the bed. Don't move because I don't wanna have to really hurt y'all."

He started opening dresser drawers until he found what he was looking for, some stockings. He called the girl who had so far cooperated and said. "I want you to take these stockings and tie your girlfriend and dude up. Tie their hands behind their backs and make sure you do it right!"

She tied them both.

"Now I want you to tie dudes ankles and hook them and his wrist together."

She did as he said then stood waiting on his next order.

"Now let's get the rest of the stuff."

She walked to the closet with him close behind her. She went to the clothes rack and pushed them aside, then reached up to where a second rack was. She twisted it then pulled it from the wall. She stuck her finger in the flange that the rod had set in. He heard a click then a small panel opened.

Kane saw that someone had built a sizable compartment.

"The dope is in the metal box." she said stepping back and pointing.

271

He grabbed her arm gently but firmly and led her back to the bed. He tied her loosely, but right. Then he tied the two women together and checked the man's bonds. He walked back into the closet, pulled the metal box out and saw a money bag and tote bag. He pulled them out and noticed the metallic clinking in the tote. He saw it contained guns and ammunition. He put they metal box and money bag inside and zipped it closed. He quickly searched the house and found a jewelry box filled with jewelry. He took the jewelry from the women and the man then put it all in the big tote bag.

Kane got the woman that helped him and took her from the room. When they got in the front room he put the bags of dope and the shotgun in the bag also. He reached in the bag of money and took out a fat wad. He removed the rubber band and spread the money out flat. He pulled the woman to him by the waist band of her jeans, and undid the top of her button and she whispered.

"Please don't hurt me."

Kane zipped her jeans down, pulled them past her hips then pulled her panties down. She looked at him with tears streaming down her face. He grabbed the stack of money put it in her panties like a pad, then pulled her panties and jeans back up. He looked in her eyes and whispered. "That's for you, keep it on the low."

He kissed her cheek then led her back to the room where he loosely tied her to the other woman, and headed back up front. When he walked in the front room he heard a knock on the door. He looked out the peephole to see who was there.

Standing there fidgeting, shifting from foot to foot was Tony. He unhooked the chain and snatched the door open, and Tony's nine was right in his face. Kane's head and hand moved with lightning quickness as he snatched the gun from Tony's hand. He couldn't help but smile.

"Put this shit up." he said handing Tony the pistol.

He tucked the .45 back in his waist, got the tote, slung it over his shoulder and they left.

"Damn Tee I thought I told you to stay in the car?"

"Shit, you was takin so long I thought you might have been in some trouble so I stepped." Tony said. "Tracy and Sonny wanted to come too but I told them to stay in the car. I know you didn't wanna leave no bodies if you didn't have to."

272

"Good lookin out Bro." Kane said, punched Tony on the shoulder and laughed.

When they got back to the car him and Tony got in the back seat. He pulled off the cap and jumper and stuffed them in the tote. About ten blocks away he said.

"Tracy stop at the next phone booth you see. I got to make a call."

A few blocks latter Tracy pulled over. He jumped out and punched in his home number. Damon answered the phone and Kane asked.

"Boy what you doin up this time of night?" It was nearly 12:00.

"I was goin to the bathroom and I heard the phone ring so I picked it up."

"Okay, get your momma for me."

The next thing Kane heard was Damon's voice yelling. "Momma! Daddy on the phone!"

He heard Leslie's voice yelling. "Boy you better stop all that hollerin in here!"

Leslie picked up the phone in their room and said. "I got it."

"I love you Daddy." Damon said.

"I love you back Dee."

Damon hung up as Leslie's voice asked. "You don't love nobody else?"

"Girl you know I love you. I'm just callin to let you know I'm alright and I should be home in bout an hour and a half. If it takes me longer I'll call and let you know."

"Alright honey I love you."

"I love you back baby." he said and hung up.

He jumped back in the car and Tracy pulled off and asked. "Where we gonna go?"

"We could go back to my girl's spot but too many eyes and I don't wanna do that."

"We can go to this chick's house I kick it with if y'all want to?" Sonny said.

"Is she cool?" Kane asked.

"She down. All we got to do is break her off."

"She got her own ride?" asked Kane.

"Yeah, she got her own shit." Sonny said.

"Alright let's do it like this. When we get to her house you go in and holla at her. Give her a yard and tell her to step off for an hour and a half. I don't want her to see me and Tee so we'll drop you off. When we see her leave we'll come to the crib and handle our business."

"That's cool." Sonny said.

They pulled up to the woman's house and Sonny jumped out and went inside. Tracy parked down the street and they sat and watched the house. When the woman came out, got in her car and left Tracy pulled in her driveway. The three men went inside and Kane sat the big tote bag on the floor.

The men looked at Kane who sat down next to the tote bag, and they all sat on the floor. Kane opened the bag and started pulling out it's contents. He sat his stuff to the side then pulled out the bag of money and sat it in front of him. The other money bag he left in the tote because he planned to split it with Tony, not the other men.

He took the guns out of the tote next. There was a .357 Magnum, three .38's, four 9mm, two .380's, a .25 automatic and ammo for all of them. Kane took his pick and passed the others out then they spilt the shells. Kane counted the money and it was $18,000. He gave them $4,000 apiece, and he kept $6,000. He thought to himself. "That girl I gave the money to got to have at least four or five grand. If she kept it to herself she straight for a minute."

When they split the jewelry Kane picked his first and kept the most. He got up and went to the kitchen with the metal box, found a screwdriver and busted the lock on the box. Inside was a key and a half of coke and about a quarter key of heroin.

"Y'all come on." Kane said and led them back to the kitchen. He looked in the cabinets and found a box of big zip lock freezer bags. He grabbed a big enamel serving platter, and sat it all on the table. He busted the key down in three parts and gave them to Tony, Tracy, and Sonny. He kept the half of key for himself.

He broke the Quarter key of heroin in half, then made three piles out of one half. He gave Tony, Tracy, and Sonny a pile each, and kept the other half for himself. After they divided the rest of the drugs Kane asked. "Y'all straight?" making eye contact with each man.

They all nodded with bright smiles.

"Hell yeah we straight!" Tracy yelled and gave Kane some dap.

They gathered up their stuff and left.

*   *   *   *

Tracy and Sonny dropped Kane and Tony off at Kane's car.

"If we hear something else how can we reach you?" Tracy asked.

"Get in touch with Tee," Kane replied. "He knows how to contact me, or just swing thru and chill. I'll come thru sooner or later.

"Alright, but we gone leave our beeper numbers just in case you wanna holla." said Tracy.

All the men shook hands and they drove off.

Sonny looked at Tracy and said. "That nigga the real deal dog."

"That he is," Tracy said shaking his head. "I done heard bout the nigga, seen him a few times, but I didn't really think the nigga was all that. The cat seem like he got his game tight."

"No shit!" Sonny said laughing. "The nigga fair as fuck too cause ain't no way in the world I would have broke a nigga off like he broke us off. A grand or two yeah, but that nigga looked out!"

"We need to keep our ear on the vine. See if we can't find another lick like this or better." Tracy said.

"You got that right" Sonny said laughing.

Tony and Kane sat in Kane's car. Kane had the tote bag in his lap. He reached in it and fished around until he found the money bag. He pulled it out and Tony's eyes grew wide.

"Slick ass nigga. What you got there?" Tony said smiling.

A NEW ERA HAS ARISED AND A NEW REGIME

HOOD WRITTENS
PUBLISHING

"A THUGS PASSION"
COMING SOON

BRINGING YOU THE BEST IN
URBAN/STREET LIT
BECAUSE ALL OUR LIVES ARE HOOD
WROTE
AND WE REFUSE TO BE DENIED

NOTE FROM THE PUBLISHER

First and foremost believe in something righteous or you will fall for anything. The world is too far gone to save, but that doesn't mean it's alright to add to the destruction. To everyone who is incarcerated we send our respect and concern, and we will do our best to give you an escape from your present reality. To all our readers abroad we hope our books are satisfying and you will continue to support our works, great thanks for your support. To anyone who is hate'en and trying to stop this flow, I thank you also for your support.

Hood Writtens C. E. O
Ausha W. Rogers